MALACHY'S GLORIAM

Merry Christmas — 2023
Thank you for all that you do for us!
C.M. Martello aka Tom

MALACHY'S GLORIAM

C.M. MARTELLO

Special thanks to Bill and Dave; to Meg for editorial support from the beginning; and to Jay for generously and patiently sharing his deep knowledge of the craft of fiction writing.

Malachy's Gloriam © Copyright 2016, C.M. Martello
All rights reserved. No part of this book may be used or reproduced in any manner whatsoever without written permission from the publisher, except in the case of brief quotations in critical articles and reviews. This book is a work of fiction. Names, characters, places, and incidents either are products of the author's imagination or are used fictitiously. Any resemblance to actual events or locales or persons, living or dead, is entirely coincidental.
First Edition   ISBN 13: 978-1-937484-42-2
AMIKA PRESS   466 Central AVE #23 Northfield IL 60093   847 920 8084
info@amikapress.com   Available for purchase on amikapress.com
Edited by Jay Amberg and Ann Wambach. Cover photography by Chunni-4691 and Stuart Monk, Shutterstock. Designed & typeset by Sarah Koz. Body in Minion Pro, designed by Robert Slimbach in 1990. Titles in Koch Antiqua, designed by Rudolph Koch in 1922, digitzed by Linotype in 2007. Thanks to Nathan Matteson.

For R.
THE BLESSING IN MY LIFE

CHAPTER I

Malachy watched Abe move slowly across the floor carrying a briefcase far too large for his short, round physique. Every year the briefcase got a little closer to the floor and Abe got a little crankier. Abe nearly bumped into an empty table because he was trying to count the house, including the back room, before he reached Malachy's office-booth. Malachy reached under the table, probing for the extra deep cigar box filled with supplier bills marked paid. He found it and placed it on the table just as Abe lowered himself into the booth and opened his briefcase. They looked at each other for a few seconds before exchanging greetings.

"You look well," Malachy said.

"I'd be better without the aggravation of this," Abe said, taking a sealed, brown-manila envelope from his briefcase.

"Nice to see you too, Abe. And I am well, thanks for asking."

"And you'd be better if that was a customer's," Abe said, pointing to a short glass of Jameson with a single melting ice cube. "Anyway, here's the report. Nothing has changed. And nothing will change if you don't fill some more seats."

Malachy took the report with one hand and flipped open the cigar box with the other and handed Abe the stack of paid bills. Abe placed them into a folder in his briefcase. Malachy put the cigar box with the unopened report on top of it under the table and braced himself for the lecture.

"And there's one more thing," Abe said. "Singer's accountant called me. He wants to know what the prospects are for the monthly payment. That and Social Security are Singer's only sources of income, and the cost of his retirement home just went up."

"Tell him things look good and increase the payment to cover the higher nut," Malachy answered.

Abe started to respond when Kevin, looking like a cross between a martial arts instructor and an affable bartender with a broad, charming smile, showed up at the booth with a half-full glass of schnapps. Abe looked at the glass, then up at Kevin and said, "So, he told you to bring that early. It won't work. Sit down, I'm getting a crick in my neck."

Kevin put the schnapps down in front of Abe, slid into the booth next to Malachy, and gestured for Abe to continue.

"Increase the payment? You should have been a politician. Revenues are down, so increase expenditures. Where's the printing press? In the storeroom?"

Abe didn't wait for any answers.

"I've been the Shamrock's accountant forever. The Irish bar business used to work in this neighborhood. No more. Every year revenues go down, costs go up. So, one more time—close the Shamrock, sell the building, run your other business out of the apartment, and you'll be money ahead, lots of money ahead."

"Cheer up," Malachy said. "Things are about to turn. We commissioned some high-powered MBAs to do an intense study of our market. Guess what? It turns out the Irish are now outnumbered, and not just on Devon but on the whole North Side of Chicago. I refused to change the Shamrock's name but we are going to fully implement the rest of their recommendations. We're adding curry, pot stickers, and tacos to the menu immediately."

"So, now you're a comedian. Good, you can make your living that way. You should close."

"Anyway, there's not enough room in the apartment for that," Malachy said, pointing to the long bar Singer imported from Ireland because of its ornate, carved shamrocks.

"Why do you need the bar?"

"Where else can I brood about my enemies?" Malachy asked in his best Yiddish joke-telling accent. "Anyway, my other business is booming. I'll increase my rent payment to the Shamrock."

"Wonderful," Abe said, sounding weary. He turned to Kevin. "You see it every day. You know it's not getting any better."

Kevin, trying to suppress a smile, responded, "He does have a point about the bar."

"You too! Why do I bother?"

"Because it's your job," Malachy said, reaching for his Jameson. "And you're good at your job. Have the drink."

Kevin, always alert to who was entering and leaving the Shamrock, focused on the doorway where an exiting regular customer was pointing out the booth to someone who just came in. He nudged Malachy.

Malachy looked up and saw a meticulously groomed man headed toward the booth. The expensive dark suit with a subtle stripe, starched light gray shirt with gold-coin cuff links, and muted tie almost seemed like a costume. The face was familiar from the newspapers. A politically wired real estate developer. Always leasing something to the state, county, or city. And somehow all the surplus property he acquired from the government turned out to have hidden value.

Kevin didn't recognize the face and moved quickly from the booth to intercept the visitor. The man stopped and took a polite step back. Kevin—a solid 210-pound, six-foot three-inch block of muscle—did not step aside.

The man addressed Malachy, trying to talk over Kevin's shoulder, which he just reached with the top of his head.

"Mr. Madden, could I speak with you in private when you are finished with your current business?"

His modulated tone was like a well-chosen fashion accessory. It enhanced the whole image of the smooth, suave, and urbane power player.

"No need," Malachy said loudly. "You have my solemn promise that next month's rent check will be on time."

Mr. Fashion Plate smiled slightly and said, "This does not concern real estate. However, my work does require me to have a traveling office in my limo. May I suggest we meet there? It is very comfortable."

"I know what you mean. Occasionally, my work requires private meetings too. I have a somewhat uncomfortable space set aside in the storeroom for that purpose. However, there are some amenities. May I suggest we meet there?"

Mr. Fashion Plate smiled again, showing a little more of his cosmetic dentistry. "Since I'm requesting the meeting and I'm on your territory, the storeroom it is. I'll wait at the bar."

"Kevin, please serve our guest whatever he wants on the house."

"Coffee is just fine," Mr. Fashion Plate said, moving toward the barstools.

Malachy looked at Abe and said, "I promise I'll look at the report and consider your advice."

"That's what you said last month. Anyway, is that who I think it is? And you're making him meet you in the storeroom? Treat the man with some respect. Maybe he wants to buy for one of his developments. If he makes a good offer, take it. Some boom you're not having," Abe said, moving his open hand in a downward arc for emphasis. "Remember, I'm your personal accountant too."

"He already said it's not about real estate."

"So, what's it about?"

"I'm about to find out. See you next month, Abe."

Malachy led the way into the storeroom. Two dilapidated armchairs, a small wooden table, a floor lamp, and a cot, all surrounded by metal shelving full of bar and kitchen supplies. They settled into the chairs. Mr. Fashion Plate sat down without inspecting his chair for dust and dirt. A man on a mission.

"Mr. Madden..."

"Mister seems a little formal for our surroundings. How about Malachy?"

"Malachy, and please call me Dino. For some reason everybody calls me that...I suppose because my first and last names are almost three times as long. I'm here as the chairman of the Committee for Justice at the Mother Cabrini Shrine. We in the community call it the Saint Shrine. Are you familiar with the recent circumstances at our church?"

"I read the newspapers, usually a day late. I like my news properly aged."

"Then you know the basics. The rector-pastor has been suspended from his duties and ordered not to perform any public priestly functions pending the investigation and a resolution of a sex abuse charge by a young man."

"Lot of that going around," Malachy said.

"Too much. And very distressing. But in this particular case Fr. Bari is innocent."

"Of course," Malachy said.

Dino started to say something, changed his mind, and asked a question instead.

"Are you familiar with Fr. Bari's activities?"

"I know he's very popular in the Italian community."

" 'Very popular' is an understatement. People are returning to church in droves. The church is packed to capacity at every Sunday Mass he celebrates. Even on weekdays the crowds are amazing. We are in constant trouble with the fire marshal. The traffic congestion and parking are worse than Soldier Field or Wrigley when the teams are winning. I've never seen anything like it."

"Must make for good collections," Malachy said, trying not to sound too cynical.

"Fr. Bari spends it on his causes as fast as we collect it. Have you read about his outreach efforts?"

"I remember reading there was some trouble with church authorities."

"Lots of trouble. Rome got involved. He has special services for divorced and remarried Catholics. Also for the gay community. When you walk into the church or one of the meeting spaces, God only knows who you might meet—Jews, Orthodox, Protestant Evangelicals, even gays with AIDS."

Malachy silently noted the "even" for the gays.

"At first, not everybody in the community approved of his outreach efforts. They thought the Shrine should just be about our heritage. But the force of his spirit just melted all opposition. He is a truly holy man, but he's canny and shrewd too."

Malachy pondered whether such a combination was possible. Then he thought of John XXIII. The Good Pope, as Italians called him, who neutralized the powerful and hostile Curia during the Vatican Council.

"Fr. Bari knows our community is the source of all the funds for his various projects, and he gives us lots of special attention with baptisms, marriages, and funerals. There were so many requests for the big three that Fr. Bari insisted we inaugurate a random system to determine his participation. It made the big donors very unhappy."

Dino paused and made a rapid back and forth gesture with the thumb and forefinger of his raised hands, silently appealing to Malachy to validate the difficulty of working with someone who ignored how the world really worked. Malachy gave an impassive look back. Dino continued, "Anyway, Fr. Bari made the system a success. And the money kept flowing in."

"And now all the good works have ground to a halt?"

"Yes. Our committee is very concerned that a grave injustice is about to be done. We know that Fr. Bari is completely innocent, but it would be very convenient for the archdiocese and Rome if somehow he was forced from his office and silenced."

"Sounds like you need a good canon lawyer."

"We already have that, here and in Rome. What we need is someone who can prove Fr. Bari's innocence in such a way that the only possible outcome is his full restoration with no restrictions. Otherwise we're concerned the church bureaucrats will win a war of attrition. And we are very concerned that Cardinal O'Grady is no friend of the Shrine and certainly no friend of Fr. Bari. There are frequent run-ins about his activities."

"Not a good man to have as an adversary," Malachy said.

"We understand you know the cardinal personally."

"Too true. We grew up in the same neighborhood. Our mothers were best friends. We were forced to play together as boys."

"Then you understand what we are up against."

"A brilliant, calculating, cold-hearted prick," Malachy said. "No doubt he has already selected the wasteland where he's going to bury Fr. Bari. Speaking metaphorically, of course."

"That is what we are concerned about and why I'm here. The committee would like to employ you to prove Fr. Bari's innocence. We understand you sometimes undertake unusual projects."

"What else do you understand?" Malachy asked.

"That you're willing to use unorthodox methods to secure a successful outcome in the projects that you undertake. That those projects usually involve people from your old neighborhood. That you keep your word. And that your late wife, Maria, was Italian and very active in our community."

Malachy winced when Dino said Maria's name. It always made him angry when strangers used her first name instead of just a euphemism like "your late wife."

Dino stopped talking when he saw Malachy's reaction.

"Anything else?" Malachy asked, trying unsuccessfully to keep the anger from his voice.

"I only meant…"

"Move on. I'm over it."

"You sometimes work with two associates. A retired professional burglar and former client named Leon Latalski nicknamed the Count. And your coworker and close friend Kevin, a fellow Vietnam veteran, who is totally loyal to you. Kevin was your chief investigator when you were still practicing law." Dino paused and then said, "There is more. I can go on."

"No need unless you know something about me that I don't know."

Dino smiled and shook his head no. "The committee has authorized me to offer you $2,000 per day, inclusive of your expenses, to act as a consultant in our efforts to prove Fr. Bari's innocence. If you accept our offer, I have a check for $50,000 with you as the payee to act as a retainer."

"Why me? Your community can handle this on its own."

"As I said, Fr. Bari is shrewd and knows the community well. He has explicitly warned us that if any intimidation, threat, or force is used against his accuser, he'll immediately resign and ask the cardinal to close the Shrine. We have assured him that none of that will happen and that the committee will hire a disinterested professional outside the community to do its investigation."

"That answers why you went outside the community. Why me?"

Dino looked down and made a slight adjustment to his left cuff link before he answered the question. "Your potential selection was somewhat controversial within the committee. But, a major donor to our group, who wishes to remain anonymous and entirely in the background, strongly recommended you and, through me, made a very persuasive argument that you are exactly the right man for the job. The final committee vote was unanimous."

"Do I know this person?"

"I don't know, but I doubt it. Will you accept our offer?"

"What's the rest of it?" Malachy asked.

"The rest of it? I don't understand."

"You have more to tell me."

"How did you know that?" Dino asked with genuine surprise.

"You told me—body language."

"Oh," he said quietly.

The idea that his scrubbed, rubbed, oiled, tanned, manicured, twice-a-week trimmed, and sartorially perfect body was telling things without his permission was a shock to Dino.

"We all do it," Malachy said.

He handed Malachy a cell phone.

"It's preprogrammed. Just press one and hold it down for a few seconds. I'll wait for your answer in the bar."

Malachy waited for Dino to leave and pressed one.

A low, distorted voice said, "Hello, Malachy. Are you by yourself?"

"Yes, all by my lonesome in the storeroom, talking with somebody I don't know."

There was a soft chuckle in Malachy's ear.

"You made Dino meet with you in the storeroom? Good for you. Did he make you wrap the chair in silk before he sat down?"

"He accepted the accommodations without complaint."

"Amazing. Let me introduce myself. I am the nameless donor to the committee and will remain anonymous in our interactions. You know me indirectly. I approved the settlement of Singer's gambling debt many years ago. I admired the way you handled that and have followed your career ever since. I have directed various clients to your practice and have always found the results satisfactory."

Malachy realized the voice was coming through a filter. A cautious, careful potential employer.

"Thanks for the referrals, I think."

"You're welcome. As to the current business, there is a success fee that goes with the assignment. Success is easily defined—Fr. Bari is found innocent and restored to his full duties at the Shrine."

Malachy stayed silent.

"Your choice: assistance with reinstatement to the bar or a $150,000 payment. You can choose after the fact."

Malachy's body language was not subtle. He almost fell off the chair. Reinstatement could ultimately be an Illinois Supreme Court decision. He clamped his mouth shut.

"Of course, I can't guarantee the reinstatement. Too many variables. I can guarantee the $150,000. It has to be one or the other, for obvious reasons."

Malachy said, "I do have two questions."

"Go ahead."

"Is this business or personal for you? And why?"

There was a long silence.

"I understand why you want to know, and I will answer your questions. But, this information is only for you."

There was another pause and then the voice went on.

"The matter is personal. I no longer have any business interests in Chicago. Some years ago, in what appeared to everyone else as a hopeless situation, Fr. Bari intervened and basically saved the life of an addicted family member. He kept my family intact, and I owe him for that. It *is* a debt of honor. There is one other thing you need to know. Any attempt to find out who I am is totally unacceptable and will terminate our relationship. And now it is decision time. Will you accept our offer?"

Malachy started to answer, hesitated, and then paused, thinking about how the word "terminate" came with a special tone and emphasis despite the filter. Then he thought about the juice Singer paid coming back with interest to help support him.

"Yes, I accept."

"Good. Hold for a minute."

Malachy waited.

"Dino has left the bar. He gave Kevin an envelope for you. It contains the check and all of Dino's contact numbers. Report to him once a week on your progress. Call him with any normal requests for information, facilitation of interviews, things like that."

"Okay."

"For anything unusual, use the cell phone you were given. It is pre-programmed with five more numbers. Use each one only once. On the first call, tell whoever answers, 'This is Malachy. I need some information.' I will call you back on that cell phone. You'll be given a new formulation for the next call. Use that exact formulation. Don't attempt to change any settings on the phone and don't lose it."

"Understood."

"Your assignment is to prove Fr. Bari innocent. Anything else you find out about Fr. Bari that is not relevant to proving his innocence, keep it to yourself."

"Of course," Malachy said with conviction.

"Good luck."

The cell phone clicked off. Malachy decided luck was not the issue.

Another problem—personal is always more dangerous than business. For everybody. Fr. Bari was either innocent of the accusation or not. That issue was already decided. If not, the high horse of holiness had thrown another rider. And that would be a major problem. The new employer definitely did not want a riderless horse. And Malachy knew the nameless voice expected those in his employ to provide what he had paid for.

"Well, Abe, business is booming," Malachy said softly to the empty room. "Now all I have to do is to keep it from boomeranging."

CHAPTER II

MALACHY STARTLED AWAKE FROM A DREAM AND IMMEDIATELY checked his left hand. There was no blood. In the dream he was playing Frisbee with a suited, masked man and suddenly the Frisbee turned into a knife-thin horseshoe just as he caught it.

"Have a good day," he said aloud.

Malachy checked the clock: 6:00 A.M. He settled back into the warm bed and tried to resume sleeping. Some days going back to sleep came easily no matter what the dream. Some days he knew sleep had fled and was not returning. He kept rubbing his fingers. A horseshoe was supposed to bring good luck, but a flying horseshoe-knife was definitely not a soporific. He considered his quick decision to take on the Bari project. Somehow Singer needing more money and the nameless voice in the storeroom introducing himself with the story of Singer's gambling debt seemed a good omen. He thought about Singer and his ironic nickname. Singer, who sounded like an off-key frog when he tried to sing, got his nickname from a strong resemblance to Dennis Day, the famous tenor on the Jack Benny show. Malachy remembered the day he got the call from Singer.

Singer asked to see Malachy in his office. Malachy was surprised because he saw Singer at least two or three times a week in the Shamrock, Singer's bar.

Singer and Malachy's father had been longtime best friends, and he treated Malachy like the son he never had. Malachy noticed Singer becoming more and more agitated and increasingly jumpy over the holidays, always switching the TV back and forth between football games. At the meeting he was distraught and incoherent, muttering to himself and alternating between pacing the office and using his chair like a trampoline by throwing himself onto it and then immediately springing up.

Malachy patiently got the story out of him. The classic betting story—double up to catch up—with the classic ending. The last minute fumble, field goal, penalty, always something, ruined the bet. And only seconds before the point spread was a friend, and the bet was in the bag.

Malachy bet heavily but only on himself. Another lesson learned from his father. Poker, liar's poker, golf. Only games where an edge was possible—from either his skill or knowledge or from a correct assessment of his opponents.

Somehow Singer's betting $50 per game turned into $500 turned into $1,500 and finally, in the last three losing games, $5,000. Singer couldn't pay. Then the juice started and the draining of cash from the Shamrock to make payments that just kept him even. Suppliers were not being paid, and the Shamrock was about to be cut off.

Malachy calmed Singer down with repeated assurances that he would find a solution, and he sent him off to lunch with a young assistant with strict orders not to let Singer out of sight, including bathroom breaks.

It took Malachy ten telephone calls and the intercession of a connected alderman to talk to somebody high enough up the food chain to make a deal and have it stick. The negotiations did not go smoothly.

Malachy finally convinced the other side that if Singer hurt himself or was hurt in the collection process, the Shamrock would close, the debt would go unpaid, and there would be lots of pissed-off Irish cops and pols from the old neighborhood. They settled on a number.

"Twenty thousand in cash. Cash, no promises, no payments. Got it? Cash. We'll pick it up from your office in three days. Yes or no?"

"Yes. Pick it up after 3:00. I'm in court in the morning."

"Okay. You understand we're done with Singer. This is now your problem."

Malachy resisted the impulse to respond in Italian with "capito." "Understood. Thursday after 3:00."

Malachy called Abe, the accountant for the Shamrock and most of the other neighborhood businesses. He explained the situation and the commitment.

"What floor are you on?" Abe asked.

"The fifth. It seemed appropriate."

"Keep Singer away from the windows. What a schmuck! I'm leaving already. So, what's with you Irishers, anyway? The booze, it doesn't cause enough problems? You need the headache of gambling too?"

The three of them assembled in the firm's conference room. Malachy told them the deal. Singer blanched and started weeping.

"I'm finished. It's all over for me."

"I've got the cash," Malachy said. "But I need it back. It's my entire private stash. It backs all my personal action. Maria runs the family finances. There's no way I'm getting a dime out of her for something like this."

"Smart cookie," Abe said. "So, Singer, how much do you owe the suppliers? And don't bullshit me. I know from bullshit."

"About twelve or thirteen thousand."

"So, we round up to fifteen thousand. Here's what we do..."

Abe outlined a complicated solution that resulted in Malachy owning the Shamrock's building but not the business and generated the cash to repay Malachy and the suppliers from a mortgage on the building.

"Where do we go to get the loan?" Malachy asked.

"One of my clients owns a bank in Uptown," Abe said, pointing north with his thumb over his shoulder. Of course, he's a businessman so he'll want some points, but so what? It's a small price to pay, and the deals he wants to do always appraise out. So, problem solved."

"Really? You're not just saying that..."

Abe interrupted Singer. "What, now I'm some kind of Dr. Feel-Good? Not on your life. This is your accountant talking. I know the numbers. It works, so calm down. One more thing, Malachy should get something for his trouble."

Singer looked at Malachy, expecting him to decline.

"I do want something," Malachy said.

Singer's face collapsed, and he buried his face in hands. "You've got me over a barrel. Whatever you want. I've got to get this over with."

"The TV goes into the back room. No TV in the main bar and no radio either."

"I don't understand," Singer said. "The TV?"

"What's to understand," Abe said. "Malachy is a smart young man. So move the TV. Less temptation. We can only do this once."

"That'll hurt business," Singer said.

"Buy a big fancy one for the back room," Malachy said. "Everybody will love it. There's enough cash in the deal for that. But I get the remote for the one over the bar, and it never goes on unless I turn it on. Not to worry, I'll turn it on if something really important happens. White Sox in the World Series, Cubs move to Peoria, the Republic invades the North, things like that. Deal?"

"Deal," Singer said, laughing for the first time that day.

As he got out of bed, Malachy consoled himself with the thought that no matter how early it started, it was still a $2,000 day. And that, according to the wisdom of the TV prophets he surfed late at night, was a good thing. Even if you had to earn it. Malachy remembered one of his father's many sayings: " 'Love what you do and you will never have to work another day of your life' is bullshit. Every job has some scut work attached to it. Doing a good job means doing the scut work well too. And nobody loves the scut work."

Malachy decided he would ask for help with some of the scut work. After all, he was a $2,000 per day consultant, and he owed his client efficiency. He would call Sheila who worked at the Business Reference Center of the Chicago Public Library. Malachy used some fancy legal footwork to get the police disciplinary charges against her husband dismissed, saving his job. She always wanted to help when he called and also enjoyed a little teasing and flirting. He moved into the kitchen and read yesterday's newspapers with his morning coffee until the kitchen clock showed 7:00. He flipped through his index cards of notes and phone numbers, found Sheila's, and called.

"Good morning, this is Sheila. How may I help you?"

"I definitely need help," Malachy answered.

"Mother of God, the hermit Malachy has emerged from the desert. How were the forty days? Did you give into the Devil's temptations?"

"Not all of them," Malachy said. "I was selective. Anyway, what desert are you referring to?"

"The one on the North Side. I haven't heard from you since God knows when. And you must be desperate to call this early. Let me guess. It was a rough night at the watering hole and you're calling to find out where you live."

Malachy laughed and said, "I'm calling from home, and I slept in my own bed and alone. And I resemble such salacious innuendo."

"Then the situation is serious," Sheila said. "Okay, out with it. What exactly do you need?"

"All print references in the local media to Fr. John Bari, the priest suspended from his duties at the Cabrini Shrine because of an allegation of sexual abuse."

"How far back?"

"The last twelve months should do it. And anything that explains church procedures in cases like this would be a bonus."

"I hope you pay property taxes," Sheila said. "This public servant will be spending a lot of time fulfilling your request."

"I was kind of hoping you could cull the articles and eliminate the redundancies and isolated references. I'm just interested in the meat and potatoes. Or in this case, the bistecca and pasta."

"And that is exactly what this effort is going to cost you. The best dinner Taylor Street has to offer."

"Capito," Malachy said. "I have a new Italian friend. I'll ask him for a recommendation. He's very fastidious about food, drink, and décor."

"Too bad the two of you don't have much in common," Sheila said. "Anyway, make sure the Shamrock's fax is loaded with ink and paper. The stuff will start spitting out at 11:00."

"Thanks, Sheila, you're a saint."

"A saint with a taste for Italian food and a long memory," Sheila said. "Don't forget to call. Bye."

Malachy moved slowly through his morning routine. His usual long hot shower took even longer as he considered and rejected scenario after scenario on how to start the investigation. By the time it came for a decision about his protective "street" clothing, he pulled out one of his everyday outfits. Research work was the order of the day. He dressed and called Dino.

"Good morning, Mr. Montegiordano's office. How may I direct your call?"

"To the man himself," Malachy answered, trying to sound wide-awake and energetic.

"May I ask who is calling and what this call is in reference to?"

"No cold calls for Dino," Malachy answered. "Just say it's Malachy calling about justice."

"Justice?" the well-modulated voice asked.

"Yes, justice. As in the blindfolded lady holding the scales."

"Very well. Please hold, Mr. Malachy."

After a couple of minutes Dino came on the phone.

"Good morning, Malachy. In the future just tell the receptionist your name and she will put your call through without any screening. What do you need?"

"I need videotape of the press conference that Fr. Bari gave about the accusation," Malachy said. "Not just the snippets they showed on TV, but as much tape as was shot."

"What for?"

"Scut work."

"Scout work? I don't understand."

"Research," Malachy said.

"I was given to understand you are action oriented," Dino said.

Malachy was silent for a while, deciding how hard to respond. Too often in the past his quick tongue made for unnecessary trouble.

"I'm a victim of my Irish grandmother who filled my head with sayings. 'Look before you leap.' 'You never get a second chance to make a first impression.' Stuff like that. I need Fr. Bari's full cooperation in order to prove his innocence. I just want to understand him better, that's all. I was hoping you could help with that monster Rolodex of yours."

Dino laughed and said, "Okay, Malachy. I get it. I'll make a few calls. My assistant will call you back with the results. I'm sure it'll be no problem."

Malachy called Kevin and the Count to schedule what he called a "joint chiefs" meeting in the back room of the Shamrock at 4:00. He gave them the background on the job and the nameless voice.

Malachy entered the Shamrock at noon. There were a few lunch customers and nobody sitting at the bar. He greeted Kevin who pointed to a thick stack of paper on the tabletop in his back office-booth, with its padded benches, extra wide table, and two wall phones.

"The fax is the most active thing in the bar," Kevin said. "It's been going strong since late morning. No courier yet."

"Dino's assistant says the courier will be here by 3:00. Ask Eduardo to bring me some fresh coffee and something to eat. I'm going to try to plow through all this stuff before our meeting. Keep it coming."

Malachy moved to his office-booth. If he picked up a piece of paper he forced himself to read it all the way through and make notes on what he read before he put it down. He sat on the visitors' side of the booth, with his back to the barroom, so he could concentrate.

By 2:30, he knew more than he ever wanted to about canon law, Rome–Chicago clerical politics, and diocesan rules and regulations concerning the use of church property. By 3:30, he knew more than he ever wanted to about sexual abuse of children by priests, including the very specific and very graphic allegations against Fr. Bari. He stopped at 3:55, knowing the Count would be distressed if the meeting started late. Punctuality and fastidious dressing were two values the short, agile Count always promulgated. And he held himself to the same standards even when he had worked nights in strangers' homes.

Kevin came over to the booth, leaned down, and said softly, "The back room is cleared and closed to the public, the tapes are ready to go, and the Count is waiting."

Malachy waited for Kevin to settle into his chair, looked at the wall clock, and at exactly 4:00 pushed the play button on the remote. The TV screen filled with a mass of reporters milling about and jockeying for position in front of the Shrine church prior to the press conference. The audio on the tape was low-level street noise from cars and trucks and mostly inaudible conversation with the occasional curse or phrase ringing out clearly. The camera slowly panned the waiting press conference microphones and the facade of the church and then did a slow circle of the surrounding area before focusing back on the bank of microphones.

The high, arched church door swung open and a tall, fit priest emerged alone and strode almost eagerly to the microphones. The reporters started yelling questions. Fr. Bari ignored the questions, raised his arms in a gesture requesting quiet, and started speaking.

"I have a statement to make. After I have given my statement I will answer your questions. Let me repeat that for those in the back who could not hear me because of the noise."

Fr. Bari repeated his remarks in a strong, resonant voice that quieted the crowd. Malachy noted that everything about Bari's figure displayed confidence and lack of fear, more like an athlete who had already won his contest than someone about to undergo an ordeal. Bari, with his relaxed stance and the calm look on his face, seemed to treat the media throng as if it was just an unruly gathering of the faithful waiting for him to preach.

"He is one of the best-looking priests I've ever seen," the Count said. "Tall, dark, and handsome. Hollywood handsome. Those types usually don't make it all the way to ordination. Too many opportunities."

"Kind of a clerical Rudolph Valentino," Malachy said. "Just as Italian with the slight accent but much taller."

When the reporters were mostly quiet, Fr. Bari started his statement.

"Sexual abuse of children is a horrific crime with terrible consequences. Some in positions of trust in the Church have committed that crime repeatedly. And some in positions of authority within the Church have facilitated the crime of sexual abuse by their failure to protect children from known abusers. Mr. Pace has accused me of such a crime. I never sexually abused him or anyone else. I repeat—I never sexually abused Anthony Pace or anyone else."

Bari paused, and immediately some reporters started yelling questions. He held up his arms again, silently appealing for the questions to stop. He continued with his statement.

"Nor do I have any personal knowledge of anyone else abusing Pace or any other minor. I will fully cooperate with all investigations of this allegation—criminal, civil, and Church. The sincerity of my accuser is self-evident. However, he is mistaken in his belief that I am the person who criminally abused him.

"I bear no ill will toward Mr. Pace. The victims of childhood sexual abuse need compassion, healing, and justice. Whatever I can do to bring healing and justice to this situation, I will do. Thank you for your attention. I will now answer questions."

The reporters erupted into a screaming match of questions. Fr. Bari let them yell for a minute. He then pointed to a reporter from one of the TV stations. After several tries, the reporter was able to get his question heard.

"You claim you didn't abuse your accuser. Did you have any contact with him at all? Were you ever alone with him? Did you know him?"

Malachy closed his eyes so he could concentrate on the pitch and timbre of Bari's voice without visual distractions.

"Pius XII is a very big parish with a large parochial school. I had no special friendship with Pace or his family. I have no memory of meeting him. But I am sure we encountered each other sometime during my regular duties at the church or school. It was never my practice to meet with children alone."

A newspaper reporter shouted a question over the end of Fr. Bari's answer. Malachy now concentrated on Bari's facial expressions to determine if they subtly contradicted Bari's words.

"Pace said the abuse started after a confession. Did you hear children's confessions?"

"Of course," Bari said. "As I said, it was and still is a very big parish and school. Every priest assigned to the parish heard adult and child confessions. I gave standard penances to children and never required a child to see me alone after confession as part of a penance or for any other reason."

Everything Malachy saw and heard pushed him toward the conclusion Bari was not the abuser.

Bari called on a cable TV commentator who Malachy knew from his days in criminal court. Snarky Steve was his nickname.

"Are you telling us in all those years at Pius XII, you were never alone with a child? Do you expect us to believe that?"

"I expect you to not misconstrue what I say out of ill will or to score points. Of course I was alone with a given child for short periods of time by happenstance. What I said was that I never asked or required a child to see me alone as part of a penance or for any other reason."

"What do you mean happenstance? Give us an example."

"The altar server before an early morning weekday Mass. There were many times I would be alone with that server for a few minutes prior to the Mass."

The press conference continued back and forth with questions, some of them openly hostile, trying to trap Bari into admission that would cast doubt on his statement of innocence. Bari's strong, clear answers dominated the exchange. Bari called on a TV network channel reporter at the back of the crowd.

"In your statement you said you never sexually abused your accuser or anyone else. What constitutes abuse is open to interpretation. Have you always lived a celibate life as a priest?"

The media crowd went immediately silent, and the camera zoomed in on Bari's face.

"My statement and this press conference are about the allegation that I committed a crime—that the horrible and criminal sexual things done to Mr. Pace were done by me. As I stated, they were not. In my adult life, I have never had sexual contact of any kind with any child."

The reporter yelled, "You didn't answer my question!"

"That is my answer to your question—in my adult life, I have never had sexual contact with any child."

The press conference broke into a maelstrom of questions about celibacy. Bari ended the conference with a "thank-you" and turned and went back into the church, passing through a line of men. Some reporters tried to follow him, but the line of tough-looking men linked arms and blocked the only open entrance to the church. The tape went blank.

Malachy clicked off the TV and said, "Ever since Starr had Clinton abusing cigars and masturbating in a sink, too many reporters act like they work for the scandal rags. Anyway, who wants to go first? Innocent or guilty?"

"A man who had his opportunities and took some of them," the Count said. "But not with children. He didn't do the crime."

"I have a question," Kevin said. "Who is this?"

Kevin took the remote from Malachy and reversed the tape until it came to the opening scenes when the camera was panning the sidewalk and street in front of the Shrine. He froze the frame. It showed a man with a camera hung around his neck leaning against a car with its windows open. He appeared to have a half-smile or smirk on his face.

"I have no idea," Malachy said. "Why? He looks like a curious bystander just trying to get a picture."

"There are a number of curious things about Mr. Curious Bystander," Kevin answered. "Look closely at the camera. The lens cap is on. Tough to get a picture that way. He's wearing large, dark sunglasses, and that day wasn't sunny. He's wearing a long-beaked hat that makes it difficult to see his entire face. And the car he's leaning against isn't from Chicago. No city sticker on the windshield."

"Surveillance of some kind?" Malachy asked.

"The camera is a prop for somebody who wants to watch but doesn't want to be recognized," Kevin said. "And that somebody uses a car that isn't required to be registered in Chicago or the suburbs."

"You saw all that the first time?" the Count asked.

"No," Kevin answered. "I was trained to look for stuff that doesn't fit the expected pattern. He didn't fit the pattern. He wasn't media because he wasn't jockeying for position. And if you're curious, you want to press closer. Not hang back. Maybe take off your sunglasses or switch to regular eyeglasses to get a better look. I saw the other stuff in the freeze-frame."

"Maybe just a neighborhood eccentric," Malachy said.

Kevin said, "I'll take that bet."

"No bet," Malachy said. "But, I'll have the picture passed around the neighborhood just to make sure. If you're right, we'll need to find out who he is and why he was there. But what about Bari?"

"I'm not sure which side he bats from, but the batboy is not part of the game," Kevin said. "What's your reaction?"

"I'm struck with the legal language," Malachy said. "It's all about crime, not sin. It's a deliberate challenge to Cardinal O'Grady who only talks about the sin of sexual abuse. It's an open invitation to the prosecutors to do their job. And he sounds angry the job has not been done."

Malachy paused trying to remember the names of two clients from his legal practice but quickly decided to use only a generic example to avoid offending the Count. "I've known a few attractive sociopaths who were persuasive and convincing in proclaiming their innocence and inviting a full investigation while simultaneously planning the next crime. Something is up with Bari, but I don't think he's a pedophile."

"So our client is not guilty by unanimous vote," the Count said. "Where do we start?"

"Research," Malachy said. "Here's the short version of what I learned."

Malachy spoke rapidly referring to his notes.

"O'Grady returned from Rome with a mandate to get the archdiocese's finances in order. It was his ticket to the red hat. He is well regarded in Rome—fellow traveler in the world of church bureaucracy. His PhD in canon law also doesn't hurt. So lots of parishes are scheduled to close. Typical O'Grady, he puts more on the chopping block than he really intends to cut. He waits to see how hard the pushback is so he can relent on a few of them and come out the good guy.

"The parish at the heart of Little Italy is slated for closure. The Italian-American community pushes back real hard, including using contacts in Rome. O'Grady compromises by forcing the parish to close, but allows the church itself to become a self-supporting Shrine. The experience rankles. Along comes Fr. Bari, and the place becomes a phenomenal success."

Malachy paused and quickly glanced at Kevin and then the Count to make sure they were still with him. He returned his gaze to Kevin, puzzled by the strange look on his face. He returned to his notes and resumed the briefing.

"But Bari is no stickler for canon law or other church rules and stirs up all kinds of trouble including attracting the attention of Rome. O'Grady uses every opportunity he can to assert his authority. Bari and O'Grady are in a constant state of conflict. Then the bombshell of the sexual abuse allegation. The perfect opportunity for O'Grady to return the Shrine to obscurity. But O'Grady has to be careful and subtle. He doesn't want to bolster Pace's case against the archdiocese."

"I know O'Grady isn't a Borgia, but I have to raise the question," the Count said. "Could he be behind the whole thing?"

"No," Malachy said firmly. "Think of him as the first Mayor Daley with a red hat but with European polish and beaucoup academic smarts. He understands power and how to use it, and has a very strong taste for it. And he could justify a lot for the greater good of the Church, but never something like that."

"What do we know about the accuser?" Kevin asked.

"Not enough," Malachy said. "His lawyer is keeping him under wraps. But we have a few facts. His mother is very pious like some we used to have in the old neighborhood. Lots of devotional practices, daily Mass. Priests on pedestals. He went to the parish school. Here's a childhood picture one of the newspapers dug up." Malachy passed around a picture of a smiling, happy-eyed boy a few years away from puberty.

"He looks familiar," Kevin said. He took the remote and put a freeze-frame close-up of Bari on the screen. He held up the boyhood picture of Pace.

"See any resemblance?" Kevin asked.

"Spooky," Malachy said. "If you didn't know better, you'd think the picture is Bari as a boy."

"Or at least his younger brother," the Count said.

"Here's a recent picture of Pace," Malachy said. He put a picture on the table of a too-thin, pale young man with a bad complexion. The smile and good looks were gone. The eyes had lost their luster.

"Jesus, what happened?" Kevin asked. "They can't be the same person."

"Drugs, alcohol, and male prostitution," Malachy said.

"Does he have AIDS?" Kevin asked.

"No, but a string of STDs, according to his attorney," Malachy answered.

"How long did the abuse last?" the Count asked.

"Three years, from eleven to fourteen. As soon as Pace hit puberty, the abuser dropped him. No contact whatsoever. Pace dropped out of high school at sixteen, ran away from home, and hit the streets. His father died in a work accident six months before the abuse started. The picture is a school photo taken before his dad's death."

Malachy, Kevin, and the Count sat in silence looking at the before and after photographs of Pace.

"What the hell happened?" Kevin asked again.

"Here is how it started in Pace's own words," Malachy said.

"The priest in the confessional started to ask me strange questions. He asked me what my name was. I told him. He asked me if I was from the family where the dad had died a few months ago. I told him yes. He seemed to know a lot about my family and me. He asked how I was doing in school and in sports. Things like that. He told me it must be hard without a dad to talk to about private things. I didn't know what he meant.

"He asked me if I ever touched myself or rubbed myself down there. I was so confused. I didn't know what to say. I stammered and hesitated. He got angry and said something like, 'You have to tell me the truth. This is confession.' I finally said, 'I sometimes touch myself there.' He immediately got nicer and told me it was okay, but there was a special penance for that and I had to meet him later. He asked me if I knew where the bathroom in the church basement was. I told him yes.

"He told me to kneel in the pew for a few minutes and then go down to the bathroom and wait inside. He said the special penance needed water and that was easiest place to get it. He would meet me there. Then he said the confessional was secret and the special penance was very secret too. I couldn't tell anyone ever or I'd commit a sin that couldn't be forgiven.

"He asked if I understood, and I whispered yes. He told me to repeat after him, 'I promise to go to the church bathroom and I promise to never tell anyone about the special penance.' I repeated what he said. He told me, 'Very good. Now go to the pew.' I went to the pew and then down to the bathroom. There was no one else around. I went inside and waited. After a while, there was a soft knock on the door and the priest said in almost a whisper, 'This is Fr. Bari. Anthony, are you in there?' I said yes. He said, 'Good, shut your eyes and turn around and face the wall.' I did it, and he came into the bathroom.

"He took some kind of a cloth or sash and tied it around my head covering my eyes. He told me to hold my hands behind my back and to turn around. He told me to keep my hands behind my back while he started the special penance. He undid the buckle of my belt and the snap on my pants and pulled my pants and underpants down. I started to grab for my pants and he said angrily, 'Keep your hands behind your back. Your hands are what caused the need for this penance.' He touched and fondled my penis and testicles over and over. I started to cry. He told me it would be over in a minute and to stop crying. He put his mouth on my penis and I felt his tongue. I told him I had to go to the bathroom. He stopped and made some moaning noises. He turned me around and said to go ahead and urinate. I did and could hear the splash of the urine in the toilet water. He flushed the toilet.

"Then he said, 'The special penance is over. That wasn't so bad, was it?' I shook my head no. 'Pull up your pants,' he said. He whispered in my ear, 'Now listen to me. The special penance is over for this week. You did fine. You must never tell anyone about this. Do you promise? It is a terrible, unforgivable sin to break a promise to a priest. Do you understand?' I nodded yes.

"'Repeat after me, I promise to never tell my mom or anyone about the special penance, and I promise to come back to this bathroom next Wednesday right after school.' I started to cry again. 'Say it now,' he said. I made the promises. I was still crying. 'Good,' Fr. Bari said. 'Remember if you break your promises, I will come and find you and it will be very bad for you.' Fr. Bari turned off the light and untied the sash. He told me to wash my hands and face after he left and go straight home. He left the bathroom, and I did what he told me. I returned to the bathroom once or twice a week after school.

"The abuse for the first couple of months was the same. Later he always started the abuse the same way, but then he also put his penis in my mouth. He whispered instructions on what to do and if I didn't do it right he would get angry. Most of the time he would ejaculate into my mouth. In the last year, he used Vaseline and penetrated my anus, first with his fingers and then his penis. It hurt and I sometimes bled. He told me I would get used to it. He always covered my eyes.

"After the first few months, he stopped talking about the special penance, but after each time he made me promise to never tell anyone what happened. He always made me repeat that promise out loud.

"I tried to get away from him a number of times. He always called me at home when my mother was out. He told me if I didn't show up where and when he told me, he would show the other priests and teachers at the school pictures of me naked doing some of the things he forced me to do. They would kick me out of the school and not allow my mother to come to Mass at the parish church anymore. And the police would come and take me away to a jail for delinquent boys. I was scared and always went back to meet him.

"It ended one day when I met him and he covered my eyes, and I started to take down my pants and he told me to stop. He said I was getting too old. He told me I was a queer and everything that he did to me would have happened anyway because I really wanted it to happen.

"He told me that it was really all my fault. He warned me that he had a lot of pictures of me doing all those things, and I would be the one everyone blamed. He repeated the threats he used to scare me into meeting him—if I ever said anything, he would mail those pictures to my mother, to the other priests, and to my teachers.

"Everybody would know I was a queer. And nobody would talk to my mother or let her be a member of any parish. She would lose her job. It would be all my fault. Everything would be okay if I just kept silent. I never told anyone until this year."

Malachy stopped reading. The three of them sat silently for a couple of minutes.

The Count spoke first. "The kid was targeted. If it's not Bari, and we don't think it is, then it has to be one of the other priests assigned to that parish during that time. That group can't be very large. We put together the list and go after them one at a time. For sure, Pace is not the only victim. Our man did it again, probably lots of times. He can't always have been so careful about disguising his identity. We will find him and quickly. The problem is going to be proving his guilt."

"I hope you're right," Malachy said. "But there are other possibilities even if they are considerably less probable. Pace could be a fraud. The priest could have been a visitor, helping out during a busy time. He could have targeted Pace and somehow arranged to hear his confession. And then used the basement bathroom for the meetings even though he was not assigned to that parish.

"Or, even less probable, what if it was a pedophile posing as a priest after he targeted Pace—maybe a member of the staff? But I agree we start with the most probable. Kevin?"

Malachy looked at Kevin, who had taken the fax and was reading the last lines over and over. Kevin answered with his head down. "We need to find this monster and stop him. He is out there doing it to some other kid. We need to put an end to it, no matter who he is and no matter what it takes."

Kevin raised his head and looked directly into Malachy's eyes. Malachy was startled to see the "battlefield stare" from their days in Vietnam.

"No matter what it takes. Are we agreed on that?"

"Yes," Malachy said.

CHAPTER III

Malachy woke early, unable to return to sleep because the day's plans were swirling in his head. The joint chiefs agreed on an initial basic plan. Kevin and the Count would attend the Mass at Pius XII church, check the layout and the access to the bathroom, and try to talk with a janitor about any change to the access from earlier years.

Malachy would obtain the names of the priests assigned to Pius XII parish and try to interview at least one of the priests on the list. He would arrange for the picture of Mr. Curious Bystander to be passed around the Taylor Street neighborhood and the Shrine. And, Malachy would continue his basic research. They would meet late in the afternoon or early evening at the Shamrock. Time to be determined by the day's events.

Malachy propped up the pillows behind his head, shut his eyes, and tried to remember his dream. But the day's plans had obliterated it. He moved to the kitchen table and at exactly 7:00 A.M. he called Sheila.

"Good morning, this is Sheila. How may I help you?"

"How do you get so cheerful so early in the morning?" Malachy asked. "It's too early to start drinking."

"Malachy, my dear, there is a direct linkage between the night before and the morning after. In your case, morning miracles would happen if the night before were more restrained and temperate in food, drink, and companionship."

"Temperance," Malachy said emphasizing each syllable and saying the word like it was from a dead language. "I will try and remember that. Anyway, I need another favor."

Sheila switched to a light brogue. "Surprised it is I am that an honorable man such as yourself would ask another favor before repaying previously granted boons. Nevertheless, I will try to help. What now?"

"I need to know the names of all the priests assigned to Pius XII Parish in March of 1991."

"Call your friend O'Grady."

"I don't think so. Anyway, he doesn't consider me a friend. But that's a long story. We need to find the answer without using official archdiocese sources."

"Can we call the parish office?" Sheila asked.

"Not if they refer the question to the pastor."

"Then we need a copy of the parish bulletin from that time," Sheila said. "Some of the parishes have archived copies on their websites, but they usually don't go back that far. But the parish definitely has a copy somewhere."

"Jesus, I don't want to do a break-in," Malachy said. "Who else might have a copy?"

"Let me think on it and make a few calls."

"Thanks, Sheila, you're the best."

"Just for the record, I have upgraded what I'm drinking at our dinner. No more Chianti, I'm thinking a really good amarone."

"Capito," Malachy said.

Malachy moved quickly through his morning routine. When he telephoned Dino the receptionist called him Mr. Malachy and transferred him immediately through to Dino's cell phone.

"Good morning, Malachy. You are certainly getting an early start these days."

"All we high-priced consultants hit the ground running early every morning," Malachy said.

"You have no idea how much I wish the many professionals I engage only charged $2,000 a day," Dino said.

"I run a low overhead operation," Malachy said. "You've seen my office."

Malachy hoped his response was only a light jab, not an uppercut. He reminded himself he needed Dino's cooperation.

Dino was ready to move on. "What do you need, Malachy?"

"I have a picture of someone who was in the background at Fr. Bari's press conference. I don't know who he is, and I want to find out. I'm calling to ask if the picture could be circulated around the neighborhood and at the Shrine to see if anybody recognizes him."

"Yes, that can be arranged. I have just the man for the job, knows everybody. Is the picture from the tape?"

"It is."

"Have five copies made and courier them to my office. I will have an answer for you in a few days."

"Yes, sir," Malachy said without a hint of sarcasm. "And thank you for the help.

"You're welcome, Malachy," Dino said pleasantly.

Malachy looked at the kitchen clock which showed 11:05. He tried to remember how much ahead he set it because he liked to leave for the Shamrock by eleven on the mornings when the bar was his first stop of the day. Malachy was getting ready to leave when Sheila called as promised.

Sheila didn't bother with any greetings. "If you head to the Shamrock right now, by the time you get there copies of the March '91 parish bulletins will be coming out of your fax."

"You're a miracle worker. How did you do it?"

"Funeral home. Advertises in a lot of parish bulletins. The owner is kind of an anal retentive type, didn't even have to go into storage. I told him a bunch of lies about a special Chicago history project. He was happy to cooperate. If I lose my job, it's on your head."

"Your family is so wired it could be a stand-alone cable company. I think my head is safe. Tell me, is there anyone in the family, on either side, over the age of ten, not on some taxpayer-supported payroll?"

Sheila laughed and said, "I come from a long line of South Side Irish dedicated to public service. You North Siders are big consumers of public services. Somebody has got to do the work. Don't forget our dinner date. Bye."

Malachy walked briskly to the Shamrock, hoping his pace would gather energy and momentum for the first interaction of the day with Bridget. As he walked in the door, he quickly scanned the bar and saw only Eduardo, the Shamrock's longtime jack-of-all-trades employee, and a few customers. Eduardo pointed to the kitchen and made a gesture indicating Bridget was wound up.

Bridget emerged from the kitchen and yelled at Malachy, "How long is Kevin going to be on your project?"

Malachy looked at Bridget with her amply filled, green Shamrock apron; smooth full face; and thick gray-white hair gathered in a bun, looking to all the world like the sweet Irish grandmother she was not, and wondered one more time how many shocked customers left the bar never to return. He motioned to Bridget to join him in his office-booth and said quietly, "For a while. You are in charge until he can return full time. Try not to make too many customers cry."

Bridget moved her volume down from yell to loud. "Shit. Drinkers nowadays are all lightweights with sensitive feelings. If you say boo, their feelings are hurt. If I'm the boss, do I get to fire somebody?"

"No."

"Do I get to change your rules?"

"No."

"Then what's the point of being boss?"

"You're helping the team. Just pretend you're Kevin and run the place like he would."

"He's way too nice. Puts up with too much shit from everybody, including you. I can't do and won't do that," Bridget said, slapping the table hard for emphasis. "I quit. Find a new boss."

"Okay, okay. You're the boss until Kevin gets back. You don't have to take shit from anybody. Deal?"

"Deal. Now quit bothering me, I have work to do."

Malachy watched Bridget stomp off toward the back room and then turned his attention to the faxes neatly stacked facedown at the side of the table. He picked up the March '91 bulletins and scanned the staff listings. Fr. Otto Grotemeyer was the pastor. Three other priests were listed—Sullivan, Cullen, Bari. He made a note on a yellow legal pad to have Sheila check that there was not a staff change recorded in later bulletins that could have happened before March.

He picked up the wall phone receiver and called his friend and confessor, Fr. Paul Kennedy. "This is Malachy. How are you?"

"I'm fine, but something tells me you're not calling to schedule a special confession."

"Well, I do need a favor. Do you know any of these priests?"

Malachy read him the list.

"Yes, two of them. I'm afraid to ask why you're asking."

"Good, that way I won't have to lie to you," Malachy said. "Somehow, lying to one's confessor doesn't seem kosher. I suppose you know the ones with Irish names."

"Of course," Kennedy said. "What do you want to know about them?"

"Which one dislikes O'Grady the most, and which one is the most talkative? You'll make my day if it is all contained in one person."

"Sorry, two names. Jim Sullivan hates O'Grady. He is laicized, and O'Grady made trouble for him in Rome as he was going through the process. Pat Cullen would talk to a rock following the cocktail hour. He is…what's your phrase…a very enthusiastic social drinker. What do you want to talk to them about?"

"Pius XII Parish and Fr. Bari," Malachy said.

"Oh, Lord, now I'm nervous. Why?"

"Background research," Malachy said.

"For what purpose?"

"Ah, now we are entering 'don't ask, don't tell' territory. I'll explain it all when it's over. Hopefully, outside the confessional. One last question—is Jim Sullivan any relationship to Peter Sullivan, my friend from the old neighborhood?"

"I don't think so."

"Too bad. It always helps to have a connection.

"Any idea where the loquacious Fr. Cullen is assigned now?" Malachy asked.

"St. Ita, not very far from you."

"And what would Fr. Cullen do for good, clean fun as the nuns used to say? Maybe a sports fan or something like that."

"I know he plays golf."

"And where might I find Jim Sullivan?"

"That's easy—he lives right here in the parish. We have a lot of laicized priests for some reason. You're really not going to tell me what this is all about?"

"Not yet. But I definitely owe you one. Thanks for helping."

Malachy decided Cullen the rock talker was probably his best bet, but he would try and talk with both of them. He wrote the two names on his yellow legal pad about four inches apart. He took an Irish sixpence wolfhound coin from the coin box he used as a paperweight and held it above the legal pad and let it drop. The coin landed on Sullivan. He searched through a cluttered file box he stored below the table, found a parish directory, located Sullivan's number, and called.

"Jim Sullivan? This is Malachy Madden calling. We don't know each other, but we're fellow parishioners. Is this a good time to talk for a minute?"

"Fr. Kennedy has been after me to serve on one of the parish committees. Is this call about that?" Sullivan sounded cordial but a little reserved.

"No, but you have my sympathy," Malachy said. "When he gets an idea someone is just right for a parish job, dynamite couldn't blast it out of his head."

Sullivan laughed and said, "You've been a victim, too. Anyway, what can I do for you?"

"I'd like to talk to you in person about something I'm working on. It wouldn't take long."

"What did you say your name is?"

"Malachy Madden. I work over at the Shamrock, maybe you've stopped in there."

"Yes, I've been in the Shamrock, but I don't remember meeting you. What is it you want to talk about?"

"Your time at Pius XII."

"How could that possibly have any connection to the Shamrock?" Sullivan asked, the friendly tone replaced with cold distance.

"It doesn't. I also have another business—let's call it project-oriented consulting." There was a long silence. Malachy decided to plunge ahead.

"Look, I know that is the long ago past for you. If you would just see me for a few minutes, I can explain the what and why." Malachy knew a bet on curiosity usually paid off. "If you decide you don't want to talk with me, I'm out of there and you'll never hear from me again unless Kennedy sticks me with some parish job."

"That sounds okay," Sullivan said. "Where and when do you want to meet?"

"Whatever makes you most comfortable."

"There's a coffee shop on the corner of Broadway and Rosemont, near my place."

"I know it well," Malachy said.

"I'll head over there now. How will I know you?"

"I look like I've spent too much time in bars. See you there."

Malachy looked down on the coin touching the name Sullivan and thought about his boyhood friend Peter Sullivan and his first "consulting" project. Peter made up his nickname, M2. He remembered how the plan to solve Peter's dilemma came to him in one piece. No research and no success fee. Clients and their projects were more complicated now. And too few knew his nickname.

Peter Sullivan came into the Shamrock for a drink on his way home to the North Shore and joined Malachy in his booth. Malachy asked after his kids. "You're the father of daughters, you understand how you worry before they're settled," Peter said.

Malachy watched Pete squirm in the booth and chop the air with his hands. Malachy had sat across from guilty clients who were less agitated than his friend. Peter continued, "Well, Kathleen is living with a druggie. He's got some kind of hold on her, the manipulative bastard. Somehow she believes she is going to save him, make him into an upstanding citizen. I'm worried sick he's going to end up converting her. She was a little wild in college, did a little experimenting, if you know what I mean."

"Whose place do they live in?"

"Hers. I co-signed the lease and help out a little with the rent, and now that worthless piece of crap is sponging off her—and me."

"You want him out of her life?"

"The sooner the better. But she won't listen to reason, not from me and not even from her mother. And she used to be very close to her mother."

"I'll take care of it," Malachy said, the plan already formulated in his head.

"Jesus, M2, I'm an attorney. I don't want the guy beat up, not that I haven't thought of that and worse."

"Just because I'm no longer practicing doesn't mean I've become a thug. I'm not going to harm him, but I'll take care of it."

"Sorry, no offense. What will you do?"

Malachy looked at Peter Sullivan for a while without answering and then said very slowly, "I'll take care of it if you want me to."

"Want you to? Damn right I want you to."

"There will be some expenses, nothing major. I would need to be reimbursed for those—in cash."

"No problem."

"Call me in a few days. I'll give you a progress report."

Peter Sullivan called Malachy three days later, sounding half-angry. "What the hell is going on? Kathleen is totally hysterical. She's been robbed. They took everything. I told her the boyfriend probably sold some stuff for drug money. She said it's not possible because everything is gone, literally, everything. There's nothing left but walls and carpet. The boyfriend is nowhere to be found, and she's heard nothing from him."

"Sounds like a wonderful opportunity for family bonding to me," Malachy said, speaking slowly so Peter would have time to adjust to the information. "Obviously, she'll need to come home for a while. All her stuff is perfectly safe. It's been carefully packed and moved to a warehouse."

"Where's the boyfriend?"

"He took a bus to New Orleans on what he believes is a drug pickup mission. When he gets there, he will report to a lawyer who will hand him an envelope with $500 in cash. He will be told the deal is not quite ready and to come back in a week. The next week the same thing will happen."

"How long will that go on?"

"Don't know. How long will it take for Kathleen to find a new boyfriend or the druggie to find a new girlfriend to prey on?"

"Thanks, M2, you're a miracle worker. I'll stop by on my way home tomorrow. Today I need to go shopping with Kathleen and her mother."

Malachy watched a wiry man with thinning, reddish-blond hair and fair skin enter the coffee shop. To Malachy something about the dark clothes and slightly ill-at-ease manner said ex-religious. Malachy waved him over to his booth at the back of the restaurant.

"Sorry, it took me a few minutes longer than I thought," Sullivan said. "I decided to check you out."

"Did I pass?"

"Kind of. Both men said essentially the same thing. You never put all your cards on the table, but you keep your word. You're known for helping out neighborhood guys with unusual problems. And sometimes the solutions can be a little unusual too."

"Fair enough," Malachy said. "And logical. Keeping one's word may not allow putting all the cards on the table."

Malachy motioned to the waitress.

"Let's get coffee or whatever you want to drink."

The waitress brought them a coffee and a Diet Coke, and Malachy started in on his pitch.

"I work for a group that wants to prove Fr. Bari is innocent. I'm looking for someone I can trust to tell me about the priests who staffed Pius XII back then and how the place really ran. Whatever you choose to tell me will stay confidential, and you will not be involved in any way because of me."

"What if he's not innocent?" Sullivan asked.

"That would be a problem."

"What would you do about the problem?" Sullivan asked.

"I don't know for sure," Malachy said. "But I wouldn't give back my fee."

Sullivan said, "A stalwart champion for the cause of justice."

Malachy looked straight at Sullivan and said, "Sometimes it works out that way."

"Sorry," Sullivan said. "Sometimes I get too bitter and sarcastic, or so my wife tells me. Okay, I'm in. What do you want to know?"

Malachy referred to his notes. "There were four priests there, including yourself and the pastor. Let's start at the top. Tell me about Fr. Otto Grotemeyer."

"Rigid, autocratic, Germanic type. Everything by the book, the old-fashioned book. Vatican II a big mistake, why do you need anything more than the Baltimore Catechism? The laity should pay, pray, and obey. Especially pay. The most important part of the day was mealtime.

"He really liked to pack it in. Things needed to run well so he could spend time at his fishing cabin in northern Wisconsin. He loved the restaurants up there. The kind of places that serve a heart attack on the plate. He left you alone as long as you didn't screw up his schedule. Innovation didn't belong in the church, the parish, or the kitchen. What else do you want to know?"

"What were his bad qualities?" Malachy asked.

Sullivan half laughed and said, "Tough to overcome the bitterness. He really wasn't a bad man or a bad priest."

"Is there any way he could have been involved in abusing Anthony Pace?"

"Impossible."

"Could he have known about it?"

"I suppose so."

"What would he have done about it?" Malachy asked.

"Slugged down some Pepto-Bismol." Sullivan stopped and looked down at his Diet Coke. "He would have seen it as a problem to be managed so that there was no public scandal. He liked to do things according to the rules, so he might have reported it downtown. But maybe not if he thought it would reflect too badly on his role as pastor."

"What if there was a problem priest?" Malachy asked.

"I suppose you mean the standard stuff—drink and women. I know the answer to the drink problem because we had one—Pat Cullen. And I guess I qualify on the woman part. The cops brought Cullen home to the rectory more than once. I don't know what a priest had to do to get arrested in those days, but drinking and driving didn't do it. Otto was remarkably tolerant on the drinking—almost as if he expected it from the Irish. A lecture during a private breakfast with the benign pastoral viewpoint—don't do it in public and cause scandal."

"How did he treat you?" Malachy asked.

"He understood an outbreak of lust, but he wanted no part of a priest struggling with his vocation. He just wanted me to go away."

"Could Cullen have abused Pace?" Malachy asked.

"I don't think so."

When Sullivan finished his last answer, Malachy decided to risk offending him.

"By the way, did you know Pace or his family?"

"By the way, I don't sexually abuse children." Sullivan stared hard at Malachy until Malachy decided to concede and looked away.

"I remember the mother because she was in church so much. I don't remember the boy."

"Had to ask," Malachy said.

"What else do you want to know?"

"About Bari."

"Dynamic, innovative, a great speaker and motivator. Charismatic and very handsome. Endless energy. Bari and Grotemeyer clashed all the time. Bari wouldn't take no for an answer. He wore the pastor down. He was always stirring things up. The young marrieds and the teenagers loved him. I'm not surprised at all by his great success at the Shrine. He got an amazing amount done under an autocratic, old-school pastor. At the Shrine, it was Bari unbound."

"Were the two of you friends?"

"We were friendly, but not friends. I supported him when I could and when it wouldn't be counterproductive. He was always on the go. He didn't socialize much with me or the other priests." Sullivan paused and again looked down at the Diet Coke. "And of course at the time, I was on my own journey."

"Pace is certain he was the abuser," Malachy said. "Abuser seems like such a lame term for whoever did what was done to him. Anyway, what do you think?"

Sullivan didn't answer right away.

"I am of two minds. I believe Pace is telling the truth about his abuse. Everything I know about Bari says he can't be the one." Sullivan hesitated, "Except, it's just...Bari is so different."

"Different, how?"

"He's so driven, so intense. It just seems more, or different, than Christian zeal. Something is going on with him, but I've no clue what it is."

"So to you, it's possible Bari is guilty."

"Very unlikely, but not impossible."

Malachy decided to keep his promise to limit the time. He wanted to be able to use Jim Sullivan as a resource in the future.

"You've been a great help. I appreciate your seeing me. And I hope everything turns out well on your journey. You had to make a tough decision."

Sullivan gave Malachy a wry smile and said, "Bad choice of greats, as in lineage."

"How so?"

"You seem like somebody who knows his Irish history. Unfortunately, my greats kept the faith during the famine. They were starving but didn't succumb to the food bribes offered by the Established Church Protestants to convert—the Soupers, the name people called the converts.

"Unfortunately?"

"Yes, if the greats had converted, I would have been raised Episcopalian. Then I could have been a married priest. And so when I converted to the one true faith, I would have been welcomed with open arms as a married priest."

Sullivan paused and then resumed in a half-sad, half-bitter tone. "Instead, I left the Catholic priesthood as a failure who didn't keep his vows."

Malachy walked back to the Shamrock, thinking about his Irish lineage. His father was an orphan, so no known grandparents on that side. On his mother's side the line was easily traced back many generations. His mother's records made it simple when he applied for an

Irish passport. He also thought about how he acted when he was hungry. He decided if any of his forefathers were anything like him they ended up with the soup, one way or another.

As he entered the Shamrock, he was relieved to see Bridget was busy behind the bar. He moved quickly to his booth, picked up the phone, and paid to have information connect him to St. Ita's. He worked his way through the automated answering service and eventually got Fr. Cullen on the phone. Malachy decided the partial truth was best.

"This is Malachy Madden calling. I run the Shamrock Pub on Devon…"

"I've driven by the place," Fr. Cullen said. "But I don't think I've ever stopped in."

"The first drink is on me, but that's not the reason for my call. I'm putting together a benefit for an injured worker who doesn't have any insurance, and somebody suggested you were just the right priest for the job."

"I see. Of course, I would want to help, but my parish schedule is so busy…"

Malachy interrupted.

"I know the Shamrock is not in your parish, but this is a citywide effort. It's a golf outing. I'm kind of a one-man committee putting this thing together. And of course, there is a stipend involved."

"A stipend?"

"Yes. The Shamrock pays the stipend so that the injured worker gets all the benefits. And of course your golf and dinner are covered. I realize it takes time out of your busy schedule, but it's for a really good cause. And it's a fun day, you know, golf, drinks, dinner. These things just work better when there's a popular priest officially involved."

"It does sound like a very good cause."

Malachy interrupted again. "Look, I know you don't know me or have enough information to make a decision. How about you let me buy you dinner, and I can explain the whole thing. Then you'll have all the information and you can think about it and make a decision. It so happens I'm free tonight. Any chance you could be my guest for dinner? I won't even make you eat at the Shamrock, although we do have a great hamburger."

Fr. Cullen laughed and said, "You're quite the salesman. Okay, Malachy, dinner it is. But I can't do it tonight. Let's set it up for early next week."

"Great," Malachy said. "The Fire Iron restaurant near you makes a good cocktail and has a decent menu. How about we meet in the bar at 6:00 on Tuesday?"

"That sounds fine. I guess we won't have that much trouble finding each other. Just so you know, I won't be wearing a collar."

"Me either."

Fr. Cullen chuckled and said, "See you at 6:00, Tuesday."

"See you then," Malachy said and hung up the phone.

Eduardo came over to the booth and asked, "Mr. Malachy, do you have your Jameson now?"

"Yes," Malachy answered, making a decision about the drink, postponing the joint chiefs' meeting and the next phase of the research all at the same time. "I need to read some depressing stuff on the Internet and the Jameson will help."

CHAPTER IV

Malachy took his research notes on pedophilia and returned to bed with his coffee. He went over his notes slowly because he needed to understand enough to talk with Rebecca Ryan, a psychiatrist. He hoped she understood how the Favor Bank operated and remembered the favor. It was more than two years since his daughter Molly asked him to help Rebecca, Molly's neighbor and friend, with a problem.

Some construction workers working on Rebecca's floor were harassing her patients as they came down the corridor to her office. She was moving offices, and the building manager promised to do something, but didn't really care. The workers were Polish, and the Count went down to reason with them accompanied by a professional wrestler known as the "Warsaw Wagon." After a slow-motion demonstration of the "Wagon Whip" on the ringleader, problem solved and deposit made in the Favor Bank.

Malachy pulled up his file box from the bottom shelf of his bedside table. He rifled through his index cards with phone numbers until he found Rebecca Ryan's. He smiled to himself with the thought how fitting it was to call a shrink while prone, even if it was on a bed and not the famous couch.

She answered on the first ring, saying, "Good morning, this is Dr. Rebecca Ryan."

"And this is Malachy Madden, Molly's father, calling with a request for a favor."

"Malachy, how good to hear from you. How are you? And how is your charming friend, Count Leon?"

"We are both doing better than many expect and some hope. The Count is still charming, and I'm still Malachy."

Rebecca laughed a little and said, "You said you have a request. What is it?"

"I'd like you to give me a short tutorial on pedophilia from a psychiatric viewpoint."

Rebecca did not respond immediately. "I have no special expertise in that subject. I could put you in touch with colleagues who stay current with the research literature and are far more knowledgeable on the subject than I am."

Malachy anticipated that answer and gave the response he had carefully formulated. "I know you and trust your insights. I'm not writing a research report, but I'm involved in a project where I want to understand pedophilia. I was hoping you could give me an hour of your time, and let me ask you a few questions about the subject."

"All right, Malachy, I'm willing to do that."

"Good, any chance you have time today?"

"Remarkably, just before you called I received a last-minute cancellation. So I have an hour free starting at noon. Because of the time constraints, we would need to meet here at my office."

"I'm willing to give up a little of my allotted hour. Could we meet in the lounge at the back of your building? Being in familiar surroundings would reduce my anxiety and therefore increase my cognitive capacity..." Malachy checked his notes and continued, "Didn't Henry Stack Sullivan say anxiety was like a blow to the head in terms of brain function?"

Rebecca gave a full laugh and said, "The Old Timer's Lounge—I haven't been in there in years. I suppose you mean in the barroom. I will be there just a few minutes after twelve. And yes, Sullivan did say something close to that. Of course there are other impediments to effective cognition that can result from barroom activity."

"I have conducted some field experiments in that area. And my preliminary conclusion is that you're correct. See you at noon. I really appreciate the favor."

Malachy decided to have Eduardo drive him to the Old Timer's. He didn't want to risk any hassle with traffic and parking that would eat into his hour.

†

Malachy entered the Shamrock and saw the Count was in his usual "casual" dress of tailored jacket, tieless monogrammed custom shirt, slacks with military-style sharp crease, and tasseled loafers. He was sitting sideways on the visitors' side of the office-booth. When the Count saw Malachy, he made an elaborate ritual of taking out his cell phone and comparing the time on the phone with that on his watch. Malachy came over and sat across from him.

"Yes, I'm early," Malachy said. "But it isn't my fault. I did the best I could."

"Tell me something. What do the Irish have against punctuality?" the Count asked.

"We believe it is reflective of a fundamental misunderstanding of the nature of time foisted upon us by the unimaginative, pragmatic, and quotidian Anglo-Saxon. Time is only linear in the apparent world."

"I see you've been spending time with Sean again. I haven't seen him in a while. How is he?" the Count asked.

"Broke and thirsty as always. And fascinating as always. He won't come in as often if he can't make a payment on his tab. So when it gets too high, I arrange for a private seminar on Irish stuff to zero it out. But of course Kevin doesn't approve."

"Why?"

"The Shamrock is cash only. Sean is the only customer who runs a tab. And Kevin is against exceptions."

"And why is Sean an exception?" the Count asked.

"He's not. It's official Shamrock policy to extend unlimited credit to all published Irish poets with an extensive knowledge of Irish culture and history, ancient and modern. It just so happens Sean is the only one who qualifies thus far."

"Does Sean really know his stuff?"

"An incredible encyclopedia of all things Irish coupled with an amazing ability to recite songs and poems and recall all kinds of historical facts. He even made six months living one Friday afternoon at the Shamrock because of it."

"That must have been some seminar," the Count said.

"A small seminar," Malachy said. "There were four trader types drinking in the Shamrock getting an early start on a Vegas junket. The upcoming Monday was a market-closing holiday. The program was to bribe the wives with a spa weekend, head to Vegas for forty-eight hours of gambling and partying, sleep it off on Monday, and be fresh for action on Tuesday."

"Ah, the energy of youth," the Count said.

Malachy continued, "There must have been something special in the firewater that afternoon because they were betting on everything in sight, playing liar's poker for big bucks, and carrying on like they were already forty hours into the junket. Sean was off in his usual spot in the corner, watching the action like everyone else in the bar, myself included.

"Somehow they get started on Irish history and then Cromwell. One thing leads to another, and suddenly it's screw Vegas, they're off to London to find Cromwell's grave and piss on it no matter where it's located, because for sure it wasn't in a Catholic church. The man who pisses on it the longest wins $10,000. Enter Sean. 'Excuse me gentleman,' Sean says, 'I do not wish to intervene but it will not be possible for you to urinate on the grave of the execrable Cromwell....'

"This is greeted with a chorus of 'Why the hell not? And who the fuck are you?'

"'Because,' Sean continues, 'there is no Cromwell grave or gravesite.'

"Sean goes on to explain how Cromwell was exhumed and executed again, so to speak, and then his remains were buried unmarked under the gallows and his head put on a pike. And how some think the skull survived down the centuries, but that claim is highly dubious.

"This news is greeted with 'They should have done that every year just to make sure the prick stayed dead,' and the like. The group decides to can the trip to London, and they invite Sean to join them. He regales them with rebel songs and poems for more than an hour."

"How did he earn all that money?" the Count asked.

"Remember, we're talking a poet's living. One of the guys says it is only fair that Sean get part of the money they all saved by not having to go to London on a futile trip. Typical trader's deal, Sean is in for one round of liar's poker at $1,500 per man, no cost to Sean if he loses."

"How did an Irish poet get so good at an American game?"

"Sean doesn't know shit about it. And he tells them that, and then with all innocence and charm, he asks if I can play the hand for him. It was a cakewalk. I'm sober, and they don't need a plane to fly to Vegas. It didn't hurt that they were playing all afternoon with the same pile of one-dollar bills. You know you can't shuffle dollar bills like you do cards."

The Count laughed and said, "You were card counting."

"Something like that. It's hard to break the habits of a lifetime. I drove Sean to the bank with $6,000 cash, all because the execrable Cromwell has no grave to piss on. But I know Kevin didn't approve because I left Sean's tab open."

"Isn't it just simpler to tell Kevin that it is no skin off his nose?"

"And offend my very good friend and loyal compatriot, and the best manager-bartender in the history of the Shamrock? No, it would not be simpler."

The Count looked at Malachy with affection and wondered how the Irish kept anything straight. Everything was like the stained glass Malachy put in the Shamrock when he took over—a whorl inside of a whorl wrapped in a circle.

"I'm surprised Kevin gives you a hard time about anything," the Count said. "He is so intensely loyal to you. Kevin told me once that you saved his life in Vietnam. And from the streets later when you both were back home."

"I only did what every Marine would do, but for Kevin everything is personal. He's the fiercest warrior I've ever known. It's like the DNA from some ancient Celt skipped forward a hundred generations and popped out in him. But, he's a black-and-white thinker and doesn't tolerate exceptions well."

"I'll try to remember to always pay my tab promptly," the Count said. "And to ask for fresh bills if we ever play liar's poker."

Malachy smiled and said, "Let's adjourn to the storeroom. We can start as soon as Kevin joins us."

Malachy looked for Eduardo so he wouldn't have to deal with Bridget. Eduardo came out of the back room and Malachy motioned him over. He asked in a low voice, "How is she today?"

Eduardo smiled and flipped his hand back and forth in a so-so gesture.

Malachy said, "When Kevin comes in, tell him we're in the storeroom. And please bring us some coffee there."

"Sí, Mr. Malachy."

Malachy and the Count settled around the storeroom table, and Malachy thought the Count looked as much out of place as Dino had. His clothing was a little less formal, but he had Dino's sense of grooming and style. And the Count deliberately dressed "younger" in terms of color, trying to knock ten years or more off his age. To Malachy's knowledge no woman, including his wife, knew for sure how old he was. And Malachy didn't either.

"I wanted you to know Dr. Ryan asked after the 'the charming Count Leon.'"

"A very attractive widow," the Count responded. "But too provincial."

"Ah," Malachy said. "She turned you down. You never told me that you asked."

"She said she didn't date married men."

"How did she know you were married?"

"She asked, and so I told her. She seemed like the type who would check an answer out."

"Well, at least she remembers you as charming."

"Perceptive, but like I said, a very provincial attitude."

Kevin entered the storeroom and said, "We were scheduled to start at four, right?"

"Correct," Malachy said. "Don't allow the fact that I'm early throw you off. I'm adopting a new policy that I understand to be standard operating procedure for some consultancies—to wit, if one is not early, one is late because there are far too many uncontrollable variables to be exactly on time."

"Bravo!" the Count exclaimed. "Let's hope that policy doesn't fall prey to nonlinear notions of time."

Malachy smiled and said, "The first agenda item is the report on your visit to Pius XII."

The Count looked at his notes and said, "Everything in the Pius XII church is exactly as Pace described it. Except now there are security cameras filming the stairs, the hallway, and the room outside of the bathroom. I drew a schematic of the layout of the church with the confessionals and the downstairs areas."

Malachy examined the drawing and asked, "Anything else?"

"The janitor wouldn't talk to us," Kevin said. "He told us everybody that works at the school or the parish was told to refer anybody asking questions to the parish office."

"Gearing up for the lawsuit," Malachy said.

There was a knock at the door and Eduardo came in with a plate of oatmeal and chocolate chip cookies and fresh coffee.

"When did we start baking cookies?" Malachy asked.

"No baking. Bridget sent me to the store after Kevin leave the kitchen."

Kevin smiled at Malachy and said, "I'm sure Bridget won't mind if you have some."

"I'm not sure. Maybe I should've spent some of my limited, Dr. Ryan time on triangular relationships."

"Tell Bridget thank you," Kevin said to Eduardo. "And please no more interruptions."

"Next item the shrink report," Malachy said.

"What are we dealing with?" Kevin asked, the warmth gone from his face and voice.

Malachy looked down at his notes. "Based on the assumption that Pace is telling the truth, we are dealing with an extremely manipulative, controlling, and clever man who sexually abuses children who are prepubescent. And who has no remorse or capacity to empathize with the children he abuses."

"Not much there," the Count said.

"She emphasized nobody in her profession does long distance diagnosis. But she was very helpful with the personality structure and traits of the typical pedophile. But I don't think we are dealing with typical. And in a way she confirmed that."

"In what way?" Kevin asked.

"Toward the end of my hour, I gave her the Pace report to read. She hadn't seen it before. Turns out she is a *New York Times* subscriber. Anyway, she took her time with it, but her only comment was, 'What a horrific ordeal for Mr. Pace.'"

"How does that confirm anything we don't know?" the Count asked.

"It doesn't. It was how she said good-bye. We spent a few minutes on Molly, the kids, and goings-on in their neighborhood. Then she said, 'Malachy I hope you will be extra cautious with this assignment. As we discussed, the typical pedophile is extremely controlling but ordinarily not violent. Please be careful and don't leave yourself vulnerable.'"

The three men were silent for a while, thinking about the warning. Kevin broke the silence.

"And you're a Marine and not a child," Kevin said in a low voice, almost as if he were talking to himself.

CHAPTER V

Malachy was startled awake by his cell phone ringing. He reached for the phone but decided to lay back and try and retrieve his dream. Nothing came. Malachy got up, grabbed the cell phone, and went into the living room with its big bay windows, where the reception was better. The call was from the Shamrock's main number. He hoped Kevin had called. He didn't want to start his day with a rant of Bridget's bitches. He called the Shamrock.

"Good morning," Kevin said cheerfully. "Shamrock Bar."

"Thank God, you called and not Bridget."

Something down the block caught Malachy's eye. It was near where he had left his car. "Hang on a second. Something is going on in the street."

Malachy put the phone down and picked up the binoculars he kept by the window. A Christmas gift from the Count for "bird watching." He focused the binoculars on his Mercury. A black pickup truck was stopped next to it in the street.

Two men climbed out of the truck. One moved to the back and one to the front of the truck. Malachy watched the one at the back put a cover over the truck's license plate. Then both men took baseball bats from the flatbed and started smashing the Merc's windows.

"Jesus fucking Christ." Malachy grabbed his cell phone and yelled, "Get your truck, and head to my place as fast as you can! Two guys are destroying my car. Make sure you have your cell phone with you."

He picked up the binoculars and watched the men smash his taillights and front lights and then take out knives and slash his tires. One man threw his bat in the back of the truck and climbed into the cab on the driver's side.

The other used his bat handle to poke a hole in the Merc's passenger-side window and then force what looked like an envelope through the hole. The man ran to the truck and jumped in the passenger side. The truck pulled away and turned into the alley and out of sight.

Malachy guessed they would stop and remove the license-plate covers and then drive away from the neighborhood. Any delay in the alley and Kevin could catch up to them. Malachy called Kevin, "The truck is in the alley near Highland. Where are you?"

"Thirty seconds away. Curb or follow them?"

"Follow. My car was targeted. Let's find out where those two goons call home. It's a black, Chevy late-model pick up. They covered the plates so I don't have a plate number."

Malachy waited and listened to sounds of Kevin's driving.

"Got 'em," Kevin said. "Wisconsin plate. Now they're headed west on Devon. Not close enough to get the number."

"Hang back," Malachy said. "They'll be nervous and checking all around. You don't want to be spotted. If you get caught at a light, assume they are going to the highway and back to Wisconsin. I'll call you back after I check out the Merc."

Malachy called the Count. "We have a situation. Two guys just smashed my car all to hell. Kevin is following their pickup truck. We think they're headed to Wisconsin. It was definitely targeted."

"What's the plan?"

"Pick me up as soon as you can, and we'll reinforce Kevin," Malachy said.

"Equipment?"

"Battle dress and a couple of baseball bats."

"I'll be in front within an hour."

Malachy pulled on some clothes and headed to his car. Some neighbors who lived in the two- and three-flats that lined both sides of the street had gathered on the parkway next to the Mercury to look at the damage. Mitch, one of the neighborhood old-timers and a Shamrock regular, stepped forward as Malachy approached the group. He was holding a large shard and wearing a tattered raincoat over his pajamas.

"Those guys did a real number on your car. I called the cops as soon as I saw what was going on."

"Thanks, Mitch. Did you get a good look at them?"

"Yeah, I can give the cops a good description when they show up."

Malachy looked at Mitch again, pointed to the knife-like shard, and said, "I'd put that down before the cops show up."

Malachy walked around the Merc, went back to the driver's side, and unlocked and opened the door. He brushed the safety glass off the seat and sat down. He picked up a white envelope off the passenger seat and stuffed it in his back pocket. A squad car came down the street with its lights flashing and stopped behind the Mercury. Malachy got out to greet the cops.

"Are you the owner?"

"Unfortunately, yes."

"What happened?" the cop asked.

"Don't know. I live over there on the third floor," Malachy said, pointing to a three-flat a half block down the street. "I saw some of my neighbors standing around my car and came down to look and found this."

Malachy gestured toward the Merc.

The cop turned to the growing group of neighbors and asked, "Anybody see what happened?"

Mitch said, "I saw the whole thing. Two guys got out of a pickup truck and beat the shit out of Malachy's car. They even slashed the tires, the bums. I'm the one who called you. They're long gone. You'll never find them."

"Anybody else see anything?"

The other neighbors shook their heads no.

"Okay. Let's break this up and everybody go about their business." The cop turned to Malachy and Mitch. "I'll need to get some more information. Sorry about your car. Hell of a way to start the day."

"Some days are better than others," Malachy said. "This one has only one way to go."

"For your sake, I hope so," the cop responded. "A detective will be contacting you later."

†

Malachy rushed through his normally slow morning routine and put on his special protective clothing—steel-toe work boots, shorts with built-in cup pouch, pants with interior nylon mesh padding from thigh to ankle, thin Kevlar vest, White Sox hat with skull shield insert. He checked himself in the mirror and approved of the lost-weight-clothes-too bulky look. Malachy checked his watch and rushed out of the apartment and down the stairs.

He made it to the curb just as the Count pulled up. Malachy climbed into the Count's van, called Kevin, and put him on the speaker.

"Where are you?"

"Just over the Wisconsin line. We stopped to have breakfast at a McDonald's. Our friends could use a little nutritional counseling. We are back on the highway headed north."

"Any chance they made you?"

"No, they're totally relaxed now that they're on home soil. I've got the plate number. Do we have anybody who can run it?"

Kevin gave the number slowly and repeated it.

"That's a huge withdrawal from the Favor Bank. We'll only do it if you lose them."

"Understood. I'll call you when they leave the highway."

Malachy looked around the front of the van hopefully.

"It's behind my seat," the Count said.

Malachy reached behind the seat and pulled out a white bakery bag with Polish pastries and coffee in it. He dunked one of the pastries in the coffee and took a big bite.

"I am now ready to consider the possibilities," Malachy said.

"Do we have any facts?" the Count asked.

"Two big, bulky white guys of an indeterminate age stopped their black truck by my Mercury, got out, covered their license plates, and mercilessly attacked my car. They poked a hole in the driver's-side window and left an envelope. They got back in the pickup and drove into the alley."

"Serendipity that you saw the whole thing," the Count said.

"As they say, 'Chance favors the fogged mind seeking better cell phone reception.'"

The Count laughed and said, "I'll add that to my book, *Malachy's Mangled Missives.*"

"Let's find out what's in the envelope," Malachy said.

He pulled the envelope from his back pocket. The Count pulled the van over to the side, parked it, and climbed into the back of the van. He turned on a light box and Malachy handed him the envelope.

"Cheap envelope, easy to see through. No explosives or inhalants," the Count said as he handed it to Malachy.

Malachy opened the envelope, pulled out a folded sheet, and read aloud the message printed in red in a large bold font:

I KNOW WHERE TO FIND YOU. STOP NOW.

"Subtle," Malachy said. "Do you suppose it's a haiku?"

The Count pulled the van back into the flow of traffic and headed toward the highway.

"Puzzling," the Count said. "The people who know you're involved in this assignment are all directly or indirectly connected to the Committee for Justice at the Shrine."

"The hardest part to any puzzle is the first few pieces," Malachy said. "Especially when you don't have a picture on the box. We'll have to ask our Wisconsin friends what the puzzle looks like."

Malachy's cell phone rang, and he put Kevin on speaker.

"They left the highway going west on Wisconsin 11. I'm about five cars back. Lot of billboards touting a casino up ahead."

"Maybe they think this is their lucky day," Malachy said. "Call back when they stop somewhere. We're on the highway coming your way."

"Do we try and get the information we want as friends or foes?" the Count asked Malachy.

"Kevin is their friend. We're their foes. I could never fake the friendly act. I like my Merc too much."

They drove to Wisconsin proposing scenarios for extracting the information. They settled on a plan just as Kevin called again.

"It's seniors' day at the casino. They open early. The parking lot is full of buses, and our friends are inside."

Malachy outlined the plan.

"Got it," Kevin said. "I'm going in to be friendly. If they start to leave, I'll call."

Malachy and the Count pulled into the casino lot. The black pickup was parked where Kevin told them. The Count pulled the van in front of it. They waited while some seniors slowly walked by them on their way into the casino.

The Count exited the van and went over to the driver's-side door of the pick-up. He worked on the lock for less than a minute, opened the door, and climbed in. Seconds later the pickup's engine started with a roar.

Malachy got out of the van with a small duffel bag and took the Count's place in the truck. Malachy drove out of the parking lot, and the Count parked the van and entered the casino. He found Kevin at the blackjack table with two other men. They all had beers in front of them. The Count calculated the two men had more than $1,000 worth of chips in front of them. He greeted Kevin like they were old friends.

"Cards falling your way?" the Count asked Kevin.

"I'm down a little, but my friends here are doing okay," Kevin said.

The Count nodded to the two men, who looked like body-type twins. An inch plus-or-minus six feet, muscular but overweight with well-developed paunches, and rough skin that said outdoor work. They were unshaven and dressed in blue jeans and work shirts. They both wore smudged ball caps, one with Packer colors and logo, and the other Brewers.

The blackjack dealer asked if the Count was joining the game. "Not just yet. I have to move around and see what game is calling to me."

The Count turned back to Kevin and the two men. "You'll never believe what I just saw."

"A big winner?" Kevin asked.

Kevin and the two men laughed.

"No, in the parking lot," the Count said.

"What about it?" Kevin asked

"A drunk staggering around trying to find his car. Looked like he was still going from last night. I asked him if I could help. He looks at me like I'm a Martian and says, 'Nah, don't need any help. I'll just take this one. Always wanted a truck.' Damned if the guy didn't get the door open to a black pickup and somehow it started...."

The Packer-hat man closest to Kevin stood up and said, "Son of a bitch, what kind of truck was it?"

The Count looked at him like he was annoyed that his funny story was interrupted.

"I said it was a fancy black pickup."

"Shit, that's our truck!"

The two men stuffed the chips in their pockets and started to run toward the exit of the casino. The Packer-hat man ran into a too-thin old man clutching a bag of quarters, scattering the coins on the floor.

"Get the fuck out of the way, goddamn it."

The men went out the door with Kevin following. The Count helped the old man pick up the spilled quarters.

"Everybody is in such a rush nowadays," the Count said. "Nobody takes their time anymore."

"I'd a whipped his ass in my younger days," the old man said defiantly. "Somebody should teach him some manners."

"You know you're right," the Count said. "I'll see what can be arranged."

The old man smiled at him, surprised.

The Count went out to the parking lot. The two men were standing and cursing in the empty space where the truck had been parked.

"He couldn't have got too far," the Count said. "He was really drunk. Probably just down the road."

"Come on," Kevin said. "I've got my truck. Let's see if we can catch him. You can always call the cops later if we can't find him."

"Fucking A, let's go," Packer hat said. "I'll kill the son of a bitch if I get my hands on him. He better not have fucked up my truck."

"Which way did he go?" Kevin asked.

"Back down that way," the Count said. "Toward the main highway. Good luck, I hope you catch him. It's not right when somebody fucks with your property."

Kevin ran toward his Ford crew-cab truck with the two men following. Kevin yelled, "One of you in front with me, the other in back behind me."

The Packer fan jumped into the front seat next to Kevin while the baseball fan scrambled to the back. Kevin peeled out of the parking lot.

"We need to cover the roadsides," Kevin said, pointing to the passenger-side window. Kevin looked in the rearview mirror. "You take the other side. We don't want to speed past your truck. The fucker is drunk and could have pulled off anywhere."

The two men grunted a response and Kevin pushed the speed up to sixty-five miles per hour.

"Stop, I just saw it!" The man on the back-bench seat said. "It's at the end of that farm road back there."

Kevin slammed on the brakes and pulled a hard U-turn.

"Right here, turn right here!" the backseat man said excitedly.

Kevin turned off the highway on to a grass-covered, two-track road that led into a clump of trees. At the end of the road was a gate that opened into a fenced field. The truck was parked at the end of the road in front of the gate.

"The truck looks okay, but I don't see the driver anywhere," Kevin said.

Kevin stopped behind the black truck. He got out slowly, letting the two men get in front of him. They ran up to the sides of the truck and started to reach for the door handles. The driver's side flew open with tremendous force and caught Packer-hat man in the upper body and face. He fell to the ground, bleeding and howling in pain. Malachy straightened up from his coiled position inside the truck's cabin, smiled, and waved to the other man.

"He's in the cab, get him!" the man shouted.

"Sure thing," Kevin said from behind the man.

Before he could turn around, Kevin aimed a powerful mule kick at the back of the man's knee, driving it into the truck's door. The man fell to the ground, cursing. Malachy unlocked the door and handed Kevin two pairs of handcuffs. Malachy climbed out of the truck's cab, shoved his man back down to the ground, grabbed the man's wrists, and twisted them up behind his back. Kevin moved around the truck and cuffed the man with his hands behind him. Then Malachy and

Kevin went back around the truck, and each grabbed an arm of the other man and Kevin cuffed him.

They returned to the driver's side, stood the man up, and Malachy went through his pockets, taking the casino chips and the identification and money from his wallet.

"Hey, those are my chips," Packer-hat man said. "You're stealing my chips."

Malachy looked at the man's ID and said, "Norm, don't think of it that way. Reframe the problem. Think of it as an out-of-court settlement of what you owe me."

"You're fucking nuts—I don't owe you anything"

"Norm, let me explain it to you. This morning you beat the shit out of my car. It's going to cost money to repair my car. Since you and your friend over there caused the damage, you and your friend are going to pay for the repairs. Got it?"

Norm looked away and said, "I don't know what you're talking about."

"Norm, you have more at stake here than these chips," Malachy said.

Malachy turned to Kevin and said, "Bring Norm's friend over here and empty his pockets. Then I'll explain the facts of life to the two of them."

Kevin went around the truck and half-dragged the cuffed man back and stood him up next to Norm. Malachy looked at the man's ID and counted the chips and money from his wallet.

"Add Jeff's contribution and we almost have enough to cover the damage to my car. We are definitely making progress."

"Are you guys fuckin' Chicago cops?" Norm asked.

"That's a good guess, Norm. And here's another good guess—the two of you are headed back to Chicago."

"You can't do that," Jeff said. "You don't have any authority in Wisconsin."

"A moot point, as lawyers like to say. Even if a judge believed your story, which I doubt, he'd just send you back to Wisconsin to be properly extradited. Somehow you two are going to end up in Chicago with videotape showing you and Norm smashing up my car. My neighbor caught the whole thing on his video cam."

Norm cursed and tried to run down the road. Kevin put out his foot and tripped him. He stumbled and fell into a clump of bushes. Kevin dragged him back and stood him up next to Jeff.

"I understand that you don't want to return to Chicago," Malachy said. "We don't have a lot of dairy farmers in our jails. Nope, no dairy farmers, but we do have bulls looking for fat heifers. Yep, I'm sure you boys would be a lot happier staying up here in Wisconsin."

"You already have all our money," Norm said. "What do you want to let us go?"

"We're willing to let bygones be bygones if we get what we're after."

"You'll let us go?" Jeff asked.

"We'll let you go. We almost have enough to pay for the damage. Give us what we're after and you go free."

"What do you want?" Norm asked.

"Sign over the truck," Malachy said, pausing to enjoy the look on Norm's face. "Just joking. We want information. Who hired you and how? The full story."

"We don't know," Norm said.

"That's not a good answer," Malachy responded.

"It's true," Jeff said. "We don't know. We…Norm got a call when we were drinking and gambling in the casino."

Malachy stepped closer to Norm.

"And?"

"The caller said he had a job for us. He needed to send someone stubborn a message. A morning's work—mess up the car and leave an envelope. Two hundred down, five hundred when the job is done."

"You got paid," Malachy said. "Who paid you?"

"We never saw him," Jeff said. "He told us to talk it over. If we accepted, go to the parking lot and open up a window and then go back into the casino. He'd put an envelope with the two hundred and directions in the cab. That's what we did."

"What about the rest?"

"When the job was done, we should go to the casino and we'd get another call telling us how to collect the five hundred."

"How did he get your cell phone number?"

"We cut and haul wood," Norm said. "The number is on the flyers we put up."

"You must have seen something in the parking lot or some of your buddies at the casino saw something. Give me something."

"We tried to look. My cell phone rang and I was told the deal was off unless we were at the tables in thirty seconds."

"What about the $500?" Malachy asked.

"When we got to the casino here this morning we got a call. We were told to look under the seat. There was an envelope taped under the seat with $500 in chips in it."

"You're not giving me much," Malachy said. "We need more. Kevin, what do you think?"

"Put them out to pasture in Chicago," Kevin said.

"Wait," Jeff said. "Tell'em, Norm."

"I didn't tell you at first. I figured you'd think I was bullshitting you. I think we were hired by a broad."

"A broad?" Malachy asked.

"It was something about the voice and the way the person talked. The voice sounded like a woman trying to disguise her voice. It just reminded me of the way broads talk. I don't like working for women, so it bothered me."

Malachy looked at Kevin who nodded yes.

"Are you letting us go?" Jeff asked.

"Reluctantly," Malachy said. "We're almost even. But no visits to Chicago. Remember, we have the tape."

"We're never going back to Chicago," Norm said. "Take off the cuffs."

"Sure. Turn around and don't move or the deal is off."

The two men turned around, and Malachy unlocked one of Jeff's cuffs and quickly slapped it on Norm. Malachy undid Norm's cuffs.

"What the hell is going on?" Norm asked.

"A lesson in social cooperation," Malachy said. "Now, turn around and watch carefully."

The two men, cuffed together awkwardly, turned around. Malachy pitched the keys to the truck into the underbrush ten yards away and pitched the keys to the cuffs ten yards in the other direction. He threw the wallets into the fenced field.

"Have a nice day," Malachy said cheerfully.

Malachy drove with Kevin on the way home. He counted the money from the cashed-in chips and the currency from the wallets.

"Do you think I can get the Mercury fixed for $1,240?"

"The Count can get it done for less than a grand," Kevin said.

"Good, then we have a little left over for gas money. What about the woman?"

"I saw her. She was driving out of the lot as I came in."

"Let me guess—young, good-looking, and Italian-American."

"Wrong."

"Which one did I miss?"

"All three."

"I'm done guessing," Malachy said.

"Over fifty, very bizarre-looking blonde."

"You're kidding?"

"No, Malachy, I'm not. The only thing attractive about this woman was the car."

Malachy was silent for a while.

"What kind?"

"Alfa Romeo. Now, I have a question. Do you have any girlfriends I don't know about?"

"None that drive Italian sport cars. And no blondes either."

CHAPTER VI

Malachy sat in his back office-booth office watching the ice melt in his second Jameson of the night, thinking about the day's events in Wisconsin. A yellow legal pad with a ballpoint on it was next to the drink, but the page was blank. He searched his memory for a connection to the woman. Nothing surfaced.

The note seemed to point conclusively to Bari. There were no other current jobs. As Kevin said, "She knows where to find you, but she doesn't really know you. Threats are an incentive."

Malachy took a sip of the Jameson to test it. He took a bigger swallow. The temperature was perfect—a little cool, but not enough to suppress the flavor. He started to doodle on the pad when he saw Matt Morse enter the bar. Matt looked warily at Bridget behind the bar and strode quickly toward the back booth. Matt was still the handsome, fit, and black-Irish-looking federal agent Malachy had known for years.

Malachy smiled to himself thinking about their last conversation on how the black Irish came to look that way with their darker complexions and hair. Matt had said, "I don't think it was from some of the Spanish Armada ships being blown off course. At that stage of Irish development, if any of the sailors made it to the Irish shore, your forefathers would have eaten them."

Malachy reminded himself that though he and Matt got along well over the years and liked each other, Matt was still FBI. It is a crime to lie to or mislead an FBI agent. And he might be wired for who knows what purpose. The Jameson would have to get warmer. He was switching to coffee.

Malachy also reminded himself not to ask Bridget for anything. She hated the FBI with a passion and went on strike the last time Matt was in the Shamrock. She blamed FBI incompetence for both Kennedy assassinations and King's murder, and that was just for starters.

"Malachy, may I join you?" Matt asked. "I hope I'm not interrupting some work."

"I'm making notes for my next confession," Malachy said, smiling and gesturing to the other side of the booth. "As you can see, the pad is blank. How about something to drink?"

Matt looked at Bridget and said, "Decaf coffee if there's some already made."

"Don't worry, Matt. I'll have Eduardo bring it."

"I don't suppose Bridget's views have softened any," Matt said. "She doesn't strike me as the type who changes her mind much."

"In terms of your employer, it's worse—9/11 and all that."

"Not our finest hour."

Malachy called Eduardo over and ordered the coffees. Bridget glared at them from behind the bar. They sat in silence until Eduardo returned with the coffees.

"We're in the middle of an investigation involving some real estate transactions with various governmental entities," Matt said. "We know from our investigation that Montegiordano was here talking with you."

Matt stopped and looked at Malachy waiting for some kind of confirmation. Malachy just smiled at him.

"What were you discussing with him?"

"The real estate guys I talk to want to know when I am going to pay my back rent."

"Seriously, Malachy, what was the meeting about?"

"Seriously, Matt, I don't discuss private meetings."

"Malachy, there's a grand jury that is hearing testimony about this investigation. We can compel your testimony."

"And I can assert my various Constitutional rights including but not limited to the Fifth Amendment. And the Feds in turn can grant limited immunity. And I in turn can file various and sundry motions attacking such a grant as insufficiently broad, and on and on. Could be fun for a frustrated, disbarred lawyer who once substitute taught the Fifth Amendment part of a course in constitutional law, and who has a file cabinet full of term papers that can easily be turned into motions with amazingly extensive citations. It would keep somebody very busy."

Matt looked at Malachy with an expression that said, "I knew you'd say that."

Malachy continued, "But I'd rather you guys spent your time more productively. After all, there are bad guys out there trying to blow things up. Moreover—I always liked that word, it seems so lawyerly—moreover, I like to cooperate when I can. So let's logic this out. If I met with Montegiordano, and if you know about the meeting, heavy odds say you already know what it was about."

Malachy paused and looked at Matt, hoping to see a flicker of confirmation. Matt's face was a pleasant, attentive blank slate.

"So," Malachy said, "conclusion number one: You are asking me questions to confirm what you already know. You've known me for a long time and know how I operate. Conclusion number two: You know there's no chance of my discussing a private meeting with you. So, my question to you is, what's really going on?"

"I told them it was a waste of time, but they insisted," Matt said. "I'm supposed to ask you to wear a wire and talk to Montegiordano."

"Talk to him about what?"

"I'm not supposed to discuss that with you unless you agree to wear the wire," Matt said. "I am authorized to offer you an inducement to wear the wire."

"I'm all ears," Malachy said.

"In return for your cooperation, the DOJ would officially support your application for reinstatement to the bar. The committee that hears those petitions and the Illinois Supreme Court are likely to find that support powerful and persuasive."

"No doubt," Malachy said.

Malachy wondered if somehow his cell phone conversation with his nameless employer was intercepted. He decided to keep the verbal jousting with Matt going to see if he could learn more. He started to respond, when a rowdy group of five young men entered the bar and started shouting at Bridget.

"Settle down and shut up," Bridget bellowed in her best foghorn voice. "You're disturbing everybody."

"I actually feel sorry for them," Matt said, as he turned around to watch the action.

"So do I," Malachy said.

"All right, one at a time," Bridget said. "What do you want to drink? You, start," Bridget ordered, pointing to one of the men.

The man pointed to the darkened TV above the bar and said, "I want to watch the end of the Cubs game."

Bridget shook her head in disgust and pointed to the next man.

"You—what do you want to drink? That's d-r-i-n-k."

"Come on, turn the TV on. The game is tied."

"Listen up, that TV stays off. House rules. Now, do you want something to drink or not?"

"Change the rules," the man said.

The man reached into his pocket and took out a wad of bills. He peeled off a bill and slapped it on the bar.

"Here's $100. We're going to have a couple of beers here at the bar and watch the end of the game. You get to keep the change. Now turn the damn TV on so we don't miss the end of the game."

"You forgot to say pretty please with sugar on top," Bridget said, picking up the hundred-dollar bill, wadding it up, and flicking it back at the man.

"I want to talk to the manager," the man said.

"That's easy—I'm the boss."

"For Christ's sake, be reasonable. All we want to do is give you a little business and watch the game on that TV."

"Not going to happen."

"We didn't mean to disturb anyone or be insulting," another man said. "We left the game early because the score was so lopsided. Then the Cubs staged an unbelievable rally and tied the game. We heard it on the radio. It's now in extra innings and we'd like to see the end of the game, that's all. How can we make that happen?"

Bridget lowered her voice and adopted a tone like she was talking with a dim-witted child. "I know this is going to be a great shock to you, but there is no slaughter rule in the major leagues. You shouldn't have left the game early."

Eduardo came out the back room with a big smile on his face.

"What's up?" Bridget asked Eduardo.

"Cubs, they win. It was very exciting—they do a squeeze play and it worked!"

"Congratulations, Eduardo."

Bridget turned her attention back to the men at the bar.

"Eduardo is a big Cubs fan."

The man with the hundred-dollar bills turned beet red with anger. Bridget smiled sweetly at him. The man started yelling at Bridget. "This is fucking ridiculous. You mean to tell me the whole time the game was on in that back room. Why didn't you tell us?"

"You never asked," Bridget said. "You were too busy demanding. Now, for the last time, what do you want to drink?"

"Nothing and thanks for fucking nothing," the man shouted. "We're out of here, and we're never coming back."

Matt turned around and asked Malachy: "How many customers a day does she drive out of here, anyway?"

"I'm afraid to do the calculations—it might bring on a clinical depression, and I'm already taking the only medicine I tolerate well."

Matt gave Malachy a smile and said, "And sometimes I think my job is difficult."

"Your job is very difficult, Matt. All law enforcement is a tough job—and dangerous. Society should value it more."

"That holds for the military, too," Matt responded.

"Don't get me started," Malachy said.

"Malachy, something tells me you have a schizoid attitude toward the law," Matt said.

"Do you think? Let's see—raised by an ardent Irish nationalist father who used to blow up things in his younger days and who fought on the Loyalist side in the Spanish Civil war, street-educated in a mostly Irish ethnic enclave with its own code and rules, trained by the Marines to combat my country's lawfully declared enemies on the battlefields of Vietnam only to have Congress change the rules and then to discover I was hated by too many fellow countrymen as the real enemy, employed as a criminal defense attorney with a sworn duty to zealously defend his guilty clients, and disbarred—in a decision I agreed with—for improper zeal in keeping an innocent client out of jail. Matt, I think you're on to something. "

Malachy smiled at Matt and asked, "If it's late at night, and there's no other traffic, do you always wait for the light to turn green?"

"Not always, and you?"

"I understand the roads would be total chaos if everybody decided for themselves what green and red meant. But in the middle of the night, if there's no other traffic, I don't wait for the green. But if a cop is hiding somewhere, and I can't talk my way out of the ticket, I accept it and pay the fine."

"Federal tickets carry heavy penalties," Matt said. "And we get really upset with lone rangers who interfere with the process."

Malachy picked up his pen and wrote a big N.B. on the pad. He turned the pad around and showed it to Matt. "Do you remember Professor N.B.? Didn't you take his course?"

"Nota bene," Matt said. "English lit, right?"

"Yes," Malachy said. "Before a big test, he'd fill the blackboard with information. Each time someone would ask a question about the test, he would silently leave the lectern and underscore the N.B."

Matt interrupted and said, "Note well. Malachy, we have always been friendly. We're alike in a lot of ways. And someday, when we're both out of the game, I hope we can swap war stories over a couple of drinks. Yes, I'm underscoring the N.B. You don't want to flunk this test."

"I did pass that course. He was tough grader, I only got a C."

"For the record, will you wear the wire?" Matt asked.

"For the record, no."

"Does our talk tonight qualify as one of your private meetings you don't discuss?" Matt asked.

"Yes, it does."

"No guarantees, but I'll try to convince them not to subpoena you for grand jury testimony."

"Thanks, Matt. What will you be drinking when we are swapping war stories?"

"Canadian Club, lots of ice."

Malachy watched Matt walk rapidly past Bridget and exit the bar. He took a long swallow of his too-warm Jameson. He made a note on the legal pad for the Count to sweep the bar, his apartment, his car, and Kevin's truck. Malachy thought about the professor and his tests.

There were never any trick questions. Everything you needed to study was on that blackboard. But, the only way to prepare for a test with a trick question is to know the question in advance or at least know that trick questions would be on the test. What did the Feds want Dino to talk about? Or was the whole thing some kind of ploy? A ploy Matt might not even know about.

He called the Count and Kevin on their cells and left a message: "Breakfast at M.C.'s."

It was code for the "operation might be compromised by surveillance." M.C. stood for Michael Collins, his father's great hero and the man who was legendary for penetrating the Crown's operations with his spies and ruthlessly eliminating the British spies who tried to penetrate his operation.

Malachy hated to invoke the code because it meant getting up at five o'clock for a six o'clock breakfast meeting with the Count and Kevin at a little diner off the expressway in Evanston. Malachy once defended the Greek owner against a gambling charge and got him cleared.

There was a small room off the kitchen, used for card games that Malachy was always welcome to use for meetings. The noise from the kitchen was the perfect shield against any external listening devices. And there was no way to plant something within the room. The owner watched it like it was the cash register.

The code also informed the Count and Kevin to meet the next morning for breakfast at the diner and to be aware they might be bugged or followed. The Count would show up earlier to make sure the site was not compromised. He would circulate and watch over Kevin's and Malachy's arrivals. The light traffic early in the morning made it easy to pick up surveillance.

Malachy looked down at his legal pad and remembered his jest to Matt that he was taking notes for his next confession. He laughed out loud as he recalled a conversation with Sam, the owner of the diner.

They were having a late lunch outdoors on the rooftop of a restaurant in Greektown. The sun was shining in a brilliant blue sky and a group of attractive, buxom women were lunching together at a nearby table. Somehow Malachy and Sam got on the topic of religion.

Sam, gesturing to their surroundings including the table laden with Greek dishes and an open bottle of Roditis wine, declared, "This is my religion. Thousands of years and thousands of religions and all of them telling you they know and own the truth. Bullshit. Right here is the truth."

Malachy said, "That's a very Irish view of life. Irish paganism viewed nature as sacred, suffused with a godlike beauty and power."

"So, how did you Irish Catholics get so screwed up about sex?" Sam said.

"Nature turned into the enemy," Malachy said. "It's a long, sad story. I blame it on the Anglo-Saxons and the Jansenists."

Sam laughed loudly, attracting the attention of the women at the nearby table. "Malachy, is there anything you don't blame on the Anglo-Saxons? Didn't those poor bastards do anything right? How about the jury trial? That's a good thing. If it had been up to that judge, I'd have been fried. And that's not good for a Greek who owns a diner."

Sam laughed even louder at his own pun. One of the women shouted over and said, "You men seem to be enjoying yourselves. Do you do this often?"

Sam smiled at her and said, "Only on days when the rooftop is filled with beautiful women and the sun is shining. It's a religious thing."

The woman turned back to her table of friends and said, "They're having a religious meeting of some kind."

The table erupted in laughter.

Sam lowered his voice and said to Malachy, "Now tell me, if we invite these women over for a little Metaxa and coffee after lunch and one thing leads to another, would you consider it a serious sin and go to confession."

"No doubt, but how serious of a sin depends on the circumstances," Malachy said.

"Really," Sam said. "I thought it was like a menu—the sins on one side

and the price on the other. Afternoon delight—cost, four Hail Marys."

"That's cheap," Malachy said, laughing. "In Catholicism, we're all sinners. But the gravity of the sin and the responsibility for it depend on the concrete circumstances."

A back and forth on confession followed with another bottle of wine. Malachy illustrated one of his points with a story about medieval confession manuals he'd read somewhere. "You know the wind that blows from North Africa?" Malachy asked. "The one the Italians call the sirocco. Well, the manuals noted that the sirocco with its fine sand was so irritating and maddening it reduced the penitent's responsibility for his sins."

"I get the idea, I really do," Sam said and gulped his wine. "The wind blew her mouth on my cock and it's not my fault. I like it—I really like it!"

Sam jumped up, clapped his hands above his head, and did a little Zorba-like dance around his chair. "Let's invite the women for Metaxa and coffee!"

Malachy decided to go home and try to get to sleep early. Then he remembered his car wasn't drivable. To get to the diner by the CTA and a bus meant getting up before 5:00 A.M. He groaned so loud Bridget heard him.

"What's the matter with you?"

"I have to get up early."

"Some people have to get up early and even go to work," Bridget said. "It wasn't that long ago. I'm sure you remember."

Malachy ignored the comment. He wasn't up to a debate on what constituted work and his strange work ethic.

"Bridget, be extra careful with anybody coming into the bar and claiming they need to fix something or with delivery men wanting access to the storeroom. The Count will be in to sweep the place tomorrow."

Bridget laughed and said, "Good, I'll make sure a broom is available."

"You know what I mean."

"What are those fascists up to now?" Bridget asked.

"I'm not sure. But whatever they're doing, they're just trying to do their job. It's not personal. Things have changed a lot since Hoover's days."

"Really? Then how come the headquarters building is still named after Hoover? That tells the tale. They're still honoring that fascist thug. You know the fatal mistake the Kennedy boys made?"

"I'm afraid to ask," Malachy said wearily.

"I'll tell you anyway. Not firing that incompetent, cross-dressing, corrupt bastard the first day in the Oval Office. They'd both be alive today and so would King. And the country would be better off."

"That would have ignited a political firestorm at the time," Malachy said. "The times and the context were different. I understand why they didn't pick that political fight."

"It was a big mistake, the biggest," Bridget said bitterly. "It cost them their lives."

"That's all hypothetical, Bridget. History doesn't tell us might-have-beens. It's hard enough to figure out what actually happened."

"We know what actually happened," Bridget said loudly. "Hoover fooled a lot of people and scared most of the rest. Nobody was willing to take him on. And it cost us big time."

"Matt's not Hoover. He's a good guy. Try to remember that the next time he's in."

"Does that include letting him plant a bug," Bridget said.

"No."

"Good. I'm glad you haven't totally lost your mind."

"I'm heading home to get some sleep," Malachy said.

"And by the way, we had a good night," Bridget said. "For days now, we're getting more business at lunch and dinner. Must be the new boss."

"Or the change in the waitstaff," Malachy said.

"And to think I was considering letting you use my car tomorrow," Bridget said

"I withdraw that foolish comment," Malachy replied. "Dealing with the FBI addled my brain."

"That'll happen," Bridget said. "Okay, you can use my car tomorrow. I'll have Eduardo drive me home and then leave it on your street. Try and bring it back in one piece."

"Yes, boss."

CHAPTER VII

"Your friends are waiting in the back room," Sam said, motioning Malachy to join him in the kitchen. "They've already ordered. How do you want your omelet?"

"With everything," Malachy said, looking around the kitchen and then back toward the counter and booths at the front of the diner. "Any strangers out there?"

"The Count asked that earlier—let me check again." Sam grabbed a coffeepot and went through the swinging doors that separated the entrance to the kitchen from the customer area and shouted, "Anybody need more coffee? It's fresh and hot! Just like Vanessa, who's late this morning!"

Sam topped off a few cups and returned to the kitchen and said, "All regulars—the usual mix of local workers and those headed downtown on the highway."

"Good. I'll join Kevin and the Count," Malachy said, starting toward the back room.

"Here take some coffee with you," Sam said, pouring from the pot into a large mug. "By the way, that Count really knows his stuff."

Malachy turned around, took the mug, and asked, "About breakfast?"

"Nah, security. He was here really early so I asked him to look at the diner like he was going to break in. I keep a lot of cash in here, makes it easier for the games. You never know when a deliveryman or somebody sees something he shouldn't."

"I hope you're keeping the game small, only people you know really well, like we discussed. The next jury might not be so friendly."

"I do everything you said," Sam answered. "No cash on the table, the whole package."

"Good. Less chance of trouble that way."

"Okay, now I make you the best omelet you've ever had."

"You said that the last time."

Sam laughed and said, "I know. I tell everybody that, and sometimes it's true."

Malachy entered the windowless room and left the door open. The noise from the kitchen, where the tempo was picking up, filled the room. Malachy greeted Kevin and the Count who were at the poker-style table with coffee and newspapers. Malachy sat down and explained the reasons for the M.C. code.

"Dino is never going to talk real estate with you," the Count said. "So, it must be about the Justice Committee—Bari and the Shrine."

"Assuming no ruse," Malachy said.

"A ruse means the wire request causes you to take a specific action they anticipate and that action moves their investigation forward," Kevin said. "I don't think breakfast at Sam's qualifies."

"Okay, let's go with the scenario that the offer was for real, and it's about Dino and the Shrine," Malachy said. "Who told them I work for the Justice Committee?"

"Maybe you did," Kevin said. "You called and asked for the Bari tapes."

"And that was picked up on a tap?" Malachy asked.

"Tap or somebody in his office is a mole," the Count said.

"So they find out I'm working on the Bari project by happenstance and decide to use that development to get Dino talking for the wire about what?"

"Something that Dino can't dodge," Kevin said.

Sam knocked on the doorjamb with his free hand.

"Here are the best omelets you've ever eaten," he said.

He carried three plates on one arm and deftly put them down one at a time in front of each man. The plates were fully covered with omelets, hash browns, and fresh fruit.

"This morning I'll settle for simple, direct, and straightforward omelets," Malachy said.

"All that and lots of feta, too," Sam said, laughing. "I'll solve your problem. Whatever it is, you have to raise, fold, or check. So pick one and your problem is solved."

Malachy raised his knife and fork high over his plate and said, "Raise!"

"See," Sam said. "Isn't life simple?"

"Sometimes," Malachy answered. "But our problem is we're playing blind. All the cards are face down."

"Then raise is definitely the right answer," Sam said. "Holler when you want more coffee."

Malachy looked at the Count and Kevin and said, "In this hand, raise means find out what the FBI was going to feed me. And nobody knows more about the Shrine than Fr. Bari. So, I guess it's time to talk."

They both nodded in agreement because they were busy eating their best-ever omelets. Over more coffee, they worked out the details of a plan.

Malachy called Dino's office from his cell phone as he drove back into the city. "This is Malachy calling."

The call was transferred through to Dino's cell phone.

"This is unbelievably early for you," Dino said. "Is there some kind of emergency?"

"Yeah, I woke up hungry," Malachy paused, "...for justice. Could you arrange a meeting with Bari? Just the two of us."

"Of course," Dino said. "When and where?"

"I'm up and out. How about this morning at the rectory?"

"Hold for a minute."

Dino came back on the line.

"Bari can see you at 8:00. But he has other appointments so he can only give you an hour today. We need to give him more lead time for a longer appointment."

"Will do. Consider this my weekly report—things are progressing."

"Are your reports always so in-depth and specific?" Dino asked.

"Yes," Malachy said. "Good-bye."

As Malachy started up the stairs to the front door of the two-story stone rectory, two men got of their car and called out to him, "Do you have a scheduled appointment? What's your name?"

Malachy turned and faced the two men: a fat Mutt and a wiry Jeff, probably off-duty cops.

"Malachy Madden. I'm expected."

"Wait there," Jeff said.

He made a call on his cell phone.

"He's okay."

Mutt started toward Malachy and said, "All visitors need to be searched."

"I'm the exception," Malachy said, indicating the man shouldn't come any closer. "I know you're just doing your job…"

"No exceptions. No search, no visit."

"Call your employer, describe me, and tell him Malachy says he is a permanent exception to the search rule. There are always exceptions. I doubt Dino lets you fuck up his perfect press job. And I don't want you spoiling my look."

Mutt looked Malachy up and down skeptically and then turned around and made a call. He closed his phone and waited with his back to Malachy. The call back took a few minutes. Malachy concluded that they indirectly worked for the same employer.

The man spun around and said, "No search for you. You can go in. Our employer said to tell you that the exception is just for you. Any colleagues get searched, no exceptions. Understood?"

"Understood. Thanks, I always wanted to be exceptional."

Neither man cracked a smile.

Malachy turned around and rang the bell and then turned back to address the two men.

"Oh, by the way, when did the death threat come in?"

Both men ignored him and just walked back to their car. Malachy figured he had the better job. He was paid well to prove Bari innocent. And his downside was limited. Who knew the downside to making a mistake that gets Bari killed?

The plan called for Malachy and Bari to leave the rectory for their meeting. It could make for an interesting procession. The security detail, the Count and Kevin, and, maybe, the FBI. No matter, this conversation had to take place outside of the rectory.

Fr. Bari answered the bell.

"Mr. Madden, welcome. John Bari, it's good to meet you. Please come in."

Malachy stared at the tall, handsome priest dressed in a sweatshirt and blue jeans. The Count had aptly called him Hollywood-handsome. When not smiling, he had a swarthy, sexually charged look resulting from combining black hair, dark eyes, and finely proportioned features.

"Please, come in," Bari urged. "My friends out there don't like me to stand in the doorway. And please excuse the dress. They don't want me to look like a priest."

"Glad to meet you, Fr. Bari. Please call me Malachy. I was hoping we could talk while we take a drive in my car. I'll explain it to your security and cooperate with them. I assume they let you go out."

"They do. I insist on it. Let me tell the housekeeper. We do need to be back by 8:55. I like to be on time for meetings. And please call me John."

"Ditto on the meetings, John. I'll arrange the drive with your security."

Malachy went out the door and walked rapidly toward the car holding the two security men. Jeff, in the driver's seat, partially lowered the window. Mutt climbed out of the front seat, came around the car, and stood next to Malachy.

"Fr. Bari wants to go for a drive. There is no particular destination. I'm thinking of driving up to Greektown and then back down to Taylor Street via the expressway and then here. With the traffic I figure the drive will take a max of forty-five minutes. Any problem with that?"

The security man in the driver's seat looked at Malachy skeptically and said, "A real joyride. Why not just stay home and save everybody the trouble?"

"Cabin fever. He really wants to get out for a few minutes."

"We stay right behind you. Make sure you don't lose us. We'll walk him from the rectory to your car. The same deal on the return. If you try to lose us, we call our employer. Got it?"

"I understand. I've got a couple of friends who will be tagging along in a white van. They'll stay back five to ten cars."

"Call and tell them to stay out of the way if there is any trouble. We don't need any help. Got it?"

Malachy flashed his Irish bullshit smile and said, "I always scored high on comprehension tests."

Malachy watched the security men escort Fr. Bari from the rectory door to his car. He pushed the passenger door open, and Fr. Bari quickly settled his long frame into the front seat and put his seat belt on. Malachy asked him to sit lower in the seat.

"We want to confuse any potential troublemakers," Malachy said. "Tell me about the death threat."

"There have been some threatening letters and a few unpleasant telephone calls. I assume they are from abuse victims who have no intention of actually doing me harm. But, Dino insisted on providing security. It seemed so ungrateful to turn him down after all he has done for the Shrine. I wouldn't have agreed if it was just my safety, but Dino convinced me others would be at risk too."

Malachy checked his rearview mirror to make sure the security was right behind them.

"Dino is right. Yours is a very high profile case. In the profound words of the world's foremost security expert, 'It *is* better to be safe than sorry.'"

Bari laughed and asked, "And who might that be?"

"Anonymous," Malachy said. "He's very prolific in a lot of fields."

"You're in a good mood. You must be a morning person."

"The paradoxical effect of sleep deprivation," Malachy said.

"All of this has a surreal aspect to it. Sometimes I feel like I'm sleepwalking."

"It's an all too-real nightmare for you and for Anthony Pace," Malachy said.

"Yes, it is."

"I believe you understand my role and why the committee has hired me," Malachy said.

"Yes, I do," Fr. Bari said. "I'm concerned that you understand and accept that any efforts on my behalf must not involve coercion. That young man has suffered too much already. I won't add to it under any circumstances. Is that clear?"

"Yes, it is. I believe we can establish your innocence using standard investigative techniques."

"Malachy, please pull over to the side of the road for a moment."

"Okay, but why? Security won't like it."

Malachy put his turn signal on and pulled into the parking lane and stopped the car. Fr. Bari reached over and lightly touched Malachy's arm. Malachy looked directly at Bari. He was startled by the intensity of the gaze.

"You just told me a lie. What you thought I wanted to hear. I ask you not to do that again."

Malachy pulled back into traffic, and they drove in silence toward Greektown. Malachy broke the silence, measuring his words carefully.

"I give my word that no coercion of any kind will be used on Pace."

"Malachy, I don't want force used to establish my innocence."

"I can't promise that," Malachy said. "Sometimes force is a necessity. For example, yesterday two men wrecked my car with baseball bats. By a stroke of luck, my associates and I were able to find them and determine some information about who hired them. That required the use of a ruse and some force. The two men were really just inconvenienced, not harmed. But, if somebody tried to harm you right now, I'd use force to stop them. That's the way I work."

"I'm sorry about your car," Fr. Bari said. "Do you believe it is related to my situation?"

"I made them pay for the car," Malachy said. "Plus a little. And yes, my best guess is that it's related to you in some way, but I don't know how yet."

"I see. I want to prove my innocence, but I'm not sure we can work together. The use of force is a real problem for me. I've accepted the security arrangements reluctantly in the hope that it will prevent a greater evil—harm to those around me."

"It is a far greater evil to allow the criminal who sexually assaulted Pace to go undetected," Malachy said in a hard, flat tone. "We both know other children will be his victims."

"Tragically, I think that's true. My heart breaks when I think of the suffering and hurt of all those children."

"Then, cooperate with me and help me prove your innocence and identify who assaulted Pace," Malachy said.

"I will pray that I make the right decision. And I will consider carefully what you've said."

"I requested this morning's meeting for a specific purpose. I need some information, and I need for my request to stay confidential. It's strictly information and will not lead to any use of force."

They drove through Greektown in silence. Malachy turned off Halsted and headed toward the highway. It was bumper to bumper, allowing plenty of time to talk during the return to Taylor Street.

"What information do you need?" Bari asked.

"What exactly does Dino do for the Shrine?"

"Why do you ask that question? You can't believe Dino is involved in some way in Pace's abuse."

"I can't tell you why I want the information. And Dino has nothing to do with the abuse as far as I know."

"Dino is chairman of the finance committee. The Shrine's outreach efforts are extensive, and we have a very large budget. We needed someone of his financial sophistication to run and supervise things. He's done a superb job."

"Are the finances audited?" Malachy asked.

"Yes, they are. And we publish the budget with a great deal of detail. We are far more open than the archdiocese. I want to earn the trust of the contributors. It is their right to know exactly where the money goes and why. Not all my causes are popular, and I don't want to hide one dime of the expenditures."

"No doubt another reason you are on O'Grady's shit list," Malachy said.

Bari laughed and said, "I understand you have a history with the cardinal."

"Too true. Even as boys we didn't see things the same way. He considers me 'a half-pagan, atavistic tribal barbarian'—and that's not a paraphrase."

"The cardinal actually said that to you?" Bari asked.

"Indeed he did, but he was only a seminarian then. I don't think his opinion has changed much. Kind of harsh for a baptized, confirmed Irish Catholic who made the nine first Fridays, don't you think?"

"Yes," Bari said, laughing again. "Very harsh."

"Back to Dino. Is the Shrine the same as most churches? Contributions via the envelopes, with the occasional large contribution by individual check or the gift of an appreciated asset? And loose cash making up the rest?"

"We are," Bari said. "Except we get more cash than most churches. We have lots of new visitors every week."

"Any chance some of the cash is being skimmed?" Malachy asked.

"No. I asked Dino to personally select the men involved in counting the collections. Some are even police."

"Sounds like you're absolutely confident the Shrine is getting a good count."

"Yes, I am."

"Could you get me a list of the top contributors without Dino or anybody else knowing?" Malachy asked.

"That's confidential information. I can't give it to you."

"I understand," Malachy said. "I'll settle for a copy of the published budget."

"Of course, I can give you that."

"Without anyone knowing?"

"I don't understand why. But yes, I can arrange that. I can fax it to you when no one else is in the rectory office."

Malachy gave Bari a business card from the Shamrock.

"The fax is always on. Don't bother with a cover sheet."

Bari handed Malachy a card and said, "Your questions are very upsetting. This card has my direct number and voice mail. Please call me if you learn anything that impacts the Shrine. I hope there's nothing going on that is going to interfere with our work."

"So do I," Malachy said. "I'll tell you whatever I can. If you decide you can work with me, we'll need to have a longer meeting. I have no facts yet, but my guess is that somehow, some way, you know the man who abused Pace. I will have a lot of questions. Some of them will be personal and difficult."

"Oh my God! Stop the car, that person is hurt!"

Malachy looked at a black man sprawled on the sidewalk, not moving. He looked around at the boarded-up housing projects on Taylor Street and the open liquor store down the block with heavy, protective steel grating on the windows.

"He's probably drunk and passed out," Malachy said.

"Malachy, stop this car. Now!"

Bari unlocked his door and started to open it.

"Okay, okay, I'm pulling over," Malachy said.

Malachy swerved to the curb, jumped out of the car, ran around, and intercepted Bari as he started across the street toward the black man prone on the sidewalk. The security men pulled up next to them.

"What the fuck is going on?" Jeff yelled. "Why did you stop?"

"He wants to help that man over there," Malachy said.

"No fucking way!" Jeff yelled even louder. "Father, get in this car. He's just a drunk."

"Malachy, let me go. That man needs help."

"I promise you I'll get him help," Malachy said. "But, please get in the car with your security. I'll call 911 and stay with him until they come."

Malachy locked eyes with Bari. Bari's face was flushed and his eyes were blazing.

Malachy said, "You know I'm not lying to you. But I'm not calling 911 until you're in the car."

"All right, I'll get in the car. But call now!"

Malachy gently moved Bari toward the open car door. He got in and Malachy slammed the door shut. The door locks clicked shut and the car sped off. Malachy took out his cell phone and called 911 as he walked toward the man slumped on the sidewalk.

"There is a man lying on the sidewalk on the south side of Taylor Street five yards from the intersection of Taylor and Racine. I don't have an exact address. He's bleeding. I think he was attacked. Send an ambulance."

Malachy answered the operator's questions and confirmed the information he gave. He reached the man and knelt down on one knee to examine him. He positioned himself a few feet away from his head to make sure he was out of flailing reach. Malachy saw signs of shallow breathing. He stood up, moved closer, and gently prodded the man's shoulder with his foot.

"Hey, are you all right? Get up."

Malachy backed away and prepared for a response. The man didn't move. Malachy nudged him again with his foot and shouted louder.

"Are you all right? Get up!"

Malachy again backed away from the man. Malachy saw two black men slowly coming toward him from the direction of the projects. He looked carefully at them for signs of a weapon. No weapon, but the bigger man's mismatched running shoes and the other's too-large trousers held up by half of a suspender confirmed addicted and homeless. And their hard-looking faces said hostile.

"Stop fuckin' kicking the brother, man. Leave him the fuck alone."

Malachy turned and fully faced the men.

"I'm not kicking him. I'm trying to find out if he's okay."

"He's all fucked-up," the suspender man said. "Get away from him."

"Okay," Malachy said, taking a few steps back.

Malachy positioned himself so he could see all three of the men and quickly checked to make sure there was nobody behind him.

"I called 911. They'll be here in a few minutes."

"You took the brother's money. Give it to us."

Malachy slowly backed away a few more steps. The white van with the Count driving pulled up, and Kevin bounded out of the front seat and ran straight at the two black men.

"Police! You two get away from the body. Now!"

The two looked at each other confused. They backed away from the man on the ground. Kevin pointed to Malachy.

"You, over to the van. Move it!"

Malachy jogged over to the van. The air filled with the siren sounds of the approaching ambulance. The two black men broke and half-ran, half-stumbled down the block and around the corner.

"Are you staying or going?" Kevin asked Malachy.

"Staying. I promised Fr. Bari I'd make sure Sleeping Beauty got help."

"What's his problem?" Kevin asked.

"Don't know. Those two said he was fucked-up. Probably drugs and alcohol. He's still breathing."

"We'll wait for you down the block," Kevin said. "I'll take Bridget's car."

Malachy nodded in agreement and went over to join the EMTs working on the man.

"How is he?" Malachy asked.

One of the EMTs looked up and asked, "Are you the one who called it in?"

"Yes."

"I thought the report said he was bleeding. I'm not finding any blood or wounds."

"I guess I was wrong," Malachy said. "It looked like that from the car."

The EMT looked at Malachy and shook his head in disbelief. The two EMTs loaded the man on the stretcher. A squad car pulled up with its lights on and two officers got out. The cop who came around the car from the driver's side looked familiar, and Malachy looked him over as he spoke into his walkie-talkie while watching the EMTs. He clicked off and surveyed the scene and recognized Malachy.

"Malachy, what the hell are you doing here? Remember me, Joey Flood?"

"Just being a Good Samaritan, Joey."

"What happened here?" Joey asked.

"As it turns out, I think it was just an overdose."

Joey went over to confer with the EMTs as they loaded the stretcher into the ambulance. He rejoined Malachy.

"Well, you saved his life this time," Joey said. "His vitals are really weak. A little more time cooking on the sidewalk and he'd be headed to the morgue instead of County."

"I'm glad he's going to make it," Malachy said.

"Temporary victory," Joey said. "That kind all kill themselves sooner or later, probably sooner."

"Maybe not," Malachy said. "He's got a new guardian angel."

"Who? You?"

"No, not me," Malachy said. "It's a long story, but that man has a powerful, new friend."

Joey motioned toward the boarded-up projects and said, "That kind never changes—to make things easy, they should just sleep in coffins."

Malachy suddenly remembered his successful defense of Joey. An on-duty auto accident involving alcohol.

"You never know, Joey. Sometimes people change after a close call."

"I guess so," Joey said, his tone a little less friendly. "I hear you're no longer in the lawyer racket."

"You heard right. But I'm thinking of getting into the Good Samaritan racket. Problem is the pay sucks."

"Whatever," Joey said. "See you later, Malachy."

Malachy climbed into the car next to Kevin. He called Bari and left the information about the comatose man on his voice mail.

"I don't have his name. I'm sure as a visiting priest you won't have any trouble locating him at County. If for some reason there's a problem, call me. I have some contacts there. Talk to you later."

"Even at County?" Kevin asked.

"Same as everywhere else," Malachy said. "I know somebody who knows somebody. And the somebody I don't know owes the somebody I do know a favor."

Kevin nodded his understanding and asked, "Where to?"

Malachy called the Count and put his cell phone on speaker.

"The Shamrock by some indirect route. Let's find out if Bridget's favorite federal agency has been involved in today's parade."

They wound their way to the Shamrock changing direction every ten minutes. As they approached the Shamrock, the Count called.

"Nobody followed you or me."

"Good," Malachy said. "Let's take the rest of the day off. I want to noodle about the current situation."

"That's a cover for nap time," the Count said.

"I do some of my best work lying down," Malachy said.

"Me, too," the Count said. "What time tomorrow?"

"Joint chiefs meeting at the crack of dawn," Malachy said.

"So, 10:00 or 10:30?" the Count and Kevin asked in unison.

"I'm surrounded by cynics and disbelievers," Malachy said. "10:30."

Malachy and Kevin were talking across the street from the Shamrock, where the truck Kevin always used for work was parked. Malachy tapped the truck's side panel and was about to ask if any new "tools" were hidden there when Kevin pointed to a group of eight well-dressed men and women headed toward the bar from the funeral home.

"Looks like we have some classy trade headed our way," Kevin said.

"We always do decent business when there's a wake for a neighborhood guy," Malachy responded. "Trouble is damn few are waked down here anymore. The gravediggers up north will rent to Conley's, so it's possible to have the traditional name and a suburban location."

"Did you know the deceased?" Kevin asked.

"Not well. He was much younger."

"Younger? That's too bad. What did him in?"

"Failure to join the right club. Lots of green and he belonged to all the exclusive clubs, even the ones that prefer you were born with a plank from the Mayflower stuck up your ass. But he never joined the Big Club."

"AA?"

"Yes. It's like the punch line from the old joke about the Irish mother who is waking her son who drank himself to death. When asked if he ever tried AA, she answers, 'No, thank God, it never got that serious.' The deceased refused to even consider going. Too low rent for him."

"What is it the Chairman says, 'Shop your meeting and keep shopping until you have a fit?'"

"That's how he got the nickname—he set up and put away so many chairs at so many meetings the name seemed a natural."

Do you want me to go in and help out?" Kevin asked.

"No," Malachy answered. "I'll go in—let's hope Bridget is in a good mood."

Kevin smiled and said, "Hope is not a plan."

Malachy watched the group settle at the big round table in the back and saw Bridget approaching the table as one woman was wiping down the seat of her chair with a handkerchief. He knew there would be trouble but decided it was already too late to intervene.

Everything went smoothly until Bridget came to the very thin, very blonde woman who had wiped down her chair.

"What'll you have?"

The question sounded like a blast from a foghorn. The woman looked up at Bridget and, without saying anything, looked back down at her menu. Bridget waited silently for just a few seconds.

"Come on dearie, pick something. The train is leaving the station. Now, what'll you have?"

The woman glared up at Bridget and said coldly, "Do not address me as dearie, and you will wait until I am ready to order."

"Well, Mrs. Mine-Doesn't-Stink, for the very last time, what will you have?" Bridget asked, emphasizing each word as the woman had.

"What did you just say to me? You can't talk to me like that!"

Bridget threw her hands up in the air in exasperation and turned to the husband.

"What's her problem? Is she feeble-minded or something? Did you forget to bring along the nursemaid? Of course I can talk to her like that. I just did."

The woman turned white with anger and said bitterly to her husband, "You insisted we come here. Do something."

The man stood up and said, "I will have an immediate apology or your job."

"I don't serve apologies. And I don't think you'd like my job. The two of you seem to have a weak hold on reality, so let me explain it to you. You are in a fading Irish dump on Devon Avenue in Chicago where people like me call people like you 'honey,' 'sweetie,' 'dearie,' and the like. If that doesn't suit you, stay away. I am sure up at the Pocahontas Club or whatever you call it, where the Mrs. has been perfecting her act, everybody pisses pink lemonade and farts Chanel No. 5, but down here on Devon Avenue, yours stink just like everybody else's. Got it?"

The husband walked toward the bar and said in a loud voice, "I demand to talk with the owner or manager."

Malachy examined the husband closely, looking for signs that he was trained in martial arts. The man was trim and fit, but Malachy figured it was from racquet sports. The man's stance was that of an athlete, not a fighter. Malachy stood up and faced the man.

"What seems to be the problem?" Malachy asked in as neutral a tone as he could muster.

"Are you the manager?"

"Well, actually I'm the bouncer, but I would like to try and resolve any problem."

"That waitress was unbelievably rude and insulting to my wife. I demand she apologize or she should be fired."

Without taking his eyes off the man, Malachy shouted, "Bridget, this customer demands you apologize to his wife."

Bridget bellowed back: "Tell him there's a better chance that monkeys will fly out of his ass, assemble a typewriter, and produce the collected works of Shakespeare."

Everybody in the bar laughed except the man's group. Malachy, fighting a smile, said, "I think the odds are against an apology from Bridget."

Malachy saw the man's face go bright red and calculated he was seconds away from charging. Malachy raised his hands palms out in a placating gesture.

"However, on behalf of the Shamrock I apologize for any offense to your wife. You know, I don't think we've got a good fit here. So why don't you and your friends find some other place to grieve?"

The other members of the group quickly took the proffered out and scrambled to get their coats on and get out the door. The husband was the last to leave and at the door he turned and said, "That loud-mouthed bitch had one thing right, this is a dump."

Malachy took a couple of quick steps toward him.

"You know how it goes, only family gets to criticize family. I'm guessing it's been a long time since your dry cleaner had to work on bloodstains, so why don't we just keep it that way and you grieve someplace else like I said before."

The man gave Malachy the finger and turned and left.

Bridget approached Malachy and said, "Just imagine at one time he thought she was a trophy."

"Just imagine," Malachy said pointing to the empty table, "that was an eight top that left without spending or tipping one red cent."

"So? I don't think there were likely to become regulars."

CHAPTER VIII

Malachy rushed into the Shamrock, checking the clock on the wall behind his office-booth. He saw Eduardo coming out of the kitchen with a coffeepot in one hand and a white bakery bag in the other.

"Damn, I suppose they're both here already."

"Sí, Mr. Malachy, they in the storeroom."

"How long?"

"Not too long, Mr. Malachy."

"I wanted to be the first."

"Maybe next time, I come get you in the car."

"Good idea, Eduardo. Anyway at least I'm not late," Malachy said, gesturing to the clock that showed 10:25."

"That clock a little slow, Mr. Malachy."

Malachy strode rapidly toward the storeroom.

Malachy passed out copies of the Saint Shrine's financial report and budget.

"Three million is a huge number," Kevin said. "How does he extract all that money from the community?"

"Charisma," Malachy answered. "It comes out of him like sweat out of a marathoner. You should see his eyes when he's charged up—it's like he's on some drug. When he's looking at you in that state, it's like he sees something no one else can see."

"Dollar signs," the Count said.

"Your Old World anticlericalism is showing," Malachy said. "Look where he spends the money. This guy is for real. Every pencil and paper clip is accounted for. But there is one strange thing that is not in the report. They get a lot of cash. And Dino is in charge of the whole show."

"And the FBI is interested in Dino," Kevin said. "What about skimming?"

"Bari says it's not possible. Of course, he could be wrong. Cash has a way of causing problems."

"Assume he's right," the Count said. "What's another explanation?"

"I don't know," Malachy said. "It's eluding me."

"Call Abe," Kevin said. "What he doesn't know about the games people play with cash is not worth knowing."

Malachy called Abe using his cell phone, clicked on the speaker function, and placed it in the center of the table.

Abe answered the phone with questions.

"So, have you come to your senses? Are you ready to close the Shamrock?"

"No and no," Malachy answered. "I need your expertise on something. And we never had this conversation."

"What conversation?" Abe said. "So, what's the deal?"

Malachy gave him the background without naming the Shrine.

"It comes back to the cash," Abe said. "Are you sure that some of the loose cash is not being credited to a giver?"

"No," Malachy said.

"Giving someone a tax deduction is just like giving them cash in their pocket. The higher their tax bracket the more the deduction is worth. If they're taking some of the loose cash and crediting it to registered envelopes, then the count is 100 percent accurate and Uncle Sam is the only loser."

"So you can manufacture charitable tax deductions," Malachy said. "And the money you are giving the donor is untraceable because it comes from owing less at tax time or a refund from Uncle Sam."

"That's the ticket," Abe said.

"What about the IRS?" Malachy asked. "Don't you need the cancelled check?"

"Not necessarily," Abe said. "The deduction needs to be backed by evidence. A statement from the church is evidence. Of course, it's fraud. But, it could go on for years undetected as long as the deductions aren't too large. Stuff like this surfaces because somebody is in trouble on something else and blows the whistle."

"Thanks, Abe. See you next month."

"Maybe by that time you'll come to your senses," Abe said.

Malachy went over Abe's theory with the Count and Kevin.

"It fits everything we know," Kevin said. "But it seems like Dino is involving a lot of people. There are lots of collections and lots of ushers."

"Dino is in charge. As long as the accounting for loose cash and envelopes is after the fact, he only needs the accountant's cooperation."

Malachy pointed to the CPA firm on the financial report.

"A small neighborhood firm donating their time to the Shrine for free, no doubt."

"What about Bari?" the Count asked. "Is he involved?"

"No way," Malachy said. "He believes Dino is giving him an honest count and he is. But this is going to complicate the hell out of our operation. The U.S. Attorney's office will have to include Bari in their investigation. If we get our wires crossed, the charge is obstruction of justice."

"If you always correctly identify and tag the wires and don't hurry, they never get crossed," the Count said.

"'Always' and 'never' are tough words to make come true," Malachy said. "We have to assume that every communication with Dino and Bari is compromised. And that the FBI may choose to follow us at any time. Yesterday they missed the parade, tomorrow they may show up."

"What about our employer?" Kevin asked. "Does he know what Dino is up to? Is he involved?"

"Those questions ruined my nap time yesterday," Malachy said. "I'm guessing no. He said it was personal. But we need to know for sure. It changes everything if he's involved."

"How do we rule him in or out?" Kevin asked.

"The list of donors," Malachy said. "If we know who is on the list, we know if it is Dino's deal or a joint play with our nameless employer. The names will tell the tale."

"Who has the list?" the Count asked.

"Bari and the accounting firm," Malachy said. "Bari has already refused to give me the list because it is confidential. So we have to procure it some other way."

The three men sat in silence for a long while.

The Count was the first to speak. "What we need is the list from two years ago. Dino could have easily modified the program if he had any inkling the Feds were interested. The accountant's office is our last resort. If the finance committee operates the way most of them do, then some of the other members have the lists."

"Here comes a proposal," Malachy said.

"I propose that I research the other members and select one to provide the list," the Count said.

"Provide how?" Malachy asked.

"Depends," the Count answered. "The operation will fit the person. The list could be on a computer or properly titled and filed in a cabinet or just thrown in a bottom desk drawer. We might get it by a ruse or it may take a break-in. I will propose the specific method after I've done the research."

Malachy looked at Kevin, who nodded yes.

"Proposal accepted," Malachy said.

"I have a proposal," Kevin said. "We need to find the Wisconsin mystery woman. I propose I try to find out who and where she is. It shouldn't take too long—there can't be that many bizarre-looking blondes driving Italian sports cars in that area of Wisconsin."

Malachy looked at the Count, who nodded yes.

"Proposal accepted," Malachy said. "Now, it's my turn. I propose I meet with Bari if he is agreeable and have the conversation about his background that might give us the connection to the actual abuser."

Kevin and the Count said "accepted" in unison.

They filed out of the storeroom and into the barroom. Bridget was behind the bar. Malachy gave her a half-salute.

"Thanks for the coffee, Bridget."

"You're very welcome. I'm glad you liked it."

"You're in a fine mood today," Malachy said.

Bridget smiled at Malachy and said, "I like it when the three of you meet. It usually means you're gone for the day, and I don't have to put up with any bullshit."

"I need to use your car again," Malachy said.

"If it means you're gone all day, that's an easy trade."

"It's nice to be wanted," Malachy said.

"I'm sure it is. Try not to wreck the car."

Malachy went to his booth and called Bari's direct line.

"Good morning, this is Malachy. How is Sleeping Beauty doing?"

"Better. He's recovering. I visited him early this morning. He'll be released in a few days. And, he has a proper name, it's Charles Moody. But, there are two problems. He'll need a place to live and a job when he's released."

"Wonderful," Malachy said.

Bari ignored Malachy's sarcastic tone.

"I've arranged for him to live at an AA first step house. But he needs a job, the sooner the better. Can you help out?"

"What can he do?"

"He'll do anything honest. But it's very important that it start as soon as he is released. I know you have a lot of contacts. Will you do something for him?"

"I was calling to ask for a meeting."

"It's very important that Charles has a job. Will you help out?"

"It's very important that I meet with you. I'm trying to prove your innocence by finding the criminal who abused Pace."

Bari ignored Malachy's comment.

"Charles needs to work. He wants to change his life, but he needs a job. I promised him I would find him one. It's hard to think about anything else when that promise is still unfulfilled."

"Okay, okay," Malachy said laughing. "I've been hammered by politicians with more finesse than that. He has a job. Dishwasher at the Shamrock. Two bucks an hour over minimum wage plus he gets tipped out. And he eats for free. It's a test run for six months. If he works out, and he wants something different, I'll help find it. Tell him to show up and ask for Bridget. Now, can I have my meeting?"

"I want your commitment that coercion won't be used to prove my innocence."

"I promise I won't torture anybody," Malachy said.

"Malachy, I'm very serious. I can't cooperate with you if you intend to use force."

"You have my commitment that I will only use force if it is absolutely necessary. And no matter what the circumstance, I will never use it on Pace. That's the best I can do. Weigh that against letting the abuser go free and destroying God knows how many more children."

"You sound confident that you'll find whoever abused Anthony Pace," Bari said.

Malachy decided to use his own hammer.

"If you fully cooperate, I will find him. I'm convinced you know him, that he has some relationship to you. I think Pace was targeted because of you."

"Because of me? Why?"

"I'll explain at our meeting," Malachy said.

Bari did not respond immediately. Malachy waited silently.

"I pray to God I'm making the right decision," Bari said. "I'll meet with you whenever you want."

"Today," Malachy said. "I'll pick you up in an hour. Let's take a walk along the lakeshore. It's supposed to be a nice day."

"All right."

"Do me a favor and let your security know," Malachy said. "They can choose the route to and from the lake and follow us as we walk. Tell them we're headed to the park at Belmont and the lake."

"I'll tell them," Bari said.

"One more thing," Malachy said. "Do you have a picture of yourself as a boy?"

"A picture? I don't know. I suppose I might have one somewhere. Why?"

"I'll explain later. A full-face shot would be best. See you in an hour."

Malachy waved Bridget over to the back booth.

"Bridget, I hired a new dishwasher. He'll be reporting to work in a few days."

"Are you deliberately trying to aggravate me? I'm the boss, and I do the hiring and firing in the kitchen. We don't need another dishwasher."

"You need more help out here," Malachy said. "Promote somebody from the kitchen and that'll make room for a new dishwasher. Anyway, it's a done deal."

"You know, Malachy, some days you really piss me off, and this is one of those days. You can take this job and shove it if you're going to constantly interfere and screw things up."

"The guy is trying to straighten out his life," Malachy said. "He just got off the sauce and needs a job."

Malachy looked at Bridget hoping his last comment would soften her reaction. She stared back at him, raised her forefinger like it was her middle finger, and said, "Great, just what we need around here—one more Irish drunk."

"He's not Irish, he's black. His name is Charles Moody."

"If he's trying to stop drinking, he shouldn't be working in a bar anyway."

"He's not. He's working in the kitchen. Tell him the bar is off-limits. And don't use him to bring up liquor from the basement."

"Anything else obvious you want to tell me?" Bridget said.

"No."

"Good. Do you have any other bullshit stunts to pull?"

"No, I'm leaving now."

"Good, don't hurry back."

†

Malachy watched the two new security men walk Bari to the car. He thought Bari looked an inch shorter and five years older as he approached the passenger side with his shoulders slumped forward, his gait slow, and his gaze vacant. Malachy figured the security were not off-duty cops. They looked more like juice collectors—big, bulky, and scowling. One of the men came around the car to talk to Malachy.

The man placed his hands on the door, leaned in, lowered his voice to a hoarse whisper and said, "Today, we're not stopping for any good deeds. Leave the hopheads on the sidewalk. I don't give a flying fuck what the good Father says, got it?"

"Got it. Today, we play Bad Samaritans all day. No problem."

"They told me you're a wiseass. We're tired and don't need any bullshit from you. Just do it by the numbers. Jackson to the Drive to Belmont and the reverse home. Max time two hours, got it?"

Malachy smiled and said, "Yes, I do indeed get it. You're not in the mood for a flying fuck. I do hope you find the lake breeze a tonic for your spirits."

Malachy hit the window control button, driving the window into the man's hands. Startled, he instinctively jumped back. Malachy pulled away from the curb and headed toward Jackson.

"No matter how hard I try I don't seem to hit it off with your security guys. I don't think they get my Irish sense of humor."

"They can be a little overbearing," Bari said. "We're all under pressure."

Malachy gave Bari a quick glance. His sweatshirt and blue jeans looked like they had been worn the day before.

"New threats?" Malachy asked.

"Yes, somebody threw a large rock through one of the back windows. There was a death threat attached."

"Anybody caught?"

"No, and I'm glad. I don't want anybody getting hurt. I'm still not sure I'm doing the right thing having private security."

"The security is the right thing, but I do have a suggestion for you. Call Dino and tell him you want only off-duty cops or ex-cops as security. The goons behind us are more likely to cause problems than prevent them."

"I'll do that," Bari said. "I've been very upset ever since you told me that Pace was targeted because of me. What did you mean?"

"Could you find a picture of yourself as a boy?"

"Yes, here it is."

Malachy reached into his shirt pocket and pulled out the newspaper picture of Pace as a boy. "Take a look at the two pictures and tell me what you see," Malachy said.

Bari held up the pictures side by side.

"Oh my God, there's a very strong resemblance."

"Well, you're both Italian. The Pace family uses the English pronunciation, but just like you Anthony is Italian on both sides."

"And you think the fact that we look alike influenced whoever attacked Pace?"

"It's a hunch—based on a meeting with my shrink consultant—not a fact."

"You consulted a psychiatrist about this?" Bari asked.

"Yeah, but I didn't have to go on the couch. She met me in a bar."

"You certainly operate in an unusual fashion," Bari said.

"I've been told that before."

They drove in silence down Jackson toward Lake Shore Drive. Malachy checked the mirror to make sure security was still behind him. The goon he startled was driving right behind him and saw Malachy checking his mirror. He gave him the finger and Malachy waved back.

"There is something you need to know about me," Bari said in a low quiet voice.

Malachy knew it was time to look straight ahead and not say anything.

"I am celibate now, but that wasn't always true. At the seminary and in my early years as a priest I had many sexual relationships. They were always age appropriate. I never sexually abused any children or teenagers. I want to make that very clear, never. No close calls, no misunderstood gestures, nothing, ever."

Malachy continued to drive in silence.

"The relationships were with both men and women," Bari said.

Malachy knew it was time to say something.

"I never figured you for a virgin."

Malachy glanced at Bari, who gave him a sad smile.

"I was a pretend priest in those days. I was immature and very confused about my sexuality. It was a witches' brew of sexual seething, sexual experimentation, shame, and guilt."

"You know, I always thought witches got a bad rap," Malachy said. "Anyway, I'm glad somebody else finds sex confusing. Tell me, is there clarity in celibacy? It's something I wouldn't know anything about."

Bari did not respond for a while. "It's not the celibacy that makes for clarity. It is truly understanding what I am supposed to be and do as a priest that makes for clarity. That makes the celibacy possible and makes it possible for the celibacy not to overwhelm me."

"I think I at least partially get it," Malachy said. "Well, my job is to make sure you can still be an active priest. What about the men you were involved with? Was anyone capable of abusing Pace?"

"I don't think so. No one ever talked about or suggested sexual activity with children. But, frankly, some of them I didn't know very well. Are you going to have to investigate all of them?"

"Not yet."

They drove up Lake Shore Drive in silence. Malachy wanted to ask about the women out of sheer curiosity but knew it wasn't relevant. He stayed silent, hoping Bari would start to talk about them. He pulled into the parking lot feeling a little ashamed of his voyeurism.

"We need to walk fast at first," Malachy said. "I don't want to give my goon friend an opportunity for a confrontation. Once we know he's going to keep his distance, we can slow down. See, I'm trying to keep my pledge."

"Good."

They exited the car and walked rapidly toward the path that wound along the lake. The security men scrambled out of their car and half-jogged to catch up to them until they were within hearing distance. Malachy turned around and gestured for them to fall back a little. Malachy and Bari resumed walking at a slower pace.

"You asked if anyone I was involved with was capable of abusing Pace," Bari said. "Some of those men are not priests. I just assumed Pace's abuser is a fellow priest."

"The abuser is a man who heard Pace's confession at least once and perhaps heard others on that day," Malachy said. "That makes it highly probable he is a priest. Probable, not certain. It also makes it probable that if a priest did it, the priest was assigned to Pius XII parish. We're in the process of checking that out. Here's a list of the priests at the parish. Do you think any of them are capable of abusing Pace?"

Bari stopped walking, took the list, and stared at it for a while. He let his hand drop and gently banged the list against his leg. He made a wide, sweeping gesture with his free arm toward the blue lake and then up to the cloudless sky. "Just look at this…how can we be talking about such…"

Malachy interrupted, "Predators only care about their prey, not the lush beauty of the forest." Malachy started to say more and stopped, not wanting to pile on.

Bari handed the list back to Malachy and said, "When I think of what was done to Pace, there is always a disconnect. I knew and worked with these men. I socialized and shared meals with them. I've searched my memory countless times for some clue that one of them was capable of such actions. After a while, paranoia sets in—well so-and-so did say or do such-and-such and didn't that have a secret meaning? Didn't that indicate he could be a moral monster? And then when I put things in context it always comes out the same—there was no indication whatsoever that any of those men were capable of such actions."

"That's too bad," Malachy said.

"I don't understand."

"Pace is very credible and very specific in his allegations against you," Malachy said. "To prove your innocence we need to prove who actually did the abuse. That will be a lot easier if the abuser is a fellow priest at the parish. If not, the possibilities start to multiply. Time is not on our side. What we're after is for Pace himself to exonerate you—the sooner the better."

"Do you really think you can get that accomplished?" Bari asked.

"Let me tell you a story about a dingy parking garage that's only a few blocks from our glorious lakefront.

"I once defended a man accused of rape. Everything pointed to the man's guilt. The woman, a devout churchgoer, claimed the man raped her in a deserted stairwell in a Loop parking garage. The woman claimed the man threatened her life with a knife. The police found a knife on my client. He had no plausible reason to be in the garage. And the rape-kit exam found his semen.

"His defense? Consensual sex. Everyone told me he was toast. But I believed him. The guy was a lot of things, but not a rapist. But even my client figured he was toast and wanted to make a deal. I told him no deals. The key was she was a Bible-believing churchgoer.

"We would make her give sworn testimony in open court and follow that up with an intense, prolonged cross-examination with the intention of cracking her story. I made sure the assistant DA knew that. And

I made sure she knew she would have to tell lie after lie on the stand. And after each lie, I'd be rubbing her nose in the Bible.

"The upshot? She recanted. She was so embarrassed and humiliated that she let herself be seduced by this guy and ended up having sex in a public place that she claimed rape—the embarrassment and the humiliation turned to rage."

"How terrible for the woman," Bari said. "She was a victimized even if it was consensual. What a horrible ordeal for her."

Malachy silently mulled over Bari's reaction. He calculated he had told the story more than 100 times and got all kinds of reactions, most of them accompanied by laughter and callous or caustic remarks about well-equipped sexual athletes and the like. One broker friend even wanted to hire his client as a cold-caller, saying he must have unbelievable powers of persuasion. But none expressed empathy for the woman. Bari interrupted his reverie with a question.

"How does your story relate to my situation? Don't you believe Pace is telling the truth about the abuse?"

"Yes, I do. The point is to find the right key to Pace exonerating you. I believe that key is his all-consuming rage. We have to convince him it is directed at the wrong person. So we have to provide him the real abuser with irrefutable, overwhelming evidence of guilt that will get Pace to see you as a victim of the abuse, just like he is."

"Me?"

"Yes. If my hunch is right that you know the abuser, then you were targeted to be the fall guy just like Pace was targeted."

"Oh, my God! Somebody hates me that much. Why?"

"We don't know who and we don't know why yet, but we will. The first step is to rule in or out all those who served with you at Pius XII."

"What if your hunch is wrong?" Bari asked.

"Then, the whole process will take longer." Malachy stopped walking and looked directly at Bari. "Whoever did this must be stopped. As I said, the sooner the better for you and for his next intended victims. But no matter how long it takes, he must be stopped."

Bari resumed walking silently. They walked for a half-mile with no conversation. Then Bari broke the silence.

"Malachy, a few of the men I was involved with have very different lives now. Some are married with children and some are higher up in the Church. I don't want your investigation to turn their lives upside down."

"Despite the way I look, I tread lightly and work discreetly. They have nothing to worry about. Odds are most of them will be eliminated without ever knowing they were investigated."

"I hope and pray that's the case," Bari said. He gestured once more toward the lake. "Somehow, it's more difficult to answer your questions in this setting. Unless you have more questions for me, I'd like to go back to the rectory now."

"Sure."

Malachy turned around and started to walk toward the two security men. There was a biker behind the security men, cycling very slowly. He looked vaguely familiar to Malachy. The man had on large dark sunglasses and a long-beaked hat, just like the man Kevin had pointed out in the background of Bari's press conference.

"We have a security problem," Malachy said in a low firm voice. "Do exactly as I say. Drop down on one knee and retie your shoe. And stay in that position. Now!"

Bari stopped and went down on one knee and started to untie his shoelace. Malachy motioned to the security men to join them, never taking his eye off the biker. The biker swung off his bike and started to walk slowly beside it. Malachy tried to spot a weapon, but couldn't see one. The security men joined them.

"Now, what the fuck are you up to?"

The biker stopped and watched the group and then turned and faced his bicycle in the opposite direction.

"Pull your weapons and shield Fr. Bari!" Malachy ordered.

Malachy started to run at full stride right at the biker, blocking the biker's view of Bari and the security men. If he spotted a gun, he intended to hit the ground and start rolling. He hoped the goons actually knew how to shoot straight.

The biker jumped on his bike and pedaled rapidly away from Malachy. He never looked back. Malachy watched him until he was out of sight and then trotted back to the group.

"You're nothing but fucking trouble. Who the hell was that?"

"Don't know."

"Was that man going to harm me?" Bari asked.

"Don't know."

"What the fuck do you know?" one of the security men angrily asked.

Malachy looked at the security goons and said, "I know it's time for you to put your weapons away and take Fr. Bari back to the rectory."

"What are you going to do?" Bari asked.

Malachy looked up and down the lakefront. There was a police cruiser moving slowly toward them. "I'm going to do my civic duty," Malachy said. "I'll call you later. Remember to call Dino."

Malachy jogged toward the cruiser waving his arms.

"You're fucking nuts," a security man yelled after him.

The two security men walked hurriedly toward their car with Bari between them.

The squad car rolled up to Malachy and stopped.

"What's the problem?" the cop asked.

"There's a guy on a bike exposing himself. He stays just far enough away so you can't grab him. As soon as you start toward him, he takes off on his bike. I can point him out if you want to look for him. He just took off headed north."

"Wait a minute," the cop said.

The cop got on his radio and called the situation in.

"Are you willing to press charges if we find him?"

"Absolutely. The little prick ruined my walk—speaking literally."

The cop laughed and said, "Climb in. Let's go hunting. What are we looking for?"

"A shorter, white guy, no more than 5'7". Over forty. Weight almost proportional to his height, but a little paunchy. He's got oversized sunglasses on and a long-beaked hiker's cap. He's wearing dark running shorts, not biker pants. Easier access, I guess. Some kind of dark collarless shirt."

The cop gave Malachy a surprised look and said, "That's very detailed, but you left out the bike. Have you done this before?"

"My name is Malachy Madden. I used to be a defense lawyer. Can't tell you very much about the bike, I got distracted."

"That name sounds familiar."

"I've defended a lot in front of the Police Board."

"Used to be?"

"It's a long story."

"They usually are," the cop said. "Okay, let's see if we can find ourselves a fresh air flasher."

The cop and Malachy cruised the lakeshore for thirty minutes to no avail.

On the drive home, Malachy mulled over the sexual information Bari revealed. He felt stronger about the hunch that Bari was targeted. The combining of an extensive, complicated sex life with Bari's extraordinary good looks was certain to have inflamed someone. Over the years in his law practice he witnessed how twisted sexuality led to all kinds of crime from the trivial to the violently bizarre. Even everyday sexual jealousy was a powerful motivator. He remembered how it led to his own first time.

Malachy rang the front doorbell to the apartment. There was no answer. He pushed the buzzer again and held it a little longer. The door swung open, and Patrick's older sister gave Malachy a confused look. Malachy could tell she had been crying. He started to explain that he was supposed to go to a Sox game when she interrupted him.

"Are you looking for Tim? I don't where he is. I don't know where any of them are. Come on in, if you want. You can wait for him."

Malachy stepped into the darkened apartment. All the curtains were pulled and all the shades were down. Malachy realized that Patty mistook him for a friend of Tim's. Patty was nineteen and the oldest. Tim was eighteen, and Patrick, Malachy's friend, was fifteen.

"Sorry it's so dark in here. Dad insists that we keep everything closed up with almost no lights on. He says it keeps it cooler and keeps the electricity bill down."

"It is nice and cool in here," Malachy said, trying to sound older. "It's really hot outside."

"I know. I was at the beach. Didn't change yet. Do you want a beer? I'm having another one. By the way, I'm Patty."

"Malachy. A beer sounds great, thanks."

Patty looked up at Malachy, searching for an answer in his face.

"That's a nice name. And I know it for some reason, but I can't think why. It's been a long day."

Malachy didn't know how to respond. All he knew was that he didn't want Patty to figure out that he was Patrick's friend, not Tim's. He tried not to stare at Patty's figure, but her cotton pullover just reached the top of her thighs and made it seem like she had nothing on underneath.

"I'll get the beers," Malachy said, moving toward the kitchen. "I know where the fridge is." Malachy moved by Patty, hoping the darkness hid his obvious erection.

"Okay. Don't take the Heinekens, they're Dad's. He lets us have Old Style."

"All right."

Malachy found a six-pack of Old Style cans in the refrigerator. He took two and opened them. There were three empty cans on the sink. He noticed the blinking message light on the answering machine.

"The message light is on," Malachy said, entering the den. Patty was sitting on the couch across from the TV. Malachy wanted to sit next to her but was afraid he wouldn't be able to talk at all if he was that close to her. He sat on the edge of a large footstool.

"Really? I better check it."

Patty got up quickly from the chair and trotted into the kitchen. She came back with tears in her eyes.

"Well, we're on our own for a while. That was Tim. The car broke down. He and Patrick are stuck way out west somewhere. They won't be home for hours."

"Won't your parents be coming home?"

"Not until much later. They're downtown at some fancy dinner. And I won't be going out tonight, that's for sure."

Patty took a big swallow of her beer. Tears rolled down her cheeks. Malachy tried desperately to think of something to say. He had to look away from Patty's cute, freckled face and glistening blue eyes so he could think at all.

"I'm sorry."

"It's not your fault. It's my boyfriend...," Patty paused and took a deep breath. "My ex-boyfriend. It's his fault, the shit."

Malachy struggled to find words that would keep the conversation going. He forced himself to stop looking into Patty's eyes and to focus on her forehead, hoping that would untie his tongue.

"Was the beach hot?" Malachy asked.

"Really hot. I think I got a little burned. It figures, burned twice. Do you have a girlfriend?"

"No, I don't."

"It won't be long. When you do, don't go out with other girls behind her back. That's what he did, the shit. Even after we…"

Patty stopped talking and began to cry. Malachy moved next to her and put his arm around her. She put her head on his shoulder and sobbed.

"You're so pretty, he must be crazy," Malachy said earnestly, able for the first time since he saw Patty to say exactly what was on his mind.

"What a sweet thing to say."

Patty reached up and put her hand on Malachy's cheek. A surge of excitement ran through him, and he felt like his hard-on would split his pants. He wanted desperately to kiss her, but not as an imposter. Patty guided him to kiss her, and Malachy quickly responded. He tried to kiss softly and keep his hands still.

"That was really nice," Patty said, pulling back from him. "Are you ready for another beer?"

"Sure, thanks."

Patty came back with the beers and sat close to Malachy.

"That name, Malachy, seems so familiar. Did we ever meet at one of Tim's parties?"

"No," Malachy said, trying to think of a way to change the subject.

"What's your last name?"

"Madden."

"That's different. Is it Irish?"

"Very. My dad is from County Clare. And my mom from County Kerry. Little towns with long names I can't pronounce."

"We're from there on my dad's side, but from way back. I don't know where."

Patty stopped talking again for a minute and then resumed with a rush.

"Johnny O'Brien is his name. It ought to be Liar-Shit. I caught them together. They were in the backseat of his car. And she's supposed to be a friend of mine. Well, screw them. They deserve each other. I just can't believe he did that to me. For her, the bitch."

The kiss and the beer made Malachy bolder.

"Screw them, they deserve each other," Malachy said, clicking his beer with hers.

Malachy chugged his beer and Patty took two big swallows of hers. Malachy put his empty can on the floor and put his arm around Patty. She put her can next to his and leaned into him. They started kissing softly, but Patty began to rapidly dart her tongue in and out of Malachy's mouth. Malachy put his hand on her breast, expecting her to pull it away as happened with so many other girls.

Patty pulled back from Malachy and reached up behind her neck and untied her bathing suit. Malachy reached under the cotton cover-up that was now riding above her waist and touched her bare nipple. Malachy throbbed with confused excitement. Kissing and touching, they slowly moved to lying side by side. Malachy put his hand between her legs.

"Don't do that," she whispered in his ear, taking his hand and putting it back on her breast. Patty kissed him in the ear with her tongue darting in and out. Malachy heard himself make a moaning, groaning sound. Patty kept kissing him in the ear while she rubbed his erection from the outside of his jeans. Patty slid under Malachy and wrapped her legs around him and pressed against his erection. They thrust against each until Malachy climaxed with a moaning sigh.

Malachy found himself speechless again. He could hardly believe he had just finished dry-docking with Patrick's older sister. "You're wonderful," Malachy finally said.

"I think we got a little carried away. I hope you don't think I..."

Malachy interrupted, "No, no, it was me. I just think you're wonderful."

"It helps that somebody thinks that. You won't tell anybody about this, will you?"

"Never. I won't tell anyone, ever."

"Thank you." Patty said. "How about something to eat? I'll make us some sandwiches. I'll meet you in the kitchen. I'm going to change."

Patty was standing at the counter making sandwiches, still barefoot but *now in bright white shorts and a hot pink top. To Malachy, with her tan, bare arms and legs, she seemed like a vision from never-ending summer. He moved quickly to sit at the kitchen table and forced himself to talk.*

"That looks good. What is it?"

"Pastrami on rye. My dad loves pastrami so there's always some in the fridge."

They ate their sandwiches, drinking more beer. Malachy tried to make small talk about the beach and the White Sox. "All the guys in the neighborhood are big Sox fans," Malachy said, concentrating on the words so he did not slur.

"Not Liar-Shit," Patty said, giggling. "He's a Cub fan."

"See, I told you he was crazy."

"You're right, he's crazy. I know, let's tear up his picture. I'll be right back."

Patty returned with a handful of photos.

"Look, there's the bitch he did it with," she said, pointing to a picture of a girl at a beach party.

"She's ugly," Malachy said, looking at the picture of a pretty, tall blonde shapely girl.

Patty tore the picture into fours and then got the kitchen scissors and cut the fours into little pieces. "Ugly bitch! Ugly bitch!"

Patty took the pieces and put then down the garbage disposal and ran it with cold water. "Good, that's done. Let's celebrate. I know—shots. Let's do some shots. Come on!"

Patty weaved slightly as she went back into the den. Malachy followed her. The room seemed even darker than before. Patty took a bottle from a silver tray and poured the whiskey into two small crystal glasses. She gave one of the glasses to Malachy and hooked her arm around his.

"I know who you are," Patty said, slurring her words. "It came to me when you talked about everybody being a Sox fan. You're Patrick's friend, not Tim's. You and Patrick were supposed to go to a Sox game tonight."

"I couldn't help myself," Malachy said. "You're so pretty and you were crying. I just wanted to be older. Do you want me to leave?"

"No, not right away. Promise me you'll never tell about anything that happens tonight."

"I promise."

They gulped down the whiskey with their arms hooked. They both coughed.

"God, that's strong stuff," Patty said.

"It sure is."

Malachy's head was reeling. His secret was out, and he was still standing close to Patty in the darkened den. He didn't know what to do or say.

"Malachy, tell me the truth about something. Have you ever done it before?"

Malachy shook his head no and said, "Not really, just things like it before."

Patty didn't respond. She went to the den closet and pulled out a thick comforter. She clumsily folded it to a double thickness and spread it on the floor. She motioned to Malachy to join her on the comforter. Malachy knelt across from her.

"I'll tell you the truth," Patty said, now fully slurring her words. "I've done it lots of times with you-know-who. I'm on the pill. This is the only way I can ever forgive him if he comes back."

"Okay," Malachy said, not understanding.

"Kiss me a lot first," Patty said. "A whole lot. And Malachy, it's not a race."

Twenty years later Malachy was standing off to the side of the bar at a family wedding, sipping his drink and surveying the dance floor when an attractive, short woman with a good figure approached him.

"Hello, Malachy, do you recognize me? It's Patty O'Brien. It's been a long time."

"Of course, I recognize you. I could never forget. You're just as pretty as ever."

Patty smiled at him and said, "Still have the charm, don't you? Well, any mother of four can use the compliments."

They talked for a while about their families and raising kids, and then Patty brought up their night together. "God, I was such a slut that night. Sometimes I can't believe it."

"Please don't talk about my first love that way," Malachy responded.

"You still say the sweetest things. No wonder I got into trouble that night. The combination of the beer and the breakup was bad enough, but we should have never done those shots."

Malachy looked down into the blue eyes he remembered so well, smiled, and said, "I've been drinking Jameson ever since."

Patty laughed and said, "At least it did make it easier to forgive Johnny when he finally got around to saying he was sorry and wanted to get back together." Patty paused and then said seriously, "I could tell you never told anybody. I really appreciate that."

"Not anybody."

Patrick and Maria approached them.

"What are you two talking so seriously about?" Patrick asked.

"I'm expounding on the merits of Jameson," Malachy said.

"Oh, God," Maria said. "The poor woman must have sore ears. I know how it goes." Maria adopted an exaggerated brogue, "If it is good enough for Michael Collins, the big fella, it is good enough for me. And then, the saints preserve us, you get the whole history of Michael Collins, Jameson's, and, as a bonus, a catalog of all the wrongdoing of the gin-swilling Anglo-Saxons."

CHAPTER IX

Kevin approached the Wisconsin summer cottage with a large, front screened-in porch. It had taken him even less time than anticipated to locate the Alfa and its owner. Only two stops—a gas station and a diner—and only two lies. The shapely woman standing behind the screen door was obviously not the bizarre blonde woman he saw driving the Alfa. But the sports car parked near a converted barn was the Alfa he spotted driving away from the casino.

"How did you find me?" the woman asked Kevin in a throaty voice.

"Good detective work," Kevin answered.

Kevin and the woman examined each other through the screen door with growing interest. The woman was dressed all in black in figure-revealing tights and top. She was definitely very Italian and very attractive.

"Please come in. My name is Antonella Swenson."

"Nice to meet you. What a pretty name. I'm Kevin."

Antonella gave Kevin an appraising look and asked, "Don't you have a last name?"

"I haven't decided which one I'm using today."

"What an interesting answer. Please sit down. May I offer you something to drink?"

"No, thank you."

Antonella sat down at one end of a long, stuffed couch. She motioned Kevin to sit in a chair across from her. As Kevin moved to the chair, he quickly scanned the cottage interior with its white walls accented with pastels looking for signs of another's presence. There were none.

"Are you a detective?"

"No. I used to be an investigator, but now I'm a bartender."

The woman smiled at Kevin and said, "Most bartenders don't have your physique. You must work out a lot."

"I do. Long, hard workouts at least three or four times a week."

"It shows. I like long, hard workouts myself. You know, you'd be a perfect model for something I'm working on."

"Are you an artist?" Kevin asked.

"No, I make my living writing soft pornography. I need to describe a pirate—you know muscles rippling, that kind of thing."

"Do I get to wear a black eye patch and a swashbuckling hat?" Kevin asked.

"That could be arranged. Do I need to provide a sword too?"

"No, I have my own sword," Kevin said. "But, I do see a problem. Most pirates are burned dark by the sun. I don't spend much time in the sun."

"That's okay. I'm a writer—I'll use my imagination to make you have a deep tan."

"I see," Kevin said. "Well, I always like to help out when I can, but it can't be today because I'm working. Maybe some other time. But the patch and the hat are a must have."

"I understand," Antonella said, smiling playfully at Kevin as she slowly raised her hands and pushed her almost jet-black hair behind her ears.

"Speaking of work," Kevin said. "Perhaps you could help me on one of my projects?"

"Perhaps."

"Why did you hire two local lowlifes to demolish my boss's beloved car?"

Antonella smiled warmly and said, "Kevin, I can't tell you why because I didn't do it."

"Your car is very distinctive—that's how I found you. Did you lend it to a friend perhaps?"

"No. Do I get to ask you a question?"

Kevin smiled back and said, "Of course."

"Do you think my sports car somehow attacked Malachy's car? It has such a good pedigree and is usually so well-behaved."

"You know Malachy?" Kevin asked, surprised.

"You asked another question without answering mine—that's not fair."

"Sorry," Kevin said. "No, I don't think your sports car directly attacked Malachy's Mercury. But the woman who hired the two local thugs to do the attack was driving an Alfa Romeo with Wisconsin plates. Unless your car has a twin, she was driving your car. How do you know Malachy?"

"I know of him. I was in the Shamrock."

"I know I never saw you in the Shamrock," Kevin said.

"I was dressed a little differently."

"As a pirate?"

"That would attract attention. I wanted to observe without being noticed myself."

"Why?"

"I wanted to find out if the Committee for Justice hired someone competent and resolute," Antonella said.

"Couldn't you have asked for references or something?"

Antonella gave Kevin an amused smile and said, "I believe in direct action. Do you believe in direct action?"

"Sometimes," Kevin said.

"What a cautious answer," Antonella said. "All the male protagonists in my fiction are direct and very forceful."

"And the women?" Kevin asked.

"They vary. Some are cold, haughty, and imperious at the start but eventually submit to the powerful male. Some are shy or submissive at the start but without fire or passion and discover their inner tigress in the arms of the adept, powerful male."

"I think I get the theme," Kevin said. "Is it ever vice versa?"

"Never in my books. I know what my readership wants. My work-in-progress is called *Yes, My Captain*."

"And what kind of woman is the pirate dealing with?"

"Haughty and imperious. The pirate has captured a ship with an

English lord, his equally highborn wife, and her serving maid as passengers. The pirate offers to spare the life of the lord and to guarantee the safety of all three if the wife and the serving maid become his willing sex slaves until he puts them safely ashore."

"So, the women have to choose between death and dishonor. Kind of like the virgin martyr saints in ancient times."

"Worse. If the women do not accept the pirate's offer, they will be turned over to the crew for their pleasure, as the ship's rules require. The pirate is handsome, healthy, and well built. The crew is a motley group of diseased, ugly men."

"I think you stacked the deck." Kevin said.

"In porn, the deck is always stacked."

"So, the highborn lady eventually submits," Kevin said.

"Yes, but first she makes a noble attempt to save her serving maid from the pirate's wicked designs with some unexpected consequences."

"Intriguing."

"I hope so. That's what I was working on when you knocked. Are you sure you won't have something to drink. I usually have some wine about now. Won't you join me?"

"No, thanks," Kevin said.

"Are you always so focused on your work?" Antonella asked.

"Only when I'm working," Kevin answered with a big smile.

Antonella got up and slowly walked by Kevin into the kitchen. She took a bottle of Frascati white wine from the refrigerator and deftly opened it.

She returned to the couch with the wine, two elegant wineglasses, and some biscotti on a tray and placed it on the table between them. She gestured toward the wineglasses.

"Just in case you change your mind."

"We pirates tend to be a resolute lot," Kevin said.

"I know. My pirate is determined to fulfill his sexual desires, not just settle for mere cold submission. Would you like to hear what I was working on? You said you were intrigued. Or would that take your focus away from your work?"

"Work is not necessarily unpleasant or uninteresting. Take right now, for instance. My work allows me to have this stimulating…," Kevin paused, "and fascinating conversation with you. After you read from *Yes, My Captain,* could you answer a few more questions about what brought me here?"

Antonella slowly sipped her wine and then nibbled on a biscotti.

"Very well, afterward I will submit to a few questions if that's what you want."

"Not mere cold submission, I hope."

"Never."

Antonella picked up a notebook from the table.

"It is easier for me to get into the reading if you just relax and close your eyes rather than watching me."

Kevin settled back in his chair and closed his eyes.

"Let me set the scene. The two women and the pirate are in his quarters. He has explained their choice in graphic terms. Lady Swanson tells the story in the first person. Are you ready?"

"Ready."

> I drew myself up and said in the most imperious manner I could, "You will hang, sir. The British Navy will find you, and you will hang. You best treat all of us with the respect and dignity that is our birthright."
>
> He emitted a raucous laugh and responded with pure sarcasm. "Your birthright commands nothing on my ship. And if I hang, you won't be there to enjoy it unless you agree to my demands. What is your answer? I have half a mind to turn you over to the crew anyway. When the tenth man climbs atop you, you can tell him about your precious birthright. But I offered you a bargain and I will let you answer."
>
> I shuddered in horror. There was no way out of the dilemma. I had to submit to save Lord Swanson and my faithful maid.
>
> "I will submit," I said coldly.
>
> "Say it right," he thundered at me.
>
> I hesitated, knowing it was the beginning of my descent into depravity.
>
> "Now, or I turn you over to crew. They won't care how you address them!"

"Yes, my captain, I will submit to your desires."

He turned to my maid and said, "And you? What is your answer?"

"Please, Captain," I said. "Spare my innocent maid your wicked intentions. She is just a child. She has no experience of the world. I beg of you to let her stay with me, but do not put her to your evil uses."

He started to laugh with such enthusiasm it seemed he would fall from his chair.

"Innocent maid? Let's put her to the test."

He drew his sword and put it to her neck. "Tell the truth on peril of your life. Do you know man?"

I expected a simple demure denial. She blushed and looked at me and started to stammer.

"Answer me! Do you know man?"

"Yes," she finally stammered out.

"Name the last man who had you. Now!"

I was shocked, but there was worse to come. She fell to her knees, crying and begging the pirate not to make her tell the name.

"I will have that name. Now!"

His voice filled me with dread. I did not know if I could keep my sanity as my world was overturned.

"Lord Swanson."

My husband, whose life I just saved with the bargain of my virtue. I shrieked in agony. She grabbed my knees and wept into my gown.

"Oh, ma'am. Please forgive me. You have been so good to me. His lordship trapped me in the parlor. I couldn't get away."

I slapped her tear-stained cheek. "You are nothing but a common harlot." I slumped to the floor, despondent.

The pirate was cruelly amused by the whole scene. "How did he take you?"

My maid started to stammer again. "From behind, Captain."

"In a hurry, was he? Did it pleasure you?"

"Not much, Captain."

I could not credit my ears. Such talk from my maid who just

minutes before I thought an innocent child. The next upheaval followed shortly.

"We will have a reenactment for my amusement—a sort of play," the pirate said. He looked impatiently at both of us.

"Have ye been struck dumb? Answer!"

"Yes, my captain," we said together.

The pirate touched my bodice with the tip of his sword.

"You shall play your husband's role. Indeed, you have more steel in you than that fop even if you are lacking a cannon."

Again he started to laugh with great energy. My face burned red with anger, but I held my tongue for fear of being turned over to the crew.

"Begin!" he ordered.

We both said, "Yes, my captain," but neither of us moved.

"Chase her!" the pirate yelled. "You are an English lord on the hunt! Chase her and make her your prize."

I whispered to my maid that we must amuse him or worse would happen to us. I told her to scamper about the cabin and I would pretend to chase her, like a child's game. She darted away from me and I went after her.

"That's it," the pirate said. "Now grab her about the waist and force a kiss on her!"

I gently grabbed my maid about the waist from the back and pretended to kiss her on the neck.

"Bah! Goddamn it, give me the real thing! Spin her about and kiss her on the mouth!"

He started to bang the hilt of his sword on his chair loudly. I knew it was no use to pretend. We must do as he commanded. I turned my maid about and lightly and quickly kissed her on the mouth.

"Follow my orders or else," he bellowed and began to bang the hilt of his sword even more loudly. "Kiss her like a real man! Tongue her!"

I knew all artifice in defense of modesty was futile. I must act the role of the lust-driven lord. I pulled my maid to me forcefully and kissed her full on the mouth. She yielded to my embrace and her lips parted. I darted my tongue in and out of her mouth. I was shocked and horrified at my ease in playing the male role and the strange excitement it generated.

"More, more," the pirate commanded. "Fondle her! Keep kissing and fondle her!"

I moved my hand to her breast and fondled her gently. The pirate kept yelling "more, more" and banging the hilt of his sword. I became more vigorous in my actions as I imagined a male might do. Suddenly my maid responded to my actions and began to push against me, kissing me with a passion I never experienced before, using her tongue aggressively.

"Disrobe each other!" the pirate commanded.

I hesitated and pulled back. I knew I stood at the edge of the abyss.

"We must obey him," my maid said urgently.

"I gave you an order. Obey it, now!"

"Yes, my captain," I said, sealing my fate.

Antonella stopped reading. Kevin opened his eyes and sat up.

"Any reaction?" Antonella asked.

"Yes," Kevin said. "Could I have a glass of ice water? It got hotter in here. It must be the afternoon sun."

"Of course. Any other reactions?"

Kevin waited for her to return with the ice water before answering.

"The transition from haughty, highborn lady to the activity with the maid seems a bit quick. But, perhaps that's a convention of the genre."

"It is a convention of the genre that seems to have made it into real life. I was reading an article the other day about how some college women make out with each other in pickup bars to sexually arouse the men they are interested in. But, I will add a detailed description of the maid's beauty and shapely figure as well. Thanks for the feedback."

"You're welcome. I've learned a lot from our resident literary scholar."

"At the Shamrock bar?"

"Yes. Sean is an Irish poet and critic. He gives informal seminars at the bar on all kinds of literary topics to cover his tab. I don't agree with the policy, but Malachy has a weakness for Irish poets."

"Why do you object?" Antonella asked.

"The Shamrock is cash only—no tabs, no credit cards, no exceptions. Except Sean is an exception. I believe no exceptions means exactly that. But Malachy is the boss."

"What's the harm?" Antonella asked.

"Exceptions always undermine morale, and bad morale leads to all kinds of problems. They tell me I'm a black-and-white thinker—no shades of gray."

"I think of morale more in terms of the military than the bar business," Antonella said.

"That's in my background," Kevin said. "It's Malachy's, too. We met in the Marines."

"How interesting," Antonella said. "So, it's no exceptions today—work only."

"Correct," Kevin said.

"Okay, to work. What are your questions?"

"Who has access to your car?"

"Only my guests. However, I must admit I'm careless about leaving the keys in the car, but only when it is parked on my property. It's a bad habit I know, but it saves me time. I'm forever misplacing keys, sunglasses, things like that."

"So, it is possible somebody else took the car two days ago and then returned it," Kevin said. "Would somebody else driving your car around town or at the casino attract attention?"

"Not necessarily. I entertain a lot and do have lots of guests up here when the weather is good. Many of my guests get a kick out of driving the Alfa. It fulfills a teenage fantasy for many of them, men and women. And a lot of them go to the casino."

"Do you have a woman friend who is over fifty, very blonde, unattractive, and somewhat bizarre looking?"

"No. Is that who was driving my car?"

"Yes," Kevin said.

"How strange and puzzling," Antonella said. "But, I was out of town for a week, and no doubt I left the keys in the car."

"Who would know your schedule?"

"Lots of people. It's not a secret. I was picked up by a shuttle to go to the airport. I chatted with the other passengers on the way to the airport. I told various folks in town as I went through my usual routine. You know the kind of thing—'See you tomorrow,' 'Not for a week, I'm going out of town.' No way to know how many people knew I'd be gone."

"What's your involvement with Fr. Bari?"

"He's my brother."

Kevin eyes widened slightly, and he glanced away from Antonella. After a few seconds, he resumed his questions.

"How did you know about Malachy's work with the Justice Committee?" Kevin asked.

"My brother told me," Antonella answered.

"You have a different last name than your brother?"

"That will happen when you get married," Antonella said. "I kept the name after I divorced."

"Is your brother a fan of your work?" Kevin asked in a cold, flat tone.

Antonella put down her wineglass and stared at it. When she returned her gaze to Kevin, she was glaring. She answered in a forceful, almost harsh manner. "I am very close to my brother despite our many lifestyle differences. He is an intense, totally committed priest. Too intense. This false accusation is destroying him. He needs to get back to his life's work and soon. I intend to do whatever I can to help make that happen."

Kevin returned the intensity of her stare.

"The best way to make that happen is to cooperate and let us do our work without interference."

"How can I be sure you'll succeed?" Antonella asked.

"You can't be. But if the man who did those things to Pace is still alive, we will find him and stop him. And finding him is the best way, and maybe the only way, to prove your brother's innocence."

"Do you believe that the attack on Malachy's car is connected somehow to my brother's situation?"

"Yes. Somebody is either trying to warn Malachy off his work for the committee or trying to cause a diversion. Do you have a place in Chicago?"

Antonella's soft, flirtatious smile and voice returned. "What did you have in mind?"

"Security. I want you someplace more secure than this until we find out exactly who took your car and why."

"How gallant of you," Antonella said. "Are you going to guard my body?"

"I'm going to follow you back to Chicago. Then I will inspect your place to make sure that it's secure, and then I'm going to…"

Antonella interrupted.

"Oh, tell me, Captain, then what are you going to do?"

"…Go back to work."

"How disappointing. You certainly are focused. I suppose that's your military training and experience."

"I've been told before that obsessive focus and black-and-white thinking may not always be appropriate for civilian life, but I did find them useful in staying alive in combat."

"I see everything in gray scale," Antonella said. "I don't think I want to return to Chicago."

"Not everything," Kevin said, gesturing first toward the white walls and then to her all black outfit.

"Well, I do like stark contrasts in color sometimes."

"It's very effective," Kevin said, hoping flattery would soften her resistance.

"Thank you, but I still think I will stay here."

Kevin decided a direct appeal had the best chance of success. "You said your brother needs to return to his work soon. If you stay here, we will need to divert resources to ensure your security. That interferes with your objective. Why not cooperate?"

Antonella took a sip of her wine, closed her eyes, and leaned back into the couch. She stayed silently in that position for a minute and then stood up and started walking toward the bedroom.

"It'll take a few minutes to get my things together. Want to help?"

"No," Kevin said. "I'll wait outside. It's cooler there."

Twenty minutes later, Antonella came out of the house carrying two bags. Kevin took the bags, placed them behind the driver's side on the floor, and gave Antonella his keys. "I'll drive the Alfa."

"You expect me to drive all the way back to Chicago in that," Antonella said with mock indignation, pointing to the four-door truck. "More security precautions I suppose."

"Not really," Kevin said, moving closer to Antonella. "That's so at least one of my teenage fantasies will be fulfilled today."

Antonella smiled and said, "Someday when you're not working you'll have to tell me about your other fantasies."

"The usual stuff," Kevin responded. "Pirates; French maids; and earthy, sexy Italian women whispering in my ear."

"In Italian or English?"

"Italian…. See you in Chicago."

CHAPTER X

The Count drove into the Loop self-park and wound his way to the top floor. He found a parking spot away from the other cars. He took out and reviewed his notes on Francis Sabatino, a member of the Shrine's finance committee. Then he listened to the brief observations he recorded as he followed Sabatini from his home to a manufacturing business on Chicago's Southwest Side. He confirmed his earlier decision that Sabatini was the right choice to provide the donor report. He checked his watch and calculated he'd enter Sabatini's office around 11:30, allowing at least two hours before Sabatini returned.

"Can I help you?" A trim, pleasant-looking, fiftyish woman asked as she looked from a computer keyboard.

The Count, hoping that his carefully selected tailored jacket, slacks, and fitted open-necked shirt made him look younger, smiled and said, "I hope so. I just fired my brother-in-law as the accountant for my firm, and I need some accounting help as soon as possible. Your firm was recommended to me."

"You're at the right place," the woman said. "We do a lot of placements in finance and accounting for family businesses."

The Count looked around the three-room office that was so neat and organized it seemed unoccupied and said, "Terrific. What do we have to do to get started? I really need to find someone soon."

"Well, the first step is to meet with Mr. Sabatino. Did you call for an appointment?"

"No, I didn't. I came downtown for some other business and just took a chance and dropped by. I hope that was all right."

"Oh, of course," the woman said with a tinge of disapproval in her tone. "Mr. Sabatino is out of the office until this afternoon. Would it be possible for you to return then? I can reach him on his cell phone and confirm an appointment time for you right now."

"Terrific," the Count said enthusiastically. "I wish everybody in my business was so client friendly, especially my lazy brother-in-law."

The woman smiled sympathetically at the Count. "May I give Mr. Sabatino your name?"

The Count handed the woman a fake business card and said, "I'm sorry, I should have introduced myself."

The woman took the card and carefully read it. She stood, held out her hand, and said, "Nice to meet you, Mr. Kaminski. I'm Gertrude, Mr. Sabatino's administrative assistant."

"Good to meet you," the Count said, taking her hand. He looked directly into her eyes hoping to spark interest. Her look back was neutral. The Count thought the office reflected Gertrude and vice versa.

The Count looked around the office with obvious admiration. "How do you keep everything so organized? Our offices are a mess—paper and files stacked everywhere. I can never find what I'm looking for. What's your secret?"

Gertrude smiled warmly at the Count and said, "We're a small office, and Mr. Sabatino is a stickler for organization. But, I do have a rule that helps a lot—what I call the rule of ones."

"Please share the rule," the Count said. "I'm choking in paper."

"One thing at a time and touch each document only once."

"Only once? What do you mean?"

"Well, it takes a lot of discipline, but I try to never pick up a document without dealing with it finally. So, if I touch it, I never put it back down without doing something with it—respond, file, shred, or put it on Mr. Sabatino's desk for review and action."

"Amazing, I have a friend with a similar rule, but he doesn't have the discipline to follow it all the time. He's always making exceptions."

"Consistency is the key," Gertrude said.

"No wonder everything piles up at my business. We operate with the rule of tens. Touch everything ten times and put it back exactly where you got it."

"Well that would make for an inefficient office," Gertrude said.

"Maybe I should have you find me a rule-of-ones specialist, too."

"We could do that," Gertrude said seriously.

"If I was that organized at the office, I'd bring all the stuff from home and get it in order, too."

"It is easier to stay organized if everything is in one place," Gertrude said.

The Count nodded in agreement. He decided the finance committee documents were one-touched and in the office. He calculated the office needed to be empty for at least thirty minutes to secure and copy the documents.

"Shall I call Mr. Sabatino?" Gertrude asked. "His schedule shows that 2:00 to 3:00 is open."

"Two o'clock works great," the Count said.

Gertrude called, explained the situation, and confirmed the appointment.

"Mr. Sabatino said to tell you he is looking forward to meeting with you at 2:00, and he's confident our firm will be able to quickly fill your open position with a highly qualified candidate. And he hopes that you will seriously consider creating an administrative assistant position at your firm."

"You bet I will," the Count said.

"Is there anything else I can help you with?"

"Actually, there is. Is possible to get a copy of this made?"

The Count took a product data sheet for his nonexistent business from his briefcase and handed it to Gertrude.

"Since I'm going to be downtown for a few more hours, I think I'll try and get some business done. Copy shops are such a hassle."

"Of course. It'll take just a second. The copy machine is in the file room."

Gertrude took the paper and started back toward the file room. The Count followed her at a distance.

"What kind of machine do you use? We're thinking of getting a new one."

The Count carefully watched her operate the machine as she explained the multifunction copier and its many features that worked well for a small office. He noted all the file cabinets were clearly labeled. After the copy was made, she made a notation in a small notebook at the side of the machine.

"Here you are."

The Count took the original and the copy.

"Thanks, that helps a lot. I hate to bother you again, but could you direct me to the men's room?"

"It's no bother. It's at the end of the hallway on the left. You'll need a key. I'll get it for you."

Gertrude returned to her desk and took out a ring with two keys on it and handed it to the Count.

"The bathroom key is the one with the red dot on it."

The Count smiled warmly at Gertrude, knowing that with her sense of organization the second key was definitely to the office door.

"Thanks, I'll be right back."

The Count took the key ring and headed to the bathroom. In a stall, he took out his kit of stock keys from the briefcase and found a replacement for the second key. He switched keys and returned to the office. He hoped Gertrude's bathroom breaks were as methodical as everything else in the office. If not, she would be locked out of her office, and he would have to find a new target. He handed her the key ring.

"I promise you this is my last request."

"How can I help?" Gertrude asked as she put the key ring back in its assigned place in the drawer organizer.

"What's your favorite lunch place nearby?"

"I usually go to Corner Bakery. I like the soups, and it's literally right around the corner, so it doesn't take too much time."

"Sounds great. Perhaps I'll see you there?"

"Oh no, not today. On Wednesdays I go to the Cultural Center for the concerts at noon, well actually 12:15."

"I hope I haven't taken up too much time and made you late."

"Oh, that's perfectly all right. If I leave now, I'll make the concert just in time."

"Well that makes me feel better. I'll tell you what, you lock up and I'll go hit the button for the elevator. I noticed they're a little slow in this building. If we get lucky, it'll arrive just as you do."

"Thank you," Gertrude said, looking at the Count with a note of warmth.

The Count let the first elevator that stopped go by and held the door of the second one, telling the irritated occupants that his associate was late for a doctor's appointment and would be there in a second. Gertrude hurried down the hallway and into the elevator. They rode to the first floor in silence and quickly exited the building.

"Enjoy your concert," the Count said. "I'll see you at 2:00."

"Thank you."

The Count walked to the Corner Bakery without looking back, went into the revolving door, and back out onto the street. He thoroughly scanned the street for Gertrude, who was nowhere in sight.

He returned to the office and thirteen minutes later emerged with a copy of all the donors to the Shrine. With the key replaced, there was no evidence left behind of his presence except the higher number of copies recorded on the copy machine. And the ever-efficient Gertrude would undoubtedly blame that on Mr. Sabatino when the time came to reconcile the notebook with the machine total.

At 1:50 he called the office and Gertrude answered.

"This is Stan Kaminski calling. I'm embarrassed to tell you there is no need for the appointment, and so I need to cancel."

"Cancel? Mr. Sabatino is expecting you at 2:00. He set aside the time for you."

"I know. But my sister tracked me down and begged me to take her husband back and give him a second chance. She was crying. She was worried about her kids and losing the house. I just couldn't turn her down. It's a bad business decision, but you know how it is when it's family. But, please tell Mr. Sabatino, I will seriously consider the administrative assistant position and will definitely use your firm for any personnel needs in the future."

"Very well, I'll tell him," Gertrude said. "Thank you for calling."

"You're welcome. And thanks for sharing the rule of ones. I intend to impose it on my worthless brother-in-law. Maybe it'll help."

"My pleasure," Gertrude said without pleasure. "Good-bye."

☦

Malachy looked at the empty tabletop in the Shamrock's storeroom and then his watch and said, "In this instance punctuality must give way to productivity."

The Count responded, "Meaning coffee and something to munch on."

"How well you translate," Kevin said, standing up. "I'll ask Bridget to send Eduardo in with the required productivity enhancers."

When Eduardo left, the Count passed out copies of the Shrine donor list.

"The code next to the name tells you where the donor works—city, county, state, and in what department," the Count said. "A few are in private business. I ignored anybody under a grand. I highlighted all the names in government or construction with donations between $1,000 and $10,000. The really big donors all check out as legit—what you would expect, successful business and professional men from the suburbs who identify with their Italian heritage."

Malachy looked over the list of highlighted, mostly Italian names and did a mental count.

"The fabulous fifteen," Malachy said. "And right in the sweet spot of the bureaucracy—not the top guys, but the ones who actually do the work…and have the information. No wonder that Dino has the golden touch."

Kevin looked over the list and gave out a low whistle when he saw Antonella's name with $20,000 next to it.

"What is it?" Malachy asked.

"I'm hoping porn is really profitable," Kevin said.

Kevin pointed to Antonella's name and told the story of his encounter.

"Some men have all the luck," the Count said. "The only stuff I heard about was organizing and efficient document handling."

"Very important subjects," Malachy said. "But a little dry when compared to pirate fantasies. Did she express any remorse that her sports car was an accessory before the fact to the attack on my Mercury?"

"No, she didn't."

"Hard-hearted," Malachy said.

"She doesn't look hard-hearted," Kevin said, smiling at Malachy. "She appears warm, sensuous, and generous. But maybe a little impulsive."

"Really, some men have all the luck," the Count said.

"One problem solved, two more created," Malachy said. "The list tells us that our anonymous employer is not part of the scheme, thank God. But, if your new friend didn't actually make a $20,000 contribution, then she has some relationship with Dino. And Bari would know about his sister's contribution."

"She answered the questions I asked, but I didn't ask about Dino," Kevin said. "I could try and find out about any relationship with Dino."

"But she might also tell Dino you were asking if she didn't make the contribution," Malachy said.

There was a series of rapid, loud knocks on the door.

"Boss, boss, problem in the bar," Eduardo shouted. "Please come quick!"

"Kevin you better come with me," Malachy said.

As they entered the front room, they saw two young men standing at the bar. Malachy had never seen them before. Tattoos and ponytails said they weren't university students. They were wet from the powerful thunderstorm that was still raging outside. The thunder and the hailstones bouncing off the windows and roof made it difficult to hear. One of them was leaning over the bar yelling at Bridget.

"Mind your own business, you fucking bitch!"

"You made it my business by yelling into your cell phone," Bridget yelled back. "I know you probably can't read, so I'll read the sign to you: 'This barroom is for the enjoyment of conversation, singing, Irish music, food, and drink only. No TV, radio, cell phones, or computers allowed. No exceptions. Use the back room for all that modern stuff.'"

Malachy stepped in front of Kevin and shouted, "What's the problem here? And you, cut out that language."

The young man spun around and glared at Malachy.

"I'll use any fucking language I want."

"Answer my question," Malachy said loudly. "What's the problem?"

"I'll tell you the problem," Bridget said. "You see what's going on outside? This knight in shining armor was using his cell phone to yell and curse at his mother to go outside and get his precious car and park it in the garage, after she pulls hers out and parks it in the street. So I told the moron he wasn't getting served and to get off his lazy, dumb ass and move the car himself."

"Sounds reasonable to me," Malachy said. He looked at the young man and asked, "Why are you still here?"

"What's a fat old fuck like you going to do about it?"

Malachy stepped aside, and Kevin moved up next to him.

"I'm going to tell you to leave, so that you don't get hurt and end up in the hospital and then jail," Malachy said.

"Fuck you! Make me leave!"

Kevin bolted forward, grabbed a chair, turned its back into a battering ram, and smashed the man into the bar. The man slumped to the floor, gasping for air. Kevin wheeled and faced the man's friend, raising the chair. The other man raised his hands in a placating gesture.

"I'm leaving, I'm leaving!"

"Move, now!" Kevin shouted.

The man ran toward the front door.

"Before you throw the other one out, get an ID," Malachy said.

Kevin reached down with one hand and pulled a wallet from the downed man's back pocket. He flipped the wallet to Bridget. She pulled out a driver's license and threw the wallet back to Kevin. Kevin rolled the man over, placed the chair over his chest, and sat down. He then stuffed the wallet in the man's mouth.

"So far your bad manners have only resulted in bruises and maybe a cracked rib or two. I'm going to escort you to the front door. Don't say or do anything. Just leave. And remember, we know who you are. Stay far away from the Shamrock. Got it?"

The man started to mumble something. Kevin grabbed the man's ponytail with his fist and pulled it over his forehead. Kevin forced the man's head in an up-and-down motion with his fist and said slowly and loudly, "Got it?"

The man nodded yes. Kevin moved the chair, and the man used it as a prop to get to his feet. He put the wallet in his pocket and stumbled toward the front door. Kevin walked next to him, holding his arm. Kevin opened the front door.

"Remember, don't get any stupid ideas when you're feeling better. Next time, I won't be so nice."

The man went out the door without looking at Kevin or saying anything.

Kevin returned to the bar and asked Bridget if she was all right.

"I'm fine, but that moron really pissed me off. Can you imagine someone cursing at his mother and sending her into that storm? To move a car? Unbelievable. Malachy, what do you want me to do with his license?"

"Keep it someplace safe. And write down the information for me. I want to make a few calls in the morning."

"I'm not your secretary, you know. I'm the boss."

"I'm glad everything is back to normal," Malachy said. He turned to Kevin, pointed toward the storeroom, and said, "Let's go."

"Do you think I'm getting fat?" Malachy asked as they walked. "No comment," Kevin said. "Who are you going to call tomorrow?"

"I'll have somebody run him for priors. Just to be sure we know what we're dealing with. And I'll call in a favor and have a social worker check on the mother. Bridget's right—there's something wrong with a son who would send his mother out into a storm like this one."

"Any storm," Kevin said.

"Indeed. Really, tell me—do you think I need to lose some weight?"

Kevin smiled and asked, "What does the scale say?"

"The scale says it's broken. How often do you weigh yourself?"

"Every morning," Kevin answered.

"Maybe I should get a working scale?"

"Maybe."

They entered the storeroom.

"Do you think I look fat?" Malachy asked the Count.

"It's your untailored, unironed clothes. They make you look bigger. Anyway, why do you ask?"

"The guy causing the trouble said I was fat."

"Very rude, I'd say. How did you handle it?"

Kevin smiled at the Count and said, "Malachy let me handle it. I escorted him to the door."

"Well, I'm sure he has a better sense of good manners now," the Count said.

"I think I'm going to buy a new scale," Malachy said.

Bridget opened the door without knocking and yelled into the room.

"Brendan is in the bar—broke, shaking, crying, and pleading for a drink. Seems his wife finally had enough and threw him out. Thought you'd like to know."

Bridget slammed the door shut.

"Jesus fucking Christ!" Malachy cursed. "This storm is worse than a full moon. How are we supposed to get our work done?"

"I thought he was going to meetings," Kevin said.

"So did I," Malachy said. "It's been a couple of years, and I thought this time it was going to stick for sure."

"Hope springs eternal...," the Count said.

Malachy gave him a hard look.

"Do you mind? He's a boyhood friend, and he's got a problem. If the fucking savage he called father had raised you, you'd have a fucking problem too."

"Sorry," the Count said. "I didn't mean to..."

Malachy cut him off.

"Kevin, give me a hand with this."

Malachy left the storeroom without waiting for an answer. Kevin got up and followed him. At the door, he turned to the Count.

"You know how he is when it's a neighborhood guy. With Brendan, it's like the younger brother he never had. And he's very close to the wife and his kids, too. It'll blow over. We'll be back in a few minutes."

Kevin joined Malachy at the entrance to the front room.

"How do want to handle this?" Kevin asked.

Malachy looked at Brendan, who was pleading loudly with Bridget.

"He looks like shit, and he's all messed up. Bring him back to my booth. You sit next to him. I'll move the people in the other two booths."

Malachy went to the couple in the booth next to his. "Sorry, folks we are closing this section. Eduardo will move you to a table in the back. Have what you want to drink on the house. Thanks, I appreciate your cooperation."

Malachy didn't wait for an answer. He waved to Eduardo and delivered the message to the next booth. Kevin walked Brendan to the booth, half supporting and half dragging him. He folded him into the booth and sat next to him. Malachy slid into the booth, examining Brendan closely. Despite all the drunks Malachy had seen over the years, Brendan's haggard, haunted face shocked him.

"Oh God, M2, you've got to help me. I'm all fucked-up. I can't think— I can't stop shaking. Give me a drink. I swear I'll check into rehab, just give me a drink now. Just one, just one. Really, I'll check into rehab tonight."

"Brendan, how many days?"

"I…I can't remember, M2. Ten, twelve, I don't know."

"What did you do about work?"

"Work, I don't know. I didn't go there, I didn't show up."

"Did you call in sick?"

"M2, I can't remember. I told you I'm all fucked-up, just get me a drink. That'll settle me down, and I'll tell you what you want to know."

Malachy reached across the booth and grabbed Brendan's face in his hand. Brendan tried to raise his hands to break Malachy's grip. Kevin grabbed both his wrists and forced them to the table.

"Brendan, listen to me. I'll get you your drink. But first, you have to tell me about work. Concentrate. It's very important. Did you call in sick or did you just not show up?"

"I called in sick the first day. I didn't call in after that."

Malachy dropped his grip.

"Good. I'll handle it at work. You're going into rehab tonight just like you promised. I'm going to take you."

"I'll do it, M2. I really will, but get me that drink. You promised."

"In a minute," Malachy said. "I need to make a call first."

Malachy got up, carrying the wall phone with a long cord with him. He took a couple steps, turned his back, and made the call. He talked for a minute, turned around, and looked at Brendan who was trying to stop his shaking hands by holding his head.

"It's all right for Brendan to have something to drink on the way to rehab. I'm going to take him up the street to get the drink and then have Eduardo drive us to the hospital."

"Let me take him," Kevin said. "You go back and square things with the Count. Anyway, you'll need to stop by and talk with Shannon tonight."

"Oh God, M2, talk to her. She'll listen to you. Get her to give me another chance."

"I'll try, Brendan. You just worry about getting straight. I'll talk to Shannon."

"Thanks, M2. I'll beat it this time. I know I will. Just get Shannon to give me another chance."

"I'm sure everything will be okay," Malachy said, knowing he was not sure at all.

Malachy had heard it before. The hard-edged tearless, "I'm done. No more. I don't give a damn if he's sober or not. I'm through. Tell him it's over." And they always meant it. No amount of talk would move that mountain—not from Malachy, not from the drunk, not from the parish priest, not from the parents, not from the kids. He dreaded talking with Shannon because her tone would tell him in the first ten seconds if that divide had been crossed.

"Okay, Kevin you take him. Just enough to keep him calm on the ride to the hospital. Call me when he's checked in."

"M2, just give me one here, now. Please, I really need it."

"No, Brendan. Kevin will take you up the street. You know the rules, no team switches. Drys can't drink alcohol in the Shamrock ever. No exceptions."

"Okay, M2. I understand. Can we leave now?" Brendan, holding the front of his jacket with both hands to stop the shaking, started to push against Kevin.

"Sure, Brendan. Kevin will take you now. Good luck. I'll come to visit when it's allowed."

"Thanks."

They got up from the booth. Malachy motioned Eduardo over and told him to bring Kevin's truck to the front door. Kevin took Brendan by the arm and started to walk him toward the door. Brendan turned around and started back toward Malachy. Kevin restrained him until Malachy nodded it was okay.

"I want you to know I really tried this time, really tried," Brendan said, his eyes filling with tears. "I didn't want to let you down. Don't give up on me. I really tried."

"I know you did, Brendan."

"I didn't tell you everything about work. I talked with my boss when I was totally gone. I totally screwed up…screamed and cursed at him. He fired me."

Malachy put his hands on Brendan's shoulders.

"Brendan, you're a friend, that's never going to change. Don't worry about the job, I'll square it with the boss. A job will be waiting for you when you're ready to leave rehab. Go with Kevin now. Everything is going to be all right."

Kevin came back and took Brendan's arm and guided him out the front door of the Shamrock. Malachy headed back to storeroom. Just as he reached the entrance, Bridget yelled at him.

"You're wanted on the phone. It's Shannon."

"How did she sound?"

"Couldn't tell."

Malachy walked back slowly to the house phone at the bar, trying to figure out what he should say. He picked up the phone like it was an enemy hand grenade.

"This is Malachy."

"Malachy, it's Shannon." Malachy heard the panic in the way she said her name. "I lost it tonight and threw Brendan out of the house right at the peak of the storm. I'm worried sick about him. I'm hoping he made to the Shamrock. Have you seen him?"

Malachy felt a surge of energy and enthusiasm.

"Yes, he made it here. He was messed up, but he'll be okay. He's on the way to rehab as we speak. Kevin is taking him."

"Thank God. Do you think he'll go through with it? He told me he'd go two or three times last week and then always backed out. He always needed one or two to stop shaking and that would get him started all over again. I wish you were taking him."

"Kevin will make sure Brendan checks into rehab. Nothing Brendan says or does will make any difference. He's going into rehab tonight. You can count on that."

"Oh, Malachy, you have no idea how relieved I am. I kept telling him to go see you. You've been such a good friend. But he wouldn't go because of the job. He was afraid you'd be mad at him after all you did to get him that job after the last time."

"He told me something about talking to the boss."

"It was really ugly," Shannon said. "Brendan was vicious and nasty. He called him every foul name in the book."

"I'll square it with his boss," Malachy said. "I know him."

"I don't think you can," Shannon said. "I called him to apologize and explain Brendan was not himself, that he was sick. He told me not to waste my breath. He had the whole thing on tape. Brendan was finished at the water department and at any city job if he had anything to say about it. And Malachy, he specifically mentioned you."

"Shannon, tell me exactly what he said."

"He said, 'And tell your friend Malachy not to bother. The shit he pulled last time won't work again.' I don't know what we're going to do. We can't get by on what I make. We still have Colleen in school."

"Shannon, his boss is just upset. Anybody would be. He'll calm down eventually. Don't worry about it. I'll take care of it. You just help Brendan get back on track. A job will be there when he's ready. Okay?"

"Okay," Shannon said without conviction. "Malachy, you've already done more than anybody could ask for or expect. But, I just don't see how Brendan can possibly keep his job. It's just not realistic. Please don't feel bad. We'll make it somehow."

Malachy's tone changed, almost as if he was giving an order.

"Shannon, Brendan needs to start work right after he leaves rehab. I'm telling you a job will be waiting for him. I'll make sure that he has a job, tape or no tape. Be sure you tell him that—tell him M2 said a job is waiting for him. Be sure and use my nickname. Do you understand?"

"I guess so. I'll tell him just like you said."

"Good. I'll call later as soon as I hear from Kevin."

"Oh, God, Malachy, I don't know how to thank you. You're a saint."

"How come I can't convince any of my girlfriends of that?"

Shannon laughed a little.

"Talk to you later, Shannon."

When he reached the storeroom, Malachy sat down and looked directly into the Count's eyes. "Are we square?"

"Yes, of course. My fault."

"No fault involved," Malachy said.

"How is Brendan?"

"On his way to rehab via the Devon Lounge up the street. But there is a problem I need your help with."

Malachy explained about Brendan and his boss at the water department.

"The guy is beyond pissed, and I don't blame him. The problem is the tape. I can get the right people to call him and apply pressure, but all he has to do is play that tape and every one of them will back off. And all I would've accomplished is to run down my fat account at the Favor Bank. We need to change the equation—can we get to the tape?"

"There's no way to get the tape if he keeps it in his office. After 9/11, the security is just too tight."

"According to Brendan, his boss has an office girlfriend," Malachy said.

"As long as they're not doing it in a water tank, I'll get what we need," the Count said. "But, it will take me away from our other project. No way to know for how many days."

"Let's hope storms make him horny."

CHAPTER XI

Malachy awoke from his dream with a feeling of panic. In the dream, he was going to a Cubs game with a young boy. His father warned him to keep the boy right at his side at all times. Suddenly as they entered Wrigley Field, the boy vanished and Malachy started to desperately search for him. But the entire crowd was dressed in white with white face masks. There were no children anywhere. Malachy tried to push his way through the crowd, but white arms kept grabbing him and pulling him down. He struggled against the arms, but felt himself being pulled down, powerless.

The panic quickly gave way to puzzlement. It was a point of pride for Malachy and his father as Sox fans that they had never stepped foot in Wrigley Field, not even when the Bears played there. So what was Wrigley Field doing in his dream? He remembered his rule about team switches and his conversation with Brendan. That triggered the memory of Brendan seeking safety with the Maddens as a boy of nine.

There was a knock at the kitchen door. Malachy, age seventeen, opened it and a crying, clearly frightened Brendan dashed into the kitchen.

"Please, M2 let me stay here. My dad is after me. He was beating me with a strap. I didn't do anything…I swear I didn't do anything, but he kept hitting me. I ran away. Please let me stay here. He'll stop looking for me. I'll go home later when he falls asleep from the drinking. Please let me stay, M2."

"Sure, sure, Brendan, you can stay. Take it easy. It'll be all right. You can have supper with us and then go home later. I know it'll be okay with my mom and dad."

Malachy's father came into the kitchen. "Well, hello, Brendan, how are you?"

Brendan didn't answer. He looked down and started to cry. Malachy explained to his father what was going on. Malachy watched his father's face flush a bright red. He walked over to Brendan, talking in a soft, almost lilting voice. "Beating you, was he? Well, of course, you can stay here just as long as you like. Mrs. Madden will be fixing a fine supper just as soon as she is home from the O'Gradys."

Malachy's father took Brendan's hands and stretched his arms out in front of him and examined Brendan's welts.

In the same soft, lilting voice Malachy's father asked, "And I suppose there are more of these on you?"

Brendan nodded yes.

"Well, now Mrs. Madden will have something to make those feel better. And Brendan, you just let Mrs. Madden treat those. No need for any embarrassment. She is used to boys in all sizes."

"Yes, sir," Brendan said.

Malachy's father gently put his hand under Brendan's chin and raised his face up.

"You are welcome in this home anytime. Anytime, for any reason. Malachy has gone and become all grown up and a big one he is—look at him."

Brendan looked up at Malachy and half smiled.

Malachy's father continued, "We miss having a fine young lad like you around the place. Just think of the Maddens as a home away from home, all right?"

Brendan nodded yes.

"Now, I'm going to go out and find your father and have a little talk with him. So, I'll see you later. Malachy here will make sure nobody bothers you. You just let Mrs. Madden take care of you. Okay, Brendan?"

"Yes, sir."

"Malachy, a word with you in the other room."

Malachy's father went over and locked the kitchen door that was never *locked until bedtime. He went to the front door and locked it. Malachy followed him into the front room.*

"I'm going to make a phone call, and then I'll be going to find that vicious bastard. Explain everything to your mother and tell her to go ahead with supper. I'll eat later. Lock the door after I go. No calls to Brendan's home until I return. And Malachy, if Brendan's father shows up here before I can find him, don't open the door. If he tries to break in, do whatever you have to do to protect Brendan. And I mean whatever it takes. That boy will not be touched again in anger this night, not under my roof. Can you handle that?"

"I can," Malachy said.

Malachy made a mental note to call and check on Brendan in rehab. He decided to spend the rest of the day at the Shamrock reviewing his account at the Favor Bank and making preliminary calls to locate potential jobs for Brendan. And then the dinner with Cullen the rock-talker.

†

At 5:30 Malachy ordered a large baked potato loaded with butter and sour cream and some bread soaked in olive oil from the Shamrock's kitchen. Eduardo brought the food to the back booth and served it with a large black coffee. Malachy told him to get the car. Bridget came over and looked at the platter.

"I see you're having your pre-drinking fortification—heavy date with a boozer?"

"Spiritual quest."

Bridget took another look at the platter and checked her watch.

"Spirits fest is more like it. Afraid the Jameson will interfere with your performance?"

"Something like that," Malachy said.

"Wouldn't it be simpler just to drink less?" Bridget asked.

"That might interfere in my getting what I'm after," Malachy said.

"Try being romantic," Bridget said. "It's easier on the liver."

When Malachy got out of the car in front of the restaurant, he said,

"Eduardo, pick me up at 9:00. If I'm not out front, come find me inside."

Malachy entered the restaurant and surveyed the bar and table area. He picked out a four top that was not too close to the other tables. It had a reservation sign on it. An obviously overworked, harassed woman approached him.

"Can I help you, sir? Do you have a reservation?"

Malachy beamed a big smile at her and said, "You sure can. I have a reservation for two at 6:30. It's for a special occasion, and I'd like to sit at this table. And I'm hoping you can make that happen." Malachy took a twenty-dollar bill and handed it to her. "You have the toughest job in the world. Everybody always wanting something special. I hope I'm not causing too much trouble for you."

The woman gave him a weary nod and a smile. "Some days are better than others. Today is not one of the good ones. But this table is yours at 6:30 and thank you. Is it a birthday or something?"

"No, nothing like that," Malachy said. "Just an old friend. We would just like to have a drink or two and a good dinner in a nice atmosphere."

"That's something we can do. Thanks again."

Malachy entered into the bar and went to the service area. He motioned to the bartender.

"Can I help you?" the bartender asked.

Malachy took out another twenty-dollar bill and held it in his hand.

"A friend of mine is joining me for a couple of drinks here before we go into dinner. He likes his drinks very heavy with little ice and I like mine light with lots of ice. I'll be drinking Jameson plain. We will be sitting at that table." Malachy turned around and pointed. "Sometimes the cocktail waitress doesn't understand. I was hoping you might be able to help."

Malachy held out the twenty. The bartender took the money.

"No problem. What's your friend drinking?"

Malachy smiled and said, "He jumps around, but you'll know the order because it will be paired with Jameson."

At 6:15 a florid-faced man in his fifties entered the bar and started to look around. He was balding with thin, wispy gray hair. He was out of shape with a thin upper body and a paunch. His shirt, jacket, and slacks were a little outdated and did not quite go together. Malachy had seen the type hundreds of times over the years in the Shamrock, including many priests. As the man's eyes adjusted to the dark bar, he spotted Malachy. Malachy stood up and put out his hand to shake. "Father, Malachy Madden. Thanks for joining me."

They shook hands, and Fr. Cullen looked down at the empty table. "Well, Malachy, nice to meet you. And please call me Pat."

Malachy motioned to the waitress and said, "I was just getting ready to order. What will you have, Pat?"

"Johnny Walker Red Label on the rocks. A little water on the side. Thanks."

Malachy gave the waitress the order, and they settled into their seats. "How did you know it was me?" Cullen asked.

Malachy noted the slight slur to the "was me." He hoped that Cullen hadn't started laying down a base too early in the day. It was too late to change the plan with the bartender. Anyway, better too much truth serum than too little.

"You were the only guy who came through the door that I was willing to go to confession to," Malachy said, smiling his best Irish smile.

Cullen smiled back and said, "Not very much call for that anymore."

"Anyway, so how's the golf game going this year, Pat? Better than mine, I hope. It's too damn cold. I need warm weather."

"No damn good at all. Don't have enough time to practice."

The waitress returned with the drinks. Malachy calculated the Walker was twice as strong as the Jameson. Malachy held up his drink and clinked glasses with Cullen.

"To a successful benefit," Malachy said.

They made small talk about golf and played "who do you know" for fifteen minutes. Malachy made sure he finished his drink before Cullen.

"How about another one before we go into dinner?" Malachy asked.

"Sure, Malachy. That's a good idea."

When the waitress returned with the drinks, Pat drained his old drink in a couple of swallows and then took a sip of his fresh drink.

"Well, Pat, let's get down to business. I really appreciate your making time to hear about the benefit."

"No problem, no problem."

Malachy could hear the Red Label starting to work. He paused and took another sip of his Jameson. "Really the whole thing is pretty simple. You are listed as an advisor to the benefit committee, and on that day you play golf and socialize with the ticket buyers. As I said, it helps a lot to have a popular priest involved. Makes everybody more comfortable, including the wives who are suspicious of these kinds of male outings. And it's all for a good cause."

"On the phone, you said something about a stipend."

"Oh, yes the stipend. It's not very much, really. I hope you find it acceptable. The Shamrock would give you $500. It's hard enough to keep the books straight for the benefit, so the $500 would be in cash, if that's all right."

Malachy looked at Cullen for his reaction. There was a smile on his face.

"That would be no problem, no problem at all," Cullen said.

"Good," said Malachy. "I'll give you a call in a few weeks when I have things more organized, and we can work out a date that works for everybody. Let's eat I'm starving."

They moved into the dining room to the table Malachy reserved. At the table, Malachy ordered another round of drinks. After they gave the waitress their dinner order, Malachy started down the road to Fr. Bari.

"Have you always been on the North Side? We must have met sometime before tonight."

Cullen rattled off three parishes including Pius XII.

"Pius XII? Haven't they been in the news? Some kind of scandal or something."

"Yeah, the famous Fr. Bari, the living Italian saint," Cullen said sarcastically. "Trust me, he's no saint. I could tell you things. I was there. He's no saint."

Malachy tried to look surprised and decided to feed the fire of Cullen's resentment.

"I haven't been paying that much attention, but that name, Bari, sounds very familiar. I remember now…some of my Italian golf buddies told me he was the real deal—a dynamic speaker, handsome, charismatic. It's hard to believe he's involved in the abuse scandal."

"Believe it," Cullen said. "He's a phony."

"Really? You saw him with the kid who's complaining?"

Cullen seemed confused. He rubbed his face a couple of times. Malachy worried he was not going to track the conversation.

"Nah, not with a kid. He had a girlfriend. Saw them in his car one time in a clench. St. Bari was involved with one of his own kind. I kept my mouth shut, not my business. Never said a word to the pastor, not my business."

"One of his own kind?"

"A real Italian type and a lot younger."

The heavy stress on the first syllable of Italian, an elongated 'eye', made it clear Italians were not Cullen's favorite priests or parishioners. The alcohol was having its effect, and Malachy reminded himself that he was the one feeding it to Cullen. Malachy decided to risk direct questions.

"You never saw him with a kid? The papers are full of the stuff about priests with kids."

"Nah, I told you. Dago broad. He was screwing a dago broad."

Malachy hoped Cullen was too drunk to notice his face flush and jaw tighten when he said dago.

"Maybe they got the wrong guy. Maybe it was one of the other priests with the kid? Ever see any of the other priests with a kid?"

Cullen tried to focus on Malachy. He rubbed his face some more.

"Why so interested?" Cullen said, now fully slurring his words.

"I don't know," Malachy said. "It just seems unfair to priests like you who are trying to do a good job."

"Unfair." Cullen repeated unfair twice and said, "The whole damn life is unfair. Shouldn't be telling you this. It's all unfair."

"It's a hard life," Malachy said. "But there's no excuse for messing with kids."

"You're right, the guys who mess with kids are sickos, real sickos."

Malachy figured Cullen was still a little alcohol short of the self-pity-tears stage or the flaring anger flashpoint. He continued to press.

"It must be real difficult to work with a sicko, knowing what they're doing to the kids, innocent kids," Malachy said.

Cullen looked confused and said, "Never worked with any. Never saw anything like that. Some guys had their problems, but never saw anything like that." Cullen's voice trailed off, and he looked down into his drink and then took a swallow. Malachy stayed quiet.

"Saw a kid crying once coming out of the bathroom in the church. He was trying to fix his pants. Asked him if anything was wrong, but he ran away. Didn't recognize him. Didn't think much about it, figured he soiled himself or something like that. Only remembered it when all that stuff came out in the paper about that kid being abused in that bathroom."

Malachy asked softly, "Did you see anybody in the area before or after you ran into the boy?"

"It was strange. I did see somebody—a woman. She hid her face from me and ran away when I approached her. Haven't thought about that in years."

"A woman?"

"Yeah, a woman. Seemed like I knew who she was, but never did figure it out."

"Could it have been his mother?"

"Don't know. Told you I didn't recognize the kid."

"Why were you outside the bathroom?" Malachy asked, switching to an aggressive tone.

Cullen's face flushed and he put down his drink. Malachy knew he had reached the anger flashpoint. "What the hell are you saying? Just what the hell are you saying about me?"

Cullen's voice was loud and angry. The diners in the surrounding tables stopped talking and started to stare.

"Sorry," Malachy said. "It was a stupid attempt at a joke. Really sorry. Here comes our dinner. Let's have a little wine and enjoy our steaks."

The food seemed to placate Cullen. They ate in silence for a while. Malachy poured some wine.

"Didn't mean to be offensive," Malachy said. "It's my fault. Wrong subject to make jokes about. Let's talk golf."

Malachy told his best golf jokes and eventually Cullen started laughing and joined in the joke telling. Malachy did not ask any more questions about Pius XII parish. When Cullen staggered to the men's room, Malachy had the table cleared. Malachy called Eduardo at the Shamrock and told him to pick him up early.

Cullen looked at the empty table upon his return with a confused look on his face. "I guess we're all done."

"I think we better call it a night," Malachy said. "They make very strong drinks here. How did you get here?"

"Taxi."

"I'm being picked up by someone from the Shamrock. We'll give you a ride to the rectory."

They dropped off Cullen at the rectory and waited while he searched his pockets over and over for his keys. Malachy watched Cullen weave and stagger as he thrust both hands into his jacket pockets so forcefully he almost toppled over. He wondered if Cullen ever prayed to St. Anthony when he couldn't locate his keys. Cullen found the keys and fumbled with them and then made several attempts to unlock the door. Finally, someone inside opened the door.

"Eduardo, drive me home. You can take the Merc home tonight and drive it to the Shamrock tomorrow. It's late and that'll save you some time in getting home to your family. Be sure to tell Bridget the extra hours you worked. You're on OT."

"Okay, Mr. Malachy."

"Eduardo, we've had this conversation before. I don't call you Mr. Eduardo, so don't call me Mr. Malachy, just Malachy. Got it?"

"Sí, okay, Mr. Malachy."

Malachy called Kevin. "We need to put off the meeting until the morning. John Jameson is forcing me to stop work early. Do me a favor and let the Count know. And while you're at it give him your measurements—like you were renting a tux. I'll explain in the morning. And for the love of God, tell him not to call me before 7:00."

CHAPTER XII

The chirping of his cell phone woke Malachy from a dream. He let the call go to voice mail because he wanted to remember the dream. He took a drink of water, propped up another pillow behind his head, closed his eyes, and worked on bringing back the dream.

He was in a church pew with a pretty Italian woman, but the pew was outside. He went to put his arms around the woman but stopped when he realized she was armless. Suddenly the pew started to move and he looked down and saw that it had wheels attached. Other pews on wheels appeared and started to bump his pew like they were in a bumper car rink.

Some of the other pews were driven by wild-looking priests and nuns and others by menacing characters from the *Godfather* movie series. He looked frantically for the steering mechanism for his pew but there was none. The other pews kept bumping his with more and more force. The pretty girl became more and more frightened and then started to scream. The girl's screaming merged into the sound of the cell phone.

Malachy thought about Fr. Cullen's claim he saw Bari and a younger Italian woman in a clinch. His employer, the nameless voice on the cell phone, sounded like a very grateful father. Would curing a drug addiction earn that gratitude no matter what the circumstances? Malachy didn't think so.

He knew how he felt about his daughter Molly's boyfriends. Either

Cullen misinterpreted the clinch or the father didn't know the sexual nature of the relationship. Another factor in an increasingly complex equation. No wonder consultants got paid so well. They were supposed to locate the steering wheels on out-of-control, moving pews.

The phone rang again and Malachy reached over and picked it up.

"I suppose it is exactly 7:00 A.M.," Malachy said as he looked at his alarm clock showing 7:09.

"It was when I called the first time. You should consider following Kevin's regimen," the Count said cheerfully. "He is in remarkably good shape according to his measurements."

"He is a much younger man."

"I thought you two joined the Marines at the same time."

"He lied about his age to get in. Call me back in thirty minutes. I have to piss and make coffee."

"Don't confuse the two operations."

Malachy settled back into his pillows, remembering the first time he met Kevin. They were new recruits in a line. Kevin was in front of him, and it was his turn to give information to Sergeant O'Rourke.

"Religion?" the sergeant barked.

Kevin looked confused and didn't say anything.

"Hey fuckhead are you fucking deaf? Religion?"

Malachy saw the back of Kevin's neck flush red, and Kevin started to stammer.

"Sir, I..."

The sergeant started to get angry.

"Are you fucking with me? Tell me your fucking religion?"

"Sir, none."

"Look fuckface, you're either a motherfucking Catholic, a motherfucking Protestant, or a motherfucking Jew. That's all the fucking religions I have. Pick one. Which is it?"

"Sir, I...I..."

The sergeant stood up and roared, "Now, I know you're fucking with me. I'm going to grind..."

Malachy intervened.

"Sir, I know the private's religion, sir."

"Who the fuck asked you?" the sergeant yelled.

"Sir, no one, sir. But a Marine should always volunteer the information the sergeant is asking for, sir."

The sergeant looked at Malachy intently.

"Do you know this stupid fuckhead?"

"Sir, no, sir."

"Then, how do you know his fucking religion?"

"Sir, by looking at the stupid fuckhead, sir."

"I'm looking at the stupid fuckhead, and I don't see his fucking religion stamped on his fucking forehead. Is it stamped on the back of his fucking head?"

"Sir, no, sir. The stupid fuckhead has the map of Ireland stamped on his face, sir. Sir, he's an Irish Catholic like me, sir."

The Sergeant half smiled and then roared at Malachy, "The two of you get the fuck out of here. And don't try that Irish bullshit with me again or I'll make your face look like the map of fucking hell."

"Sir, yes, sir," Malachy and Kevin said in unison.

The Count's admonition made Malachy wash his hands extra carefully in the bathroom. He was drinking his first cup of coffee and scanning yesterday's paper when the phone rang. The kitchen clock showed 7:33. Malachy made a mental note to set all the clocks ahead the same. Malachy answered and explained about the measurements.

"I can get that accomplished by 10:30," the Count said. "Let's say another three hours for the recon work and drive time to the Shamrock. I propose a joint chiefs meeting in the storeroom at 2:00 which allows time for unforeseen contingencies."

"Proposal accepted. Let me ask you a question. Do you find time-talk erotic?"

"No. I find it semiotic. I'll send a signal if there are any changes."

When Malachy opened the door to the Shamrock, Bridget started yelling at him. "You took Eduardo away for too many hours last night. I needed him here. Don't do that again."

"I needed him more than you did," Malachy said.

"What the hell am I supposed to do for help? You know being the boss of this place is a shit job. If you don't stop interfering, I quit."

"Kevin will be here for the lunch hour and will be available for a couple of hours," Malachy said.

Bridget glowered at him.

"And I promise if I take Eduardo, I'll make sure some of the other kitchen workers stay to help. How did we do last night?"

"We had a good night. Probably because you weren't here to screw it up. You look like shit. You better eat something. Do you want some breakfast?"

"We don't serve breakfast, only lunch," Malachy answered.

"I'm the boss, remember. And I say today we serve breakfast."

Malachy ordered breakfast and moved to his office-booth. He kept going over the information he learned from Cullen. Fr. Pat Cullen was not a pedophile. If the celibate life got to be too much for him, Malachy guessed he got drunk and looked for a hooker. But what about that woman that he saw following Pace?

"Bridget, I want to ask your opinion on something."

"Okay, here it is. Abe is right, close the Shamrock."

"Your vote is duly noted and recorded. Do you remember Mrs. O'Malley from the old neighborhood?"

"Of course. Rumor had it she bathed in holy water. And when that ball-less, sad-sack husband of hers was allaying his concupiscence once or twice a year, she said the sorrowful mysteries of the rosary. Not my kind. What about her?"

"If a priest was abusing one of her kids and she found out, what would she do about it?"

"Are you serious?"

"Yes."

"Well, let's start with the negatives, the things she wouldn't do. She wouldn't crack the priest's head open with a baseball bat, as any mother worthy of the name should do. She definitely wouldn't call the cops. And she wouldn't confront the priest. She would either bring it into the confessional or go up the ladder. If it was a parish priest, she would go to the pastor with her spiritual problem, the cross she was carrying."

"Grist for the mill," Malachy said. "Thanks."

"One more thing. She would blame the kid, big time. Either openly or with the silent treatment. Any other questions?"

Malachy shook his head no. The odds were that woman was Pace's mother. And whoever she was, odds were she saw who came out of that bathroom before her son. That woman knew what the pedophile looked like. The plan was clear—find her and get her to talk.

Eduardo approached the booth with the Merc's keys in his hand. He looked nervously at Bridget and said to Malachy, "I parked the car where you told me."

"It's okay, Eduardo. Kevin will be here to help out with the lunch hour. Anyway, she's not mad at you. She's pissed off at me as usual."

Malachy joined Kevin and the Count in the storeroom. He briefed them on the previous night with Cullen. The Count reported on his recon work.

"I have located Pace's mother. She lives by herself in a small bungalow in the Pius XII parish a mile and tenth from the church. She works a few miles away in a consignment resale store, mostly clothes for women and children. I went shopping in the store. She reminds me of some of the older women you see on Catholic cable—pleasant, nondescript, slightly depressed, and totally committed to some fringe devotional practice."

"What about the rest of the family?" Malachy asked

"Split right down the middle. Pace has four siblings, two brothers and two sisters. One brother and a sister are not talking to Anthony, and the other two are not talking to the mother. This is according to one very talkative neighbor. And obviously from what I have already reported, Mrs. Pace has no romantic life and, worse, no sex life." The Count delivered the last sentence like a doctor telling a patient there was no hope—some empathy and a great deal of relief that it did not apply to him.

"Will she buy our story?" Malachy asked.

"I think so. She's not too inquisitive. It's clearly worth attempting, and I don't see any downside. But I do think we should disable her phone as a precaution."

Malachy got up and removed the plastic bag from the clothes hanger behind the Count.

"What do think, Fr. Kevin?"

Kevin looked at the perfectly pressed priest's garb and clerical collar.

"Let's hope she doesn't want to go to confession," Kevin said.

"We're after a kind of confession—who did she see come out of that bathroom before her son, what did he look like, and who did she tell about it."

"The resale shop closes at 6:00," the Count said. "I propose the following plan. Malachy and I head to her neighborhood in my van and fix her phone and put her under surveillance from 5:00 on. As soon as we are certain she is headed home after work, Kevin times his arrival to almost coincide with hers. We keep the house under surveillance while Father Kevin charms the confession out of her."

"Accepted," Malachy and Kevin said simultaneously.

"What's my name?" Kevin asked.

"Monsignor Sean O'Grady," Malachy said, handing him some business cards. Kevin looked at one of the cards with his new name on it and official looking seal.

"The same as the cardinal?" Kevin asked

"Nepotism," Malachy said with a big smile. "Not in the literal sense. You are the cardinal's cousin on a special assignment from the cardinal himself. If we're right that Bari is innocent, then Mrs. Pace knows that and she has stayed silent. Why? We don't know, but it is a good bet that the red hat will trump whatever the reason is for the silence. If not, we have a problem."

"It's too bad she is not Polish," Kevin said, looking at the Count.

As they left the storeroom laughing, they encountered Bridget.

"When you're forced to close the Shamrock, you can always reopen as a comedy club," Bridget said.

"Well, at least we'd leave the customers in tears from laughing," Malachy said. "In the meantime, we are still an Irish bar—you know, the kind with a warm welcome for everyone, especially paying customers."

"You told me I didn't have to take shit from anyone," Bridget said loudly. "Including paying customers."

"Too true, too true," Malachy said over his shoulder as he followed Kevin and the Count out the back entrance of the Shamrock.

†

Kevin answered his cell phone.

"Mrs. CC went grocery shopping. She's now four blocks away. She parks in front of the house. Where are you?"

"Mrs. CC?"

"Code name—Mrs. Catholic Cable," the Count said.

"I think you've been watching too much Mother Angelica. Anyway, I'm parked a few houses down from her place. Just got here."

"How's the car?"

Kevin looked at the almost-new, dark-blue Buick with muted interior colors. It was rented, but the Count switched the plates "just in case."

"Respectable and boring, just the transportation ticket for an important chancery official like myself."

"I've found that false identities are the most believable when you fulfill the target's expectations," the Count said. "What your identity actually drives doesn't matter—that Buick is exactly what Mrs. CC thinks you drive."

"Here she is," Kevin said. "Mic is on, start taping."

Kevin timed his approach just as Mrs. Pace took the single bag of groceries from the backseat. "Excuse me, are you Mrs. Pace?" he asked.

Mrs. Pace looked at Kevin nervously and then quickly peered into the grocery bag as if she was looking for a particular item. "Yes, I am," she said without looking up.

"I'm Monsignor Sean O'Grady from the chancery office. I'm here on business from the cardinal. Could I talk with you in private? It is quite important."

"The cardinal?"

"Yes. I apologize for not calling ahead to see if this is a convenient time. Here, let me take that for you."

Kevin reached for the grocery bag as he handed Mrs. Pace a business card. She hesitated for a second and then gave him the bag and took the card. Kevin immediately started to walk to the front door of the house. She followed him, trying to read the card at the same time. At the front door, he held open the storm door as a silent invitation for her to unlock the front door.

"You're an O'Grady, too?"

"Yes. I'm the cardinal's cousin. He asked me to speak with you on his behalf."

"I don't understand what this is all about."

"Could we talk inside?" Kevin said with a tone of authority. "This is a private matter."

"Excuse me. Of course, please come in."

She unlocked the door. Kevin followed her inside and shut the front door.

He was taken aback by the interior. He quickly counted more than a dozen shrines and altars with pictures and statues, some to saints whose names he had never heard before. He knew some comment would be expected. With the grocery bag in the crook of his arm, he looked at each one.

"This is a very impressive collection. I must admit a few of these saints I am not as familiar with as I should be. The saints are our advocates in heaven. Our fallen heroes, so to speak. It is good they are so honored in your home."

"Thank you. I try to spend a few minutes a day with each one."

"That's to be admired." Kevin moved into the kitchen and put the bag down on the table. "Could I have a glass of water?"

Mrs. Pace quickly gave him a glass of ice water. Kevin settled in at the kitchen table as she put the groceries away.

"As I said, I'm here at the cardinal's request. A report has surfaced at the chancery office concerning you."

"Concerning me? I don't understand."

"Please sit down. This concerns your son and his alleged abuse by Fr. Bari. We're in possession of a report that states you saw your son and his abuser come out of the bathroom in the basement of the Pius XII church. Is that true?"

Mrs. Pace crossed herself and murmured some prayers.

Kevin adopted a stronger tone and said, "It is very important to the Church that we know the truth, the whole truth. Is that report true?"

"I prayed and prayed that this day would never come. I don't know what to do. I can't talk about it."

"I understand," Kevin said softly. "It is a very difficult subject, but we must know the truth."

"I...I can't talk about it." She moved quickly across the kitchen to a pantry area with two soup cans shaking in her trembling hands. As she returned to the kitchen, Kevin stood up and played his trump card.

"The cardinal is aware that you've been sworn to secrecy." Kevin raised his hand high in the air in an exaggerated start to the sign of the cross and said, "Cardinal O'Grady by the power vested in him as your bishop and spiritual leader hereby releases you from all prior oaths and promises of secrecy and commands you to tell the whole truth about this incident."

Kevin finished the sign of the cross. "Now, tell me what happened that day."

Mrs. Pace slumped into the kitchen chair and held her hands together to stop the trembling. She looked down at her hands for a while, staying silent.

"The pastor swore me to secrecy. He said it would be a very grave sin for me to ever talk about it to anybody, so I never did. Not to anybody. I wish the pastor were here to talk to. It's all so confusing."

Kevin sat down and replayed his trump card. "The cardinal has made your duty to the Church very clear. Nothing the pastor told you can bind the cardinal. The cardinal is your spiritual leader. You owe him obedience. We know you saw your son that day. The answer to your prayers is to tell the truth. What happened that day?"

Mrs. Pace put her face in her hands and sobbed quietly. Kevin patted her arm. "You'll feel better once you tell the truth," Kevin said gently.

Mrs. Pace raised her head and fixed her eyes on a picture of Pope Pius XII and started to speak in a flat, emotionless tone as if she was reading a report scrolling across the picture.

"He had been acting so strangely. Quiet and secretive. Sometimes I heard him crying. At first, I thought it was about his father's accident. But sometimes he disobeyed me about coming right home after school. So that day, I decided to follow him after school. He never saw me.

"I followed him to the church and down into the bathroom. He closed the door. I hid myself so that he wouldn't see me when he came out. Then a priest knocked on the door, and the door opened and he went inside. I listened at the door. I could tell they were doing disgusting things. I ran back to my hiding place, crying. First, the priest came out and then Anthony. I stayed in my hiding place crying and praying.

"After a few minutes, I started to leave and I saw Fr. Cullen. I hid my face and ran away from him. I was so ashamed. I didn't want anybody to see me. I walked and prayed for an hour. I didn't know what to do. Finally, I decided to go see the pastor. I went to the rectory and asked to see him. I told the priest it was an emergency. Finally, the pastor, Fr. Grotemeyer, saw me.

"I was surprised. He seemed so angry with me. He questioned me about who and what I saw. He told me Anthony was involved in a very grave mortal sin and so was the priest..." Mrs. Pace's voice broke and she started to sob again. Then she picked up a holy card from a small dish on the table and started to murmur the prayer written on it.

"Please continue," Kevin said with a slight tone of authority in his voice. "What did the pastor say next?"

Mrs. Pace turned the holy card over, stared blankly at it, and resumed speaking as if she was talking to the picture of the praying saint on the back of the card. "He told me he would make it stop and that he would speak to both Anthony and the priest. He said we must make sure that no scandal touches the Church. He told me to get on my knees and swear an oath that I would never reveal to anybody what I saw and never talk to anybody about what happened on pain of excommunication. I fell to my knees and repeated the oath after him."

Mrs. Pace started to sob again. Kevin patted her arm again.

"You did the right thing. There are a few things that are not clear. Was the priest you saw coming out of the bathroom Fr. Bari?"

Mrs. Pace shook her head no. Kevin realized he needed the answer on the tape.

"What was the name of the priest you saw come out of the bathroom?"

"I don't know. I didn't recognize him. He was not a Pius XII priest. I don't think I ever saw him before."

"You're absolutely sure the priest was not Fr. Bari?"

"Yes, I'm sure. That priest wasn't tall. Fr. Bari is very tall. And Fr. Bari is very Italian looking. This priest looked sort of Irish."

"What did the pastor ask about the priest you saw?"

"He asked me who it was. When I told him I didn't know, he asked me what he looked like."

"How did you describe him?"

"Just like I just told you—that he was shorter and kind of Irish looking. And that I didn't get a good look at him. I really didn't see his face."

"Did Fr. Grotemeyer say anything about him?"

"After I gave him the description, he said, 'I know who it is, and I'll put a stop to it.'"

"Did he ever say a name?"

"No, no name."

Kevin patted her arm again and said, "The Church is truly grateful for your cooperation. The Church is trying to identify the priest who abused your son. Is there anything else you can remember that would help? You said that you listened at the door. I know this is very difficult for you, but what did the priest say?"

Mrs. Pace started to sob.

"Please don't make me repeat it. It's so disgusting, so sinful. Please, I can't. I have nightmares about Anthony going to hell because of those sins. And the ones he is still committing. Sometimes I think he's possessed."

Kevin's faced flushed with anger. He bit down on his lower lip, increasing the pressure until the impulse to lash out at Mrs. Pace passed. Kevin tried to sound empathic. "The priest told your son to do sexual things."

Mrs. Pace nodded her head yes.

"I understand," Kevin said. "You don't have to say any more. Just one more question. What did the priest's voice sound like?"

"That's very strange," Mrs. Pace said. "He sounded like Fr. Bari. It wasn't Fr. Bari, but he sounded just like him."

"Thank you," Kevin said. "I'll be leaving now. The cardinal will be very pleased with your cooperation."

"What happens now?" Mrs. Pace asked.

Kevin tried to sound like a monsignor from the chancery office.

"If you are called on to testify in any official proceeding, tell the truth about your son's abuse just like you have today. Otherwise, the cardinal would appreciate if you did not talk about our meeting. The cardinal does not want you to be burdened like before so that is just a request. You are free to do whatever you think is best as long as you tell the truth."

Mrs. Pace looked confused. Kevin stayed silent.

"All right," Mrs. Pace said.

"One more thing," Kevin said.

Kevin paused and tried to focus on his role as a priest, but could not contain his anger.

"The man you saw coming out of the bathroom used his authority and status as a priest to horribly abuse your son. Anthony was a child who was preyed on by that priest. There was no sin on his part. The pastor was wrong. I suggest you pray for reconciliation with your son and pray that he forgives you and all the other adults who failed to protect him."

Mrs. Pace looked at Kevin like he was speaking a bizarre-sounding foreign language.

"I don't understand," she said.

Kevin's tone went flat and hard. "I think you do."

Mrs. Pace started to weep, and Kevin walked out of the kitchen. He left the house without looking back.

CHAPTER XIII

"You fucking bastard! How did you get this?" John Crowley, Brendan's boss, growled in a low voice at Malachy, trying not to be overheard in the crowded Loop restaurant not far from city hall.

Malachy looked up from the pictures showing Crowley entering and leaving a motel room with a large-breasted coworker and said in a carefully modulated voice, "An enemy of yours gave it to me."

"Enemy? Who? That's bullshit. You're trying to blackmail me. You fucking son of a bitch, I should call the FBI."

Malachy knew from poker there are some bluffs so transparent that the attempt should be given another name. "I'll save you the trouble," Malachy said, looking around the restaurant. "See that young man at the table near the window. He's FBI. I know him from my days as a lawyer. Here take the pictures and go tell him I'm blackmailing you. I'll wait here. Anyway, I'm not blackmailing you."

Crowley glared at Malachy.

"Spare me all your double-talk bullshit," Crowley said in a hushed angry voice. "Next comes the threat to show it to my wife. It's fucking blackmail and you know it!"

"On the contrary, I'm here to tell you I would never use this picture to harm you in any way," Malachy responded.

"Right! Now, you're my goddamn protector. Do you expect me to believe that bullshit?"

"I expect you to remember what you learned about me when you checked me out the last time," Malachy said, still speaking in a quiet, even tone. "I keep my word. And I give you my word I will never use this picture to cause you any trouble at home or at work. Period."

Crowley looked at Malachy like he was a particularly difficult crossword puzzle. "What game are you playing? What do you want? The tape back?"

"No, I don't want the tape," Malachy said.

"What the fuck do you want?"

"A favor," Malachy said.

"What kind of favor? Take Brendan back?"

"No. It wouldn't be fair to ask that. Brendan was way out of line. And no boss should have to put up with what's on that tape."

"What then?" Crowley asked, the anger gone from his voice for the first time.

Malachy put the pictures back in the manila envelope and slid it to Crowley.

"You have my word there are no copies and no negatives."

"What kind of favor?" Crowley repeated, grabbing the envelope.

"Let Brendan resign instead of firing him. I have his resignation right here."

Malachy put a white envelope on the table.

"And if I don't?"

"I will have to work extra hard to get him another city job. And you will miss the opportunity to call on me to repay the favor in the future. As the airline attendants say, 'Shift happens.' So you never know, maybe it's good insurance to have me as a friend who owes you. I hear the water department may have some problems that require some management changes."

Crowley picked up both envelopes.

"I never want to lay eyes on Brendan again. After all I did for him, I can't believe the names he called me, the things he said to me."

Malachy stood up from the table.

"Don't visit the aviation department, then. Brendan will be working there. The resignation makes that possible. Call me at the Shamrock if I can do anything for you."

Crowley didn't say anything. Malachy picked up the check from the table.

"I'll take care of this."

Malachy headed toward the cash register. He caught the eye of the young man by the window and waved. The young man half waved back with a puzzled look on his face. Malachy hoped he would not lose any sleep trying to figure out who waved to him.

Malachy drove to his appointment with Bari thinking about another Crowley, a friend of his father's. That Crowley was politically powerful, a fierce Irish nationalist like his father, and possessed of a legendary quick wit. His father told him the story about a meeting between Crowley and the first Mayor Daley, a man not known for his sense of humor, especially when the reputation of Chicago was involved.

Daley called Crowley to the fifth floor at city hall because he was concerned about the Queen's visit to Chicago in 1959. Daley wanted to make sure that the local Irish groups affiliated with the IRA did not embarrass Daley and the city during the visit. His father loved to tell the story, imitating both Crowley and Daley in their back and forth.

After the usual exchange of pleasantries about family, Daley got down to business.

Daley: Thanks for coming in. There is a small matter I want your help on. The Queen's visit is a major event for the city, recognition of the international importance of Chicago. I've been informed that some protests are being planned. Now, I understand about the North and all that, but I don't want any trouble. Do you understand what I'm telling you? No trouble, nothing that embarrasses the city.

Crowley: Well, as a protest, I was thinking of pissing on one of those ridiculous hats she wears, hopefully with her head under it. I'd prefer to piss on her crown but I'm sure she left that at home.

Daley: Now, cut that kind of talk out. I'm being serious here. I don't need none of your jokes. This is important to the city, very important. And I want your cooperation in this matter.

Crowley: Okay. I won't piss on her hat or any other part of her.

Daley: Everything is a joke to you, isn't it? You're not funny. Got it?

No trouble. Take care of it with all your groups, all of them. I'm dead serious about this.

Crowley: Alas, poor George!

Daley: George? George Dunne? What's he got to do with this?

Crowley: Not that George, he only runs the county board. I'm talking about King George III. They say he went insane with grief over the disloyalty of his subjects and the loss of his American colonies. If only he could have known—he still has loyal subjects in Chicago!

Daley (his voice quivering with anger and his face flushed red): I'm as good an Irishman as any of youse. And I've done more for our people than any of youse!

Crowley: No need to get mad, I was just having a little fun…

Daley (pulling out an index card from his desk, his hand shaking): Make a joke out of this. You've got seven family members on the payroll. They are all on this card. If there is any trouble, none of them have a job the day after. Now, get the hell out of my office, Mr. Comedian.

When Malachy turned the corner onto Bari's street, two squad cars with lights flashing were in front of the rectory. Malachy parked his car and jogged to the front of the residence. He approached the two private security guards and asked what was going on.

"Who are you?" asked the older, portly guard.

"Malachy Madden. I'm working with Fr. Bari. What happened here?"

The younger, fitter guard opened a notebook with pictures in it and then looked at Malachy. He said, "It's okay, no search needed."

They motioned for Malachy to get in the back of their car. They climbed in the front.

"We have ourselves a strange situation here," said the portly man in the driver's seat. "There was a report that an intruder was in the rectory. We know nobody got by us. And we don't think it is possible for someone to enter from the back or sides without being detected. The place is secured from the inside like Fort Knox, and there are alarms on the outside. So if somebody is in there, they were let in."

"Who called it in?" Malachy asked.

"We don't know," the other security man said. "They are going through the place now, room by room. Here they come now."

The two security men climbed out of the car and approached the officers coming down the stairs. Malachy recognized one of the officers.

"Jesus," Malachy murmured to himself. Malachy couldn't remember the cop's name or rank, but knew he was too high up to be assigned to a squad. All Malachy could remember was that the cop had testified against a client in a trial years ago and at that time was already moving up in the ranks. The officers and the security men talked for a couple of minutes and then returned to their vehicles. The squad cars turned off their lights and pulled away.

"What's the deal?" Malachy asked.

"Some neighbor thought they saw someone going in through the back door and called it in. It must have been the housekeeper. There was nobody inside."

"Did you guys know the cops?" Malachy asked.

Both men shook their heads no.

"We're not from the city. We work in Cicero. By the way, I'm Sal," the older man said. "And this is Tony."

"Always good to meet fellow Irishmen," Malachy said, giving them a big grin. "Did my name come up?"

"I don't think they ever saw you," Sal said. "They had their backs to the car. We didn't mention you. Why? Is there some problem with them?"

"No problem," Malachy said. "I just thought I recognized one of them. You know I was going to meet Fr. Bari in the rectory, but I have a hankering for an Italian beef. You guys know Al's?"

"Who doesn't? But your track record on trips isn't too good. There's been enough excitement for today. How about you bring the sandwiches back here. I'll take mine with extra peppers and dipped good, nice and messy."

"Me, too," Tony said.

"Done deal," Malachy said. "I'll be back in twenty minutes. But Fr. Bari does like to get out even if we don't go far. How about the park down the street? We'll never even get out of my car, unless you give the okay. Everybody can enjoy their sandwiches with Columbus providing security for all of us. After all, he is the patron saint of Italian beef."

"I didn't know he was a saint," Tony said.

"It's kind of like popes—you Italians have so many sometimes I get mixed up," Malachy said. "Anyway, how about it?"

"From what I've heard you could get in trouble on a trip between here and the front door so I suppose going one block won't make any difference," Sal said. "But no strolling around the park. It's not Columbus's pigeon-pecked ass that's on the line—it's ours."

"Deal," Malachy said.

Fr. Bari and Malachy sat on a park bench looking at the imposing statue of Columbus and trying to balance their beef sandwiches on their laps. "I hear you had some excitement at the rectory," Malachy said.

"It was very confusing," Bari said. "A neighbor thought they saw someone breaking in through the back door and called the police. The officers said it must have been the housekeeper coming in from the outside. But, I talked with her and she never left the house. I guess the neighbor was just being overly protective and thought he saw something."

"I hope you like Italian beef from Al's," Malachy said. "I ordered yours just like all the others—extra peppers with lots of juice. Tough to eat without making a mess, though."

"It's fine," Bari said. "Before all this started, I used to go there at least once a week. It's a neighborhood institution."

Malachy took a big bite of his sandwich and pretended to take his time chewing it. He was trying to decide how to handle the incident with the cops.

He looked at Columbus, thinking about the numerous problems the explorer confronted. Malachy decided to set sail for a new world. There was no time to consult with the joint chiefs, but Malachy knew any plan that was bold and forced the issue would get their backing. He wondered if Columbus ever had to worry about obstruction of justice charges.

"There're two things I need to tell you. But I need the first one to be held in strict confidence. It needs to be a priest-penitent kind of thing so that no authority has a right to any answer from you concerning it."

"I don't understand," Bari said. "But I will keep your confidence in that strict manner."

"I think the police coming to the rectory was a setup. They were planting bugs. And your phone is probably tapped, too."

"Oh, my God, what's going on?"

"I think it's the Feds. The Chicago Police were cooperating in the placement of the bugs. All done legally, of course, with a proper warrant. But I'm sure the supposed call from the neighbor was a ruse to get into the rectory and have free access to all the rooms without you present. I suppose you were guarded in one location while the police searched for the intruder."

"Yes, in the walk-in closet off the entry hallway. The police said it was for my safety. This is very distressing. Are you sure it was a ruse?"

"Yes," Malachy said. "But I don't want the Feds to know that you know. And that means you need to leave the rectory. There's no way for your conversations to seem normal once it's in your head that they're listening. No matter how hard you try, you'll give it away."

Bari moved the sandwich to the bench, his hands trembling, and then started to gesture and point toward the rectory. "Leave? Where would I go? That's my home."

"I want you to go up to your sister's place in Wisconsin today."

"My sister's place? I don't want my family involved in this."

"She already is. Whoever ordered the attack on my car was driving your sister's fancy sports car. That's how we found her."

Malachy explained about Antonella's return to Chicago.

"I don't understand. Is my sister in some kind of danger because of me?"

"We don't know what kind of person we are dealing with. A bizarre-looking blonde stole your sister's car, which isn't hard to do, and used it in arranging the attack on my car. A note was left warning me to stop. But it didn't say stop what. I wasn't even certain that the attack was related to my work for the committee until I found out your sister's sports car was involved. That can't be a coincidence."

"Why can't I just stay in the rectory? I'm innocent and nothing I say in the rectory will make me guilty of anything."

Malachy thought about reciting chapter and verse about how investigators looking for a certain pattern often found it regardless of the facts or intentions of those being investigated. But he decided to keep it simple. "Look, the Feds have a program and we have a program. They're not the same program. Let's just leave it at that."

Bari was silent. Malachy decided to let him have the time to mull over the news. Malachy returned to eating his sandwich. After a few minutes, Bari asked the question Malachy knew would come eventually. "Why send me to Wisconsin if your colleague wanted my sister to return to Chicago for security reasons?"

"I want to go fishing, and you're the bait," Malachy said.

"I want to make sure my sister is protected. If this helps, I'll do it."

"No guarantees," Malachy said. "But it could help by attracting the woman who stole your sister's sports car. It'll get around town that you're staying at Antonella's place."

"All right, I'll do it. When do you want to leave?"

"I'll come back and pick you up in a couple of hours," Malachy said. "I need to make a few arrangements. And remember everything you say is being picked up. Just tell the housekeeper you're going away for a few days. Don't say where."

"What if she asks where?"

"Just tell her you're not supposed to tell because of security."

Malachy took one more big bite of his sandwich, got up, and placed the remains in a trash basket. Bari carefully wrapped up his sandwich and joined Malachy in the short walk back to the car, carrying his mostly uneaten sandwich. Malachy started up the car, waved goodbye to the statue of Columbus, and drove toward the rectory.

"You said there were two things you needed to tell me about," Bari said.

"This one is good news," Malachy said. "We have a partial identification of the man who actually abused Anthony Pace."

"Why didn't you tell me that first? That's great news! I've been praying that you'd find him. What do you mean partial identification?"

"He's shorter than you," Malachy said.

"Shorter? That's it? He's shorter! For God's sake, is this one of your jokes?"

"No, it's not," Malachy said. "Actually, it's very important."

"Why?"

"Because you're very tall. Also, because we learned that Fr. Grotemeyer knew the shorter man. And that makes it almost certain that the shorter man who abused Pace is a priest. So that makes for a partial ID. For the moment, we're looking for a not-too-tall priest who knew Fr. Grotemeyer and who has it in for you. Any ideas?"

"I'm sorry I was sharp with you a moment ago, but sometimes you can be very exasperating."

"That must be true," Malachy said. "My confessor has told me the same thing."

"The problem is most priests are shorter than I am," Bari said. "Nobody in particular comes to mind. How short is short?"

"Good question," Malachy said. "Do you still have some contacts at the seminary? I want to stop there on our way up to Wisconsin."

"I do. Why?"

"To look at mug shots," Malachy said.

"Mug shots?"

"Class pictures."

†

Malachy called Dino. "We're making progress. To move things along, I want to take Bari to his sister's place in Wisconsin. Let your security know. We won't need them until we return. I'll give you plenty of advance warning of that so you can get things set up. I'll be picking Bari up in two hours."

"I don't think that's a good idea," Dino said. "Bari is much safer staying put in the rectory. It is secure and far safer than Antonella's old cottage in Wisconsin."

"You know his sister's place?" Malachy asked.

"Yes, I've been there a few times. It's not suitable for Bari under these circumstances. I must veto your plan. Bari stays put."

"Don't make a hasty decision," Malachy said. "Think it over and call me back."

"I have thought it over—Bari stays in the rectory. Move things along some other way."

"Think it over again and call me back," Malachy said, clicking off the cell phone. Malachy pulled out the cell phone his nameless employer arranged for him. He pushed the first preprogrammed number.

He could tell the call was automatically transferred to another number. After five rings, the call was picked up, but nobody said anything. Malachy broke the silence.

"This is Malachy. I need some information."

"Hang up," a voice said.

Malachy clicked off and waited. The cell phone rang ten minutes later. "This is Malachy."

"What do you need?" a distorted voice asked.

Malachy explained that Dino vetoed his plan to take Bari to Wisconsin.

"Do you agree to take full responsibility for Bari's safety until he returns to the rectory?"

"Yes."

"I'll arrange it. If you need to call again add 'special' to the formulation. Good luck."

Malachy wondered if his employer actually believed in luck. Malachy knew if something happened to Bari, his employer would not just write it off to bad luck. That was a certainty.

Malachy remembered an interaction he had with a gambler who was tracking the numbers that came up on a roulette wheel and recording them in a notebook. Malachy had made some trite comment about the wheel being unfriendly.

"Do you really think the laws of physics have emotions? The ball lands exactly where it should land. Nothing in life is more certain than that. The only thing to be determined is if any physical condition is causing a bias greater than the house's edge."

"Tell that to Mr. Happy over there," Malachy said, gesturing to a drunken gambler with stacks of chips in front of him.

"If he stays at this table or any other, he'll end up a loser. The only way he wins is to quit right now while he's ahead. The longer he continues to play, the more certain his loss."

Malachy decided Bari was staying at the cottage for three nights only. He would figure out later what to do about the bugged rectory.

CHAPTER XIV

Malachy and Bari drove under an arch topped by a large cross and onto a wide, tree-lined roadway leading to the main buildings of the seminary. Malachy had sent the Count and Kevin ahead to Wisconsin to check out Antonella's cottage and to prepare the security arrangements.

"Beautiful grounds," Malachy said.

"And you haven't even seen the lake yet," Bari said. "The grounds are truly inspirational. But, sometimes when I think of my time here I cringe. I was supposed to be engaged in formation for the priesthood. But, it was a time of upheaval for the Church and for me personally. It was not a good mix. Looking back, I can hardly believe I was so young and so immature. It's like I was an actor in a play."

"Comedy or tragedy?" Malachy asked.

"More soap opera than anything else, I'm afraid. I literally had no idea what it really meant to be a priest. And now that I finally do, I am embroiled in all this."

"Somebody wanted you on the hot spot," Malachy said. "Let see if we can find a picture of that somebody."

Malachy parked the car, and they walked slowly toward the massive, stone administration building.

"I still can't believe that some classmate or colleague could do such evil things. And on top of it, hate me so much."

"Believe it," Malachy said. "That type is out there."

They entered the administrative building and Bari told the receptionist he had an appointment with Fr. Robert Keane. After a few minutes, a frail looking priest entered the area using a cane and warmly greeted Bari. Malachy was introduced as somebody who was investigating the charges against Bari.

"It is good to meet you," Keane said to Malachy in a weak voice. "I am glad someone is trying to get to the truth. Do you have a lot of experience in this field?"

"I was a criminal defense attorney for a long time," Malachy said. "Investigating to establish facts is part of the job."

"Thank you for the work you're doing on John's behalf," Keane said. "How can I help?"

"We would like to look at class pictures," Malachy said. "If a seminarian could have crossed paths with Bari, then we want to look at his picture. In a group photo, if possible."

"Yes, that's possible," Keane said. "I think what you want is hanging on the wall in the rec room. Please, follow me. I'm afraid that some of the photographs have aged quite a bit—just like me."

They adjusted their pace to Keane's and made their way through a maze of hallways to a rec room with two Ping-Pong tables, a pool table, solid wood tables with chess sets, and groupings of couches and chairs.

"Here we are," Keane said. "The pictures are in order by year. When you find John's year, the classes who were here at the same time will be on either side. Feel free to take them off the wall and look at them under the lamp. If you need to, you can take them out of their frames."

They found Bari's class picture. The clerical garb and the backdrop did not diminish Bari's striking good looks—it was as if somebody slipped a still life from a film into the frame. Malachy realized the headshots made it impossible to tell the height of any individual. Keane saw the look of dismay come over Malachy's face.

"May I ask what you are looking for?" Keane asked. "Perhaps I could be of help."

"I know it sounds strange, but I am looking for someone shorter than Fr. Bari and probably a little shorter than the average seminarian."

Keane took in the information. He slowly looked around the room.

"May I make a suggestion?" Keane asked politely.

"Of course," Malachy said.

"There are a number of group photographs on these walls and in some other rooms. Some are posed and some are not. I believe we will able to tell the relative height of the subjects in those pictures. Unfortunately, they are not arranged by class year. Many of the photographs have some class year identification on them. If we…"

"Jesus…how fucking stupid!" Malachy exclaimed.

Keane blanched, and Bari forcefully grabbed Malachy's arm.

"Malachy, watch your language!" Bari said sternly. "I'm sorry," Malachy said to Keane. "I was speaking about myself. I missed something obvious. John, I need to talk with you privately for a minute."

"If it is about my life here, you can speak openly. Fr. Keane knows everything about my time here."

"Did you have a particularly intense relationship with anyone?" Malachy asked.

Bari answered without hesitation.

"In my first year, I was completely infatuated with one of my teachers. He was very dynamic, a forceful personality with a commanding physical presence."

"Students told me he was absolutely mesmerizing in the classroom," Keane said.

"He was very facile when it came to the history and development of the Church," Bari said. "He compared the Church to a very long train moving very slowly on a track to the future. Because of the drag of the weight from past practices nonessential to the Church's mission, it was difficult for the train to get any traction. It was up to progressives to uncouple the unnecessary cars so the engine could make progress." Bari paused and looked down and then at some of the pictures and continued in a slower, sadder tone.

"And it was up to a very few select visionaries to get out ahead of the engine and lay new track. And of course, he was one of those visionaries. He would cite arcane beliefs and practices that took years for the Church to discard. He made it seem that if you were struggling to be celibate, you were just one of those at the end of the train weighing it down to no purpose."

"What happened?" Malachy asked.

"It turned out he was a leader of a kind of sex club. He targeted me for seduction. I'm afraid I wasn't much of a challenge. I was naive enough to think it was a special relationship. I lost that belief soon enough. After a few months, it was time to pass me on to other members of the club. He made sure that happened in a fog of alcohol and marijuana."

"What is his name, and where is he now?" Malachy asked.

"His name is Adam Fischer and I believe he's in California," Keane said. "He started a New Age church with an ex-nun. I believe it is some kind of a synthesis of Native American religious tradition, Buddhism, and Christianity."

"Makes sense," Malachy said. "Twisted track is part of the California religious tradition. Somehow, I don't think he would cooperate in our investigation. My hunch is that the short man with the...," Malachy caught himself. "The short man is on these walls somewhere. But I want to focus on Fischer rather than John."

"Fischer was an avid Ping-Pong player," Keane said. "He used to hold a tournament. If you wanted to be in his good graces, you entered the tournament no matter your level of skill. I think some of those pictures are in a drawer here. Perhaps we should start there."

"Great idea," Malachy said enthusiastically.

Keane led them to a built-in cabinet with drawers beneath the doors. He pulled open a drawer full of pictures, most unframed. They each took a handful and spread them on the Ping-Pong table.

"Malachy, take a look at this," Bari said, placing a picture on the table.

It was a picture of Fischer surrounded by young men. The young man right next to Fischer was shorter than all the others in the row. Fischer had his arm around the man. Malachy picked up the picture and examined it closely, trying to imagine the young man years older.

He looked at his mouth and realized he had seen that half-smile, half-smirk before. It was in the picture he had sent to Dino to circulate in the Taylor Street neighborhood.

"That's him!" Malachy said. "That's the son of a bitch we're after!"

"Malachy, control your language," Bari said.

Keane smiled gently at Bari and said, "I've heard the term before. Truth to tell, I've used it myself from time to time."

Keane picked up the picture and looked at it closely.

"He looks so young and innocent."

"Who is he?" Malachy asked.

"I don't remember him," Keane said.

He handed the picture to Bari.

"I don't think I've ever seen him before," Bari said, handing the picture back to Malachy.

Malachy examined it front and back. There were no notations.

"No hat in this picture. We'll be able to find him on the wall."

"Malachy, you sound like you've seen him before," Bari said.

"I have, and so have you. He was the man on the bicycle who followed us when we walked by the lake. He was also at your press conference. We have the picture of him pretending to be curious bystander."

"But I don't know him," Bari protested. "Why is he interested in me?"

"I'll ask him when we find him," Malachy said. "Now, let's go put a name on him."

The three men started to check the wall with Malachy placing the picture next to the class pictures on the wall.

"Here he is," Bari said. "Reginald Flynn. He graduated two years before I arrived here. I don't understand what's going on."

"Reginald? What the hell kind of name is that to give to an Irish Catholic kid? No wonder the man is so screwed up."

"Reginald Pole was the last Roman Catholic Archbishop of Canterbury," Keane said. "Or perhaps someone in the family was a P.G. Wodehouse fan. Jeeves's first name was Reginald."

"No Irish Catholic should be named after an English servant," Malachy said. "An English cardinal is bad enough. Anyway, Fr. Keane, may I keep the picture?"

Keane hesitated before answering and then said, "I move so much slower I'll start back to the reception area. John, could you accompany me? And Malachy would you mind putting everything back to rights?"

"I'll take care of it," Malachy said.

Malachy waited for the two men to turn their backs to him as they started for the reception room. He put the picture of Fischer in his pocket and went back to the cabinet. He carefully and slowly returned all the others to the drawer. He decided not to try and catch up to Bari and Keane so they would have a chance to talk. He hoped the use of force would not be the topic of conversation.

When Malachy entered the reception room, Bari immediately asked him, "Are you sure he's the one?"

"Positive," Malachy said. "The facts are falling into a pattern, and the pattern says Fr. Reginald Flynn is the priest who criminally abused Pace. But I'm not the jury. The jury of one we have to convince is Anthony Pace. And not beyond a reasonable doubt, but beyond any doubt."

"Isn't that going to be very difficult?" Keane asked

"Yes," Malachy said. "But there is good news—there are no rules of evidence."

"John was just telling me of your somewhat unorthodox methods," Keane said.

"When in Rome…," Malachy said.

"We are forbidden to fight evil with evil," Keane said.

"We are not forbidden to fight," Malachy responded quickly. "If proving John innocent and stopping Flynn from abusing another child requires a little rule breaking, so be it."

"Bureaucratic rules are made for bureaucratic purposes," Keane said. "Moral rules are for God's purpose."

"Then, we agree," Malachy said. "And I'm hoping you agree that the rules that protect Flynn's seminary personnel file are bureaucratic."

"Those files are confidential for more than bureaucratic reasons," Keane said. "What do you want to obtain from the file?"

"Personal information that will expedite the investigation. Information we can and will obtain eventually based on what we already know, but that process takes time and resources. And during that time, more children are put at risk."

"I promise you I will consider your request seriously and pray about it," Keane said.

"That's all I can ask for," Malachy said.

†

Bari broke the silence as they drove north to Antonella's place.

"Malachy, for the life of me, I cannot come up with a connection to Reginald Flynn. I know you know things you can't share with me, but there must be some connection I can understand. If, he's the right person."

"There is—your former teacher, Fr. Adam Fischer. Do you know why high school and college reunions are so charged?"

"School reunions? Malachy, please be serious."

"I'm serious. They are charged because of the volatile combination of the erotic and the longing. The longing for a different life by those who are unhappy and the memories of intense passions, fulfilled or not. Add in a lot of alcohol, and combustion is a certainty."

"What are you saying?"

"Fischer's sexual activities didn't start or end with you. We know Flynn is twisted sexually. How do you fit in? Take a look in a mirror. You're tough competition."

Malachy continued after a minute of silence.

"Maybe Flynn tried to get Fischer interested again and you were in the way. Maybe he heard through the grapevine that you were Fischer's new favorite and started to obsess about that, and maybe it's something we could never imagine. But when we find Flynn, we'll figure out some way to get the answer. Because the answer will be important in convincing Anthony Pace you are innocent."

"It makes me sick to think of Pace being targeted because of something I've done," Bari said.

"Flynn would have fixed on some other child if it hadn't been Pace," Malachy said. "There is nothing we can do about the past. Our job is to find Flynn and obtain enough evidence to convince Pace that you are a victim too."

Malachy paused, checked the rearview mirror to make sure nobody was behind him, and slowed the car down. He glanced at Bari, who was staring blankly out the window. He considered his words carefully and said in a louder voice, "And we have to make sure that Flynn never abuses another child."

Bari shifted in the seat and returned his attention to Malachy as he resumed driving at the speed limit. "We are forbidden by Jesus to fight evil with evil, just as Fr. Keane said. No matter what, I must live by that command."

"I'm not a theologian," Malachy said. "All I know is that sometimes we are forced to choose between two evils. And not to make a choice may cause even greater evil."

"It's easy to use that to rationalize what serves our interest," Bari said with an increasing intensity. "The Gospel demands more of us."

They drove in silence for fifteen minutes. Malachy mulled over the next steps in trying to locate Flynn. He needed to know if Keane would get him the personnel file.

"Do you think Fr. Keane will give me the contents of Flynn's file?" Malachy asked.

"No, I don't. It's a step too far for him. And, no, I won't try to change his mind."

Malachy silently cursed to himself. He wondered how the Count —an anticlerical Polish Catholic—would feel about breaking into a seminary.

"I guess we'll do it the hard way," Malachy said.

They drove in silence again.

"What happens when we get to Antonella's cottage?" Bari asked, breaking the silence.

"My colleague Kevin will be staying with you in the cottage. He'll have his dog with him. He'll make sure you're secure. Another colleague will be floating around, but not staying with you. You may never see him."

"A dog? What kind of dog?"

"Irish wolfhound, especially trained."

"Trained how?"

Malachy flashed a big grin at Bari.

"Moral theology—he's a whiz! No conundrums for him. He always knows the right choice to make."

"Do you always make a joke out of everything?" Bari asked

"It's an Irish thing," Malachy said. "We tend to get depressed and self-medicate if we stay too serious, too long. Anyway, as many others have noted, we know that God has a sense of humor—otherwise, why did She create sex?"

Bari shook his head in disbelief.

"To answer your question, Kevin trained his dog in providing protection. Kevin will know immediately if someone unauthorized is on the property. It makes for better sleeping."

"What will you be doing?" Bari asked.

"Going to church, a lot. In fact, every mass they have today and tomorrow. Tonight at 5:00 is fine, but I'm certainly hoping they don't start too early tomorrow. I hate getting up early."

"That parish church is a very interesting building," Bari said. "Not what you would expect from a country church—tons of marble, very elaborate—more what you would expect in a wealthy suburban parish. It's modeled after a church in Italy. A local man was wounded in the Italian campaign and sought refuge in the prototype in Italy. He vowed if he survived his wounds he'd build a replica in his hometown to replace the converted barn that served as the church."

"A battlefield bargain with God that someone actually fulfilled," Malachy said.

"I think the church's history somehow affected the pastor. He is a church militant. Everything is a crusade and a battle."

"I know the type," Malachy said.

"Do you think the woman who stole Antonella's car will come to the church?"

"You never know who might show up."

"Flynn?"

"He seems to go where you go. We know he likes church bathrooms. By the way, where is the bathroom in that church?"

"I don't know."

Bari's cell phone rang and he answered it. "It's Fr. Keane, he wants to talk to you."

Malachy took the phone, hoping the quick response meant cooperation.

"There is some information about the file I can share with you," Keane said. "The entire file is missing. There is a note indicating that no information on Flynn is to be given to anyone, and all inquiries should be directed to the Office of Legal Affairs in the chancery."

"The long arm of O'Grady," Malachy said.

"It would seem so," Keane said.

"Why circle the wagons unless you expect an attack?" Malachy asked. "And why expect an attack unless you know you are in hostile territory? Just thinking out loud. Thank you, that information is very helpful."

"That note was definitely for bureaucratic purposes," Keane said. "I will pray that you are successful in establishing John's innocence. He is a good priest, doing good work. The sooner he returns to his work, the better."

"Amen," Malachy said.

He handed the phone back to Bari.

"I could hear what he told you, but what does it mean?"

"It means O'Grady knows he has a problem."

"What kind of problem?" Bari asked.

"A big problem," Malachy said. "We don't know the dimensions yet, but we will. This is progress."

"But you wanted to know the information in the file," Bari said.

"I still do. We'll find another way to get it."

There was another stretch of silent driving that Bari broke with a question.

"Does all this ever cause you to question your faith?"

"I was inoculated against that growing up," Malachy said. "Almost on a daily basis at the dinner table."

"Your parents?"

"Yes. I get my faith from my mom. My dad was an anticlerical lefty whose religion was unionism. He would recite chapter and verse about every idiotic thing the institutional Church did and taught. Mom just treated all that stuff as irrelevant. Her faith was unshakeable. 'Of course, the Church does stupid and sinful things,' she would say."

Malachy continued trying to imitate her light Irish accent. " 'Peter denied Jesus three times and he was the first pope. Why would you expect the rest of the lot to do any better? And anyway your precious unions are just as bad. But in the end, unions at their best can only give bread, but people don't live by bread alone. The Church at its best is doing God's work and bringing God's grace into people's lives.' "

"Not everyone has such faith," Bari said. "The Church is driving many away. Sometimes the Church's leaders seem willfully obtuse about the actual lives of the faithful."

"All entrenched, self-perpetuating bureaucracies tend to act that way," Malachy said. "But, as my mom used to say, 'In the end, God always prevails.'"

"Are your parents still living?"

"No, they both have passed, God rest their souls. They were older when they had me."

"They seem like such an unlikely pairing," Bari said.

"A thousand census takers could not find two more opposite people from the south of Ireland."

"How do you mean?"

"You name it and they were on opposite sides with a couple of notable exceptions, thanks to the Holy Family, as my mom would say. Those notable exceptions include love of the White Sox and traditional Irish music and dancing. It was the dancing that led to yours truly, because in the beginning if they had to talk about anything other than baseball and Irish music and dancing my name would be Schmidt, if I had a name."

"Malachy Schmidt just doesn't have the same ring to it," Bari said. "How in the world did they ever meet?"

"Now, you understand, I wasn't there, but according to my half-brothers, the story goes this way. Schmidt was courting my mom. She was a widow with four kids. Her husband was killed in the war in the Pacific. Now Schmidt is a good, decent man with some means. But something didn't click, and there wasn't any chemistry.

"So the courtship is going on two years with no resolution. And then she meets Martin Madden at the County Kerry annual dance. He is ten years older and a widower with three kids. Tough luck for Schmidt because he's not a dancer of any kind, and my dad is a great dancer. So my parents-to-be are out on the dance floor, dance after dance, and Schmidt is left at the table twiddling his thumbs.

"So Schmidt sees his whole courtship dancing away from him, and he decides urgent action is required. He fortifies himself with a lot of beer and heads out to the dance floor, red-faced and agitated, where he confronts his nemesis."

Malachy adopted a slight German accent. "'I brought Shannon to the dance. It is not right that you take all her time on the dance floor, so I am cutting in. And you can leave now because I'll be taking her home after we're done dancing.'"

Malachy switched to a soft brogue and imitated a woman's voice.

"'The dancing has been just wonderful, Martin, but I do really need to be getting home after this dance. Please don't ruin a lovely evening with a scene.'

"My dad gives a curt nod to Schmidt and moves to the side of the dance floor, where he watches Schmidt try to dance. Then he disappears from the hall. A few minutes later, two big uniformed coppers show up, go out on the dance floor and arrest Schmidt, and start to take him away.

"When my mom tries to find out what's going on, all they will tell her is that Schmidt is a dangerous criminal and she is fortunate to be out of his clutches. My dad reappears, offers to take my mom home, and the rest is history, as they say in chemistry class."

"What was Schmidt charged with?" Bari asked.

"Criminal assault on the Irish step dance."

Bari laughed.

"The two cops were friends of my dad. They held Schmidt until my dad left with my mom, and then they let him go. Schmidt tried to raise hell about false arrest and all that, but he didn't get very far. The krauts didn't have any clout after the war. And, anyway, all the witnesses said the charge was fully justified."

"I think your dad had a great influence on you too," Bari said in a serious tone. "Did your father ever relent about religion?"

"No. Mom loved her faith and simply ignored the faults of the clergy as not important. That attitude drove my father crazy, particularly when she would say, 'The loving and merciful God, because of the intercession of Jesus and His mother Mary, is going to forgive them just as He is going to forgive you your heathen ways.'

"Dad outlived my mom by a few years year. He made me promise I wouldn't go sentimental and bury him in consecrated ground next to my mom. He wanted to be cremated and his ashes spread at Kilmainham jail in Dublin—and that's what I did."

"A jail?"

"The place where so many from the Easter Rebellion were executed. One of his heroes, Connolly, was shot there. He was a labor leader. He was too weak from his wounds to stand so they shot him in a chair. My father used to say the jeering of the Dublin workingman as the rebels were marched off was harder for Connolly to bear than the English bullets that killed him."

"I can understand that," Bari said.

"Don't worry, O'Grady won't shoot you."

"Are you sure?" Bari asked, laughing.

"On that doctrine, I'm infallible," Malachy said. "And I'm not even Italian. That's another thing my mother used to say, 'Why don't they try an Irishman? They couldn't do any worse than that run of popes Pius.' On that even my father agreed, at least until O'Grady started to move up the ladder. 'If the white smoke ever goes up for O'Grady, it will be proof positive that the Vatican is Ghost free,' he would say."

CHAPTER XV

Malachy watched in disbelief as the priest left the altar and disappeared from view only to reappear from behind the curtains that served as a backdrop for the ornate pulpit that loomed over the congregation. Few celebrants now even used the modest pulpits at the side of most altars for their sermons. He thought of his friend and confessor, Fr. Kennedy.

Kennedy always started out on the top step leading to the altar and then started moving as he talked. The sermons were like his movements—sudden twists and turns, unexpected ascents and descents, and the stray digression that seemed totally unconnected to what went before. Kennedy told stories on himself to illustrate the relevance of the Gospel to today's life. He could be forcefully challenging, mostly about social justice issues. A Kennedy sermon sometimes lacked coherence, but it never lacked compassion.

This priest was Kennedy's opposite in every way Malachy concluded. He looked and sounded like a prosperous, too-well-fed Wisconsin dairy farmer of German descent expounding on his superior knowledge of all things agricultural.

The priest paused after the gospel, making a show of looking over the congregation. After an overly long period of silence, he began his sermon. "Our parish and church are named Christ the King after the feast day established by that great pope, Pius XI. In today's world when those who reject Christ as King besiege us on every side, when so-called leaders in every field, especially government, are more aptly termed betrayers, and when too many who call themselves Catholic reject Church teaching, we do well to listen with open ears to the wisdom of Pius XI from his encyclical." Then he read:

> If princes and magistrates duly elected are filled with the persuasion that they rule, not by their own right, but by the mandate and in the place of the Divine King, they will exercise their authority piously and wisely, and they will make laws and administer them, having in view the common good and also the human dignity of their subjects. The result will be a stable peace and tranquility, for there will be no longer any cause of discontent.

The pastor stopped speaking and bowed his head in silence and then resumed.

"Alas, we know those wise words were not heeded by the rulers of those days. In fact, instead of acknowledging the necessity of installing Christ as King and Ruler, the dark storms gathered strength and soon attacked the Church itself in many countries. There were a few leaders who heeded the pope's words and defended Christ and the Church. In Spain, the forces of atheistic communism and socialism combined with others who hated Christ, and they attempted to eradicate the Church.

"How fortunate the Church was in that day to have a stalwart defender like Franco, who gave Christ His proper place as King, and because of that was able to defeat the forces of atheism and to secure the Church's rightful place in that country.

"Today the Church is under severe attack by the forces of secularism —a malevolent philosophy that attempts to remove Christ the King who reigns over all from every aspect of civil life and daily life. Who will defend the Church in this later day? Who will fight to ensure that Christ the King has His rightful place in our country? In every country?"

Malachy looked around to see if anyone was paying attention to the pastor's sermon. The glazed look on most faces said they had heard it all before. The pastor again quoted Pius XI.

...the Church, founded by Christ as a perfect society, has a natural and inalienable right to perfect freedom and immunity from the power of the state; and that in fulfilling the task committed to her by God of teaching, ruling, and guiding to eternal bliss those who belong to the kingdom of Christ, she cannot be subject to any external power.

Malachy gripped the edge of the pew with both hands and pulled until the powerful impulse to stand and challenge the pastor passed. He knew that loyalty to his father required him to confront the priest, but he would wait until after Mass. Malachy joined the rest of the faithful and tuned out the remainder of the sermon.

At the end of Mass, Malachy positioned himself so he was the last to file past the pastor. He noted how few parishioners lingered to chat—most just nodded and quickly moved to exit the church. As he approached the pastor, Malachy adopted his father's lilting tone and accent.

"That was a hell of a sermon, Father. But I was a little confused and I have a question."

The priest looked at Malachy quizzically. "Of course. What is it?"

"This Franco fellow, the one who made Christ his King. I'm confused about him."

"How so?"

"Is Franco a common name over there in Spain like Smith here in the States? Or would your Franco be the same Franco whose German air force terror bombed civilians at Guernica? Whose forces slaughtered Basque priests? Who was an ally of Hitler and Mussolini and sent forces to fight with Hitler's armies in the invasion of Russia? Is that the Franco you're talking about?"

"Are you a..."

Malachy interrupted.

"Because if it is, then your Franco should have met the same fate as his good buddies Mussolini and Hitler."

The pastor's face turned red as he sputtered out his question, "Are you a parishioner?"

Malachy gave the priest a big smile. "No, God has spared me that affliction. Despite our differences, I wish you well with your operation."

"Operation? I'm not having an operation."

Malachy gave the pastor another big smile.

"Really? I just assumed your case of cranial-posterior inversion was so severe that it would take a team of surgeons to pull your head out. Well anyway, have a nice day!"

Malachy inhibited the impulse to clap the pastor on the shoulder out of concern he would end up knocking him over. He walked rapidly out of the church and into the parking lot. The lot was almost empty. Out of habit, he surveyed the remaining cars. There was nobody in the cars parked near the church. There was one occupied car at the far end of the lot. On a hunch, Malachy returned to the interior of the church.

The pastor was gone, and the only activity came from two women volunteers on the altar. Malachy positioned himself in the corner of the vestibule, out of the line of sight of anyone entering the church through the main doors, and waited.

After few minutes, a man of medium height and build entered the church. Malachy did not recognize him. Malachy stepped out from his secluded spot.

"I'm afraid you're too late for Mass," Malachy said loudly. "But trust me, the sermon was definitely not a showstopper."

The man startled and spun around to face Malachy.

"I'm not here for Mass," the man said bitterly.

"Who are you? Why are you here?" Malachy asked.

The man ignored Malachy's questions and countered with an angry question of his own.

"Where is Fr. Bari?"

"All right, let's play twenty questions," Malachy said. "I'll answer your question and then you answer mine. Fr. Bari is at his sister's cottage with an associate of mine. Your turn."

The man looked around the church with a scowl on his face. "It's been a long time since I was in a church. Let's go outside and talk."

"Lead the way."

The man turned his back on Malachy and strode out of the church. Malachy followed at a distance, examining the man closely trying to spot a weapon. He didn't see an obvious one. Malachy figured the man at 5'10", a little overweight and out of shape, and no fighter of any kind. He waited for Malachy in the parking lot.

"To answer your question, I'm here to make sure Fr. Bari doesn't abuse any more children."

"How do you know he ever abused any children?" Malachy asked. "Did he abuse you?"

The man glared at Malachy. "I hate your type—victimizing the victim all over again. No, he didn't personally abuse me. But I've met with Pace, and I believe him. He's telling the truth."

"I also believe Pace is telling the truth," Malachy said.

"Then how can you stomach defending Fr. Bari? Even being in the same room with him. He makes me sick!"

"Pace is telling the truth about his sexual abuse, but he has the wrong priest. Fr. Bari never abused Pace or anybody else."

"You just don't get it, do you?" the man shouted. "They're all liars. That's how they're able to dupe everybody—they're great liars!"

Malachy realized he was losing by arguing. The man had access to Pace—he was the key to the lock. Malachy needed to keep the key available.

"Your goal is to make sure Fr. Bari has no opportunity to abuse another child, is that right?"

"You're goddamn right, that's right."

"Good," Malachy said. "Move in with him."

The man stared at Malachy, speechless.

"Look," Malachy said. "I'm responsible for Bari's security. Having you wander around up here makes my job harder. You can watch Bari and we can watch you. It works for everybody."

"I couldn't stand being in the same house with him."

Malachy guessed the man would revert to the stomach argument. "Okay. We'll keep you informed of his whereabouts."

"Why should I trust you? Your job is to protect a sexual predator."

"Where are you from?" Malachy asked.

"The western suburbs of Chicago," the man said. "Why?"

"I take it you're a Catholic," Malachy said.

"I was. Again, why?"

"Because you need somebody you trust to tell you that I keep my word. I'm trying to find the common link."

"I know who you are," the man said. "You're Malachy Madden, a disbarred lawyer."

Malachy smiled at the man. "Believe it or not, I do know some folks who would find that a recommendation."

"I already checked you out," the man said. "When I found out you were involved with Fr. Bari. You don't have the best of reputations, but people did say you kept your commitments."

"Well, I'm making this commitment to you—I will keep you informed of Bari's whereabouts. Provided you have no weapons, you can be as close to him as you want. But I do need to know who you are and why you're involved."

The man pointed at the church and started to speak in a loud voice again and then abruptly stopped and said, "My name is Joe Valquist and I'm a member of the Chicago chapter of Fight Abuse. The members are all victims of abuse and have pledged to help other victims and to do everything possible to prevent future abuse. We got a report that Fr. Bari was up here, and we were concerned there might be the potential for more abuse of children from him. I came up here to investigate."

Malachy realized the report must have come from Flynn.

"Anonymous tip no doubt."

"Yes. How did you know?"

"Lucky guess. Why were you following me?"

"I wasn't. I was checking to see if Fr. Bari came to the Mass when I spotted you. I thought maybe he was with you. When you didn't come out after Mass I came in to investigate."

"You want to do your job and I want to do mine," Malachy said. "Let's drive back to the cottage and you can confirm that Bari is there."

"What happens after that?"

"Let's take things one step at a time. How about it? Follow me back to the cottage."

"I just want to confirm his whereabouts."

"Good," Malachy said. "Let's go."

As Malachy drove toward the cottage, he called Kevin and explained the situation. Malachy wanted to make sure that Valquist was forced to interact with Bari once they were at the cottage. They called the Count on a conference call and quickly settled on a plan. As they drove through the town, Malachy signaled he was pulling into a gas station. Valquist pulled up on the street and waited.

The Count approached Valquist's car on foot on the passenger side and pretended to ask for directions. Valquist rolled down the window. The Count leaned against the car as he was talking and unobtrusively kicked the tire. Valquist explained he didn't know the area. The Count thanked him and walked away. Malachy finished filling his car with gas and resumed the trip with Valquist following.

At the cottage, Malachy pulled into the long driveway and drove up to the parking area close to the front door. Valquist followed into the driveway, but stopped his car far from the front door and waited. When Malachy walked back to the car, Valquist rolled down the window.

"I think you picked up something in your front tire on the drive here," Malachy said. "It looked a little flat to me as I came down the driveway. Do you have a spare?"

"Damn! I hope the spare is still good," Valquist said as he got out of the car. "I've never had to use it."

Valquist joined Malachy in examining the front tire.

"It's definitely losing air," Malachy said. "You won't be able to drive on it. Let's change it and then you can deal with Bari."

Valquist went to the trunk and pulled out the spare, a lug wrench, and a jack. He bounced the spare on the driveway.

"It seems like it's okay," Valquist said.

Valquist started to position the jack under the front of the car.

"Let's loosen the lug nuts first," Malachy said. "It's easier when the tire is still on the ground."

Malachy took the wrench, pried the hubcap off, and started loosening a lug nut. Valquist stood behind Malachy, watching. Suddenly Kevin, Bari, and the Irish wolfhound emerged from a wooded area and started toward the car.

"Who's that?" Valquist asked in a panicky voice.

Malachy stood up and waved to the group.

"It's my associate Kevin with Fr. Bari. I didn't know they were out for a walk. The dog is skittish with strangers. Just stand completely still until Kevin talks with you and reassures the dog you're all right."

Valquist stood frozen in place, eyeing the dog nervously. When the group reached the car, Malachy introduced Valquist.

"This is my associate Kevin and, of course, Fr. Bari. This is Joe Valquist. He's a member of Fight Abuse. We ran into each other at church. Kevin, would you make sure Fergus knows Joe is not a threat?"

Kevin walked over to Joe with his hand held out.

"Nice to meet you, Joe," Kevin said, shaking Joe's partially extended hand. "Shake with Fergus that way he knows you're a friend."

"Friendshake," Kevin said firmly to the dog.

Fergus sat and raised his paw, and Valquist briefly shook it as Fergus sniffed his hand.

Bari started toward Valquist with his hand out.

"I'm glad to meet you," Bari said.

"Keep your distance," Valquist said angrily.

Bari stopped and gave Malachy a puzzled look.

"He has met with Pace as part of his work with the Fight Abuse organization," Malachy said. "He believes you are responsible for Pace's abuse. He only came here to verify your whereabouts. Unfortunately, he also believes you're a psychopathic liar who has successfully duped me."

Malachy turned to Valquist and asked pleasantly, "Does that about sum it up, Joe?"

Valquist looked warily at the three men and the dog without responding.

"I didn't understand," Bari said. "I apologize for causing you any distress. I wouldn't have approached the car if I had known the situation."

"I just want to fix my flat and get the hell out of here," Valquist said.

"Will do," Malachy said.

Malachy resumed loosening the lug nuts. A pickup truck stopped on the road and then backed into the driveway. A loud backfiring noise filled the air.

"Weapon!" Kevin shouted. "Everybody down!"

Malachy grabbed Valquist and pulled him to the ground. Kevin pushed Bari to the ground behind the car and then shouted at Fergus to attack. Barking furiously, the dog bounded up the driveway toward the backed-up truck. The truck shot forward with the tires squealing.

"Everybody to the cottage!" Kevin commanded. "Now!"

Kevin ran down the driveway toward the road calling to Fergus. Malachy leaped up and shouted at Valquist and Bari to run to the house.

"Stay away from the windows," Malachy said. "I'm going to help Kevin."

The two men ran to the house. Malachy joined Kevin at the end of the driveway.

"Not too bad for off Broadway," Malachy said. "I just hope Bari doesn't ask too many questions. He has an uncanny ability to know when I'm lying."

"Nothing like a common cause to create camaraderie," Kevin said. "Why don't you take your car and give chase? The Count could probably use a decent cup of coffee by now. I'll go back to the cottage and tell them it will take a little longer to secure the property. Hopefully all the adrenalin got them talking."

"Valquist wants to talk," Malachy said. "Let's hope that all the action loosened the right part of the anatomy."

Kevin entered the cottage and found Valquist and Bari sitting on the kitchen floor.

"Was that really gunfire? Valquist asked.

"There was a weapon—a rifle," Kevin said. "But I think the truck was rigged to backfire."

"Was it Flynn?" Bari asked.

"I don't think so," Kevin said. "That was an amateur stunt, and I don't think Flynn is an amateur at anything he puts his mind to. Malachy is trying to find the truck. I'm going to secure the property with Fergus. I'll be back. Just stay put."

"Aren't you going to call the police?" Valquist asked.

"Absolutely not," Kevin said. "The whole purpose in coming up here is to attract Flynn. We don't want the police involved in anyway."

"Who is Flynn?" Valquist asked.
"I'll let Fr. Bari explain," Kevin said.

Kevin returned in a half hour. Bari and Valquist were still sitting on the kitchen floor.

"Everything checked out. Joe, I changed your tire. Malachy called, he didn't have any luck in finding the intruder. But, he did find a gas station that is open and will fix your flat. He says there is no way you should try and drive home on that temporary spare, if you're going home. The gas station is just this side of the interstate. He'll wait for you there."

"I'm going home," Valquist said.

Valquist got up from the floor and started toward the front door of the cottage.

"Please wait," Bari said.

Valquist stopped and turned around. Bari quickly wrote a number on a notepad and offered it to him.

"No matter what you want to say to me, I hope you'll call."

Valquist took the note. "I'll think about it."

Malachy waved to Valquist as he pulled into the station and directed him to park at the side of the station.

"Pop the trunk and I'll grab the flat," Malachy said.

"That's not necessary," Valquist said.

"I feel kind of responsible for your flat and for subjecting you to that show at the cottage. I was the one who encouraged you to follow me back to the cottage. Let me take care of the flat."

"All right, if you insist."

Malachy took the flat and went into the garage and returned with two cups of coffee.

"He got right on it. It won't be long. Hope you like the coffee. I'm going to head back to the cottage."

"Thanks," Valquist said, taking the paper cup. "I'd like to ask you a question."

"Shoot," Malachy said.

"Do you really believe this Flynn is the priest who abused Pace? His name has never surfaced in any of our work. And we keep track of every allegation and report. Our files are very extensive and comprehensive for the Chicago area."

"Before I was disbarred, I was involved in hundreds of criminal cases," Malachy said. "At my peak, I had two investigators working for me full time and some part-time help. In every case I was going to take to trial we followed the same basic method. We researched the facts—what actually happened. That is hard, painstaking, detailed work but it pays off at trial. I always knew more than the prosecution.

"Then we established facts and possible interpretations of facts that could lead to reasonable doubt. I can't tell you all the facts we have established about Bari and Flynn, but I can tell you this...," Malachy paused, drained his coffee cup, and then looked directly into Valquist's eyes, "Flynn is the priest who abused Pace and that is beyond doubt. And the files suggest Flynn's name will surface soon enough."

"What do you mean?"

"It's never just one child."

"I am going to try and keep an open mind about all of this," Valquist said.

"Good," Malachy said. "Safe home."

CHAPTER XVI

Malachy entered the Shamrock and looked for Bridget, who was behind the empty bar. There were a few customers at tables in the barroom and in the back room. He approached the bar and winced when Bridget started in at him in a low voice.

"The absentee landlord deigns to visit the peasants. We *are* honored! How were things in London?"

"I was in Wisconsin," Malachy said. "And things there were fine, but busy. No time to check in, but I knew things would run right with you in charge."

"That bullshit buys you nothing."

"I figured if you had a problem, you'd call on my cell," Malachy said.

Bridget picked up the bar telephone and energetically punched in a number. Malachy's cell phone rang. He dug the phone out of his pocket.

"This is Malachy."

"Your Lordship, there was a problem on the Estate."

"What kind of a problem?" Malachy asked, talking into the phone and looking at Bridget.

"A knife fight."

"Jesus!" Malachy said. "What happened?"

"Mayhem, your Lordship, mayhem!"

"Bridget, for the love of God, will you drop this lordship shit, and tell me what the hell happened?"

Malachy clicked his phone off and headed to his office-booth, yelling at Eduardo. "Take over the bar!"

Bridget followed Malachy to the booth and sat across from him.

"So, what happened?" Malachy asked.

"The new dishwasher, Charles, and one of the busboys, Jose, got into it. Not sure how it happened, but a bucketful of dishes fell on the floor and shattered. Words and curses were exchanged, and things escalated quickly. That Jose is a hothead. He grabbed a kitchen knife and backed Charles through the swinging doors and into the barroom—and that's when Sean got involved."

"Sean? Now I'm getting nervous."

"Sean stepped between them and pulled out that switchblade he carries, clicked it open, and ordered Jose to drop the knife and go back into the kitchen. All in Spanish and very forceful."

"And?"

"Jose dropped the knife, returned to the kitchen, and started to clean up the dishes."

"Where were you?" Malachy asked.

"Behind the bar getting the baseball bat. I sent both of them home just to make sure there wasn't another flare-up."

"I didn't know Sean speaks Spanish."

"Neither did I."

"Anyway, no real harm done. So, what's the problem?" Malachy asked.

Bridget looked exasperated and said, "Let me spell it out for you." She began to write with her forefinger in the air.

"Just tell me," Malachy said.

"I'm not allowed to fire anybody without your permission."

"Who do you want to fire?"

"Take a guess."

"He's an illegal with a family," Malachy said.

"Whose problem is that?"

"Isn't there another solution?" Malachy asked

"Sure," Bridget said. "Have Sean patrol the kitchen, switchblade in hand. And that has another advantage—it would keep his unpaid bar bill from increasing so rapidly."

"When did this happen?"

"Yesterday."

"Are they both due to work today?"

"Yes, in about an hour."

"Close the back room to the public," Malachy said. "Kevin will be here in a few minutes. When they show up, send them to the back room with Kevin to babysit. Tell Kevin to make sure neither one has any kind of a weapon. He'll know what to do."

"Then what?" Bridget asked.

"A bench trial," Malachy said.

"Do I get a say?"

"No, you're biased against Jose."

"I knew you'd piss me off and you've only been back for twenty minutes," Bridget said. "This job sucks."

"But think of all the tremendous fringe benefits," Malachy said.

"Like what?"

"How happy you are when I'm not here. And guess what? I'm not going to be here a whole lot over the next few weeks."

"Good," Bridget said. "Are you hungry? Want something to eat?"

"I'm starving," Malachy said. "I'd love some breakfast after the trial—in about an hour. A hungry judge makes for a short trial."

"We don't serve breakfast, remember?"

"Yeah, but you're the boss and can make it happen if you choose to," Malachy said.

Bridget got up and headed back to the bar, shaking her head and talking to Malachy over her shoulder. "What kind of boss can't fire anybody? I'm telling you this job sucks."

Malachy decided silence was the best way to earn breakfast.

†

Malachy went out the Shamrock's front entrance and looked up and down the street for the Count. He wasn't sure which vehicle from the Count's small fleet would be in use, but he knew whether converted cab, modified truck, or van it would be clean and shiny. He spotted a clean white van across the street and started toward it. The Count climbed out of the passenger side and waited for Malachy on the sidewalk.

"How did it go?" Malachy asked.

"As planned," the Count said.

"How many?"

"Two crews of three and one ringer," the Count said. "Each crew thinks the ringer works for the other crew. I guarantee you that rectory will be so clean it will squeak in Polish."

"I hope the Italian housekeeper isn't too insulted," Malachy said.

"She'll be insulted after the fact. We picked her day off."

"You know I have to ask," Malachy said.

"Yes," the Count said. "They will find every bug. Relax. The ringer has the special equipment and knows how to use it. If the Feds examine the trash, they will find their bugs nestled next to empty bottles of Mr. Clean."

"And there is no way to trace the ringer?"

"Absolutely not. She'll pay the cleaning crews in cash, get paid in cash herself, and be on the plane back to Poland tonight. She very much appreciated the chance to visit with some of her family before the operation started. Even if the Feds have surveillance on who enters and leaves, all they will get is a picture of a rather plain-looking cleaning lady with a nondescript figure. Too bad."

"Why too bad?" Malachy asked.

The Count turned and gave Malachy a smug, satisfied smile.

"Because she is a rather handsome woman who stays in shape," the Count said.

"What happened to the no-fraternization rule?"

"Operational necessity," the Count said.

"Of course," Malachy said. "Necessity is the father of erection or however that saying goes."

"How true, how true," the Count said happily. "Now I have a question."

"Yes," Malachy said. "The cover story will hold up at least until we have completed the job. Hopefully by that point the Feds will have established for themselves that Bari is not involved in Dino's scheme, and they won't want to spend any resources on finding out how their bugging operation got screwed up. But it might piss off somebody."

"Then you get a visit," the Count said.

"For sure, and you too. They know I'm involved and they know we work together and they know you're Polish. So they'll try to find a link to the cleaning crews."

"Doesn't exist," the Count said.

"So then they question the private security on why they let the crews in, and the trail heads back to Dino, their employer. And by that time, Dino will only be talking to his lawyer. And an additional count of obstruction of justice will be the least of his problems."

"And what will be his greatest problem?"

"How our nameless employer reacts to the news that Dino involved Fr. Bari and the Shrine in his tax fraud scheme. For Dino's sake, I hope they are boyhood friends or something."

"Me too," the Count said. "The man dresses well—has a sense of style."

"Unlike your present company?"

"What do you have against pressed clothes? That practice antedates the Anglo-Saxon so it can't be an ethnic prejudice."

"The time it takes... Let's head back in to the Shamrock. I don't want to be late for the bench trial."

"Punctuality and unwrinkled robes befit a judge," the Count said.

"Funny thing," Malachy said. "Monihan was the most sartorially perfect and punctual judge I ever appeared before—and the most crooked."

"As you argued to many a jury, correlation does not imply causation," the Count said.

†

Malachy entered the Shamrock's backroom and greeted Kevin. "How are the prisoners in the dock behaving?" Malachy asked.

"Showing signs of anxiety about their fate," Kevin said.

"Approach the bench," Malachy said to Jose and Charles, indicating an imaginary bench with his hands. "Kevin, please translate for Jose. Jose, what happened in the kitchen?"

Kevin translated the question, and Jose responded in a stream of rapid, excited Spanish with an exaggerated mimicking of Charles, with his hands shaking violently, dropping the bucket of dishes.

"Charles dropped the bucket because his hands were shaking," Kevin said.

"Charles, were your hands shaking?" Malachy asked

"They've been shaking pretty bad this last week," Charles answered. "But, Jose didn't wait until I had both hands on the bucket—he let it go when I had only one hand on it, that's why it dropped."

"Jose, what did you say to Charles after the dishes broke?" Malachy asked.

Jose gave another long answer in Spanish without waiting for the translation.

"He doesn't remember exactly what he said because he was very mad and upset," Kevin said. "He was afraid of Bridget—that she would yell at him and make him pay for the dishes, and he needs the money to send to his family in Mexico."

"The judge rules that fear of Bridget is most definitely an extenuating circumstance, and the judge notes that he personally has witnessed such fear causing irrational behavior in otherwise rational persons," Malachy said.

Kevin translated that into Spanish as "the boss understands what you're saying."

"Charles, what did Jose say to you and what did you say to him after the dishes broke?" Malachy asked.

"He started yelling in Spanish but kept saying nigger in English. I told him to shut his motherfucking mouth and that's when he picked up the knife."

"Okay," Malachy said. "I think we know what happened and why. We don't need any testimony about the knife because there is no disagreement on that. I am ready to rule. Both of you sit down."

Kevin translated, and Jose and Charles sat down with Kevin standing between them with a hand gripping the back of each man's chair. Malachy looked at Jose and guessed his weight at a maximum of 140 and no taller than 5'6". Charles had four inches and forty pounds on him. No wonder he chose a knife over taking a swing.

"Jose, you made the right decision to follow Sean's orders and end the incident and that is in your favor. And it's a good thing you did so because otherwise you would now be jobless with a broken arm."

Malachy paused and let Kevin translate.

"But the Shamrock cannot have working conditions where any employee is in fear of life or limb from any other employee with the notable exception of Bridget as the fear inducer."

Kevin translated this as "nobody working at the Shamrock should have to be afraid of being stabbed when they come to work."

"Therefore, I rule that your continued employment is up to Charles and Kevin. Both must agree."

Kevin translated this as "you still have a job if Charles and I agree. Now don't say a word in Spanish or in English."

Malachy turned to Charles.

"Are you willing to give Jose another chance, or do you want him to be fired?"

"I don't want anybody fired on my account," Charles said.

"Kevin?"

Kevin grabbed Jose by the collar and dragged him into a corner of the room. Kevin faced Jose to him, thrust his hands under his armpits, and bumped him up the wall until he was eye level with Kevin. After two minutes of hushed, intense conversation in Spanish, they returned and stood in front of Malachy.

"I agree to Jose keeping his job," Kevin said.

"So be it," Malachy said. "One more ruling. Jose, do not hand any more buckets to Charles. Place them on the counter next to the sink. If the counter is full, place them on the floor. Do you understand?"

Kevin translated and Jose nodded his head yes.

"Okay, everybody back to work," Malachy said. "With great hope that breakfast is waiting, this court is adjourned."

Jose and Charles headed toward the kitchen.

"What did you say to Jose?" Malachy asked Kevin.

"We had a 'come to Jesus' moment," Kevin said. "Literally. I made him hold the cross he wears around his neck and swear he would never pick up a kitchen knife in anger again. And I gave him permission to leave the kitchen and go outside anytime he was upset no matter what was going on. And I promised I would talk to Bridget about easing up on him in my absence."

"Do you think it will work?"

"I do," Kevin said. "I could tell by the look in his eyes when I had him up against the wall that I was getting through."

"Good," Malachy said. "I don't want to fire him. He's a hard worker with a big family. I'll leave it to you to explain the program to Bridget."

"A wise and rational decision, Judge."

Malachy entered the barroom, moved to his office-booth, and asked Eduardo for coffee.

"Mr. Malachy, I bring the breakfast in five minutes."

"The judge will wait patiently," Malachy responded.

Eduardo left to go into the kitchen and Malachy drank his coffee and thought about the punctual, corrupt Monihan, who the Feds eventually wired up, and his innocent client Daniel.

"Make sure the kid gets off," Jack Lynch said. *"It will kill Louise if her kid does time and I need her. She runs the whole household and does the cooking. You know what my stomach is like—I'm telling you I need her. I'll pay what it takes, but make sure the kid gets off. Do what you have to do, but no jail time."*

Louise Tate worked cleaning and cooking for North Shore families, doing everything she could to keep Daniel straight and get him an education. And then the full-time and more job with the Lynch family. Ten years, never a Christmas just with her own family, but good pay. And every spare dime into savings for Daniel's education.

"Can you help him, Mr. Madden, can you help him?" she asked, fretting, nervous. *"I know he's innocent. I pray you can help him."*

Malachy determined Daniel was in fact innocent. Not as in "not guilty beyond a reasonable doubt," not as in innocent this time but did it many times before, but innocent as in not there, nothing to do with it. Truly innocent beyond any doubt. A trifecta of cross-checking established that fact. First, Malachy did everything but torture Daniel to crack his story. There were no inconsistencies, no gaps, everything computed. Second, Kevin went through his life with a fine-tooth comb in one hand and a vacuum cleaner in the other.

He turned up nothing. Third, Malachy pressed his private cop network for an answer off-the-record. The network was strangely silent. Malachy pressed even harder, calling in old favors. Finally, he got the call.

The arresting detective had made an undercover buy of cocaine from a young black male who bolted before the arrest could be made. Daniel and two friends were smoking pot in the vicinity after coming out of a music club. The detective, boozed and pissed off, cruised the neighborhood looking for his collar and spotted Daniel and his friends and ID'd Daniel as the cocaine seller. The detective's testimony was locked in and would not change, and good luck in trying to impeach it. Detective Francis Boyle—when sober—delivers compelling testimony. Juries think he is Sergeant Joe Friday reincarnated—no bias, all facts. Plead it down and move on.

The counter to Boyle is the testimony of two pothead friends with no jobs and too many priors. Malachy filed every motion he could think, stalling until something could change the equation. Eventually the trial took place. Malachy could not shake Boyle's "testilying." Malachy knew he was losing the jury and that he had no defense case to put on to bring the jury back. But a corrupt judge trumps a corrupt detective—directed verdict of not guilty.

Sean approached him in the office-booth. Malachy was surprised to see him carrying a small overnight bag.

"Sean, is something wrong? You're never here this early."

"Could I speak with you in private?" Sean asked.

"Of course," Malachy said. "Let's go into the storeroom. It is the most private place in the Shamrock. Follow me. Do you want something to drink?"

"Could I get just a half glass of red wine?"

"Done," Malachy said.

Malachy yelled to Eduardo to bring wine and coffee to the storeroom for both of them and to put his breakfast on hold. After Eduardo closed the storeroom door, Malachy raised his glass in salute.

"Thanks for your intervention the other day," Malachy said. "Your decisive action kept things under control."

"I could do no less under the circumstances," Sean said. "May I speak to you in confidence about a matter of the heart?"

Malachy put down his glass and tried to match Sean's serious tone and formal language.

"I will reveal nothing of what you tell me without your prior permission."

"I have told you in the past in bits and pieces about some of my romantic interests…"

"Yes, I recall," Malachy said.

"That younger Italian woman I was so infatuated with is returning to Chicago for a visit, and I have a problem."

Sean paused and took a drink of his wine.

"As I recall, she is first generation Italian-American and a professor of literature in Italy somewhere," Malachy said.

"Yes," Sean said. "In Rome. She is also a poet—albeit a struggling one—and much admires my work."

"As does any serious student of poetry," Malachy said.

"Thank you," Sean said. "She is coming to Chicago for a conference at the University of Chicago. And she wants to meet with me to go over her latest work. We have been corresponding since she left for Rome. The problem is…I have not been forthcoming about my current domestic situation."

"That you are now living with Sarah," Malachy said.

"Yes," Sean said. "As you know, that's a very complicated situation."

Malachy knew "complicated" was code for the apartment and most everything in it belonged to Sarah, that Sarah paid the rent, that Sean could not afford his own place, that Sean often sought refuge in the Shamrock from Sarah's loud bitching, but that there was some connection between Sean and Sarah that worked for both of them.

"In truth," Sean said, "that is not the real problem. The real problem is I don't want to tell Carla about Sarah. I don't want that to potentially affect our meeting. I often dream about a meeting with Carla with— well with Eros unbound. It never happened in our past meetings. I believe she could be attracted to me in that way, but we were never in circumstances that allowed for any romance."

"I take it you would like for that to change on this visit," Malachy said.

"Precisely. You are a man of the world. May I speak frankly about this?"

"Certainly," Malachy said, still trying to match Sean's serious tone.

Malachy enjoyed his friendship with Sean for many reasons including talks like this one when he felt he was suddenly transported into a 1940s movie.

"Carla's poems suggest there have been more than a few intense, brief erotic encounters—passions of the moment that she has reveled in, rode the whirlwind so to speak, and then moved on. I have often imagined myself as one of those passions. I...I yearn to be one of those passions. But, as you know, my pecuniary resources are limited. Sarah watches for my pension check like a hawk. I hesitated to come to you because my unpaid bill here at the Shamrock is already substantial...."

Malachy interrupted. "Consider that cancelled as a small way of saying thanks for your intervention of the other day. If things had gotten out of hand, God only knows what the financial consequences would have been."

"That is very generous, thank you," Sean said. "Would it be possible to advance me $300 in cash? I could pay it back by..."

Malachy interrupted again.

"Sean, the $300 is no problem. We'll worry about the repayment program later. But is that enough?"

"I have made some discreet inquiries into the cost of a dinner with wine and a room afterward, and I believe if I managed prudently..."

"Isn't passionate prudence a kind of oxymoron?" Malachy asked.

Sean gave a shy smile and said, "Yes, I suppose it is. What do you suggest?"

"I suggest we call in my colleague the Count. He is very experienced in these matters. In fact, one could even term him an expert."

"If you think that is best, I concur," Sean said.

"Good. I will call and ask him to return to the Shamrock. We can reconvene our meeting in about an hour. In the meantime, please join me for breakfast in my booth."

The Count listened to Sean carefully without interrupting. When Sean finished, he got up and paced back and forth in the narrow space of the storeroom without saying a word. Then he sat down and gave his opinion.

"Sean, you have constructed an excellent plan given the circumstances and resources. But I believe it does not maximize the probability of success. May I suggest an alternative?"

"As you know my resources are constrained," Sean said, "but I am open to new ideas."

"Good," the Count said. "The resources expended in my plan are not great and even do double duty. First, in this type of operation, commercial establishments are fraught with dangerous potential. We will use Malachy's place instead."

"We will?" Malachy asked.

The Count shot Malachy a look that asked "are we going to do this right or not?"

"Of course, my place is available," a chastened Malachy said.

"Its present condition is unacceptable, but I will arrange for that to be corrected—and that's the double duty part," the Count said. "Malachy will benefit permanently from the changes we make to his place."

Malachy rolled his eyes but kept silent.

"Second, we will transport Carla from the university to Malachy's by private car. To say the least, the CTA, subway or elevated, does not qualify as romantic."

"I do not own an automobile," Sean said.

"Of course not," the Count said. "Why would you? But in my plan you won't be fetching Carla anyway. We will be sending Eduardo. I will provide a suitable vehicle. You see that way we are setting the right mood and tone. Naturally, there will be a small welcoming basket for her on the backseat containing bottled water, some fresh fruit, dark chocolate, and, most important, a welcoming note from you—or better yet a short poem. Is that possible?"

"Yes," Sean said. "I can do that."

"Good," the Count said. "Now we are making progress. What's Carla's favorite festive drink?"

"One poem refers to prosecco," Sean said.

"Excellent," the Count said. "That is what you'll welcome her with at the apartment and sip while you do your critique of her poetry. After the review of her work, there will be a more formal cocktail hour with caviar and the like. You will be dining in. Is she a vegetarian?"

"No," Sean said.

"Good," the Count said. "That makes planning easier. Give me a little time here to make a list."

Malachy and Sean made small talk while the Count made a series of notes. After ten minutes, the Count announced the plan was ready.

"The apartment will be totally reworked. I will not bother you with all the details except to say the end result will be comfortable and sensuous."

"What happens to my stuff?" Malachy asked.

"All of your…," the Count smiled at Malachy, "stuff we don't use will be locked in the spare bedroom."

"That bedroom doesn't have a lock," Malachy said.

"It will when we are done," the Count said.

"Who is this 'we'?" Malachy asked suspiciously.

"A cleaning crew of three, two all-purpose handymen who will double as movers, and me," the Count said.

"Jesus," Malachy said. "No paint, and I mean it. No paint!"

"Very well," the Count said, scratching an item from his list. "Touch up paint only. In order of priority, we will redo the bathroom, the bedroom, the living room, and then the kitchen."

"I keep a clean bathroom," Malachy said.

"Of course you do," the Count said. "That's not the point. We need a place that invites a woman to bathe or shower before or after."

Sean interrupted and said, "I think there's a misunderstanding. I am supposed to meet Carla this afternoon."

"No misunderstanding," the Count said. "As they say in the military, 'amateurs talk strategy, professionals talk logistics.' Under my supervision, six hours is more than enough time to purchase sheets, towels, robes, fixtures, etc.; to install everything; and to transform the apartment."

Sean turned to Malachy and said, "I don't want to cause…"

Malachy said, "Sean, the Count is the expert. And anyway he's right. My place could use a little work. Double duty is the order of the day."

"Good," the Count said. "Back to the list. For music, I suggest harp music in the background while the two of you are working. And for the more formal cocktail hour, of course, Chopin. After that it depends on the how the campaign is going. My recommendation is for the dinner to be celebratory rather than anticipatory. But in these matters, opportunity must rule."

"I understand," Sean said.

The Count checked his watch.

"Time for action. I won't bother you with the rest of the list now. Sean, I will explain everything when we walk the terrain together at 3:00 P.M."

"Can I help in some way?" Sean asked.

The Count consulted his list.

"In fact I have you scheduled for several trips. To my barber and then to the Russian baths for a good sweat, a rubdown, and a short nap. And we need to fit in a light lunch and time to compose your welcoming poem."

"Sarah will question me about my changed appearance," Sean said.

"Tell her the truth," the Count said. "Just not the whole truth."

"What did you tell Sarah about being away overnight?" Malachy asked.

"I had a reading in Milwaukee," Sean said. "And the discussion afterward would likely extend past the time of the last train home. She wasn't that interested—just told me not to call late and wake her up."

"Time to launch," the Count said.

The Count made three cell phone calls in quick succession, speaking rapid Polish each time. All Malachy could make out was his address, which the Count made each listener repeat in English.

"Two more things," the Count said to Malachy. "I will need Eduardo for the whole day until he escorts Carla to your apartment, and the key to your place would make things easier."

Malachy reluctantly handed over the key.

"I think we'll let Kevin explain to Bridget why Eduardo will be unavailable for the day," Malachy said.

"Where will you spend the night?" Sean asked.

"A rectory," Malachy said. "Ironic, don't you think?"

"Under the circumstances, better you than Sean," the Count said.

CHAPTER XVII

"Malachy, Malachy, wake up," Fr. Bari said in a whisper.

Malachy raised his head from the pillow and tried to see Bari in the darkness.

"What's the matter?" Malachy asked in a low voice.

"I heard something downstairs. I think there's somebody down there. I couldn't sleep. I know I heard something—not just normal house noises. And nothing in my room works."

Malachy motioned for Bari to sit in the chair next to the bed and put his finger to his lips to signal silence. Malachy checked the room. The clock radio and the night-light in the bathroom were off. Malachy checked his cell phone and unplugged the charger and plugged it back in. Nothing happened.

Malachy slid from the bed and found his oversized gym bag with his equipment. Malachy quickly put on his special protective clothing, including a policeman's Kevlar vest, steel-toed boots, and a kind of tool belt. He clipped cuffs and other equipment to his belt. When he was fully dressed, Malachy pulled Bari close to him and whispered in his ear.

"You need to stay here. I am going to check things out. Where is the main fuse box?"

"In the center of the west wall in the basement," Bari whispered back.

Malachy reached into his bag and pulled out a wedge and a cell phone. He took two pillows and a blanket from the bed and handed it all to Bari.

"I will close the bedroom door behind me. Put the wedge under the door and lock the door, and then go into the bathroom, lock that door, and get into the tub. Keep your whole body below the top of the bathtub, especially your head.

"Check the time on the phone when you get into the bathtub. If I don't call you within thirty minutes exactly, call 911 and tell the operator there's a fire in the rectory and you're trapped in the upstairs guest bathroom and give the address. Don't get out of the bathtub until you are sure it's a fireman outside the door, no matter what you hear. Understand?"

Bari nodded yes.

"Good," Malachy said. "Now repeat to me what you are going to do."

Bari repeated the instructions. Malachy reached into the bag and pulled out a combination flashlight–stun gun and clipped it to his belt. He took out night-vision goggles from the bag and put them on. He motioned for Bari to follow him to the door and to flatten himself against the wall. Malachy unclipped a black, folding-cane device from his belt, bent it staircase-style, placed his baseball cap on the vertical arm, and slowly opened the door. Malachy positioned the hat so it matched his height and slowly pushed it out the door and held it there. Nothing happened. Malachy slipped through the door, closing it behind him.

Malachy stood still and slowly and methodically examined the hallway from one end to the other. Everything seemed normal. Bari's bedroom door was closed. He realized there was no way to secure the second floor in the allotted time—too many rooms. And there was no way to know if the security men outside were neutralized or involved.

He silently dropped to the floor and began to gradually move down the hallway toward Bari's room. He stopped every few feet and listened. On the third stop he heard the sounds of someone in Bari's room. He military crawled to the wall next to Bari's bedroom door, sat on the floor with his back against the wall, and listened.

It sounded as if someone was moving around the room scraping the walls. From the pattern of the noises, Malachy guessed there was only one intruder in the bedroom. Malachy concentrated on examining the staircase and trying to listen for noise from the first floor. He calculated any backup was far enough away that he could incapacitate the bedroom intruder and still have time to deal with any threat from a backup charging up the stairs.

Malachy primed the stun gun and waited.

The bedroom door opened and a flashlight beam swept the hallway and staircase. The intruder stepped into the hallway. Malachy grabbed a leg, drove the stun gun into the intruder's thigh, and fired. The intruder howled and fell hard on the floor writhing in pain. Malachy waited a few seconds and then threw himself on top of the intruder with his full weight. The intruder was wearing a lightweight rain suit with slip-on covers over his shoes.

Malachy quickly forced the man on his stomach and cuffed his hands behind his back. He slapped a piece of tape on his mouth and taped his ankles together. He grabbed the intruder's flashlight, clicked it off, and rolled over to the opposite wall that intersected with the staircase. He braced himself against the wall and listened for sounds of a backup. He heard nothing.

After a few minutes, the bound intruder started to stir. Malachy rolled over next to him, jammed the stun gun between his legs and into his crotch. He put his head close to the intruder's.

"Is there anybody with you?" Malachy whispered in the intruder's ear. "Nod yes or no. The wrong answer gets you another zap."

Malachy prodded him with the stun gun. The intruder vigorously shook his head no.

"Now, listen carefully," Malachy whispered. "I'm leaving for a few minutes. Don't make any noise or move your position while I'm gone. Understand?"

Malachy prodded him again with the stun–flashlight. He nodded yes.

"Good," Malachy said.

Malachy clipped the stun gun to his belt, rolled to the top of the stairs, and started to slide down the steps. At the landing, he paused and checked the time on his cell phone. There were thirteen minutes until Bari called the fire department.

He slid down the remainder of the stairs to the first floor, crawled over to the wall next to the basement door, and stood up. The house was still silent with no signs of another intruder and the only light coming from the outside. He pushed the basement door open. There was no response. He attached the flashlight to his folding rod device, turned it on, and quickly moved it three feet away from his body.

He moved the flashlight into the entranceway to the basement. Again, there was no response. He went down the basement stairs on his back with the flashlight high above him, scanning the basement. At the bottom of the stairs, he found the fuse box with the flashlight beam. He decided to change tactics.

He strode quickly to the box, threw the switch to on, ran back and up the stairs two at a time. At the top of the stairs, he paused for a second to listen, dropped down, and rolled out the door. He jumped up, closed the basement door, and placed a wedge under it. He called Bari.

"Everything is okay. Don't call the fire department, just stay put. I'll be there in a few minutes."

"What was that scream? It sounded horrible."

"I'll show you in a minute," Malachy said. "But, don't worry, nobody is really hurt."

Malachy moved into the kitchen and turned the lights on. He went from room to room on the first floor turning on lights.

The rectory phone rang.

"This is Malachy."

"What the hell is going on? Why are all the lights going on?"

Malachy considered letting the security detail check out the house, but rejected the idea because he didn't know how the intruder got in.

"Bad nightmares," Malachy said. "My screaming woke Fr. Bari up. So we decided to have an early breakfast and get started on the day. Sorry, I should've called you, but I didn't want to wake you up."

"You're definitely a fucking fruitcake. And we were awake, asshole."

"Well, anyway, everything is fine here. I bid you a good morning."

Malachy charged up the stairs to the second floor, taking the steps two at a time. He stepped over the bound intruder.

"Just stay still. I'll be back to talk with you in a second."

He entered Bari's bedroom and clicked on the overhead light. He primed the stun gun and pulled the closet door open. Empty. He checked under the bed and found nothing.

Suddenly he stopped his adrenalin-fueled search and looked at the walls. They were covered with enlarged photographs of Bari engaged in homosexual sex acts. Malachy turned on the rest of the lights and began to examine the photographs.

The photos were of Bari as a younger man with a clearly older man. Malachy recognized Fischer, Bari's teacher at the seminary. Malachy examined the photos' background and the foreground. Most were in a woods or park-like setting.

In all the photographs with Fischer, Bari was the one performing oral sex. There were two photographs of Bari in a picnic *ménage à trios* with men his own age. In both of those Bari was the man in the middle.

There was a note printed on the clearest photograph of Bari engaged in anal intercourse with Fischer. "Tell Malachy to stop now or all of these will be released on the Internet."

"Jesus fucking Christ," Malachy muttered. "Win the battle, lose the war."

Malachy short-circuited an impulse to rip the pictures down. He decided to let the Count remove them to preserve anything that might help. He went out into the hall, closing the bedroom door behind him. He ignored the intruder and moved rapidly down the hall to the other bedrooms.

In each room, he turned on all the lights, did a quick check of the closets and under the beds, and then taped the doors shut. He decided it was safe enough to let Bari out of the bathtub. He called his cell phone.

"Bath time is over," Malachy said. "You can move into the room, but keep the door locked and closed with the wedge and the lights off."

"Is everything all right?" Bari asked. "Is anybody hurt?"

"Nobody hurt," Malachy said, adding a silent *yet*. "See you in ten minutes."

He went to the end of the hallway out of earshot of both the intruder and Bari and called the Count.

"Good morning, this is Malachy. Somebody broke into the rectory in order to put up some incriminating photos of Bari. The intruder is packaged up, awaiting questioning. I need you and Kevin to do a full security check of the rectory and to figure out how he got in. And to deal with the photographs. Bring what you think you'll need. There won't be any security check, just ring the front doorbell."

"I'll call you when we're twenty minutes away," the Count said. "And I hope the morning's activity doesn't put you off early rising."

"I'm just about to go dig for worms," Malachy said. "See you when you get here."

Malachy took the cell phone he was given by his nameless, faceless employer from his belt and pushed the preprogrammed number. The phone rang a couple of times and was automatically transferred twice before it was answered.

"This is Malachy. I need some special information as soon as possible."

"Hang up."

Malachy clicked off the phone and waited. A few minutes later the phone rang.

"What do you need?"

"Somebody broke into the rectory. I have the situation under control. There are a number of yet unanswered questions about how and why. I need Fr. Bari to be taken as soon as possible to a secure location that only you know about. I want the current security to be removed without causing any alarm. I will take full responsibility for Fr. Bari's security until you pick him up."

"Hold."

Malachy waited.

"The security is gone. We will pick him up in ninety minutes. The man who comes to the door will hand you an index card with a circled number eleven on it. Tell Fr. Bari to pack some reading materials. There's no TV or Internet at the new location. Call when you want him back. Add 'important' to the formulation when you call. Good luck."

Malachy knew the new location might be two blocks or two hundred miles away. But he wouldn't have to worry about Bari for the duration. All resources would be needed to find Flynn and his stash of pictures. And the shortest route to Flynn was through the intruder. Time for that talk.

Malachy knocked on his bedroom door.

"It's Malachy. Stay put. I need some more time."

"What going on?" Bari asked. "Is anybody hurt?"

"Nobody is hurt. I just need a few more minutes to make sure everything is secure. It will be over soon, just stay put."

"All right. Be careful."

Malachy grabbed the bound intruder by the collar of his rain suit and dragged him into Bari's bedroom, closing the door behind him. He propped him up in a chair and closed the bedroom door. Malachy set another chair across from him and sat so close their knees were touching. Malachy unclipped his stun gun and started to toss it methodically between his hands, staring into the intruder's eyes and saying nothing.

Malachy reached a silent count of fifty when he thought he saw the right amount of fear in the young man's eyes.

"I am going to ask you some questions," Malachy said in a low intense voice. "If you tell the truth, only good things will happen to you. If you lie or withhold, only bad things will happen to you. Do not shout or yell. Understand?"

The young man nodded his head up and down. Malachy reached up and ripped the tape from his mouth.

"Please don't…"

"Shut up and listen to me. What's your name?"

"Conrad."

"Who gave you those pictures?"

"He called himself Jonah."

"Describe him," Malachy commanded.

"I don't…"

"Young or old?"

"Older."

"Fat or thin?"

"Medium."

"Tall or short?"

"Shorter."

Malachy wanted to make sure Conrad's memory was not impaired by too much stress.

"So far, so good," Malachy said. "I'm going to put this away as long as you're telling the truth and cooperating."

Malachy ostentatiously clipped the stun gun to his belt.

"Where does this Jonah live?" Malachy asked in a friendlier voice.

"I don't know."

Malachy frowned.

"He made me put on a mask before we went to his place."

"How did you meet him?" Malachy asked.

"I was on the street."

"Where?"

"On the North Side, by Clark and Belmont. He picked me up. Showed me a hundred dollar bill, said I could have that and more, but he didn't want me to know where he lived so I had to wear the mask."

"How long did you drive?"

"I'm not sure. I was really strung out. All I wanted was to get the money and get some junk."

"What happened at Jonah's place?"

"Sex games, some of them weird. I had to shave down there."

"How long were you there?"

"A couple of days, I think. It was all a blur. He gave me junk, and I'd do what he wanted. I didn't care what it was."

"Did Jonah use any of the junk himself?"

"I don't think so—he didn't act like it. He seemed more interested in his games."

"Tell me about breaking in here and the photos," Malachy said. "Start at the beginning and don't leave anything out."

"I was getting desperate for a hit, begging him to give me some more. He told me I would have to earn it. If I did it right, he'd give me a week's supply and three hundred dollars. All I had to do was break into an empty old house and tape up some photos on the wall of the main bedroom. He made me wear the mask again until we got close."

"How did you get in?" Malachy asked.

"A tunnel in the basement."

"What kind of tunnel?" Malachy asked.

"I don't know. We went into an old building and down into the basement. Jonah said I would have to crawl about a hundred feet…"

"You told me you're alone," Malachy said.

"I am…I am! Jonah didn't come with me. He told me after I was done he would pick me up a block from the old building and then give me the money and the junk."

"What else did he tell you?" Malachy asked.

"He gave me a bag with this in it…," Conrad gestured to his outfit. "And he told me I'd get dirty crawling through the tunnel and should put this on before coming up stairs."

"What else?" Malachy asked.

"I should relock the swinging door that led to the tunnel when I came back and not to make any mess in the basement."

"This is important," Malachy said. "So get it right. Are you saying the door to the tunnel in the basement locks from the tunnel side?"

"Yeah," Conrad said. "It's more like a half door. There's a bolt on the tunnel side. I unlocked it to get into the basement—that's what I was supposed to relock when I left."

"Where is it in the basement?" Malachy asked.

"In the back."

"Okay, Conrad, you can relax—only good things are going to happen to you. You're doing really good. This next question is really important, so take your time. What kind of car was Jonah driving when he picked you up?"

A blank look came over Conrad's face.

"I…I've no idea. I was really strung out. It was nothing fancy, just a car."

"All right, Conrad. Here are the rules. Stay put and don't make any noise. I don't want to have to tape your mouth. Understood?"

"Yeah."

"I'll be back."

"Are you going to call the cops?"

"No, Conrad. No cops. I figure you've got enough problems. Like I said, cooperate and only good things will happen to you."

Malachy went out into the hallway, closing the door behind him. He called the Count.

"I just picked up Kevin," the Count said. "We'll be there in twenty minutes."

"Have Kevin drop you off and tell him to drive around the immediate neighborhood looking for Flynn. Start with the area within a block of the old school. Flynn is probably driving the same car that was in the video of Bari's press conference."

"What's the plan if he finds him?" the Count asked.

Malachy did not answer immediately.

"Did you hear my question?"

"I heard," Malachy said, still making up his mind. "The plan is not to let him get away. Tell Kevin to do whatever is necessary to hold him, including ramming the car. If it goes public, Kevin is making a citizen's arrest for kidnapping. I'll explain later."

"The plan is understood," the Count said. "No questions."

Malachy stood still for a minute, trying to figure his next moves. He knew the attempt to find Flynn was a real long shot. He probably parked somewhere he could see the rectory. Once all the lights started to go on, he would flee the area for home. Unless home was in the area.

Time to deal with Bari. Malachy knocked on the bedroom door.

"It's Malachy. Open up."

Malachy entered the room, locked and secured the door with the wedge just in case he was wrong about Flynn's whereabouts, and turned on the lights. He gave Bari a brief explanation of the situation, leaving out the photos on the wall.

"So after my colleague gets here and we're certain the rectory is secure, you'll need to pack," Malachy said. "Be sure to include lots of reading materials. You're going to be picked up in about an hour."

Malachy braced himself for lots of questions about where Bari was going and who was taking him.

"I want to talk to that young man," Bari said.

"I don't think that's a good idea," Malachy said.

"Malachy, I know you are trying to protect me, and I truly appreciate that. And I'll cooperate with you, but I must do my work as a priest. I must talk to that young man before I leave. He needs help."

Malachy started to curse and checked himself. He looked at Bari, whose eyes blazed with strange intensity.

"All right. I'll bring him in here. But he stays cuffed the whole time. He's jumpy because of withdrawal."

"Bring him to me."

Malachy pulled himself up to Conrad so their knees were touching.

"What's the matter?" Conrad asked.

"I need to explain something to you, and I need you to fully cooperate."

"Okay."

"This place is a rectory. The priest who lives here wants to talk with you. He's concerned about your welfare. If you want to, you can share your story with him. It's entirely up to you. But not the photos. The photos do not exist. Do you understand? The photos don't exist."

"Are the photos of him?" Conrad asked.

Malachy unclipped the stun gun from his belt.

"I don't think you understand. The photos don't exist."

"I get it. But what do I say if he asks why I broke in."

"You tell the truth," Malachy said. "You tell him that I ordered you not to talk about that to anybody, including him."

"Can I tell him about Jonah?"

"Yes. Anything else you want, but not the photos. Got it?"

"Yeah, not the photos."

"Okay, let's go."

"Malachy, leave us alone, please," Bari said.

"Okay, as long as Conrad here obeys the rules," Malachy said, as he put his hand on Conrad's shoulder and squeezed. "You have about a half hour. Do the door routine after I leave."

Malachy went downstairs to wait for the Count. When he heard a car come down the street, he checked his watch. It was eighteen minutes since he clicked off from the Count. Malachy opened the door just as the Count was going to ring the bell.

"God, it's good to see you," Malachy said. "The situation is getting complicated."

"One tree at a time and soon the forest is felled."

"The first tree is in the front bedroom—the photographs," Malachy said.

As they climbed the stairs, Malachy gave a quick summary of everything that happened and the actions he took in response. When they entered the bedroom, the Count began to examine the photographs.

"No need for imagination with these," the Count said. "And they look real. No way to tell for sure until I get them under a powerful microscope."

The Count put on white gloves and began to carefully remove the photos from the wall and place them in individual oversized folders. He placed the folders in a small suitcase. When he finished he turned to Malachy.

"Next tree?"

"Secure the premises," Malachy said. "This room and the other bedroom where Bari and the intruder are talking are the only two rooms I'm sure are secure. I think Flynn is nowhere near the rectory, but we need to be certain. From his note, I'd say his obsession is getting more intense and his behavior more dangerous."

"For everybody," the Count said. "We'll start on this floor and work down. The only thing that bothers me is the tunnel. What if there are other hiding places. From my days in Warsaw, I can tell you it is impossible to find them from a visual inspection."

"Somehow, Flynn found out about the tunnel. It's probably a tunnel for heating pipes when all the buildings in the complex were heated from a central source. The odds are no other hiding places exist. Bari is leaving soon. Let's just make sure Flynn is not somewhere obvious."

"You stand guard in the hallway. I'll check the rooms. We'll follow the same procedure all the way down to the basement. I brought you this. It's untraceable. Put on these."

The Count handed Malachy a small gun wrapped in a pair of gloves.

"Don't let the size fool you. I've modified it. One shot will stop anything under four hundred pounds in its tracks."

Malachy put on the gloves and carefully examined the gun.

"Ready."

Malachy and the Count climbed up the basement stairs.

"Next tree?"

"You stay with Fr. Bari while he packs. I'll make sure Conrad has followed the rules."

Malachy put the gun in his pocket.

"Fr. Bari is something of a pacifist."

The Count pointed to the small suitcase stored by the front door containing the sex pictures.

"Make love, not war. I happily agree, but the Nazis of this world, no matter nationality or ethnicity, operate with a different slogan—Make death, destruction, and devastation in order to dominate—and only greater force stops them."

"Too true," Malachy said. "Even in our little world, love of any kind is not going to stop Flynn."

"No, it's not," the Count said. "That's our job."

Malachy knocked on the bedroom door. "The rectory is secure. Time to pack."

"Malachy, I need to talk with you about Conrad," Bari said, opening the door. Bari stepped out into the hallway and closed the door behind him.

"He's decided to return home and enter rehabilitation. I must take him home."

"That's impossible," Malachy said.

"Conrad needs to be escorted home immediately. He's willing to call his parents to try and reconcile with them. They have the resources to pay for his stay in rehab."

"Wonderful," Malachy said without enthusiasm. "But someone else has to do it."

"He is afraid of you," Bari said, frowning slightly at Malachy.

"He should be," Malachy said. "Let's try and remember I didn't break into his bedroom."

"Malachy, I know you're protecting me. But Conrad needs my help. He needs someone to intervene with his parents. It's a difficult situation. I must help."

"That's not possible," Malachy said. "You're being picked up in thirty minutes. You need to pack."

"I'm not going anywhere," Bari said, his eyes blazing. "I promised Conrad I'd go home with him."

Malachy knew it was a simple decision—force Bari to leave or take Conrad home.

"Where's home?"

"Lake Bluff."

"Home it is," Malachy said. "But, Conrad stays cuffed with his hands in front of him on the trip. He can take them off before he goes inside. Now go and pack."

"All right," Bari said. "I'm glad you're cooperating."

"Me, too," Malachy said.

Bari smiled at Malachy and placed his hand on his shoulder. "I thought we agreed you're not going to lie to me."

"Well this isn't a lie," Malachy said. "I don't need any more dishwashers."

Bari gave a laugh and said, "And I promise I won't ask. I'll go and pack now. Where am I going?"

"First to Lake Bluff, then somewhere secure."

"Okay, Malachy, I understand. I won't ask any more questions."

"Good," Malachy said. "And that's not a lie."

When the doorbell rang, Malachy opened the door to a young, very muscular Hispanic man. The man handed Malachy an index card with the number eleven circled on it. The man stepped in and closed the door behind him.

"I am here to pick up a religious package," the man said.

"There's been a change in the plan," Malachy said.

"No changes. I have my instructions."

"You can call or I can call, but the plan needs to change."

The man called on his cell phone and spoke in rapid Spanish and then handed the phone to Malachy. Malachy listened as the call was passed through two forwarding cycles.

"What do you need?"

"There's an extra passenger that needs to be taken with Fr. Bari to a private home in Lake Bluff. They need to ride together. Fr. Bari will need to spend some time in the Lake Bluff residence. Then he'll be ready to travel to the final destination."

"Everything is still under control?"

"Yes," Malachy said.

"The instructions will be changed. Click off and give the phone back. Good luck."

Malachy handed the phone back. It immediately rang. The man turned around and answered without saying anything. Malachy could just hear someone speaking in Spanish. The man listened carefully and then speaking slowly seemed to be repeating his instructions. When he finished he turned back to Malachy.

"We will bring them both out at the same time. Tell them to keep pace with their escorts. The escorts will be using large umbrellas."

"It's not raining," Malachy said, handing him the key to the cuffs.

The man ignored the comment.

Malachy and the Count watched the group move toward the vehicles. Fr. Bari and Conrad were each accompanied by a man carrying a large open umbrella with two hands and pointing it like there was heavy rain coming sideways right at them. Another man was in front of the group with one hand in a jacket pocket. The Hispanic man who first came to the door stood on the stairs with his coat folded over his half-raised arm. Bari and Conrad climbed into the back of the SUV without incident.

"Forty seconds from door to door," the Count said. "Very impressive."

"And puzzling," Malachy said. "They were all Hispanic."

"Subcontracted?"

"Who knows," Malachy said. "I just hope Bari doesn't reconvert all of them. We have enough problems."

Malachy's cell phone rang. It was Kevin.

"Any sign of Flynn?" Malachy asked.

"No," Kevin said. "But, I think you are about to have some visitors."

"That group is not returning," Malachy said.

"The Feds I'm looking at just got here. They're drinking coffee and look to be waiting."

"Jesus fucking Christ, where is here?"

"Down by the statue of Columbus."

Malachy put his cell phone on speaker.

"The Count will exit through the tunnel with all of our equipment. Pick him up on the other side of the school. I'll wait for the Feds. Was there any sign the rectory was being watched before?"

"No."

"Good. Call both of us when they start to move."

The Count pulled out his checklist. "You take the suitcase and your equipment down to the tunnel. I'll start at the top floor and work down. I'll head to the basement if my phone rings."

"Why are you smiling?" Malachy asked.

"I was hoping I'd get to use that tunnel. Brings back the old days in Warsaw."

"Ah, the good old days," Malachy said. "Death, destruction, and devastation instead of obstruction of justice. I kind of miss them myself."

"You weren't born yet," the Count said cheerfully over his shoulder, as he headed up the stairs.

CHAPTER XVIII

Malachy watched the Feds' vans roll up in front of the rectory and the agents jump out and charge the stairs. He opened the door just as the lead agent reached it.

"Good morning to you and a fine one it is," Malachy said to a very lean, very young agent with a this-is-serious-business look on his face.

"We are executing a search warrant on these premises. Out of the way. And who the hell are you?"

Malachy opened the door wider and stepped back. The other agents poured through the door and began to search the rectory. Malachy counted a total of eight.

"Identify yourself."

"Malachy Madden."

"Where is Fr. Bari?"

"He left early this morning."

"Who else is in the rectory?"

"No one."

The agent stepped away from Malachy and spoke into a walkie-talkie. Malachy headed for the kitchen.

"Where the hell are you going?"

"To the kitchen. My coffee is cold."

"Just stay put."

"I am sure you're aware as an agent of the federal government that every American has a constitutionally protected right to coffee in the morning, especially early morning. Without waiving any of my constitutional rights, I will comply with your request."

The FBI agent gave Malachy a bewildered look but said nothing. Malachy beamed a big smile at him. The agent spoke into his walkie-talkie again. After a minute Malachy saw another agent come up the stairs. Matt Morse walked through the open door.

"Good morning, Matt. I'm glad you're here. Your colleague here doesn't seem to understand I'm not a morning person."

"Good morning, Malachy. We weren't expecting to find you here. Where is Fr. Bari?"

"Join me in the kitchen nearer the coffeepot, and I'll tell what I know."

"That should make my job easier," Matt said, gesturing toward the kitchen. "But somehow I doubt it."

In the kitchen, Malachy poured himself and Matt coffee.

"What do you want to know?" Malachy asked.

"Where is Fr. Bari?"

"I don't know. He left this morning with a young man he was helping with a drug problem. Somebody I don't know picked him up. He didn't say when he would be back."

"Why are you here?" Matt asked.

"Because I needed a place to sleep for a night. I thought it would be a good chance to get to know Fr. Bari better."

"What's wrong with your place?"

"Sean needed a place for a tryst, so I let him use my place."

"Sean? The Irish poet? You're kidding!"

"I am not using hyperbole, litotes, or any figure of speech despite the subject being a poet. My statement was literal fact."

"Who's his partner? Sadie the lady from the Old People's Home."

"*Au contraire, mon frère*. The intended paramour is a very attractive younger poetess whose identity must remain confidential as a matter of honor. I say intended because as of yet I do not know if the campaign was successful."

"Will wonders never cease? There must be magic in poetry."

Malachy raised his right arm high, wrote in the air with a flourish, and said, "As the great poet wrote:

> God guard me from those thoughts men think
> In the mind alone;
> He that sings a lasting song
> Thinks in a marrow bone…

"Does that mean what I think it means?" Matt asked.

"That too," Malachy said.

"Who's the great poet?"

"Yeats."

"There wasn't any security in front of the rectory when we pulled up," Matt said.

"Perhaps you scared them off. I'm not in charge of that, so you'll have to ask somebody else."

Matt stepped closer to Malachy and lowered his voice so only Malachy could hear it.

"Some weird stuff has happened concerning the rectory. And now you're here and underfoot. You are at the very edge of the envelope. And that's a dangerous place to be."

Matt stepped back and Malachy silently mouthed, "Understood."

"What happens now?" Malachy asked.

"We execute the warrant and leave," Matt said.

"What do you want me to do?"

"Stay out of the way."

"How long do you think it will take?" Malachy asked.

"Less than an hour."

"Is it all right if I stay? I want to make sure the place is properly locked up before I leave."

"You are a guest of Fr. Bari. I've no authority to tell you to leave. Just stay out of the way."

"Will do," Malachy said. "What else can I do to help out?"

"Submit to a search of your person," Matt said. "And then find a comfortable chair, move it into the hallway, and stay put until we're ready to leave. And don't give any lectures on your constitutional rights."

"I agree to it all as long as I can have coffee and the morning papers while I wait."

Matt called to the other agent. "He has agreed to a search. Then he's going to wait in the hallway until we're done."

The other agent came into the kitchen and approached Malachy. Malachy emptied his pockets on to the kitchen counter and then raised his arms. The agent examined the collection from Malachy's pockets and then patted Malachy down.

"There's nothing on him. He's clean," the agent said.

Malachy moved a comfortable armchair into the middle of the hallway and settled into reading the papers. The morning news was thin and Malachy started in on the crossword puzzle. He usually got totally frustrated within ten minutes of starting a puzzle, muttering to himself that there was something wrong with the brains of the people who constructed such weird connections.

"Hey Matt," Malachy yelled. "I need some help."

Matt leaned over the second-floor banister and looked down at Malachy.

"What's the problem?"

"It's too early in the morning or the coffee is decaf. How are you at Greek mythology? I need the name of a Greek hero—five letters."

Matt came down the stairs and said, "Let me see. I need the context."

Malachy gave him the puzzle. Matt looked at the down and across numbers and the clues.

"Gyros," Matt said.

"Jesus...a sandwich!"

"There is no indefinite article in the clue—just Greek hero," Matt said.

"Thanks," Malachy said. "I'd starve if I had to solve those things for a living. How's the search coming? Finding what you're looking for?"

Matt gave a wry smile and said in a low voice, "You know, Malachy, it might be better to be hungry than to be in the crosshairs of an angry prosecutor. Some occupations are safer than others."

"I've noted that over the years," Malachy said. "But somehow those safe occupations have eluded me. You know, my girls are always trying to marry me off to a country-club, golf-playing, North Shore widow of Irish or Italian heritage. I can't rationally explain it, but somehow that seems more dangerous to me than my current occupation."

Matt laughed and asked, "And how would you define your current occupation?"

"Constitutional scholar and house sitter?"

"If only those were full time," Matt said. "Malachy, we'll be leaving in a few minutes. Try and remember what happens to test pilots who push beyond the edge of the envelope."

"Remind me again," Malachy said.

"They crash and burn."

"A suboptimal outcome, as we consultants like to say."

"So now you're a consultant," Matt said. "That sounds more lucrative than house sitting."

"The per diem is quite adequate," Malachy said. "But there are hazards."

"Like what?" Matt asked.

"Like sometimes you piss off powerful people just by doing your job."

"Maybe you should consider just taking a pass sometimes," Matt said.

"Too late in this case," Malachy said. "I'm constrained by genetics."

"Genetics?"

"It's one of those inbreeding things—I got it from both sides. Once I start something I'm forced to see it through to the end. Nothing I can do about it. Preprogrammed, no free will. But let's look on the bright side."

"And what would that be?" Matt asked.

"Every puzzle has a solution," Malachy said.

"And the dark side?"

"Sometime the solution turns out to be a messy sandwich," Malachy said.

Malachy locked the door to the rectory and called Kevin.

"Are all my federal friends gone?"

"No," Kevin said. "At least one car left with two agents. Can't tell if they're watching the rectory or for you."

"Let's keep it simple," Malachy said. "We'll meet in the Shamrock's storeroom. I'll take a bus and the el. You two secure the equipment and the photographs."

"What's on the meeting agenda?" Kevin asked.

"How to find Flynn and his trove of pictures without triggering their release."

"We propose meeting at 3:00 P.M.," Kevin said. "We want to spend a few hours looking for Flynn's car in the neighborhood."

"Great!" Malachy said. "It will give me time for a nap. This early morning consulting is taxing my system."

"Don't forget that Sean may still be using your place," Kevin said. "There is always the cot in the storeroom."

Malachy muttered some curses into the cell phone.

"What was it you told me about Sean's bar bill?" Kevin asked cheerfully. "Oh yes, I remember—it is important to support traditional Irish culture because it is under attack from every side."

"Yes, but I want my own bed."

"Remember what our great spiritual leader Sergeant O'Rourke told us so many times," Kevin said.

"Your memory is hyperactive this morning," Malachy said. "What did the good Sergeant tell us?"

Sergeant O'Rourke's voice from long ago boomed out of Malachy's cell phone. "You fuckfaces have only one fucking need and that is to stay fucking alive, the rest are wants and your wants don't count for fucking shit."

"Thank you for that empathic message," Malachy said.

"You are most welcome. Enjoy your nap on the cot."

†

Bridget's loud voice woke Malachy from his dream.

"Now hear this, now hear this!" Bridget yelled into the darkened storeroom.

Malachy did not answer until he secured a fragment of the dream in his memory so he could use it as the key to remembering more of the dream later.

"All right, all right, I'm hearing—what the hell is it?"

"The following information," Bridget said. "Are you sure you're not going to fall back asleep?"

"Your greeting isn't exactly a lullaby," Malachy said. "Trust me, sleep is gone and not returning."

"Sean is in the bar with a happy face," Bridget said. "He wants to thank you in person for use of the Love Palace. Earlier, Sarah called looking for Sean. She sounded pissed she hadn't heard from him. I told her we expected him shortly because he had a scheduled meeting with you. Kevin called, and he and the Count will be here for the 3:00 meeting. And not that you give a damn, but business remains good. That's the full report. Do you want coffee?"

"I'll be out in ten minutes and have the coffee with Sean, thanks."

"Ten minutes? You must be getting older—if it takes that long to scratch yourself and make sure everything is still intact."

"Not exactly. I need to think about something."

"Contemplation before action," Bridget said. "You are getting older."

Bridget closed the storeroom door with a bang. Malachy put his hands behind his head, settled back on the pillow, and recalled the dream fragment and then the dream.

He was a fighter pilot in a World War II vintage plane. He was flying low over enemy ground troops on some kind of strafing mission. His guns were stuck and wouldn't fire no matter how hard he pulled the trigger. The enemy was firing at him, but instead of bullets or flack, the fire was little black envelopes, a blizzard of black envelopes. He was worried he would get disoriented and lose control of the plane. He headed back to base, but he was greeted with more envelope fire.

This fire was larger kelly-green envelopes that started to foul his propellers. He put the plane into a steep climb to get away from the fire. Suddenly all his instruments started to go haywire. He realized he had no parachute.

That's when Bridget's voice woke him up.

Malachy decided that jammed guns, everybody firing at you, and no parachute made for a difficult mission. He got up, grabbed his spare Dopp kit, and headed to the bathroom to wash up and brush his teeth.

Malachy strode into barroom and waved Sean over to join him in his booth.

"Sean, you are positively glowing!"

Sean smiled and said:

> An aged man is but a paltry thing
> A tattered coat upon a stick, unless
> Soul clap its hands and sing, and louder sing…

"Funny thing. I was quoting Yeats myself early this morning. But I don't think my one-man audience was very receptive. Not a romantic at heart. I believe his occupation—he's in law enforcement—has caused that part of him to atrophy."

"When we always walk on concrete with our feet shod, it is difficult to recall the feel of grass," Sean said. "Malachy, it was a splendid afternoon, evening, and morning. Your colleague has an unerring eye for what pleases a woman. I only hope it was not too much bother for you. I am truly grateful for all you have done. Those twenty-plus hours are burned into my memory, and my heart will always sing when I recall them. Thank you."

Malachy started to acknowledge Sean's thanks when he saw Sarah enter the Shamrock followed at a distance by Kevin and the Count.

"I think we have a situation developing," Malachy said. "Sarah is headed our way. See if you can get her to join you at one of the back tables."

Sean reluctantly stood up and faced the fast-approaching Sarah.

"Sean, you selfish son of a bitch," Sarah yelled as she approached him. "You never called this morning. Where the hell have you been?"

"Now, Sarah…"

Sarah looked Sean up and down and laughed.

"You look ridiculous. I have a good mind to throw your ass…"

Suddenly, the Count appeared at Sarah's side.

"Madame, it is all my fault," the Count said in a loud, accented voice.

"Who the hell are you?" Sarah asked belligerently.

"Count Leon Latalski, at your service."

The Count took Sarah's hand and clicked his heels. He looked into her eyes for a moment and then with a slight bow kissed her hand.

"It is an honor to meet you. Sean told me of your steadfast support for his work. Please, allow me to explain. And please join me at one of the tables."

Without waiting for an answer, the Count gently took Sarah's arm and guided her to an out-of-the-way table. He pulled out a chair and with a sweeping gesture indicated Sarah should sit down. He deftly took a chair and pulled it close to Sarah and sat down. Malachy and Sean approached the table, and the Count indicated Sean should sit down across from Sarah. The Count then looked up at Malachy.

"Would it be possible for someone to bring us a little refreshment? I find business discussions proceed more smoothly when everyone is comfortable."

"What business discussions?" Sarah asked, with some of the shrillness gone from her tone.

"That's what I wanted to explain, but first what would you like to drink? I'd be honored if you would join me in a little champagne. Somehow it seems appropriate to celebrate today."

"I guess I could drink a little champagne," Sarah said.

"Excellent. A bottle of your best champagne with three glasses," the Count said to Malachy.

"I will have it brought to the table immediately, Count. Anything else?"

"Some appropriate appetizers," the Count said. "I will leave that to your discretion."

Malachy headed to the bar.

The Count turned to Sarah.

"You see I was at the reading last night in Milwaukee. I was overwhelmed with emotion and insisted on driving Sean to Chicago this morning. I am afraid I monopolized all of his time with my enthusiasm for his work and the project I proposed. It is entirely my fault he failed to call you."

"I wondered what happened," Sarah said. "What's this project you keep talking about?"

"Before I explain, I must apologize. It was selfish of me to allow my enthusiasm to interfere with your domestic life, especially after Sean told me how important you are to his work. I'm sorry. Will you forgive me?"

The Count reached over and covered Sarah's hand with his. "Please?"

Sarah gave a little embarrassed laugh and said, "Yes, okay."

"Good. Ah, here is our champagne and an ice bucket. Wonderful."

The Count took the bottle from Eduardo. He carefully examined it and then opened it with a flourish. He poured a little in his own glass, took a mouthful, and chewed on it.

"If you explode the bubbles by a slight chewing action, it helps to get the full flavor. As one might expect, it is a domestic. However, it is quite acceptable. In my cellar in Warsaw I mostly stock French champagne with the occasional Italian sparkling wine. I do find prosecco quite refreshing on occasion."

The Count poured champagne for Sarah and Sean and returned the bottle to the ice bucket.

"Let me propose a toast," the Count said. "To the friendships that flourish from poetry."

They all clinked glasses and drank. The Count pulled his chair even closer to Sarah's.

"Let me explain. You know, the Poles and the Irish have much in common. Two great Catholic nations that have known much adversity. Of course, Ireland is blessed because it's an island. Unfortunately, Poland lies between a viscous bear to the east and a ferocious wolf to the west. Still, we both have survived and mostly prevailed in our historical struggles. So, when I heard Sean read from his recent work last night in Milwaukee, a thunderbolt struck me."

"About the business discussions you mentioned?" Sarah asked.

"Indeed," the Count said. "An anthology of Irish poetry, from both the Irish and English, translated into Polish with Sean as both the editor and a contributor. Now of course as you both know only too well, the market for poetry is limited. Nevertheless, if done well with an eye toward the textbook market, I think it could be commercially successful."

"Sean is absolutely hopeless when it comes to money and business," Sarah said. "He is always wasting time on projects that never bring in any money. What kind of upfront payment are you talking about?"

Sean started to protest, but the Count interrupted him.

"That is not his job," the Count said. "His talent requires he spend his time creating poetry, not coining money. Sarah, I like a woman who speaks her mind directly. And I understand your concern. I cannot guarantee the project will be commercially viable or guarantee a specified upfront payment. However, I am involved in various commercial enterprises, and I believe one of those may allay your concern."

"I don't understand," Sarah said.

"What I propose will become clear in a moment. But first I must obtain something from my vehicle. Excuse me, and please enjoy some more champagne. I will inquire about our appetizers on my way out."

The Count strode over to Malachy, who was sitting at the bar listening to the conversation at the table. They walked toward the front door together.

"I think you have extracted Sean from the quicksand, but you are in the pit and sinking fast," Malachy said.

"First, quicksand is denser than the human body so if you do not panic and flail about, you will float. Second, as you will shortly see, I am nowhere near the quicksand. Third, where are the appetizers?"

"At the table as we speak. What are getting from your car?"

"Something for Sarah," the Count said. "Do you know where Eduardo parked my limo?"

"It is in the funeral parking lot. I thought it would be safer there. Eduardo says that it's quite something, very plush and quite distinctive."

The Count smiled and said, "Yes, it has a number of special features. Converted cabs give you a lot of space to work with."

The Count checked his watch.

"And yes, I will be on time for the meeting."

The Count returned to the table with a closed jewelry box. He put it on the table in front of Sarah.

"I am in the jewelry business along with various other enterprises. In the box is a sample I use for special selling purposes. Here is what I propose. You take what is in the box on loan—as a kind of security guarantee. If Sean is required to put in substantial time and energy into my project and it does not pan out financially, you can keep what is in the box as payment."

The Count flipped open the box.

"Oh my God, what beautiful diamond earrings," Sarah said. "Are they real?"

"Very real."

"They must be worth thousands."

The Count didn't respond.

"On loan, you said."

"Well, I prefer security deposit," the Count said. "Of course, you may treat them as your own. Wear them whenever you want. They are insured so you don't need to worry about wearing them."

"I can take them home today?"

"Of course, they are yours to use. Do we have a deal?"

"When do we decide if the project is working or not?" Sarah asked.

"I'd say about eighteen months from now. That will be enough time to tell for sure."

"Deal," Sarah said, picking up the earrings.

"You two stay and finish the champagne and appetizers," the Count said. "Unfortunately, I must attend a business meeting. I would much rather spend the time with my new friends, but duty calls. Sean, I will be in touch."

The Count walked into the storeroom at 2:59 and greeted Kevin and Malachy.

"How did you leave the happy couple?" Malachy asked.

"They are drinking champagne and conversing amiably," the Count answered. "I had to intervene. Sarah was about to ruin a perfectly planned and executed operation and those are hard to come by in any of life's endeavors."

"I was watching Sean watching you," Kevin said. "He was like a child mesmerized by the snake charmer, but keeping a wary eye on the snake.

"Sarah is tough and difficult, a ballbuster in slang terms, but she is still a woman," the Count said.

"I have to ask," Malachy said. "Are they truly real?"

"Do you think I would deceive the lady?"

"Yes."

"Very real," the Count said.

"Are they hot?" Malachy asked.

"Only slightly lukewarm. They are from a long-ago operation. The fence made a totally inadequate offer so I kept them. Under a jeweler's eye, there are some distinctive markings and that reduced their street value."

"What if they are recognized when Sarah is wearing them?"

"Their previous owner and Sarah do not travel in the same social or geographic circles. My calculators do not have enough places to calculate the infinitesimal chance that someone would recognize them."

"Will you miss them?"

"I have other jewelry hidden in the limo that will substitute when needed," the Count said.

"What happens in eighteen months?" Malachy asked.

"You know, once I talked about the project out loud, I kind of liked the idea," the Count said. "So, I may pursue it. I've been spending so much time with you I think I've been infected by this Irish stuff."

"It happens," Malachy said, laughing.

"Anyway, a year and a half is a long time away. Who knows what will happen? But I can always come out of retirement if I need them back for some reason."

"Back to our current business," Malachy said. "How did the search go?"

"No luck," Kevin said. "We split up. I was on foot and the Count in the car. We methodically went through the entire neighborhood. Nothing."

"Back to the drawing board," the Count said.

"Let's start with the facts we know," Malachy said. "Somehow Flynn found out about the tunnel. We know Bari didn't tell him. Flynn was never stationed at the Shrine when it was a regular parish, and his other assignments were nowhere near the neighborhood. So who told him?"

"Maybe somebody from a facilities committee or its equivalent," Kevin said. "Or how about Dino?"

"Dino has his own Shrine scheme going," the Count said. "He's not sharing Shrine info with anyone."

"That tunnel has not been in use for years," Malachy said. "It is older than everybody on that committee. Do they even know it exists? After all, it doesn't require any maintenance and it was sealed off. And how would Flynn get to meet with and question somebody on a committee like that?"

"Older…older," the Count repeated. "In my war years in Warsaw, we always talked to the elderly about the buildings. They always knew the most amazing things—hiding places, trapdoors, walled-up windows, chimneys, even staircases, and, of course, tunnels.

"It was quite instructive about memory. They couldn't tell you what they ate for breakfast yesterday, or if they had breakfast, but they could describe in vivid detail the places their childhood games took them and how those buildings changed over the years."

Malachy and Kevin gave each other a bemused look.

"Where do we find somebody older than the tunnel?" Malachy asked.

"Not older than the tunnel necessarily, just old enough to know it existed," the Count answered. "But also somebody who is connected to Bari and who Flynn could approach."

"Who?" Malachy and Kevin asked together.

"The housekeeper," the Count said.

"Jesus," Malachy said in a muted whisper.

"I propose that Kevin and I talk with the housekeeper tomorrow first thing in the morning," the Count said. "You can stay in bed and follow your usual routine."

"Enthusiastically accepted," Malachy said.

"Me, too," Kevin said.

"Talk to her as what?" Malachy asked.

"Good cop, better cop," the Count said.

"Let me guess," Malachy said. "You're the better cop."

"Of course," the Count said. "An older woman is still a woman."

"There is one more item on the agenda," Kevin said. "Flynn. When we find him, what are we going to do with him?"

"Keep him," Malachy said.

"Where?" Kevin asked.

"We could give him to our employer for safekeeping," Malachy said. "But we need easy access to him. Obviously, it can't be anyplace the Feds might visit. And it needs to be isolated."

"I have a storage warehouse in Indiana we can use," the Count said. "The former owner lived on the premises. He put in a small bedroom and kitchen. It was a violation of zoning so he disguised it. No windows. I'll send a crew there to get it ready and make sure everything works."

"What do you store there?" Malachy asked.

"Not to worry," the Count said. "Everything in there has been legally acquired. There won't be any unexpected visits from the law."

"Legally acquired? Now, I'm really curious."

"The principle is simple—it has to be large, difficult to move, and storable in an unheated warehouse. I have the manpower, equipment, and expertise to move it and store it. So I pay next to nothing for it and wait. Boats, farm equipment, building supplies, you name it and you'll find it in the warehouse. Buy it in the fall, sell it in the spring."

"I don't think Flynn qualifies," Malachy said.

"That's okay, the Count said. "I don't expect we'll be keeping him in inventory."

CHAPTER XIX

Kevin and the Count watched a short, stout elderly woman pulling a two-wheel, open shopping cart in the direction of their parked car.

"Is that her?" Kevin asked the Count.

The Count looked at the woman's dark dress, sweater, and her all-black walking shoes and answered, "That's the housekeeper. I watched her enter the rectory at 7:00 a.m. She has a firm step for her age—over eighty I'm guessing. She could pass for the widowed grandmother in any country west of the Rhine."

"I assume that's not your opening line," Kevin said.

The Count turned his head toward Kevin, smiled, and responded, "Join us on the park bench that faces Columbus in five minutes."

"You should be retired," the housekeeper said, shifting her gaze from the statue of Columbus and turning on the park bench toward the Count. "How come you're still working?"

"You know you're right," the Count said. "Sitting in the sun in a nice park with a protector," the Count swept his hand up toward the Columbus statue, "is nice for a little while but then what do you do? So I work and try to teach the younger ones. But they're stubborn and know-it-alls. And they like to do everything too fast."

"He doesn't look so young," the housekeeper said, pointing at Kevin at the end of the bench.

"He's not. He's even older than he looks. But this is a special assignment. They actually gave me somebody with a little experience to work with."

"I don't know if I should talk to you without my daughter."

"We only want to talk with people who can help our investigation," Kevin said in an even tone. "It's confidential."

"I'm not sure," the housekeeper said.

"See what I mean?" the Count said. "Even with his experience he still wants to go too fast. Of course, we'll be happy to talk with you with your daughter present. Please tell her there is nothing to be alarmed about. We just need to ask a few simple questions. It will only take a couple of minutes."

"Questions? What kind of questions?"

The Count lowered his voice and leaned in toward the housekeeper.

"We are looking for a man who has done something I can't talk about. We think you might have seen him."

The housekeeper gave a scoffing laugh. "Me? I don't see any men. You don't know what you're talking about."

"We haven't even described him yet," Kevin said in the same even tone.

The Count shook his head in dismay and asked, "See what I mean? No patience even at his age. Of course, I'm surprised a woman like you doesn't have at least a couple of male friends, but that's not what I meant. I meant maybe he came to the rectory or you saw him in the neighborhood, maybe in a shop?"

"What did he do?"

"It was bad," the Count said.

"It's against regulations to tell you," Kevin said. "We can't do it."

"See what I mean?" the Count asked. "Everything by the book. People like us, we know better."

The Count leaned in again and said in a whisper in Italian, "You don't know this."

A bus went by behind them, and the housekeeper turned her head a little so she could hear better.

"He hurt little children," the Count whispered in English. "A lot of them. We need to find him before he does it again."

The Count pulled back and adopted an official tone. "Anything you can do to help is appreciated."

"Children? What does he look like?"

Kevin reached over and handed her a copy of a cropped picture of Flynn from the seminary. "This is a picture of him as a young man," Kevin said.

"He is a little taller than I am," the Count said, gesturing to himself.

The housekeeper brought the picture close to her face and looked at it for a while in silence.

"He talked to me," she said. "Here in the park."

Kevin and the Count stayed silent. The Count nodded his head very slightly up and down.

"He asked me if I was the housekeeper at the rectory. He said he went to Sunday Mass at the Shrine. He seemed nice."

"Only that once?" Kevin asked abruptly.

The Count shook his head again. He adopted a reassuring tone. "What he means is that it would help us to know what you talked about when he talked with you."

"He said he worked at the university. He asked me a lot of questions about the old days. What the school and the Shrine were like when I was a girl. I didn't understand him sometimes. I told him it wasn't right that they destroyed the neighborhood to build the university. He said it was wrong too, and he was doing research to prove it was wrong."

"So you saw him every day in the park," Kevin said in a firm tone.

The Count did not intervene.

"No, no, not every day," the housekeeper said. "Let me count."

She talked to herself in Italian and counted out the times on her fingers.

"Four or five times," she said. "He was very polite and nice to me. I didn't know."

"Of course not," the Count said. "But it's very important for us to know what you talked about. It will help us catch him before he can… well, before he finds another child."

"He asked questions about Fr. Bari and the rectory and the Shrine. I don't remember everything."

"What did you tell him?" Kevin asked.

"I don't know...I don't remember. It gets lonely in the rectory. We just talked. Things like how big the house is and how hard it is to keep it clean. Things like that."

"Of course, you don't remember," the Count said, shaking his head at Kevin again. "You are just making conversation with a parishioner who seems nice. Something you should do, something Fr. Bari would want you to do. What my young, impatient friend means is was there anything that he seemed particularly interested in or even excited about?"

"Well, he was interested in a story I told him about the old convent and rectory."

"Really?" the Count said. "Could you tell us?"

"Some of the older boys in the neighborhood said there was a tunnel that connected the convent and the rectory and that's how the priests and the nuns got together at night. I was shocked and asked my father about it. He laughed and told me the priests and nuns were too fancy to climb through a small, dirty heating tunnel full of spiders and mice."

"That's interesting," the Count said. "When I was a young boy we thought the priests and nuns didn't even have private parts."

The housekeeper gave a snorting laugh and said, "Nobody thinks that today."

"Did he say where he lived?" Kevin asked.

"I asked him that one day because I saw him in the neighborhood. My daughter picked me up and we were driving through the neighborhood to get to the expressway, and I saw him going into an apartment building. I asked him if he lived there when we met in the park the next day."

"What did he say?" the Count gently prompted.

"He said no, that he lived on the North Side. He was just visiting a friend."

"Do you think you could show us that building?" the Count asked.

"It's not hard to find."

"Good," the Count said. "That will be a big help in the investigation."

†

Malachy looked up at the third-floor apartment. There was nothing to distinguish the older brick building from so many others like it in the neighborhood and the city. He moved the binoculars from window to window. No lights, no movement. He checked in with the Count and Kevin with his cell phone.

"No signs of life," Malachy said.

"No sign of his car within three square blocks," Kevin said. "And you need a permit to park. Probably keeps the car outside of the neighborhood. Stairwell totally quiet."

"Time to go in," the Count said. "But, I don't want to open a door. He probably knows we caught his young friend. He may have rigged the front and back doors. We need time to examine the apartment and to prepare for his return."

"Okay, I'll bite. How do we get in without opening the door?"

"Through the transom" the Count said. "A window would be less work, but my Batman act in daytime would attract too much attention."

"There's a transom?"

"Sort of. Walled up, over the back door. Easy to cut through with the right equipment. If done right, it will come out in one piece. It's the top floor so we shouldn't attract too much attention. We'll hang drop cloths to block the view. I'll be inside within thirty minutes. Once I check out the doors, we can operate normally."

"What about the noise?" Malachy asked.

"Have you ever noticed, it's difficult to hear anything when a jackhammer is operating nearby? Two jackhammers in the alley should do the trick. I'll adjust the silencers just to make sure."

"What are they going to hammer?" Malachy asked.

"Concrete. I'll have them bring some."

"Good," Malachy said. "The alley is city property and it's against the law to destroy city property."

"Kevin?"

"How long will it take to get your crew in place?" Kevin asked. "We need to cover the building."

"Two hours. I'll prep the back porch. We'll be safely inside within two and a half hours. Agreed?"

"Agreed," Malachy and Kevin said in unison.

"Last item," Malachy said. "If something unexpected happens, everything has been authorized by the landlord."

"Does the landlord know that?" the Count asked.

"Not yet and hopefully never. But if it's necessary, I'll call Dino. He owns the building. Not too surprising, since he owns half the neighborhood. But the Feds are his silent partner in every communication, so we keep him out of it if we can."

Malachy closed his windows against the noise of the jackhammers. He watched the workers bust up big blocks of concrete. He looked at his watch. He trained his binoculars on the porch. The drop cloths waved a little, but nothing was visible. Two ordinary work projects going forth together by coincidence. Twenty minutes later the jackhammers stopped, and he answered his cell phone.

"In, and no problems," the Count said. "Do-it-yourself alarms on the doors. It will take a few minutes to neutralize them. See you at the front door."

Malachy watched the workers carefully clean up the concrete they had busted and load it in the truck. An old man was watching them from the entrance of the alley. The workers swept the alley, attached the compressor to the back of their truck, and drove away. Malachy exited the car and headed for the entrance to the apartment building. He walked by the old man.

"Did you see that?" the old man asked Malachy. "City freeloaders. Probably on time and a half. Can you believe it? They had their own concrete. I should've called the newspaper. Taxes go up every year, and the mayor does nothing about shit like that. The city that works. I should call the newspaper."

Malachy stopped and motioned to the old man to join him.

"I wouldn't do that if I were you," Malachy said in a low voice. "You never know whose spoon is in that bowl."

Malachy placed his finger under his right eye and pulled it down. "Capishe?"

The old man looked at Malachy, muttered something in Italian, and shuffled off. Malachy wondered if it was possible to add to the old man's cynical view of the world. He doubted it.

As Malachy approached Flynn's apartment, the front door swung open. Malachy paused for a moment; quickly slipped on gloves, plastic covers for his shoes, and a shower cap for his head; and entered the apartment.

"Spartan, not to say monastic," Malachy said.

"Not his permanent home," the Count responded. "Just a forward operating base. Only the minimum necessary. And unfortunately, no computer. Probably uses a laptop."

"Anything of help at all?"

"Nothing," the Count said. "It's like he knew we were coming."

Malachy walked into the kitchen and looked up at the Count's handiwork over the door. He opened the refrigerator.

"Nothing but baking soda. Anything in the garbage cans?"

"Nothing," the Count said.

"Any telephone?" Malachy asked.

"No."

"So what have we got?"

"The alarm system," the Count said. "It gives off a signal Flynn can pick up outside the building. No too bad for an amateur."

"Great," Malachy said without enthusiasm. "If the son of a bitch ever returns, we can surprise him. In the meantime, God only knows what damage he can cause to Bari. We need to find him and those pictures. And soon. What the hell do we do?"

"I propose two operations," the Count said. "Police work—canvass the building, maybe somebody saw something that will help. And a microscopic search of this apartment. I need some of my special equipment for that."

Malachy paced around the apartment in silence. The Count waited.

"For sure we do the search," Malachy finally said. "But I counterpropose we look for his car. We know he used a car. He had to park it somewhere within walking distance. The street parking requires a permit. Too much trouble to get one. We know there's no city sticker on his car. We know he operates in Wisconsin. Maybe that's home.

Monthly parkers need to register their cars—description and plates."

"You should play the lieutenant on *Law and Order*. Now you tell Briscoe and the other guy to canvass all the parking garages within walking distance of the apartment."

"Let's keep it simple. Assume he parks at his make-believe work. Didn't he tell the housekeeper he worked at the university. That's within walking distance. Before we shift to the scene with you exchanging sarcastic remarks with a garage manager, let me make a call."

Malachy took out his cell phone and pushed a speed-dial number.

"Good afternoon, Business Research Center, this is Sheila. How may I help you?"

"I'm out on Taylor Street researching restaurants for that dinner I owe you, but I need a little help in figuring out where to park."

"Prevaricator," Sheila said, laughing. "And if that's too many syllables for you, try liar."

"I am on the West Side. I need a favor. Is there monthly parking available at the university?"

"God, I'm afraid to ask why you're asking! Just tell me she's a teacher and not a student."

"Neither, I'm researching a script for *Law and Order*."

"In your case, disorder. Hold a second.... Is your parker a student or a faculty member?"

"Unlikely," Malachy said.

"Parking is restricted," Sheila said. "Your parker gets to pay on entry or exit depending on the lot."

"Thanks, Sheila. I'll call soon to arrange our dinner."

"It's congenital with you, isn't it?"

"Well, one thing is for certain, it's not my fault. Bye."

Malachy turned to the Count and said, "The plotline just got fucked up. So, it's police work. Canvass the building, maybe somebody saw something that will help."

"Sure thing, Lieutenant. What about the apartment search?"

"You go get the equipment you need. Kevin can do the canvass."

"I'll wait here."

"What about the kitchen?" the Count asked. "He could come up the back way."

"Put the piece back in. He won't notice any change from the outside. Once he opens the door he's mine."

Malachy called Kevin and explained the plan.

"What if I see him in the hall?" Kevin asked.

"Grab him up if he tries to bolt and bring him to the apartment," Malachy answered. "Just make sure he doesn't make too much noise."

"Understood."

Kevin lightly knocked on the door of the apartment. Malachy partially opened it. From the hallway, Kevin looked at Malachy and the Count.

"You two look like demented escapees from a sandwich prep line," Kevin said.

"You are adding insult to injury—we have nothing," Malachy said.

"He left this morning in a cab," Kevin said to Malachy. "The woman who lives in front on the second floor passed him as she entered the building from shopping. He was carrying a suitcase and a small case. He got into a waiting a cab. She doesn't know what kind."

Malachy gave a big smile.

"So we get to canvass those parking lots after all. Unless he took the cab to his car, if that car is parked somewhere we can find it. So let's go find it."

"We still need to cover the building," the Count said.

"Can you rig the alarms so the signal can reach the university?" Malachy asked.

"It will take twenty minutes," the Count said. "I need to get some more stuff from my van. I propose you put the kitchen back to rights while I fix the alarm. And Kevin covers the building from the street. That way he won't immediately suspect anything if he does return."

"A woman's work is never done," Malachy said. "The kitchen it is."

The Count drove slowly up the ramp of the parking garage. Malachy sat in the front passenger seat with Kevin on the opposite side in the back.

"How many more garages are there?" the Count asked. "It is depressing to see how many drivers never wash their cars."

Malachy started to answer when Kevin shouted, "Wisconsin plate, there!"

The Count pulled the van next to the car, and Kevin got out and examined the windshield and walked around the car and got back in the van.

"Nothing on the windshield. It looks like the car in the video of the press conference. No student stuff visible anywhere."

"How about we take a look at the glove compartment?" Malachy asked.

"Easy enough to look," the Count said. "I'll go in on the driver's side. I'll be back with my treasures in four minutes."

The Count slipped into a vest that held various tools in Velcro-sealed pockets on the inside. He exited the van and worked at the window of the car for thirty seconds. He pulled the car door open, climbed into the driver's seat, and closed the door.

The Count pulled a tool from his vest and then opened the glove compartment, scooped up the contents, and folded them into his vest. He exited the car and got into the van. He sorted the stuff in his vest and handed Malachy an envelope.

"And the winner is...," Malachy said.

Malachy opened the unsealed envelope and examined the registration and insurance cards.

"Registration and insurance cards for one Reginald Flynn. We now know where the son of a bitch lives. Where the hell is Mine Point, Wisconsin?"

The Count took out a map and located the town.

"About ten miles west of Kevin's new girlfriend's cottage."

"We need to thoroughly search his car and his place," Malachy said. "We need to find the originals of those pictures. Dino's committee can always claim any copies are phonies if we have the originals."

"I'll take the car to my warehouse," the Count said. "We can do his place tomorrow. But we can't leave the apartment uncovered."

A device clipped to the Count's belt starting flashing red and making a loud, intermittent buzzing sound.

"What the hell is that?" Malachy asked.

"A door to Flynn's apartment was just opened," the Count said.

"Jesus...he's returned. Let's go!"

The Count maneuvered the van out of the parking lot, carefully obeying all the rules for paying and exiting. He drove at exactly the speed limit toward the apartment. Malachy knew it was futile to ask for greater speed.

"We need to surprise him," Malachy said. "Going in at the same time from the front and the back. Do we have keys?"

"Of course," the Count said. "That was one of the first things I did."

"What about latches?" Malachy asked.

"They're rigged," the Count said. "They won't hold against any pressure. The front door is not latched because Flynn went out that way."

"Looks like you thought of everything," Malachy said.

"Of course," the Count said. "Professionalism resides in just such details. Like not speeding to your destination even if the impatience in the air is thick enough to cut with a knife."

"Okay, okay," Malachy said. "I'll calm down. I propose Kevin take the back, I take the front, and you cover the hallway."

"Agreed," the Count said.

"Agreed," Kevin said.

"What if he is already on his way back out?" the Count asked.

"Just like before, grab him and return to the apartment. Where are you going to park?"

"First available and risk the ticket," the Count said. "The plates cannot be traced."

The Count parked the van across the street from the apartment building. Malachy and Kevin bolted from the van before it was fully stopped and ran to the building.

"I'll go in on your signal," Kevin said.

"Okay," Malachy said.

Kevin rapidly climbed up the back stairs for two floors. At the third floor, he dropped down and crawled up the steps. He peered over the last step. The kitchen door was open and the lights were on. The kitchen was empty, but he could hear someone in the apartment. From his perch, he carefully examined the doorjamb. The door had been forced open. He went back down the stairs and called Malachy.

"The back door was forced open and all the lights are on."

"I'll call the Count and tell him to cut the power to the apartment. When the apartment goes dark, call my cell. We'll go in on that signal.

I'll follow you in after one minute. Go in low. Whoever is in there might have a weapon. No one gets to leave."

"Understood."

Kevin crawled back up the stairs and waited. After fifteen minutes, the apartment went totally dark. Kevin heard a curse from the apartment. He pressed a speed dial on his cell and quickly crawled into the kitchen. He closed the door behind him to cut down on the light from the outside. He crawled into the dining area.

The front door opened and Malachy crawled into the living room and quickly closed the door behind him. In the few seconds of light from the hallway, they spotted each other and Kevin motioned toward the bedroom. They both slowly and quietly military crawled toward the bedroom.

A figure emerged from the bedroom, moving slowly and groping the living room wall. Kevin shifted his position to a coiled crouch and launched himself at the figure's legs. He smashed his shoulder into the legs, and the figure hit the wall and fell hard to the floor with a loud curse. It was a male voice.

Malachy threw himself on the prone figure with his full weight. He was surprised at how slight the person was. Malachy rolled off, and Kevin grabbed his wrists and cuffed the intruder. The man was gasping for air. Malachy waited for a few seconds and then slapped a piece of tape on his mouth.

Malachy called the Count. "Power on and join us."

The lights in the apartment went on. Kevin quickly strode through the apartment, checking for an accomplice, and then turned off all the lights and secured the kitchen door. Malachy propped the man against the living room wall and turned a flashlight on him.

A boy's frightened eyes tried to see who was behind the flashlight. Malachy clicked off the light, and Kevin pulled the boy away from the wall and went through the pockets of his blue jeans. Kevin found a wallet and seven dollar bills.

Kevin took a license from the wallet, and Malachy clicked the flashlight back on to see it. He shone the light on the boy just below his eyes. The boy started to shake and his eyes darted wildly about the room.

"Calm down, Roy. We're not going to hurt you. We have some questions. And you, Roy, have some answers. Now listen carefully, real carefully. We are in a hurry, a big hurry. So we don't have time for bullshit answers. Understand?"

The boy started to shake again. Kevin grabbed his head and forced it into an up-and-down yes motion.

"Good. You can't answer questions with that tape on your mouth. So if I remove the tape, you're not going to scream, are you?"

Kevin grabbed Roy's head and made it wag no. "Good," Malachy said.

The front door opened and quickly closed. The Count joined Malachy and Kevin, standing behind them in the darkness.

"The person behind will know if you're telling the truth. Got it?"

This time Roy nodded yes for himself.

"Excellent," Malachy said. "Ready for the tape to come off without yelling?"

Roy nodded yes again. Malachy reached over and ripped the tape off the boy's mouth.

"I...I..."

Kevin gently put his hand over Roy's mouth.

"Roy, just listen and then answer the questions," Kevin said. "Are you ready to listen?"

Roy vigorously nodded yes. "Are you by yourself? Is there anybody with you inside the building or outside?"

"No, no, I'm by myself," Roy said.

"Why did you break into this apartment?" Malachy asked.

Kevin held his hand over Roy's mouth while Malachy repeated the question.

"Ready to answer?" Kevin asked.

Roy moved his head up and down. Kevin removed his hand.

"I needed some crank—bad. Jonah keeps it in the closest. I came to get it. I..."

Kevin quickly covered his mouth again.

"Did Jonah use you for sex games?" Malachy asked.

Kevin removed his hand, but Roy didn't answer. After a moment, he nodded his head yes. "How many times?"

"Five or six."

"How did he find you?"

"He would look for me on the street."

"When was the last time?" Malachy asked.

"About a week ago," Roy said.

"How did you find the apartment?"

Roy looked surprised. "I was shaking all over and the blindfold moved."

"How did you know the apartment would be empty tonight?" Malachy asked.

"I heard him on the phone last time. He said something about going to California for a meeting this week."

"What kind of meeting?"

"I don't know. He didn't say."

"Roy, this is very important," Malachy said. "Relax and take your time. Think back to your last time and tell us anything he said about the meeting."

Roy started to answer, but Kevin covered his mouth.

"Roy, take your time and think, really think and try to remember," Kevin said.

After a minute, Kevin withdrew his hand.

"After the phone call, when he started playing with me again, he did say something."

"What did he say?"

"He said he should take me to the meeting, but I was too old."

"Did you have to shave yourself?" Malachy asked.

"Each time. He was weird about it. I had to do it while he watched."

"Roy, you've done good. Are you sixteen like the license says? You have a birthday coming up."

"Yeah."

"It's time for you to go home, Roy," Malachy said. "We will make sure you get home safely."

"I can't," Roy said.

"Why not?" Malachy asked.

"At least I get paid on the street."

Malachy and Kevin looked at each other. Kevin pointed to the kitchen.

"Roy, don't move," Malachy said. "We'll be back in a minute. Our friend here will keep an eye on you. You're doing great, don't screw it up."

"I need crank real bad," Roy said. "Real bad."

"We don't have any," Kevin said.

Malachy and Kevin went into kitchen.

"We can't turn him back out on the streets in this condition," Kevin said.

Malachy knew Kevin's tone meant "I won't do that."

"What do you want to do?"

"He can come home with me for a few days," Kevin said. "If I can't convince him to stay off the streets at least when he goes back he won't be so desperate. The way he is now he is going to get himself seriously hurt or killed."

"We could send him to a hospital," Malachy said.

"They'll let him go. He needs somebody to sit on him for a few days. I know the symptoms. On the street, he'll take big risks to get a hit."

"Okay," Malachy said. "It's home to sweat it out with you."

Malachy turned on the lights in the living room. He pulled Roy to his feet and sat him on the couch.

"Roy, do you know what your name means in Irish?" Malachy asked.

Roy looked bewildered and shook his head no.

"Well, it means Red. So Red, here's the deal. I'm Malachy, that's Kevin, and that's Count Leon. Red, we can't let you go back on the street because you're going to end up getting hurt big time. And we can't turn you over to the cops because that won't be good for you either. So, Red, consider yourself adopted for a few days. You are going home with Kevin. He won't hurt or abuse you, and if you choose the street later, so be it. Got it?"

"No, no, I won't go. You've no right to do that. You've got to let me go now. I need..."

Kevin put his hand over Red's mouth and said, "Listen to Malachy, Red."

"Red, you don't think I understand, but I do. You really have only one need right now and that is to stay alive. And you're not capable of doing that on your own. So we are intervening. Is that right? I'll tell you what…you can give me the answer to that question later on, and I promise I won't argue the point."

"I won't go. You can't make me."

"Well, Red, there you go making my point for me…"

Malachy signaled to Kevin who quickly slapped the tape back on Red's mouth, bound his thrashing feet, and then lifted Red off the couch and held him in the air.

"…You're just not capable of understanding reality right now."

CHAPTER XX

Malachy's landline rang. He forced himself awake, cursing and struggling to make out the time. The clock showed 7:10 a.m. He picked up the phone.

"Malachy, are you awake?" Bridget asked.

"I am now. What's going on?"

"There's something happening I thought you'd want to know about. Are you sure you're awake?"

Malachy did not like the tone in Bridget's voice. He sat up in bed.

"Bridget, what's wrong? Just tell me."

"Fr. Kennedy is being held hostage in the church. There are some others with him, nobody knows how many."

"Jesus…"

Malachy caught himself and didn't finish the curse. He bolted from the bed, punched the speakerphone button, and began to pull on yesterday's clothes. He stopped and went to the closet to get his special protective gear. He pulled all of it from the closet and threw it on the bed.

"Tell me everything you know. Don't leave anything out."

"The sirens woke me up, and I looked out the window. There were cops everywhere. They have all the streets blocked off. Nobody is allowed within a block of the church. I went downstairs to find out what was going on, and they wouldn't let me leave the building. They told me to go back upstairs, close the front drapes, and stay away from the windows. They'd make an announcement when things were safe. All they would say is there is a problem in the church."

"How did you find out about Kennedy?"

"I went out the back and down the alley. There are two squads blocking off the street, and I recognized a couple of the cops. They come in for the discounted lunch. They know not to give me any shit. So I asked what was going on."

"Tell me everything they said," Malachy yelled at the phone from the bathroom.

"All they knew was that some nutcase had taken Fr. Kennedy hostage at the start of 6:30 Mass. And that he is also holding some of the people who were there for the Mass. Nobody knows how many, but it can't be more than a handful nowadays."

"Did they say what kind of weapons he had?" Malachy asked.

"I asked because I knew you'd want to know. They said they heard it was a handgun, but they weren't sure."

"Who called the cops?" Malachy asked.

"A businessman came in late for Mass through the side door. When he saw what was happening he ran out and called the cops on his cell phone."

"Has there been any communication with the hostage taker?"

"The cops are on bullhorns. He sent out one woman. I guess as a messenger. My cops didn't know what the message was."

"I can guess," Malachy said.

"The thing is, Malachy, I think I might know who the hostage taker is. What should I do? Go to the cops?"

"Who?"

"I think it might be Holy Holleran."

"Who the hell is that?"

"You've seen him a few times in the Shamrock. He's a lot younger than you. A neighborhood guy who got tossed from the seminary years back. Emotionally unstable. He never got over it. Started down the conspiracy road. He got the nickname because he was always going to church, always trying to get Kennedy to start some old-fashioned devotional practice. You know the type, Opus Dei is too liberal for him."

"Why do you think it's Holleran?" Malachy asked as he selected what to wear and started to dress.

"I heard he was becoming obsessed with Kennedy, complaining to the archdiocese and even to Rome. Last week I heard he started yelling at Kennedy during one of his sermons. Said he was preaching heresy, that kind of thing. You know what Kennedy is like."

Malachy was silent, his mind churning.

"Malachy, are you still there? Should I go to the cops with my suspicion? Maybe they don't know yet who he is, maybe it would help."

Malachy picked up the phone and spoke firmly.

"No, don't go to the police. Here's what I want you to do. Call the Count and explain the situation in detail and tell him to meet me at your place with full equipment. Then go back to those cops you know and find out who's in charge. And then call whoever you know who knows Holleran and his family. Gossip with them. Find out as much as you can about him. Take notes. Can you do that?"

"Yes. What are you going to do?"

"I'm not sure yet. I'll be at your place soon. Leave your back door open. One other thing, would Holleran know who I am?"

"Of course, everyone in the neighborhood knows who you are."

Malachy carefully checked himself in the mirror. He was dressed in his full "armor." He thought he looked a little bulked up but passable. Under the circumstances, even the Count wouldn't criticize.

Malachy entered the kitchen and waved to Bridget who was on the phone. He went to the front room, pulled back the curtains, and surveyed the scene three floors below.

"Jesus," Malachy said softly to himself.

There were squad cars everywhere with blue lights flashing, yellow "Police Line Do Not Cross" tape blocking every approach to the church, cops with bullhorns ordering the gawkers in the apartment windows to move back, a canine unit, SWAT team officers lined up on the sides of the front and side entrances to the church at the ready, and ambulances waiting a half block down the street.

Malachy figured there was also a team ready to storm through the dressing area and into the church proper. If they all went in at once, the odds of a friendly-fire incident increased greatly, especially if they didn't know exactly where Holleran and the hostages were located in the church.

Malachy cracked open the window to listen to a bullhorn. The negotiator was giving a telephone number and asking that hostage taker to open negotiations by using any cell phone available. No name was used. After a few minutes, the negotiator returned to the bullhorn.

"We understand your message. There will be no attempt to enter the church. We understand the church is a sanctuary. We respect that. We are asking that you stay in contact via the cell phone directly. We are asking to talk with you directly, not through messages."

Malachy pictured the inside of the church in his mind. He knew exactly where he would hole up if under siege—the side windowless area near the middle where the confessionals are located. There was no way for a sniper to get off a shot through a window or from entranceways into the pew area. A determined gunman could get off many rounds before the SWAT team would be in a position to fire a lethal shot. And Holleran would start with Kennedy. Heretics are always the first to go.

If the church was stormed, Malachy figured the hostages for no help. At 6:30 Mass on a weekday, probably few under sixty and mostly women. He searched his memory for neighborhood retired cops who might be at the Mass. None came to mind. Lent was long over, and with the good weather the early risers would be at the golf course or fishing at the lake. He returned to the kitchen. He motioned to Bridget he wanted to talk. She ended her conversation and picked up her notebook.

"There's a Captain Ronan in charge, not the normal commander of the SWAT team."

"No luck there. I don't know him. What about Holleran?"

"Holleran's family—three sisters, father dead, mother living with one of the sisters in Lake of the Ozarks, Missouri. The other two are married, one living here and one out of town. Major crack-up after being tossed from the seminary. Never had any serious girlfriends even in high school. Family normal Irish-Catholics—if there is such a thing. Not highly religious or pious, but Sunday Mass types. Doesn't talk to one sister who's been married twice, both times outside the Church—she's the one who lives here.

"Lives alone in a one bedroom. Too strange to hold a normal job. Used to make a low-rent living delivering newspapers in the very early morning in the burbs. Got fired for putting pro-life flyers in papers that editorially supported abortion rights. Does odd jobs for various pro-life groups. Mom sends him money every month. Has grown progressively weirder over the last year. Lately two things have really obsessed him—Kennedy and the Baltimore Catechism."

"What's Kennedy got to do with the Baltimore Catechism?" Malachy interjected.

"Nothing," Bridget said. "Separate obsessions. Over the last three months he's been at almost every Mass said by Kennedy taking notes, documenting Kennedy's heretical preaching—Holleran's words—and then sending long complaints to the archdiocese and Rome quoting canon law statutes Kennedy violated."

"I'm sure O'Grady finds those entertaining," Malachy said. "So, what's the deal with the Baltimore Catechism?"

"He's committing it to memory," Bridget said. "The long version."

"Joining the union of tortured Catholic school children," Malachy said. "Myself included."

"Me, too," Bridget said. "Anyway, he believes Vatican II is an invalid council, its reforms are the work of the Devil, and only by returning to the Latin Mass and the Baltimore Catechism can the Church be rescued. Got the picture?"

"I do and I've an idea," Malachy said. "Please tell me you have a computer."

"Okay, I have a computer. But it's dial-up and it's slow."

"No problem," Malachy said. "Just point me in the right direction."

Bridget opened a cabinet and pointed.

"How about making some breakfast while I'm online."

"God, Malachy, you're a strange one. How can you think about food?"

"Low blood sugar leads to confusion," Malachy said, sitting down in front of the computer. "There is already enough confusion in that church."

Malachy worked at the computer for twenty minutes, slowly and methodically eating his breakfast. He stationed Bridget at the front window, and she gave a running commentary on the happenings at the church. The Count came through the kitchen door, carrying two cases of what appeared to be TV or photographic equipment.

"Bridget, keep telling us what you see," Malachy said, closing the kitchen door. "We can hear you."

Malachy quickly briefed the Count on the situation and his idea. The Count paced the kitchen silently for a couple of minutes before responding.

"I propose you give the negotiator some more time. He's just getting started. The ideal solution is no involvement by you and Kennedy is safe. But, you're right, Kennedy will be the first one harmed in any storming operation, if Holleran is not bluffing. And there's no way to know that until some kind of action starts."

"Action can erupt at any time with somebody like that," Malachy said. "I need to get in there so Kennedy has a chance. Those SWAT guys are pros, but they'll get no help from the hostages, including Kennedy. And I don't think they get any easy shots."

"If the snipers had an easy shot, they would have already taken it," the Count said.

"If my idea works, I get the shot," Malachy said. "But first I have to get by the SWAT commander. There is no way they let me into the church with a weapon. What do I use?"

"Let's start with the goal and work backward to the means. You need something that forces Holleran to act instinctively with his hands, an involuntary action that makes it near impossible for him to deliberately fire his weapon for a few seconds. Time enough for you to get to him. We'll have to risk an accidental discharge."

"But whatever it is, it can't trigger an attack by the SWAT team," Malachy said. "So nothing that sounds like gunfire or anything that makes them think the hostages are under attack."

"Something small and normal-looking," the Count said.

The Count opened one of his equipment cases. It was full of carefully arranged, clearly labeled, small packages. The names on the closed packages were generic and innocuous—meter, battery backup, lens, special lights, etc. He selected one labeled "cell phone" and opened it.

"If you can get close enough, this will do the trick," the Count said. "But you only get one shot."

"No explosives," Malachy said.

"I understood the first time," the Count said. "It is spring-loaded and shoots a capsule. You target his face. The capsule is under pressure. When it hits, it will silently explode, releasing an eye-burning mist. If he breathes in enough of the mist, he will lose consciousness. No way to guarantee that—too many variables."

"Are you two listening to me?" Bridget yelled from the front room. "Everything is status quo. There still talking with him through the bullhorn. They are trying to persuade him to let all the women go. No response yet."

"Yes, we're listening," Malachy said, opening the kitchen door.

"Why was the door closed?" Bridget asked.

"So you are not part of it if anything goes wrong."

"You're using my apartment with my permission," Bridget said. "I'm already in. Leave the door open."

"Okay."

The Count looked at his watch.

"I propose practice with blanks. If Kennedy is not safe by then, you try and talk your way into the church."

"Show me how it works," Malachy said. "I try and talk my way in as soon as I can hit the target."

"How about three times in a row?" the Count asked.

"Reluctantly agreed," Malachy said.

The Count loaded the cell phone with a blank, held the phone in his hand palm up, and turned his back on Malachy.

"Make a fist with your left hand and hold that arm straight out," the Count instructed.

Malachy complied, and the Count spun around and fired at close range, hitting Malachy's fist with the blank capsule.

"Jesus, that hurts!" Malachy half-yelled, instinctively pulling his fist toward his chest.

"Exactly," the Count said. "Now you have some sense of its force and how the physical reaction cannot be controlled."

"I believed you when you just told me," Malachy said.

"That's not the kind of knowledge you need to have to be successful," the Count said, reloading the phone and handing it to Malachy.

The Count reached into the other case and pulled out a plastic face mask without any openings and put it on.

"Back up five feet and try to hit me in the face," the Count said.

Malachy backed up, fired, and missed.

"You need to get a sense of the trajectory," the Count said. "Try again, same distance."

Malachy and the Count repeated the firings until Malachy could hit the face mask three times in a row from ten feet, standing or crouching.

"Okay," the Count said. "We're there. The ideal is to have Holleran reach for the phone as if he is getting a call and fire it right into his face. Otherwise, fire at the face if you're within ten feet. From a longer distance, fire at the chest and pray he breathes in."

"Understood," Malachy said. "I'm ready to go."

"Not yet," the Count said. "You need to take off all your armor. You're just an ordinary citizen, rushing over to help out because you know Holleran and can talk him down. Ordinary citizens don't dress like that. Let the SWAT team give you a vest to wear."

Malachy knew the Count was right but was reluctant to give up his special protective clothing and vest. It served him well in past confrontations, and he connected it to safe outcomes.

"I'm keeping the cup, the boots, and the White Sox hat," Malachy said.

The Count eyed the hat skeptically and said, "Reluctantly agreed. The way you dress no one will notice the hat is a little too bulky."

Malachy quickly removed the vest and the protective, thin plastic guards from his clothing. He looked like somebody who had lost weight and was wearing clothing a size too big.

The Count examined him and delivered his judgment.

"Perfect. You look just like the good citizen who threw on whatever was available and rushed over to help. Stuff the phone in your front pocket."

Malachy emerged from the front door of the apartment building, and a cop waved and yelled at him to get back inside. Malachy walked rapidly directly toward the cop.

"I'm Malachy Madden. I know the hostage taker, and he'll listen to me. I can help."

"Are you a relative?"

"No," Malachy said. "I know him from the neighborhood and from the Shamrock bar. He's a lot younger than I am, but I know him and his family well. I really can help. He'll listen to me."

"Okay," the cop said. "Follow me."

Malachy followed the cop through a gap in the police line of tape and sawhorses. The cop motioned Malachy to stop. The cop continued to a makeshift command post a few yards away.

"Captain this guy says he knows the hostage taker well. He wants to help," the cop said.

The captain put down his walkie-talkie and came over to Malachy. "Who is he?"

"Holy Holleran," Malachy said.

"Holy? What the hell kind of a name is that?"

"Neighborhood nickname," Malachy said. His real name is Henry Michael Holleran. Hank to his friends."

"How do you know he's the hostage taker?"

"Because he's been stalking Fr. Kennedy for more than three months. He thinks Kennedy is a dangerous heretic."

"Who are you?"

"Malachy Madden. I've lived in the neighborhood my whole life. I run the Shamrock over on Devon. Holleran comes in there all the time. I know the family really well."

"I've heard your name before," the captain said.

"I used to defend before the Police Board," Malachy said.

"Wait a second."

The captain yelled for the negotiator to join them. A young man, not in uniform, put down a bullhorn and quickly moved to the captain's side.

"This is Malachy Madden. He thinks he knows who the hostage taker is," the captain said as he turned toward Malachy. "Tell him."

Malachy repeated the information, filling in some more detail about the family and Holleran.

"Good," the negotiator said. "Let's get the sister down here and see if she can talk to him and defuse the situation."

"That won't work," Malachy said. "He's not talking with that sister—she married outside of the Church twice—she's part of the problem as far as he's concerned. Let me talk with him. I think he'll listen to me. I'm old enough to be his father."

"It's worth a try," the negotiator said, looking at the captain. "We've had no luck establishing phone contact. We've broadcast our number over the bullhorn, but he hasn't called. We know some of the hostages have cell phones, but they are all turned off. Let's put Malachy on the bullhorn and see if he can establish phone contact. We need to get the guy talking."

"We haven't even established Holleran as the hostage taker for certain," the captain said.

Malachy decided it was time to ratchet things up.

"Look, it's Holleran for sure. Like I said, I know the guy really well. He's kind of jumpy. At the Shamrock he'd be quiet for anywhere up to a couple of hours and then he'd start to act weird. And I'd have to intervene and calm him down. Walk around with him a little bit, talking and listening."

The negotiator turned to the captain and said in a deferential tone, "Your decision, but right now we're stymied, and any kind of talk is better than none."

"Okay," the captain said. "We'll put him on the bullhorn—not much risk in that."

Malachy decided to ratchet it up one more notch. "That might've worked an hour ago, but now you're running out of time. If he's where I figure him to be and he starts to get jumpy, a lot of people are going to get hurt before you get to him."

"What the hell are you talking about?" the captain asked sharply.

"That's my church too," Malachy said. "I figure he has Kennedy and the hostages over by the confessionals where you can't get a shot and it'll take too long to get to him. The guy is nutty about religion, but he's not stupid."

Malachy decided to let his last statement percolate for a while before he made his pitch. He looked at the captain as if he expected him to say something.

"Well, he's somewhere we can't get a sight on him," the captain said.

"And you're running out of time," Malachy said. "Let me talk to him."

"You just said it was too late for that," the negotiator said.

"It is too late, over the bullhorn," Malachy said. "Let me talk to him at the entry to the church where he can see me. He's used to me from the Shamrock. Just tell him over the bullhorn I'm coming into the church—that I need to talk to him about something religious. Once I'm in there I'll use the Baltimore Catechism to get him talking and to persuade him to let the hostages go. If he turns me down once he sees me, I'll leave."

"What's the Baltimore Catechism, and why is that important?" the negotiator asked in an aggressive tone.

Malachy knew he had his wedge. The negotiator was not a Catholic.

"It's what Catholic kids used to have to learn about the faith," the captain said. "But Holleran is too young for that."

"He's obsessed with it," Malachy said. "Kennedy probably said something in his sermon that Holleran thought contradicted it and it triggered him. I remember enough of it to be able to talk to Holleran without setting him off. I think I can use it to get him to let the hostages go." Malachy raised his voice a little, "But, I'm telling you, you're running out of time."

"Give us a moment," the negotiator said.

Malachy quickly stepped away. The negotiator turned his back to Malachy and talked intensely to the captain. After a minute of back and forth, they motioned to Malachy to join them.

"We're going to give your idea a try," the captain said. "You'll have to wear a vest, and we'll give you an earpiece and wire you up so we can hear what's going on. You need to follow our instructions to the letter. Basically, you talk only from the entryway. And if he shows the slightest sign of being agitated, you get the hell out of there."

"I understand," Malachy said.

"Malachy Madden needs to talk to you about a religious subject," the negotiator announced over the bullhorn. "Something we don't understand. He will be coming into the church from the front door. He is unarmed and just wants to talk to you. He will be entering the church in three minutes."

Malachy opened the church door and stepped into the vestibule. He stopped and let his eyes adjust to the light in the church. He pulled open the door to the pew area, raised his arms up with his palms out, and went through the door.

"Stop right there!" Holleran yelled. "Don't take another step."

Malachy stopped, still holding his arms up.

"Is it all right if I put my arms down?" Malachy asked in a loud voice. "They're getting tired."

"Okay," Holleran said. "But no tricks. Satan is finally controlled."

Malachy lowered his voice and turned to the source of the voice. As he expected, Holleran was by the confessionals, pacing back and forth with a gun in his hand. He didn't see any hostages, but he heard them. There were sounds of muffled crying and praying coming from the pews in front of Holleran.

"Good job," the negotiator said through the earpiece. "Keep him talking."

"What do you want to talk to me about?" Holleran yelled.

"I need to finish my confession with Fr. Kennedy," Malachy said. "He didn't give me final absolution. I'm worried. Where is he?"

"He's right here," Holleran said, pointing with his gun to a pew. "Kennedy is in league with Satan. Satan controls him now. And I control Satan."

"That may be," Malachy said, "but he is still a priest and will always be a priest, no matter what he says or does."

The way Holleran pointed the gun Malachy calculated that Kennedy and the other hostages were forced to lay down, probably one per pew, facedown. Holleran could easily and quickly shoot them all just by taking a few steps. He hardly even needed to aim.

"I am just trying to do what the Baltimore Catechism tells me to do," Malachy said. "Isn't that what you want everybody to do?"

"You're trying to confuse me," Holleran said, putting his gun hand to the side of his head. He grabbed his forehead with the other hand and quickened his pacing. "No confusion, no confusion," he muttered.

"Don't you want me to do what the catechism teaches?" Malachy asked.

"You're a friend of Kennedy's—it's some kind of trick!"

"I just want to do what the catechism says," Malachy responded.

"What do you mean?"

"The catechism teaches that the penitent should return to the priest who gave the conditional absolution—that's why I need to see Fr. Kennedy."

"Persuade him to let Kennedy come to you," the negotiator said into the earpiece. "Don't go to Kennedy, don't go farther into the church. Do you hear me?"

"Just let me talk with Fr. Kennedy," Malachy said loudly, ignoring the earpiece. "It won't take long."

"I know you're trying to trick me," Holleran shouted.

"I'm not," Malachy said. "I'm just trying to do what I was taught."

"Why are you wearing a vest, then?"

"The cops made me. They wouldn't let come in here without one. I'll take it off. All I care about is the chance to finish my confession and return to a state of grace."

Malachy slowly undid the vest and threw it underhand up the aisle.

Malachy's ear was filled with a loud voice, "No, no, you're not following the script. Get him to let Kennedy come to you!"

Malachy chose his words carefully for both audiences.

"Look, everything is going to work out. It's not a trick. I just need to talk with Fr. Kennedy. I'll follow your instructions after that."

Holleran stopped pacing and in a calm, almost ceremonious, tone asked, "Are you willing to swear by the soul of your dead wife Maria that this is not a trick?"

Malachy felt the breath go out of him as if he'd been hit hard in the stomach. He silently gasped for air as his mind whirled trying to come up with an answer. Then he remembered something Maria told him when they were courting. "You know, Malachy, I'm really more pragmatic than you are. You've a strong streak of other-world, romantic–

mystical in you. I guess it's the difference between Sicily and Ireland."

"I am willing to so swear," Malachy said.

"Say the words," Holleran responded.

"I swear by the soul of my wife Maria that this is not a trick."

Malachy's voice was strong, firm, resonant, and convincing.

"All right, you can see Kennedy. Come up the side aisle slowly."

Malachy ignored the squawking in his earpiece and started walking up the side aisle. He concentrated on Holleran who backed away from the pews. When he reached the confessionals he stopped.

"Where is he?" Malachy asked Holleran.

"Over here, Malachy," Kennedy said, lifting his head above the end piece of the pew.

"Quiet, Satan!"

Malachy motioned toward Kennedy.

"I'll just kneel at the end of the pew," Malachy said, moving slowly toward Kennedy. As soon as Malachy was positioned between the pews holding the hostages and Holleran he stopped, turned, and faced Holleran.

"My cell phone is vibrating," Malachy said. "I need to answer it."

Malachy did not wait for a response. He quickly put one arm in the air with the palm out and with his other hand reached into his front pocket for the phone. He showed the phone to Holleran and then put it to his ear.

"Yes, he's here. Just a moment. It's for you."

Malachy held the phone out to Holleran.

"Who is it?"

"It's your mom calling from Lake of the Ozarks. She wants to talk to you."

"My mom?"

"Yeah, your mom. You can talk to her while I finish my confession."

Malachy held out the phone and turned toward Kennedy's pew. Holleran dropped his gun hand slightly and came over to take the phone from Malachy. As Holleran reached for the phone, Malachy swung the other arm rapidly, and hit Holleran hard in the side of the throat with the heel of his fisted hand. Holleran dropped the gun and staggered backward gagging and gasping, unable to breathe. He collapsed on the church floor still gasping for air. Malachy picked up the gun, emptied the chamber, and stuffed the gun in his belt. He ran over to Holleran, thoroughly patted him down, and then methodically stomped each hand into the stone floor, mangling his fingers. Holleran writhed in pain and made a strange, suppressed screaming sound.

"What's going on? What going on?" It was now the captain's voice in the earpiece. "If you don't tell us right now, we're coming in!"

"This is Malachy. Everything is under control. Hold your positions. Kennedy is coming out with the hostages. Repeating, hold your positions. The hostages are coming out. Everything is under control."

Malachy put his hand over the mic and approached the pews. Heads began to pop up above the edge of the pews.

"Okay everybody, it's safe to get up. Holleran has been disarmed. Is everybody able to walk out on their own?"

"Oh my God, are we safe?" a woman asked, crying. "I prayed and prayed…it's a miracle."

Malachy saw another old woman struggling to right herself in the pew with her cane. She was frail but had a determined look on her face. It was ninety-year-old Sis O'Brien, a regular at the Shamrock and one of the few who could tame Bridget.

"Sis, are you okay?" Malachy asked.

"I'm fine," Sis said. "Good job, Malachy. I was going to whack that fruit loop with my cane, but I was afraid I'd miss and he'd shoot somebody. Surprised he didn't given the mewling and crying from the sob sisters here. I thought they'd never shut up. Not a fighter among them."

Kennedy started toward Holleran.

"Leave him be," Malachy commanded. "I'll see to him. You need to lead these folks out of the church."

"God, Malachy, don't hurt that poor, crazy man anymore."

Malachy looked at his friend without rancor. From long experience he knew that those who had never faced a lethal adversary often reacted to necessary force like it was gratuitous violence.

"Holleran will fully recover from all his injuries," Malachy said. "But if he shoots somebody in the head, the funeral mass would probably interfere with the recovery process. I was just making certain he was out of action."

"Oh God, Malachy, I'm sorry I didn't mean... It's just all so upsetting. I'm truly grateful you rescued us. Forgive me."

"It's all right, Paul," Malachy said, using Kennedy's first name. "Okay, everybody listen up. Line up behind Fr. Kennedy, single file. As you exit the church, keep your arms up, palms out, hands empty. Then do exactly what the police tell you. Everybody understand? Good, line up!"

Three women and one man lined up behind Kennedy in his vestments. Malachy watched as they filed into the vestibule. It almost looked like the procession after Mass except Kennedy was first in line.

"The hostages are coming out," Malachy said. "Hostages coming out behind Kennedy."

"What about Holleran?" the captain asked. "Where's Holleran?"

"Disarmed," Malachy said. "On the church floor. Better send in the paramedics, he's having a hard time breathing."

"Are you hurt?"

"No," Malachy said. "Everything went according to plan. Holleran is the only one hurt."

Malachy put the gun on the floor and waited for the SWAT team.

Malachy came through the church's now open doors escorted by two fully armed SWAT team members. They steered him over to where the captain and negotiator were waiting by themselves.

"You lied to me—you had no intention of following the plan," the captain nearly shouted at Malachy.

Malachy let the captain glare angrily at him for a short time before responding with a mild, "Well, everything turned out all right." Malachy was going to use his all's-well-that ends-well line, but thought it might put the captain over the edge.

"You put hostages' lives at risk with your bullshit stunt," the negotiator said. "Innocent people could have been killed. You were lucky."

Malachy ignored the negotiator who could cause him no trouble and looked the captain in the eyes and said, "It wasn't luck. I did my homework and had better intelligence than you did because of the neighborhood. You trusted me, and you made the right decision. Holleran dealt with me just like I said he would. He could've sent me away, but he didn't. So, what's the difference?"

"The fucking difference is, I'm the one who makes the decision about the use of force," the captain shouted at Malachy. "You were supposed to just talk to Holleran, that's the fucking difference. I should have you arrested!"

"You might want to check with your PR department before you do that," Malachy responded. "The last time I looked, the department was getting lambasted by everybody because a rogue cop beat the shit out of some innocent schmuck, and it was all caught on video surveillance. Made for really nasty pictures in the papers. You have an unqualified win here. You took the risk, why not reap the reward?"

The captain started to answer and then abruptly stopped. He carefully looked Malachy up and down. "Give me your hat," he ordered. Malachy took the White Sox hat from his head and handed it over.

"Cub's fan?" Malachy asked.

"Shut the fuck up," the captain said, as he rapped the hat with his knuckles. "You're Kennedy's friend. You probably never interacted with Holleran in your life. You came down here and lied to us to get a chance to save Kennedy, putting lives at risk."

"Can't argue with that," Malachy said, putting his hands out in front of him like he was going to be cuffed.

"Fuck you," the captain said, ignoring Malachy's outstretched hands. He hurled the hat at Malachy's face. Malachy instinctively raised his arms and ducked, partially blocking the hat with his forearm. It grazed his face and fell to the ground.

The captain turned, stomped a few feet away, and then turned around to address Malachy again.

"Just fuck you and your PR."

Malachy leaned down, picked up his hat, and brushed it off before putting it on his head.

"You just made an enemy," the negotiator said.

"That's too bad. I already have more than I need. Look I understand he's pissed and with good reason. Nobody likes having their authority undercut. But the department can use a win right now. The captain has one here, that's all I'm saying."

Malachy and Fr. Kennedy walked toward the reporters and TV cameras gathered behind the police barricade.

"Do me a favor and praise the police, especially the captain in charge," Malachy said. "He's a little pissed at me."

"More than a little, the way I heard it," Kennedy said.

They stopped in front of the barricade, and the reporters started shouting questions.

"Would it be all right if I gave a few remarks?" Kennedy asked.

When the group quieted down, Kennedy started.

"I just came from the church where all of us who were taken hostage gathered to thank God for His mercy and grace during this morning's rescue operation. We also prayed for Hank Holleran, the deluded man who threatened us. We prayed that he would be healed in every way."

To Malachy, Kennedy's voice and intonation sounded just like the start to one of his sermons. Malachy half-expected Kennedy to start pacing, turning, and twisting as he often did on Sundays.

Kennedy continued, "For most of us, the day-to-day outstanding work of the Chicago Police Department is invisible. Today it was visible, front and present. Without the wisdom and patience of the SWAT team led by Captain Michael Ronan, the outcome could have been quite different.

"Captain Ronan and his team demonstrated today the best the Chicago Police Department has to offer, and we are grateful. And of course special thanks to my good friend Malachy Madden, who under the leadership of Captain Ronan, performed the actual rescue."

Kennedy put his hand on Malachy's shoulder and shook his hand. The photographers asked them to hold the pose so they could capture the moment. Then the questions started. Malachy kept parrying the questions about the details of the rescue with a standard response.

"You are asking about tactics. Captain Ronan is the only one who can speak to that if he chooses to. Remember, it helps if Ronan and his team can achieve tactical surprise in these types of situations in the future. So don't expect too many details."

Eventually, the questions turned to Malachy's motivation and his friendship with Kennedy. "Friendship was not the only reason I was part of the rescue effort," Malachy said in answer to a question.

"What was? Why did you do it?" a reporter shouted.

"I guess you can say it was an environmental imperative," Malachy said, knowing he was only half-joking.

That answer stimulated a new torrent of questions about chemical weapons and the like.

Malachy paused for quiet before answering.

"Good confessors are very scarce and difficult to find. If they're not on the Federal Endangered Species list, they should be."

CHAPTER XXI

Malachy bolted awake from his dream and looked down at his hands. In the dream he was mercilessly beating a crippled boy, who kept trying to speak but couldn't. He thought about Holleran and the oath he was forced to pronounce in church. He settled back in the bed and made himself remember a good time with Maria. He chose the beginning of their courtship when he was just out of the Marines. They had met at a dance because bawdy Aunt Theresa told Maria to date the Irish if she wanted a talker: "Your ears will be more sore than the other part."

They were in Aunt Theresa's apartment in the double bed that almost filled the guest bedroom. They had finished making love for the first time and Malachy was telling Maria stories about his youth. Maria said, "Tell me another story."

"I call this the Factory Boy Story—a tale of ingratitude. We were playing our greatest rival, the Academy. Christian Brothers versus Jesuits. Early in the game I sack their star quarterback, just smother him. I am a little slow getting off him and he says, 'Off me, factory boy, get off me.' I push him back down and draw a personal foul. The coach benches me, yelling at me like I just lost the game with that penalty. I watch the QB like a hawk and then I see the tell."

"Isn't that a poker term?" Maria asked.

"My dad taught me about it because of poker, but it applies to all kinds of situations. So I plead with the coach to put me back in, but he just ignores me. Finally, with just minutes to go, when we are on the wrong side of 7 to 6 and the Academy has the ball and looks to score again, I get in his face and announce, 'I think I can get the ball back.' At first, I think he is going to punch me, but then he just pushes me onto the field. I substitute for the end instead of my usual tackle position. That sets the coach into a yelling frenzy, but it is too late.

"The ball is snapped and I run for the spot where the tell indicates there will be a pitchout. My timing is perfect, and I grab the ball and head up the field with dreams of glory in my head. I'm moving as fast as I can but I'm big and not that fast, and when I look back the QB is gaining on me. It's a footrace I'm going to lose.

"I wish I had something to throw at him besides the football. I know if I can stay on my feet, I score. But if he tackles me low, I go down and time runs out. I start to slow down and then suddenly stop, plant my right foot, crouch, and brace myself for the impact.

"The QB hits me going full stride and just as he makes contact I thrust my free elbow into his gut as hard as I can. That takes the starch out of his shorts, and it is all he can do to just hang on to me. I head toward the goal line dragging the QB with a single thought in my head to keep my legs pumping. The goal line is less than ten yards away.

"Suddenly, I'm hit from the side, and the ball pops straight up in the air. As I go down, I see Belmont, our other end, reach for the ball, and I'm dead certain that he will catch it and carry it over the goal line. And he did. We win!"

"Why a tale of ingratitude?" Maria asked.

"Because, when all the excitement calms down, the coach claps me on the back, and says, 'Not elegant, Madden, but you got the job done.' I set up the win for him against our greatest rival and all he can muster is a 'not elegant.' I call that rank ingratitude!"

"There should've been a better reward than that," Maria said, starting to stroke his thigh.

When they finished making love for the second time, Maria said something in Italian.

"How does that translate?"

Maria gave an exaggerated sigh of contentment and said, "In colloquial English, 'not elegant, Madden, but you got the job done.'"

†

"How was the well-deserved day off?" Kevin asked Malachy. "It seems in my absence you went to church and it wasn't even a holy day. I hear there was a little excitement there."

Malachy settled into the front seat of Kevin's truck and looked for coffee for his empty cup before answering.

"Coffee is in the thermos on the floor behind me," Kevin said, as he drove off. "And a bakery bag."

Malachy poured himself coffee, selected a sweet roll, and gave a sigh.

"My day off was brilliant, just brilliant," Malachy answered. "The morning in bed with day-old newspapers, channel surfing, and additional sleep. Then a very late breakfast with Fr. Kennedy followed by an early dinner with the girls and the grandkids, aka Cuchullain's band. And that followed by a moderate amount of Jameson at a competitive watering hole and then early to bed. Ain't life grand?"

Kevin pulled onto the highway and headed toward Wisconsin. "Indeed it is," Kevin answered. "And what did you and the good Father discuss?

"Mostly his namesake," Malachy responded. "You know, the one who took the road to Damascus. Are you aware that there is no clear, compelling biblical evidence that St. Paul believed in the divinity of Jesus in the Trinitarian sense?"

"Not a bit of it," Kevin said. "That was no part of my religion classes."

"Mine either," Malachy said. "The Brothers and their hired hands were not into complexity in theological matters. In fact, based on their teaching one could conclude the New Testament was some kind of sexual rule book."

"A strict one, too," Kevin said. "At least my version was."

"Mine, too. And speaking of sex, drugs, and rock and roll, how is our young friend Red?"

"He had a very rough couple of days."

"Unfortunate, but not unexpected," Malachy said. "Will he bolt?"

"I don't think so. I think he actually like his new digs. I told him he could stay as long as he wants."

"Who is with him now?"

"Antonella."

"Bari's sister?" Malachy asked, surprised.

"The one and the same," Kevin said. "I called her and explained the situation. She was eager to help. Turns out she is an outstanding cook in addition to her literary skills. So she and Red are cooking at my place as we speak. If all goes well in Wisconsin, I will be dining with them tonight."

"That situation would tend to make for ambivalence on wanting Red to stay or bolt," Malachy said.

"No ambivalence," Kevin said seriously. "I want Red to stay. A return to the streets will end up killing him."

"If he stays, what's next?"

"Work. I want to hire him for the Shamrock, if it is okay with you."

"Sure," Malachy said. "But you tell Bridget."

"I already did," Kevin said. "He starts as a busboy."

"And if I told her that, she'd yell at me like I was an FBI agent, but with you it is all sweetness and light. I don't get it."

"Irish charm," Kevin said.

"What? I'm a thoroughbred."

"Only in the Irish part," Kevin said.

"Are you implying I suffer from a charm deficit?"

"I'm taking the Fifth," Kevin answered. "It's a long ride to Wisconsin."

"Speaking of Wisconsin, what did you hear from the Count?"

"He has been scoping out the area, the police capacity, and Flynn's place for the last four hours. The plan is a go so far."

"Jesus, the man suffers from some kind of insomnia. That means he got up at 4:00 A.M."

"And he believes you suffer from some kind of thyroid disorder—on the underactive side of the ledger."

"Circadian rhythms are a mysterious thing," Malachy said. "One imperils good health by fighting what nature has ordained. I'm not a morning person."

Kevin turned and gave Malachy a big, charming smile.

"It is rumored that John Jameson is not either," Kevin said.

"Alas, the rumor is too often true," Malachy said. "Let's stop for more coffee before we cross the border."

"Will do," Kevin said. "The Count does have one problem you should be aware of. It seems he's a little offended you didn't use his device to subdue Holleran. He thought your method, while effective enough, lacked a certain subtly. He made some allusion to 'crude.'"

"Guilty as charged," Malachy said. "Holleran really pissed me off. But it was also a matter of training. The venerable Sergeant O'Rourke must take some of the blame."

"How so?" Kevin asked.

"How many times did the good Sergeant tell us—'Fuck fancy, fucking fancy will get you a fucking funeral'?"

"Too many to count," Kevin said.

"Rote learning is not subtle, but it can be effective. I still know my multiplication tables, and, better yet, I'm still alive to recite them."

†

Kevin and Malachy found the Count waiting for them at an isolated picnic table in a rest area off the two-lane highway leading to Flynn's cottage. They greeted each other and then the Count spread out an elaborate lunch from a cooler. Their dress, demeanor, and lunch all planned to assure any observers that the meeting was nothing more than old friends with hardy appetites meeting to talk over old times.

The Count watched Malachy eye the sandwiches with his hand hovering over the triple-decker pumpernickel and smoked salmon. He knew Malachy would interrupt him once he attempted to discuss business. "I propose…"

Malachy raised his hand in a stop gesture and asked, "Are those capers?"

"Yes, of course."

Malachy picked up the sandwich and started to eat. After he swallowed the first large bite, he delivered his verdict. "Delicious. Please proceed."

"I propose we block the driveway with my van and Kevin covers the highway from his car," the Count said. "There is a sheltered area at the back of the cottage where we can change into our outfits unseen. We will need no more than three hours in the cottage with full equipment to find the originals of the photos if they are there."

"For sure he didn't travel with them," Malachy said. "So they're someplace he controls."

"I'm hoping for a safety deposit box in the local bank," the Count said.

"Jesus, I'm hoping not," Malachy said. "Remember, there's a three initial reason why you never did banks—FBI. Even Bridget allows they do a good job on bank robberies."

"Just a professional hopeful aspiration, not a proposal," the Count said.

"How do we get the equipment into the cottage?" Malachy asked.

"It's all packed in a large cart on bicycle tires. Rolls rapidly and easily. I've calculated all the distances. With the driveway blocked, if Kevin signals trouble we will have just enough time to exit the house, change, and put the equipment away."

"What are we, anyway?" Malachy asked.

"Septic system experts. We're testing the leach lines. We set that up before we enter the cottage."

"And if a county cop shows up for some reason?"

"Kevin waits until we are talking with him and then calls in an emergency that pulls him away. The sheriff's department has a lot of territory to cover. Odds are we never see him. Kevin's car will have the hood up so if he is just cruising, he will most likely stop to see if help is needed. I am using the masculine, but one deputy is an attractive female. If she stops, Kevin will just have to charm her."

"No problem," Kevin said, looking at Malachy.

"What about plates?" Malachy asked.

"We use false IDs and plates. They will all check out to a non-traceable front business."

"So what goes wrong?" Malachy asked.

"Flynn returns from his trip and comes directly here via airport shuttle while we are in the cottage. He calls the sheriff and/or the state police before he investigates why a van is parked at the beginning of his long driveway. He persuades the driver of the shuttle to block our van. The van malfunctions because we are forced to drive over the rough field and crash through his fence. The police arrive and we are arrested and charged with being fraudulent shit detectors."

Kevin and Malachy laughed, and Malachy said, "I'll take that risk."

"You know what's interesting about that bank?" the Count asked. "It is not housed in a stand-alone building, but shares a common wall with a store."

Malachy smiled at the Count and said, "Mr. William Sutton, could you please keep your aspirations to yourself? I'm trying to digest the excellent luncheon thoughtfully provided by my friend and colleague, the risk-aversive Count Leon Latalski!"

†

In the basement of Flynn's cottage, Malachy and the Count methodically looked for hiding places with the detection equipment. Malachy visually looked for telltale signs of tampering with spaces created by pipes, vents, and appliances. The Count was methodically examining the walls with a large, boxlike machine.

"What's that?" Malachy asked in a low voice.

Malachy and the Count stopped their search and listened. There was a soft knock at the cottage's back door. Malachy called Kevin on his cell phone.

"Somebody is knocking at the back door. Is there any way somebody got by you?"

"No," Kevin said. "Whoever it is must have come through the woods at the back of the property. Nobody went down the driveway. I've got the binoculars on the cottage now and can't see anybody. Wait a second...somebody is coming around the side of the house...it's a kid. He's headed to the front door."

"Is there any way he can see me if I stand behind the door?"

"No. The front windows are too far apart."

"Okay," Malachy said. "Keep me posted."

Malachy went up the stairs two at a time and quietly moved behind the front door. The doorbell rang.

"Who is it?" Malachy said loudly, trying to sound hoarse.

"Mr. Flynn, it's me, Billy. You said to come by. I can do that gardening work if you want."

"Can't do it today, Billy. I'm real sick."

"Sorry, Mr. Flynn. I'll come back another day after my camp."

"No need for that Billy. I've decided not to do the garden. I'm going to be away too much. But, if I need you, I'll call you."

Malachy stopped talking for a few seconds.

"Billy, I don't want you just stopping by. If I need you, I'll call you, understand?"

"Sure, Mr. Flynn," Billy said in a disappointed voice.

"Sorry, Billy, but that's the way it has to be."

"That's okay, Mr. Flynn. I was just hoping to see the Hank Aaron card you were telling me about."

Malachy spun around and looked at the Count who signaled no he hadn't found a baseball-card collection. Malachy turned back to face the front door. His face had a fierce, determined look but his voice was very gentle.

"Billy can't do it today. But I'll send it to you in the mail just as soon as I'm better. Look for it next week some time."

"Geez, that'd be great. I promise I'll bring it back."

"No, Billy, you can keep it. It's a gift. But no more just coming by, Billy. Do you understand?"

"Sure thing, Mr. Flynn. Wow, thanks, that'll be terrific."

"That's okay, Billy. You better go now. I need to rest."

"Thanks again, Mr. Flynn. I'm going now."

"Good-bye, Billy."

Malachy turned to the Count with the same look on his face.

"The plan has changed. Pack everything up. Bring his computer and all his financial records and files with us, but first create a hiding place about this big." Malachy cupped his hands and held them a few inches apart and then continued, "One made by an amateur."

"What about the pictures?"

"We'll let Flynn tell us where they are," Malachy said. "Is your place in Indiana ready?"

The Count looked at Malachy's face again and decided against a sarcastic answer.

"Yes."

"Good, we'll be using it soon."

The Count went back to the basement. Malachy called Kevin.

"The plan has changed. We are coming out with some of Flynn's stuff in about thirty minutes. Did you get a good look at the kid? Could you pick him out?"

"I did. And it will be easy to pick him out."

"Why?"

"He's black."

Malachy and the Count rolled the cart up the tracks and into the back of the van. They unloaded the equipment and returned to the back of the cottage with the cart. They carefully loaded up Flynn's computer and records and brought them to the van. They worked in silence. When everything was secured, the Count took out his clipboard.

"I need to go back to the cottage. I think it would be a good idea to rake out the cart's tracks and the van's after we pull out."

"I'll take care of it," Malachy said.

"Remember to keep your shoe covers on," the Count said.

"I will," Malachy answered, his tone and face softening for the first time since Billy mentioned the baseball card.

†

Malachy, Kevin, and the Count sat at the same picnic table as before in the deserted area. This time a casual observer would think they were three workers with a serious technical problem interfering with their work.

"We'll pick him up as soon as he returns to Chicago and take him to the warehouse in Indiana," Malachy said. "He must be stopped now."

Kevin remained silent and let the Count ask the obvious question.

"We don't know where he is, when he's returning, or by what means of transportation. So how do we grab him?"

"That's why we took the computer and the records," Malachy responded. "We know he didn't drive, so he purchased a ticket—probably on a plane. If the information is not on the computer, we will get it online using his financial records."

"That's not my area of expertise," the Count said. "I'll need to get help."

"Not necessary," Malachy said. "I'm going to call our employer on the cell phone. I'll request overnight service. I figure we'll have the information by the end of the morning at the latest."

"For planning purposes, let's assume we know when and how he is returning," the Count said. "How do we take him?"

"Arrest him."

"Who does the arrest?" Kevin asked. "He'll bolt if he sees either one of us."

"Cops he doesn't know and has never seen," Malachy said.

"You have that much on deposit in the Favor Bank?" Kevin asked in surprise.

"I have a big account, but not that big," Malachy said. "I kind of liked the style and efficiency of our Hispanic friends who picked up Fr. Bari. They aren't warm and fuzzy, but who cares? They'll be convincing to Flynn, totally convincing."

The Count got up from the bench and started to pace around the table. After a minute, he sat down and addressed Malachy.

"The cell phone you were given had five preprogrammed numbers. This is number three. If we get to five, do you get another cell phone?"

"You know, I've thought about that question and I don't know the answer. And I don't want to find out the answer. That's why I'm going to make this call count."

Malachy described in detail what else he was going to request. Kevin gave out a low, long whistle. The Count jumped up and proceeded to resume pacing around the picnic table in wider and wider loops. After a few minutes of watching the Count pace, Kevin checked his watch and waited for the Count to be out of earshot.

"We are now approaching a personal best for the Count," Kevin said.

"What's your reaction?" Malachy asked quietly.

"Flynn must be stopped. Whatever it takes, no matter what."

"No matter what," Malachy repeated slowly, looking directly into Kevin's eyes.

The Count returned to the table.

"I think the plan works. Any needed modifications will be minor."

"I'll make the call."

Malachy placed the call and gave the code. A few minutes later, the cell phone rang. Malachy explained his requests. There was a long period of silence.

"Is everything you requested essential for success?"

"Yes."

"I will call you back," the voice said to Malachy.

"He calling back," Malachy said to Kevin and the Count. "Are there coffee and treats in the van?"

"Of course," the Count said. "And the coffee is even hot."

They waited at the table, drinking coffee, eating homemade cookies, and constructing wagers about the return call. When there was no call after an hour, Malachy worried he had gone too far and their nameless employer had lost confidence. To keep busy, they constructed even more elaborate bets on the return call.

The cell phone rang just seconds after their last bet and Malachy answered. The voice sounded like that of their nameless employer, but Malachy couldn't be sure.

"Arrangements have been made for all your requests. Where are you calling from?"

"Wisconsin, just over the state line."

"Start back to the city, heading to the West Side. You will be called on your cell with the address to drop off the computer and records. You can pick them up from the same address tomorrow morning between 10:00 and 10:15, no earlier, no later. Once we have the information on the person's return, those arrangements will be made. We will need participation on the arrest to make sure there is no mistake on the identity. The other things you requested will be delivered to you, and only you. You will be called on the cell with the time and place. Is everything clear and understood?"

"Yes."

"If needed, no formulation for the next call. Just your name." The phone clicked off without a wish for good luck.

"Everything's a go," Malachy said. "But something tells me if we get to number five it's our last call. No new phone. Anyway, who won?"

"Kevin," the Count said. "He got the over on the time of the return call and total time elapsed for the call. You lost to me on his final salutation. The other four bets are a wash."

Malachy explained all the instructions and then turned to Kevin.

"I want you to find Billy's home and warn his parents about Flynn. Tell them you are in the middle of an investigation and have Flynn and his place under surveillance. Tell them Billy has been stopping by and that must stop. Billy should never go anywhere near Flynn or his cottage."

"Is that necessary?" the Count asked. "We don't need panicky parents spreading rumors or calling the authorities."

"Flynn has abused his last victim," Malachy said. "Yes, it's necessary, just in case the son of a bitch eludes us somehow."

"Who and what am I?" Kevin asked.

"How about regional Child Protective Services Agency?"

"CPSA? Do you have your badge and identity equipment in the van?" Kevin asked the Count.

"Of course," the Count said. "Don't leave home without it."

†

Malachy's special phone rang just as the Count pulled the van onto the Eisenhower expressway. Malachy answered with his name.

"Copy that," Malachy said, writing the address and instructions.

"Where are we headed?" the Count asked.

"To a warehouse in Berwyn. We'll be met at the dock. Guess who? Bari's escort of the other day."

"Do you think Bari's inside?" the Count asked.

"You never know, but I don't think we're going to find out. That young man is all business. I say we are at the dock for no more than five minutes. The voice said to back into the dock, but not all the way, open the door, and point out whatever is to be unloaded. You're not supposed to leave the driver's seat."

The Count slowly backed the van toward the empty dock. As the van stopped, three Hispanic men appeared with a cart. Malachy exited the van and climbed the stairs to the dock. He nodded to the leader.

"Good evening," Malachy said. "Nice to see you again."

The man looked at Malachy without responding. He pointed to the van's back door. Malachy signaled to the Count, and the back door popped open. Malachy pointed to the computer and the three boxes of financial records.

"That's everything."

One of the men hopped off the dock and rapidly passed the computer and the boxes up to the second man who carefully stacked them on the cart. When they were finished Malachy turned to the leader.

"Say hello to Fr. Bari for me, will you?"

The man looked at Malachy without expression and said, "Tomorrow between 10:00 and 10:15."

"Loquacious fella, aren't you? See you then."

"Did you see the cart?" Malachy asked the Count as they drove toward the expressway.

"What about it? My view was partially blocked."

"It had padded sides and bottom. No way was the computer going to be damaged in transport or the records spilled. I think they went to the same school you did."

"Excellent," the Count said. "We want the arrest to be flawless. And Flynn will be jumpy and hypersensitive. It will be interesting to watch their plan in execution and to see what equipment they use."

"One thing for sure," Malachy said. "Our friend won't be talking his way out of any problems."

CHAPTER XXII

The Count watched Flynn looking for his bag as the carousel started to move. He politely moved through the crowd and stood next to Flynn. He pretended to reach for a bag and slightly bumped Flynn.

"Sorry, I guess I was a little anxious. They lost my bag the last time."

"That's okay," Flynn said, not taking his eyes off the moving belt filled with luggage.

The Count moved away and nodded to the team leader. He tried to spot the other members of the team that were going to make the arrest. There were three men dressed in suits who appeared to be discussing transportation to the city. They were vaguely Hispanic looking. Flynn picked up his bag from the carousel.

Flynn pulled out the handle and began to wheel the bag toward the exit. The Count followed a few steps behind. The three men were in front of Flynn walking in a line. As they approached the exit door, they slowed their pace. Just at that moment, the Count yelled out to Flynn.

"Excuse me, but I think you picked up my bag by mistake."

Flynn turned around and gave the Count an exasperated look.

Two men rushed by the Count and confronted Flynn.

"Stop right there," one of the men said. "Let's see some identification."

"Look, there's been some mistake. This is my bag. Here let me show you," Flynn said, fumbling in his coat pocket for his airline ticket.

"Sir, I asked you for identification. Show it to me now, please."

The three men in suits positioned themselves behind Flynn, saying nothing.

Flynn started to stammer, "I...I...what's this all about?"

"That's it," the man said. "You're under arrest."

All the men converged on Flynn. Two of the men behind Flynn grabbed an arm each and cuffed him. The third man directed passersby to keep moving through the door, saying curtly, "Police business, keep moving."

Flynn started to protest. All the men moved even closer to Flynn, blocking him from public view. One of the men quickly slapped flesh-colored tape over his mouth. The men spun Flynn around, and the two biggest grabbed him under the arms, lifting him off his feet.

The group moved rapidly through the exit door with one man in front, two men moving Flynn with his feet not touching the ground, and one man in the rear carrying Flynn's bag. The men moved toward a van parked at the curb with its sliding door open.

They pushed Flynn into the van, placed the bag inside the door, pulled the door shut, and knocked on the roof. The van pulled away.

The five men dispersed in different directions. One strode quickly across the inner drive to the passenger pickup road and climbed into a waiting car. One returned to the terminal and went up the escalator. Two of the men walked in opposite directions along the front of the terminal. The fifth man climbed onto a courtesy bus from a nearby hotel that was ready to depart.

Inside the terminal, the team leader answered his cell phone and then nodded to the Count. The Count checked his watch. The entire operation had taken less than fifteen minutes from the time he bumped Flynn.

"The most interesting aspect was their van," the Count said to Malachy as he climbed into his own van in the O'Hare parking garage.

"How so?"

"It was either marked up as a Streets and San vehicle or it was a real one. It looked authentic."

"Allows you to park curbside even with heightened security," Malachy said. "I don't know if the vehicle was the real thing, but I'd bet the plates were."

"That team was not just some street crew on temporary assignment," the Count said. "Too professional. They are extremely well trained and have worked together before. I'd say they are some kind of security professionals."

"A puzzlement," Malachy said. "Our employer controls Dino's involvement in our assignment, but doesn't know about Dino's Shrine scam. Our mystery man used to be involved in Outfit gambling operations long ago, but his guys are Hispanic. Yet some of the security provided by Dino for Fr. Bari is almost too obviously local, connected types including the off-duty cops."

"So where does that leave us?"

"On the way to the warehouse without all the answers."

"Well, we have an answer to the most important question," the Count said.

"What's that?"

"Where in the world is Flynn?"

Malachy pulled up next to the Streets and Sanitation van at the warehouse dock. He got out and opened the back door. Two men emerged carrying Flynn and placed him in the van. They did not acknowledge Malachy's presence. Malachy checked the dock for the leader, but didn't see anybody. The men got back in their vehicle, and it pulled away from the dock. Malachy climbed into the back of the almost pitch-black van next to Flynn. The Count moved next to Malachy.

The Count checked the cuffs and binding on Flynn's feet with a small flashlight. They maneuvered him into a big, soundproofed moving box with a long, large diameter tube attached to it. Malachy placed a black eye mask over Flynn's eyes and then ripped the tape off his mouth.

"Help!" Flynn screamed. "Somebody help me! I'm being kidnapped!"

"Save your breath," Malachy said. "Nobody can hear you, but just in case I'm going to give you a little musical accompaniment."

"Who are you?" Flynn shouted in a loud, scared voice. "Where are you taking me?"

Malachy ignored the questions. The Count gave Malachy a headset attached to a modified CD player. Malachy turned it on and checked that it was playing sound both through the speakers and the headset. He turned up the volume.

"It's a Wagner opera," Malachy said to Flynn. "But, it's not meant as torture. We just don't want anything but singing voices or music coming from the box. Who knows? Maybe you'll enjoy it. By all accounts, he was an obsessive, ruthless, no-good bastard so at least you have that in common. See you in a few hours."

Malachy secured the headset on Flynn with a tight elastic strap and secured the player to a hook at the top of the box. The Count closed the box and taped it shut. He climbed back into the front seat with the tube. He checked the cap on the end of the tube, opened it, and listened for a second.

"God, I hate Wagner," the Count said, closing the cap.

"Me, too," Malachy said. "He caused one of my biggest fights with Maria."

Malachy pulled the van away from the dock and headed for the expressway. As the van picked up speed, the Count opened the window, took the cap off the tube, and held it out the window, renewing the air in the box. As soon as Malachy started the story, he closed the cap.

"Maria was a big opera fan, it didn't make any difference what was playing as long as it wasn't modern. And she would never leave early. I think it was partially a money thing. We had great seats, and our package included every opera. They cost a small fortune. Occasionally she let me off the hook and went with a girlfriend, but that night it was me and I was tired and in no mood for four hours of Wagner and getting to bed after midnight.

"It was opening night for *Tristan*. As we approached the entrance to the Civic Opera House, there were some very polite and restrained protesters with signs linking Wagner to the Nazis and Hitler and urging a boycott of the performance. I told Maria they were right and we shouldn't go in—that it was kind of like crossing a picket line."

"Have you ever crossed a picket line?" the Count asked.

"No, unless both the union and the cause were corrupt. If there had been a strike at the hospital where I was born, my dad would have delivered me himself in the parking lot. I was on lines before I was old enough to walk."

"Did Maria buy the argument?"

Malachy shook his head no and said, "She didn't even respond. She just glared, handed me my ticket, and told me she would see me at the seats. Her glare was something to behold—dark and threatening. And her father was so mild-mannered. I don't where she got it."

"So what did you do?"

"I gave the lead protestor twenty bucks and told him to keep up the good work and to try and shut down the performance. And then I went to the bar inside the Opera House and fortified myself for the onslaught of Wagner. I was hoping to catch a nap after the lights went down, but the singing was terrible. No nap was possible. Then the first intermission."

"I'm guessing escalation is on the program," the Count said.

"Good guess. I head to the bar for refortification and then joined Maria with a group of her opera friends. One of the women asked, 'Isn't it a wonderful opening night? Everybody is in such good voice and Wagner's themes are so dramatic. Aren't we fortunate to be here?'

"'No,' I said, in a way-too-loud voice. 'I think the protestors are the lucky ones. They're outside in the fresh air and don't have to listen to the god-awful screeching.'

"'Oh, Malachy, you don't really mean that,' another woman said. 'You're just trying to be funny and sarcastic.'

"One of the men clapped me on the back and said, 'Why don't you tell us what you really think?'

"'Okay,' I said, in even a louder voice, 'I will.'

"'No, do not do that,' Maria responded. But I ignored her and proceeded to tell the group how I really felt."

"The fatal mistake," the Count intoned. "Proceed."

"Now I was loud enough to attract the attention of everybody around us, and of course they fell silent as I boomed out: 'I'd rather somebody stick a gun up my ass and pull the trigger than endure three more hours of this crap.'"

"What did Maria say and do?" the Count asked, laughing.

"She glared at me and said, 'I wish I had a gun,' and then she asked her friend for a ride home and stomped off. She didn't talk to me for a week."

"A well-deserved punishment," the Count said. "Wagner and the terrible singing are extenuating circumstances, but not exonerating ones. You were rude and embarrassed Maria in front of her friends. Did you learn your lesson?"

"Yes, I did," Malachy said. "I never went to another Wagner opera."

Malachy stopped the van in front of the warehouse's overhead door.

"Is the room ready?" Malachy asked.

"Just as you specified," the Count said. "The color scheme is a little monochromatic. What do you call the procedure we are using?"

"The *Moby Dick* Interrogation Model."

"Why? Are you going to harpoon him?"

"No violence, no torture," Malachy said. "We are employing Melvillian psychology, just the never-ending whiteness of the whale. Melville has quite a riff on whiteness in *Moby Dick*. Everything Flynn sees once we take the mask off will be some shade of white."

"How did you come up with this program?"

"I saw the movie with Gregory Peck the other night when I was channel surfing, and the idea came to me."

"Well, once we take his mask off everything Flynn sees will be white, but he won't see much," the Count said. "Walls, ceiling, cot, toilet, sink."

"Good," Malachy said. "I want this over with as fast as possible. No offense to your warehouse, but it's not exactly the Ritz."

"No offense taken," the Count said, climbing out of the van to unlock and open the door. "I've actually stayed at the Ritz and had occasion to spend some time in their equivalent of my warehouse. Mine is more comfortable."

Malachy and the Count pulled Flynn from the moving box, took off his headset and cassette player, unbound his feet, and guided him toward the white room.

"Where are you taking me? What are you going to do to me?"

"We are going to listen to you," Malachy said. "And when you tell us the truth about what we need to know, we're going to let you go and return you to your home."

"It's you, Madden, isn't it? You've no right to do this to me—it's wrong! Let me go! Now!"

"I think Wagner has ruined your hearing," Malachy said. "So let me repeat—you get to go home when you tell us what we need to know and not before."

At the door, Malachy and the Count each grabbed one of Flynn's arms and Malachy uncuffed him. They pushed him into the pitch-black room and slammed and locked the door. The Count flipped a switch and the room was flooded with an intense bright light. Through a one-way mirror, they watched Flynn rip off his eye mask and try to adjust to the light. He closed his eyes and started yelling.

"Let me out of here! Let me out of here!"

The Count picked up a microphone and his amplified voice boomed into the small white room.

"Strip off all your clothes. Take the eye mask and all your clothes and put them on the shelf. Put on the clothes provided for you. They are on the cot. After you have done that, you'll be given something to eat and drink."

"No! Go to hell, I'm not doing it!"

The Count switched off the mike and clicked another switch.

"We can hear him, but he can't hear us."

Malachy looked at the white underwear and scrubs neatly folded on the cot.

"Was it difficult to bleach the scrubs white?"

"No, it wasn't difficult, but the laundress was surprised. She's used to dyeing my stuff midnight blue."

"What's for dinner?" Malachy asked. "I'm hungry."

"Special pasta followed by veal Marsala and then salad. It won't take long to prepare it. The veal is already pounded."

"Any chance for a Jameson before dinner?" Malachy asked.

"Of course."

"I hope he holds out all the way through dinner," Malachy said. "I hate it when a good meal is interrupted."

"Me, too," the Count said.

Malachy dipped his biscotti into espresso, took a small bite, and then sipped his after-dinner drink.

"Chocolate biscotti and black sambuca, what a great dessert," Malachy proclaimed.

They heard Flynn on the speaker.

"Alas, duty calls," Malachy said.

The Count checked his watch and said, "Only two hours and fourteen minutes. I forecast we are out of here tomorrow by 5:00 P.M."

Malachy pointed to the case of vanilla-flavored meal substitute on the counter.

"I calculate it as a maximum of eight cans. Even the TV ads for that stuff say to have a normal dinner."

"Have you ever tried it?" the Count asked.

"Never," Malachy said. "My system wouldn't know what to do with a balanced meal."

The Count reversed the revolving shelf, bringing Flynn's clothes out of the room and returning an empty shelf.

"Where's my dinner?" Flynn yelled. "You said I'd get dinner."

The Count clicked on the microphone and said, "Eye mask."

"I need the eye mask—the goddamn light is too bright."

The Count clicked off the microphone and said, "Let's finish our dessert."

Malachy smiled and headed for their dining area.

Malachy was finishing up the dishes when Flynn started yelling and banging on the door. The Count turned up the volume on the speaker.

"Let me out of here, now! I'm thirsty! There's no water in the faucets! Let me out of here!"

The Count turned the speaker back down.

"Did it take a long time to rig the faucets that way?" Malachy asked.

"No, it's just a simple valve on the pipes going into the room. There's no water in the toilet either."

"He's used to control and manipulation," Malachy said. "We'll have the eye mask in no more than an hour. And tomorrow we'll get all the information we need. It's going to be less than an eight-can job."

Twenty minutes later, Flynn started talking in a subdued, defeated tone.

"The eye mask is on the shelf. Please give me something to eat and drink. I'm really thirsty."

The Count took the eye mask off the shelf and placed two large white plastic cups filled with the meal substitute on it and sent them into the room. Flynn quickly grabbed one of the cups and drank half of it.

"Give me some water," Flynn pleaded.

The Count opened the valve and the faucets and the toilet gurgled with water. Flynn went over and placed his mouth on the faucet and gulped in the water. He stopped drinking and flushed the toilet. The Count shut off the valve.

"No, no, leave it on," Flynn said.

The Count did not respond.

"I won't talk to you until I get more water."

"Nothing like food and drink to revive the spirits," Malachy said to the Count. "Let's see if the whiteness does its job."

Malachy looked at the Hollywood gin rummy score and said, "We may have to set up another game with a higher score to win. Flynn is proving stronger than I anticipated."

The Count looked at a separate tally sheet he was keeping and responded, "I'm not so sure. We've had six angry outbursts in a row, but in the last three the cursing was subdued. I figure we get some pleading and appeals to fairness next. We don't need full-blown Stockholm Syndrome, just some cooperation."

"Okay," Malachy said, drawing lines on the sheet. "One hundred and fifty points it is, but this time I'm not going to let you win out of appreciation for that fine dinner."

"Right," the Count said, shuffling and then presenting the deck for cutting.

The Count put down his cards and listened carefully to Flynn on the speaker. "That one is different, no appeals to fairness just pleading. We're getting close."

Malachy looked at score sheet and said, "Maybe if I make a plea for mercy too, it will move things along."

"You're just hoping he cracks before I win the third game—under our rules then no money changes hands."

"Fortunately, there's no delay of game penalty in gin," Malachy said, standing up. "Bathroom break time."

As Malachy returned to the table, the speaker crackled with sound.

"I'm ready to talk," Flynn said in a weary, defeated voice. "What do you want to know?"

The Count threw his cards on the table and followed Malachy to the white room.

The Count turned up the volume on the amplifier and repeated five times, very slowly: "Only the truth." The walls vibrated with sound.

Flynn winced and asked in a whining tone, "What truth? What do you want to know? How can I tell you the truth if I don't know what you want to know?"

The Count looked at Malachy. Malachy shrugged and mouthed, "Why not?" The Count handed Malachy the mike and Malachy announced, "Here are the rules: you answer every question with the truth. Even the smallest deception will cause all interaction, including food and water, to stop. When you have answered all of our questions, and we have verified the answers, you will be returned to your home. Understand?"

"Yes, yes, I understand. What do you want to know?"

Malachy did not respond immediately. He pulled out several long lists of questions from his pocket. Malachy decided to skip the list that was intended to condition Flynn to give truthful answers before asking about Bari.

"Where are the original pictures of Bari that you had posted on his bedroom wall?"

"My car, in my car," Flynn said eagerly. "They're in my car."

"Where exactly?"

"They're locked in a box under the front seat on the passenger side."

"How many copies are there?" Malachy asked.

"Three, only three."

"We have information you made far more than three copies," Malachy said.

"No, no, I swear I didn't," Flynn said in a panic. "Only three. I made them myself on the computer."

"Where are all the copies?" Malachy asked.

"I hid one in my apartment building in the city. And I mailed one."

"Mailed where?"

"To the chancery office."

"When and from where?"

"From the airport when I left on my trip to California."

"What kind of postage?"

"First class."

"What return address?" Malachy asked.

"I put Bari's address on it—at the rectory."

"That only accounts for two copies," Malachy said.

"The wall…Bari's bedroom…a copy there."

Malachy looked at his list of questions and selected one.

"Why do you make the street boys you pick up shave their genital area?"

"I…I…"

Malachy boomed an angry voice into the room.

"No hesitations, no lies! Tell the truth now, or we're done with you!"

"I wanted them to look like children," Flynn said in a quiet voice.

Malachy followed with five rapid-fire questions about Flynn's days in the seminary that only required one or two word answers. Flynn answered them all quickly and truthfully. Malachy continued asking questions for another forty minutes about the surface facts of Flynn's life, only allowing Flynn one break to drink water. At the end of the time, he asked a test question.

"Exactly where in the apartment did you hide the two copies of Bari's photos?"

"I…it…was only one copy. It's in the storage area in the basement. I taped it underneath an old kitchen chair."

Malachy decided it was time for the end-game moves. He asked questions that forced Flynn into longer and longer answers about his targeting and sexual abuse of children. Malachy strived to keep his tone neutral no matter what Flynn revealed. He kept his follow-up questions short until Flynn gave answers about his transfers from parish to parish and then he bore in.

"When did the cardinal learn of your activity?" Malachy asked.

"When he was still the archbishop, I'm not sure of the exact date. Some parents complained to the chancery office and I was called in. I denied it and said it was a misunderstanding. I was transferred and sent for psychological counseling."

"Did you meet with O'Grady at the time of the first complaint?" Malachy asked.

"No, I didn't."

Malachy's tone became hard and he raised the volume on the microphone.

"You are contradicting yourself."

"No, no, I'm not. Right after that, there was a general meeting of the Archdiocesan Priests Advisory Council. He met with me privately after the meeting. It was not an official meeting. It seemed like it was spontaneous, but it wasn't. I was told in no uncertain terms to keep myself available after the meeting."

"Do you have a clear memory of the meeting?"

"Yes, I do."

"Exactly what did O'Grady say to you? Do not paraphrase. Tell me exactly what he said."

"He said, 'I am aware of your problem and I hope and pray you are making good progress resolving it. There must not be scandal. Do you understand? There must not be any scandal. The Church cannot afford it. We have dealt with the complaining parents, and there must not be any other incidents. I am instructing you to never be alone with any child. Will you promise that?"

"What did you say and do?"

"I thanked him and made the promise."

"How long did your promise last?"

"I'm not sure...about a week."

Malachy kept close track of the total time of questioning. He knew from long experience as a lawyer that there was an optimum time to ask the crucial questions. It always came when the information was flowing freely and before fatigue caused a mindless rebellion. He judged they were approaching the apex.

"We are almost finished and then you can rest," Malachy said.

Malachy signaled for the Count to turn on the backup taping system.

"Why did you target Anthony Pace?"

Malachy listened carefully to the answer, decided no follow up question was necessary, and asked the next question in his choreographed list. He carefully and slowly took Flynn through his entire list of the why, how, and when questions that spanned the time of Pace's abuse. Malachy pushed hard with follow-up questions on everything Flynn did to assume Bari's identity. Toward the end of the questioning, Malachy could sense the fatigue and resentment building up.

Malachy took time to look over the list of questions. Even though they had the entire history, something eluded him. Malachy knew he had left something off the list.

"I'm tired," Flynn said. "I've told you everything. There can't be any more. Leave me alone!"

Malachy looked over the lists again. He saw the very first question he asked about Bari's photos. He realized what was missing.

"Last question," Malachy said.

"Where are the photographs of you and Pace naked together?"

Flynn blurted out the answer.

Malachy clicked off the microphone, turned to the Count, and threw the lists up in the air.

"Pay dirt!" Malachy exclaimed.

CHAPTER XXIII

Malachy drove into the garage at Midway airport. He found an isolated parking space as instructed. He tried to spot if he was followed but didn't see any candidates. He unlocked the car doors and waited. He positioned his rearview mirror and side mirrors so he could see as much of the garage as possible.

Out of nowhere, the Hispanic team leader approached the car, carrying a computer case. He opened the back driver's-side door and placed the case on the floor. As he closed the door, a car pulled up. The team leader took a few seconds to look around the garage and then climbed into the front seat of the waiting car. The car drove off. Malachy waited the full five minutes he was told to wait and then headed for the garage exit. Once out of the garage, he drove toward the toll road to Wisconsin.

On the toll road, Malachy called Kevin.

"I have my package. How is yours doing?"

"Very unhappy and grumpy. He didn't like his breakfast and doesn't like his accommodations. I told him not to cause any trouble and he'd sleep in his own bed tonight."

"For the last time," Malachy said, "if the plan works. See you at the picnic site."

Malachy, the Count, and Kevin sat at an isolated table eating a late lunch of deli sandwiches. Malachy looked at the van flanked by his car and Flynn's car.

"Any trouble getting Flynn's car out of the lot?"

"None. And the pictures of Bari were exactly where he told us. They are now secure at my place."

"Let's hope the pictures with Pace are just as easy to find," Malachy said. "What's the timeline for tonight's plan?"

"One hour at the church max, two hours at Flynn's, assuming we find the pictures on the first try and that the information in your package is correct."

"I'd rather bet the next pope is from Utah than bet against our employer," Malachy said.

"The timeline and the operational aspects don't concern me," the Count said. "It is the cumulative impact of the whole plan that I'm worried about—it could look contrived. Are we piling on?"

"Yes," Malachy said. "But it's necessary. We can't chance Flynn unmonitored. Anyway, I think we can count on two things. After his experience in the white room, Flynn will become unhinged and start talking to defend himself."

"And two?" the Count asked.

"No one will believe the story he'll tell. My only concern is what he does immediately after we let him go. I'm hoping it's to climb into bed and go to sleep."

"I propose we give him real food for dinner with a double dose of a sleeping aid in it just before we let him go," the Count said.

"Good idea," Malachy said. "Are we in agreement on the whole plan?"

Kevin and the Count nodded their assent.

"How are you going to pass the time?" Malachy asked Kevin.

"Work out. I brought my weights and a jump rope in the van."

"And I'd drink coffee, eat cookies, and read yesterday's papers. Where did I go wrong?"

"You don't heed Sergeant O'Rourke's advice on fitness," Kevin said.

"Do tell me. What did the venerable and learned O'Rourke preach about fitness?"

"Stop flapping your fucking gums and fucking move!"

"Such wisdom and so pithy in expression," Malachy said. "I will fucking reflect on it for fucking sure."

†

Malachy watched the Christ the King church from a block away, listening to the two-way radio and to the idling sounds of Flynn's car. Malachy could tell by the rhythmic purring of the engine that the Count had worked on the car in his shop. Malachy figured at a minimum the Count changed the air filter and oil, replaced the battery, and tuned the engine. Also, the tires would have had to pass inspection or be replaced. After all, the function of a getaway car was to get away.

Malachy saw the Count emerge from the side door of the church, carrying a dark-blue duffel slung over his shoulder. Malachy put the car in gear and placed one foot on the brake and the other lightly on the speed pedal. He watched the Count walk toward him looking like a sailor on leave, moving at a brisk pace but without giving the impression he was in a hurry. In the darkness, he was difficult to track. Nothing he had on reflected light.

As the Count approached the car, Malachy pulled a lever, popping open the trunk. The Count placed the duffel in the trunk, quietly closed the trunk, and climbed into the passenger seat. He slid down so far in the seat, he was not visible from outside and then checked his watch.

"About thirty minutes, including the locks on the side door and the cabinet. Not too bad, but I did feel a little rusty."

"Gold medal performance," Malachy said, pulling the car onto the main part of the road. "Any problems?"

"Well, the paper ID tag from the duffel got snagged on the metal insert in the doorjamb. I was in a hurry so I left it there with a piece of rubber band hanging from it."

"I know…it's piling on," Malachy said. "And if our time line wasn't so tight, I too would like to be more subtle. All I can tell you is I've defended guys who left even more obvious and stupid markers."

"Present company excepted, I hope," the Count said.

"Not one of them even owned a clipboard," Malachy said. "Was everything available?"

"Chalices, vestments, the whole works. I propose we just leave it in the trunk in the duffel."

"Agreed. Phase two, coming up."

Malachy pulled the car under Flynn's carport and stopped. With the engine and lights off, they carefully checked the property for signs of visitors. The cottage looked the same as their last visit with the acreage around it somewhat overgrown.

"There's the shed. I'll take that, you get started with the computer in the house."

Malachy turned to the Count when he did not hear an immediate agreement.

"Malachy, sometimes you go too fast. I'm concerned the shed could be booby-trapped. Let me check it out first."

"Unlikely, but not impossible. I promise I'll go slow. But we are time limited."

Malachy handed the Count the materials from the computer case.

"You need time to load this stuff in and then contact the websites," Malachy said. "And we don't want to overstay our welcome. We know what that leads to."

"Reluctantly agreed," the Count said, taking the folders and climbing out of the car. "Just go slow."

"Understood."

The Count worked at the back door for a few seconds and then it swung open. He returned to the car, picked up the computer, and entered the house. Malachy headed for the shed with the Count's toolbox. He circled the shed slowly looking for anything out of the ordinary. Everything seemed normal. He took a telescoping rod from the toolbox and from fifteen feet away probed the shed door with a series of increasingly hard thrusts. On the final thrust, the door creaked open.

Malachy moved closer, shortened the rod, and began methodically moving the rod around the interior of the shed, trying to set off any trip wires or other devices. He waited a few minutes and approached the entrance to the shed.

He took an infrared light from the toolbox, mentally divided the shed into sections, and examined each section. It was a normal under-used shed, full of cobwebs and some rusty gardening equipment, and in the corner a stack of bicycles—children's bikes in various heights.

"Jesus...," Malachy muttered.

The two-way responded with the Count's anxious voice, "What's wrong? Are you okay?"

"I'm fine," Malachy said. "There are five kids' bikes in here, all polished and wrapped in plastic."

"Stay cautious," the Count said.

Malachy continued to examine the shed, looking for the hidden storage site of the pictures. As he examined the planked floor, he found a section where the cracks between the boards looked different. He took a very thin-edged wedge from the toolbox and tested the boards. There was a two-foot-square section held together. He fastened a metal loop to the middle of the section, tied a wire to it, and ran the wire outside the shed. He pulled hard on the wire, and the section came up in one piece.

He re-entered the shed and found a metal box in the revealed space. He replaced the square section without the loop, stamped around on the floor to make the floor conditions look the same in all areas, jerry-rigged the broken door latch, and left the shed with the box, closing the door behind him.

"I have the box," Malachy said.

"Don't open it! Let me examine it. Bring the toolbox with you."

The two men sat at the kitchen table looking at the box with pencil flashlights. The Count closely examined the box with a powerful magnifying glass. "If it is rigged, there has to be a way to defuse it from the outside."

The Count found what looked like small rivets on the bottom of the box. "These did not come with the box," he said.

The Count took a small screwdriver and pried out the rivets. He took a battery-operated, miniature metal saw and cut through the hinges. He lifted the top of the box one inch from the hinged side and examined the interior. He took long-handled clippers, inserted them in the box, and clipped.

"Not bad for an amateur," he said, pointing to a small bottle of liquid he took from the box. If the box is opened normally, the liquid, probably some kind of acid, spills out and destroys the pictures."

The Count pulled out the stack of pictures and spread them out on the kitchen table.

"Mother of God," Malachy said, almost in a whisper.

On the table were dozens of photos of a naked or half-clothed man with naked children in a variety of sexual poses. Most of the photos showed the child's face, and none showed the man's. Malachy lined up the pictures of Anthony Pace. There were eight of them, more than any other victim. He picked them up one by one and closely examined them.

"How the hell do we prove it's Flynn? None of them show any part of the face."

"Look at it the other way around," the Count said.

"I'm not following you," Malachy said.

"We have to prove to Pace that it was not Bari who abused him."

"And?" Malachy said impatiently.

"And these are not the only photos we have in our possession." We have Bari naked, and it shows his face. Look at Flynn in these photos. We blow up the photos and compare the body types. There's no way anybody, including Pace, will conclude that it is Bari in these faceless photos. The body types are just too different. Bari is at least 6'3" and very lean. Flynn is a maximum of 5'7" and pudgy. Case closed."

"It might just work," Malachy said. "We have Pace's mother to corroborate it was not Bari she saw come out of the bathroom. It might be enough."

"I'm going back to work," the Count said, looking at the photos on the table. "These are almost as bad as the stuff I'm working with."

Malachy gathered up the photos and placed them in a large sealable plastic bag.

"What do we do with the box?" Malachy asked.

"Take it with us," the Count said. "You're sure there's no evidence that you were in the shed?"

"None," Malachy said, looking at his gloved hands. "I assume we are burning everything we have on."

"Of course," the Count said. "Everything is loaded into the computer.

It will take another thirty minutes to contact all the websites we were given and to leave the appropriate messages. And another fifteen minutes to hide the rest of the stuff. I propose you call Kevin and tell him to give Flynn his special dinner."

"Accepted," Malachy said.

†

Kevin guided Flynn through the door and into the kitchen.

"Where am I?" Flynn asked, slurring his words and yawning. "What have you done to me?"

"You're in your home in Wisconsin, as I promised," Malachy said. "You're just very tired. It was a long ordeal. Soon you will be in your own bed and able to sleep."

Malachy and Kevin took Flynn up the stairs to the bedroom and placed him on the bed. Kevin held him down while Malachy made sure the room was totally dark.

"Here are the rules," Malachy said. "I am going to take off all your restraints, everything but the eye mask. Do not get up from the bed for one hour. We have set the alarm so you will know when an hour is up. We will be watching from the outside for that hour. If we see any movement or light, we will come back and get you. Stay in bed for the hour. Do you understand?"

"Yeah, an hour," Flynn said in a barely audible voice. "Hour, don't move."

"Right," Malachy said.

The Count drove Flynn's car in reverse up the long driveway and then went forward and parked under the carport. He went to the back porch and retrieved a half-empty bottle of Scotch he took from the kitchen. He opened the trunk, poured some on the duffel, and closed the trunk. He poured some on the sides of the front seats and left the open bottle between the door and the driver's seat. He walked back to the waiting van along the side of the driveway. At the van, he went over the list on his clipboard.

"Everything's done," he said to Malachy and Kevin. "Any sign of life from the house?"

"None," Malachy answered, putting down the binoculars.

"Ready for phase three," the Count said, climbing into the van.

They drove back to the picnic area. They shed their jumpsuits, hats, gloves, and special shoes and placed them in a burn bag. Malachy gave the Count the keys to his car and then climbed into the van for the ride back to Chicago.

"I will call you in the morning as things develop," the Count said.

†

Malachy's cell phone rang, waking him from a dream. A fragment of the dream stuck with him as he answered the call—a large adult riding a child's bike with training wheels. He checked the time: 8:30.

"Awake enough to listen to something I taped?" the Count asked.

"How do you know I haven't been up for hours methodically checking off items on my to-do list?"

"The unlikely is not the impossible," the Count responded. "But it is still the unlikely, and in this instance, the very highly unlikely. It is also unlikely that a small-town police department could solve a crime within hours of its discovery. However, lucky breaks do occur. Listen to this from a local radio station."

Malachy put his cell phone on speaker, turned up the volume, and carried it into the kitchen. He propped it up on the counter and poured himself a cup of coffee.

"There was a break-in at Christ the King church sometime last night. It was discovered early this morning. The intruder took vestments, chalices, and other religious articles used in the celebration of Mass. The sheriff's department has already made an arrest in the case and recovered all the stolen items. The department has scheduled a news conference for this afternoon at 3:00. We will bring you more information as soon as it is available. And congratulations to Sheriff Grimes on the quick results in this case!"

"Good work, Sheriff Grimes!" Malachy said in a loud voice aimed at the cell phone.

"And just as important, the good sheriff did it all according to Hoyle," the Count said. "Or at least that was the talk at the local coffee shop where law enforcement gets caffeinated. Proper search warrant and complete Mirandizing."

"Good," Malachy said. "I was hoping for that. Maybe we'll be lucky enough to win the trifecta—a thorough search even though they recovered the stolen items."

"The trifecta is a tough bet, but in this case the race is fixed. When they process Flynn, the stuff they find on his person will trigger a very complete search."

"How about bringing Bari home?" Malachy asked.

"I consider it safe now. I suppose it's not impossible for Flynn to make bail, but I'd rather bet you would rise at 6:00 A.M. for one hundred consecutive days."

"I'd consider five days a major achievement," Malachy said.

"As would all who know you," the Count said. "Talk to you when I know more."

Malachy used the special cell phone and gave his name. The call back came quickly.

"It is safe to bring Fr. Bari back to the rectory," Malachy said. "But we will need to resume the normal security arrangements."

"Where is Flynn?"

"In jail," Malachy said.

"What about bail?"

"Not going to happen," Malachy said.

"Fr. Bari will be dropped off at the rectory between 5:00 and 5:30 this evening. Security will check out the rectory prior to that and will be in place upon his return."

"I request that the security check include searching for bugs."

There was no immediate response. Malachy waited silently.

"That will be done. If needed, use the formulation 'this is five calling.' Good luck."

Malachy clicked off, relieved he did not get questioned about why there might be listening devices planted in the rectory. Malachy took his coffee, returned to bed, and stared at his favorite spot on the ceiling. It was a relief to know Flynn was no longer a threat to Bari or any child, but that fact alone did not get the job done.

Flynn was no longer in the game. Time to focus on Pace and the cardinal. But with what game plan? After three hours, two coffee and bathroom breaks, and a lot of pacing, he was satisfied with his proposed opening play. And he was hungry.

†

Malachy looked up at Bridget who was standing next to his office-booth in the Shamrock.

"Brunch? Now what in God's name are you talking about?" Bridget asked.

"You asked me what I wanted to eat," Malachy said to Bridget. "It's too late for breakfast, and I haven't eaten anything yet. Somehow, I can't just start the day with lunch food. I figured brunch was the right answer."

"Wrong answer," Bridget said. "And to think I was in a good mood."

Bridget turned and yelled to Eduardo, "Bring the lord of the manor one piece of dry, whole-wheat toast and a cup of coffee. Now, after you break your fast with the toast, what do you want for lunch?"

"The usual," Malachy answered.

"Thank God, a straight answer."

"How's business?" Malachy asked. "Any problems?"

"Business has been okay. And you've been gone, so of course the problems have been minimal."

"I'm glad you missed me," Malachy said.

"I'll get all the mail and the other crap you ignored in your absence. Maybe you can actually do some Shamrock work today. The business doesn't just run itself you know."

"All right, I'll do some Shamrock work after my lunch."

"I hope you survive the ordeal," Bridget said.

Malachy looked up from his work and watched a man cross the floor and head toward the bar. He did not look like a patron. He was dressed in a cheap suit, shirt, and a bad-fitting tie. His manner said he wanted something. Malachy figured he was in his fifties. He was overweight and looked like he didn't get much exercise. He seemed nervous. Malachy got up and moved to a booth closer to the bar.

"Excuse me," the man said to Bridget. "I understand that Roy Arbussy works here."

"And?"

"I need to talk with him about a family matter."

"And who are you?" Bridget asked.

"I'm family."

"What kind of family exactly?" Bridget demanded.

"Could you just tell me where I can find him?" the man said in a louder voice.

"No, I can't," Bridget said in an even louder voice. "Until you tell me who the hell you are and why the hell you're here."

The man looked around the almost-empty bar nervously.

"Roy's mother is sick and would like to see him. She asked me to give him that message."

"And you are?"

"I'm married to Roy's mother. I'm his stepfather."

Bridget gave the man a hard stare and then without taking her eyes off the man shouted to Eduardo.

"Tell Red to come to the kitchen door, just to the door. Understand?"

Eduardo answered sí and went into the kitchen. Bridget reached down under the bar, grabbed the baseball bat, and slammed it on the bar.

"When he comes to the door, don't you move. Got it? Don't move an inch."

"I...I," the man stammered.

"Shut up," Bridget said. "I'm not interested in your bullshit. Just wait for Red."

Red stepped through the swinging doors and stopped.

"This man has a message for you," Bridget said.

"He can go to hell," Red said.

"Red, listen to the message," Bridget said, using the bat to point at the man. "Go ahead and tell him."

"Roy, your mom is sick and wants to see you. I promised her I'd find you and tell you."

"You both can go to hell," Red yelled.

"Red, go back to work," Bridget ordered.

Red backed through the swinging doors, giving the man the finger with both hands.

"Is his mom really sick? Don't give me any bullshit."

"Yes, she is," the man said. "She's in Mercy Hospital. It's too bad there's a misunderstanding between Roy…"

Bridget held up her hand to indicate the man should stop talking. She put the bat on the bar and motioned to him to lean in closer as if she had something private to tell him.

As he leaned over, Bridget reached across the bar, grabbed the man's tie with both hands, and yanked hard, slamming his face into the beer spigots. The man yelped in pain, and his nose began to bleed.

"There's no misunderstanding about this," Bridget said. "If you ever come within ten yards of that kid again, I'll take this baseball bat and turn you into Humpty Dumpty! Now get the hell out of here!"

Bridget released the man's tie and pushed his face hard with both hands. He yelled in pain, stumbled over the barstool, and fell to the floor. Malachy went over, picked him up by the collar of his suit coat, and dragged him to the front door.

"I know you'll find this hard to believe," Malachy said to the man, "but today is really your lucky day. If my colleague Kevin were here, you'd be headed to the hospital at best. I'll let you figure out the worst, but a clue is the funeral home across the street."

Malachy opened the door and the man stumbled through it. Malachy returned to his booth to find Bridget waiting for him.

"Malachy can you handle things for a few hours? I'm going to take Red to the hospital to see his mom."

"What if he doesn't want to go?"

"He doesn't get a choice. He doesn't have to go back, but he's going at least this one time."

"Okay. I'll take care of things until you get back."

"Stay out of the kitchen. I finally have everything running smoothly."

"Will do. And Bridget, I liked the tie maneuver. Very effective."

"You should—I learned it from you."

Malachy tried to remember when he had used it in the Shamrock. Nothing came immediately to mind. He figured it would come to him eventually, and he went back to his book work. At 4:00, he fixed himself a Jameson, slowly sipped his drink, and remembered past confrontations. When his cell phone rang, Malachy answered with a question.

"Did I ever tell you about yanking a guy's tie in a fight?"

"No," the Count said. "Unfortunately, there wouldn't be much opportunity for that with today's too-informal dress. Why?"

"Damn," Malachy said. "Bridget said she learned it from me, and I can't ever remember using it in the Shamrock."

"Sounds like it was an interesting afternoon. Perhaps you were drinking when you used it and that's why you don't remember. If you work hard enough on it, it will surface. Ready to hear the latest local news?"

"Drinking and fighting, now there's an unlikely combination. Pray tell, what's the news of the hour?"

"According the sheriff and the local prosecutor, the Feds have been called in. They wouldn't say why other than their investigation has found materials that required bringing in the Feds. The prosecutor is going to oppose any application for bail at the arraignment. They believe Flynn is a flight risk and a risk to the community."

"Anybody with a forged foreign passport qualifies as a flight risk," Malachy said.

"And anybody in possession of child pornography is a risk to the community," the Count said.

"Not to mention various controlled substances used for sexual stimulation purposes and illegal drugs," Malachy said. "Still worried about piling on?"

"Yes, very worried. Too much of a good thing is a bad thing."

"I must admit I'm prone to excess," Malachy said.

"Do tell," the Count said.

Malachy took a large swallow of his drink and said, "Okay. I must admit I'm prone to excess."

CHAPTER XXIV

Malachy dreamed of a man on stilts who was working puppets with both hands. The puppets were moving up and down, first one side and then the other. Malachy's cell phone rang, waking him and driving the dream away. He let the phone ring and said aloud "puppets" and then answered his phone.

"Good morning, Malachy. This is Joe Valquist from Fight Abuse calling. I hope you don't mind my calling your cell phone. I got the number from Fr. Bari."

"Glad you called, what can I do for you?"

"I'm calling to tell you I believe you're right about Fr. Bari, and I told him the same thing. I read in the papers this morning about Flynn."

"I am sure your call meant a lot to Fr. Bari," Malachy said, still struggling to wake up. Malachy sat on the side of the bed rapidly scissoring his legs.

"The story in the paper just confirmed what I was finding out about Flynn."

"How so?"

"After our talk, I started making inquiries through our network. It turns out he was transferred from at least two parishes and maybe more after parents complained. The chancery office knew he was abusing children and just moved him on without any warning to the new parishioners."

"Have you actually talked with the parents?" Malachy asked.

"Only some of them on the telephone. But we have scheduled a meeting and are inviting all the parents we know about so far. Of course some won't show up. They were bullied by chancery officials and are afraid of the consequences, spiritual and otherwise, of taking on the Church. Would you like to come to the meeting?"

Malachy was silent for a few seconds, trying to formulate his answer. He wished he'd been up for an hour with two cups of coffee in him. Valquist was the key to Pace, and he needed that key.

"Joe, I want to help in any way I can. If you want me at that meeting, I'll be there. But the parents would need to know up-front who I am and what my role is. Think back to your own reaction when you found out I'm a disbarred lawyer. Those parents are going to be hyperemotional."

"You make a good point, Malachy. Maybe we could meet for coffee and explore the plusses and minuses."

"For sure. Can't do it today—I'm going to try and talk to O'Grady."

"The cardinal? You have a meeting scheduled with the cardinal?"

"Not scheduled. I intend to confront him at lunch."

"About what?" Valquist asked.

"Flynn," Malachy said. "I want to know if his arrest changes things for Fr. Bari."

"Aren't you wasting your time? He'll never talk to you."

"Joe, you're probably right. But, maybe I'll learn something useful even if he freezes me out. How about I call you after the meeting and we can set a time for coffee?"

"Tell the cardinal from me that he should be sitting in the cell next to Flynn," Valquist said. "I'll talk to you later."

Malachy clicked off his cell phone and started thinking about the puppets in his dream. Suddenly, the entire "tie" incident came back to him. It didn't happen in the Shamrock, and it took place many years before. He must have told Bridget the story when he was only a customer.

Malachy was crossing the bridge over the Chicago River on his way to a bar in the Transportation Center. A fellow criminal defense lawyer wanted to meet about a case, and they agreed on that location so the other lawyer wouldn't miss his train home. As Malachy approached the walkway to the main terminal, he saw a very tall, obviously drunk man with three young black kids around him, jumping up at the man's outstretched arms. The man had a bunch of twenty-dollar bills interweaved in his fingers and was taunting the kids with the money.

When Malachy was a few feet away, the man shouted, "Look at the little niglets jump!" The man lowered his hands so they were almost in reach and then quickly raised them as the black kids tried to grab the bills. Malachy realized the man had no intention of ending his sadistic game by giving the kids any money, and he decided to even the playing field.

Malachy looked at his watch and said in a loud voice, "Jesus, I'm late for my train." He started to run toward the door to the walkway. As he drew even with the man, he pretended to stumble, and then he collided with the man. The man lowered his arms to keep his balance, and the kids quickly stripped the bills from his fingers and ran away. The man started cursing and took a few steps after the kids yelling, "Give me back my goddamn money!"

Malachy didn't say anything and just kept going at a fast walk into the main terminal. He found his colleague and joined him at the bar. They intended to have one drink and then move to a table to discuss the case. He ordered a drink and put his money clip on the bar so he could pay, when he heard someone yelling at him from behind.

"You son of a bitch, you did that on purpose! You owe me the goddamn money. Give it to me!"

Malachy spun around and said in an even, controlled tone, "I have no idea what you're talking about. You're obviously drunk. Why don't you just go home and not cause any trouble?"

The man, his tie askew and with sweat beaded on his forehead, yelled, "Fuck you!" He lunged for Malachy's money clip. Malachy grabbed his tie and yanked down and aimed a kick at the man's knee. The man crashed into the bar face first. He grunted and fell to the floor, bleeding from the mouth.

Malachy told the bartender, "You'd better call the cops. You don't want him suing, claiming the floor was wet or some other bullshit. I'll wait over at that table."

Malachy told his colleague to catch an early train and they'd try again tomorrow. The cops arrived quickly and came over to talk to Malachy after getting the story from the bartender and talking to the attacker who was still slurring his words.

"He's not making much sense and he stinks of alcohol," the cop said. "He's mumbling something about you helping some black kids rob him. The bartender said you told him to go away and not cause any trouble, but he went for you and slipped and crashed into the bar. Do you know the guy? Do you have any history with him? Do you have any idea what he's talking about with the black kids?"

"To answer your questions directly, no, no, and no. But I do have a theory because I'm in the business," Malachy said, handing the cop one of his cards.

"Okay," the cop said, examining the card. "What's your theory?"

"When you're looking down at people from that height all you can see is the top of their heads. Mix in too much booze and it's a sure recipe for mistaken identity."

The cop laughed and said, "You don't seem very upset about the whole deal. Do you want to press charges?"

"Nah," Malachy said. "It not his fault he's so tall. But there is one thing I don't understand."

"What's that?"

"Like I said, I'm in the business and I've never heard of street thugs, white or black, needing the help of a guy like me to roll a drunk. I mean, how drunk is the guy? Maybe he's mixing other shit in there, too, but whatever he's doing, it fucks with your head and I want no part of it."

Malachy wasn't sure what the bartender actually saw, but he figured the twenty dollars he left on the bar as a tip helped keep the story simple and straightforward.

Malachy looked at the clock and calculated how much time he needed to prepare for his "meeting" with the cardinal. He mused about confronting O'Grady at his favorite restaurant, the Pump Room in the Ambassador East hotel.

Malachy checked his closet and confirmed a pressed jacket and slacks were available so he could pass the dress code. He wondered if O'Grady walked or took the chauffeured limo there. He guessed the limo. Malachy didn't know what to expect out of O'Grady when he confronted him. It could range from a phony hospitality to an immediate call for security. But at least one thing was certain. If O'Grady came at him, he wouldn't be wearing a tie.

†

Malachy quickened his pace as he went up the marble steps leading to the entrance of the Pump Room. He breezed by the maître d' with a "very late for a meeting with the cardinal" and maintained his pace as he entered the elegant, dark-wood-dominated room. He scanned the room and spotted the cardinal with an associate in one of the large booths far from the entrance and the celebrity-famous Booth One.

"Hello, Augustine," Malachy said to Cardinal O'Grady.

O'Grady looked up from his meal and looked at Malachy without saying anything. Malachy looked back letting the silence build to uncomfortable while silently playing the "over/under" on a $1,000 for the finely tailored black suit and soft-looking white collar that held in O'Grady's ample girth. He kept the "over" to himself and said, "Nice booth you have there. A good spot for a private talk."

"Hello, Malachy. In fact that's just what I'm engaged in at the moment—discussing some archdiocesan business. So please excuse us." O'Grady looked down at his plate and began to slowly cut one of the lobster pieces covered in a thick white sauce.

"I understand," Malachy said. "Lots of good news to discuss I'm sure."

The other cleric at the table, beefy with a red face and a definite "way under" in clerical suits, looked up at Malachy and said, "His Eminence and I would like to have some privacy. Thank you for understanding."

"I do understand, and I won't be long," Malachy said, sitting down at the end of the booth. "That's the great thing about this setup—plenty of room. And thanks for the warm welcome."

"You were not invited to sit down," the other cleric said. "Please do not force me to call security. Just leave quietly."

"No," Malachy said, looking at O'Grady.

O'Grady stopped cutting his lobster, looked at Malachy, and said, "I see you haven't changed much. What is it that you want?"

"A few minutes of private conversation," Malachy said.

"You can't just barge in, sit down, and demand His Eminence's time," the other cleric said, his voice rising in anger. "Leave now!"

"It is okay, Phillip," O'Grady said. "Malachy thinks he has that right because of the old neighborhood, but he will not cause a scene. Will you?"

"Like you said, I haven't changed much so we can't be too sure of that. But speaking of the old neighborhood, I would've thought that I earned a few minutes at your table because of our families' friendship."

Phillip started to say something and Malachy interrupted him, never taking his eyes off O'Grady. "In case you forgot, my mother nursed your mother every day of her illness, and my father and I made sure your father was fed, cleaned up, and half sober when he saw your mother. While you were out at the seminary learning how to be holy, I was cleaning up your old man's vomit."

O'Grady's pallid face turned a little red, and he said quietly, "I haven't forgotten. You and your parents were very good to both my parents, and I deeply appreciate that. Unfortunately, you and I have never seen eye to eye about much. How much time do you require?"

"No more than ten minutes."

"Very well."

"I will be back in ten minutes," Phillip said, standing up.

"Before we start, Malachy, I do want to say two things. I was sincere in expressing my appreciation for all you and your family did for my parents. And, your rescue of Paul Kennedy was very courageous if unorthodox."

"Maybe you've heard the saying, 'No better friend, no worse enemy,'" Malachy said.

"I believe that was Sully's epitaph," O'Grady said. "The Roman general and dictator."

"Always the scholar," Malachy said in a neutral tone.

"But the way you said it made it seem like a warning," O'Grady said. "We don't seem to be able to get along even for a few minutes of conversation. What is it you want to talk about?"

"Flynn and Bari."

O'Grady gave a smile and said, "Malachy, we are not playing poker like we did when we were kids. You don't need to watch me quite so intensely."

Malachy smiled back and responded, "We didn't even see eye to eye about that. You played the cards, always calculating the odds. I played the people, always looking for the tell."

"What about them?" O'Grady asked

"Flynn was the priest who abused Anthony Pace. Bari is completely innocent of the charge against him. He should be restored to his role at the Shrine."

O'Grady bristled. "Malachy, there is a procedure in place to deal with these issues, and Fr. Bari will be treated fairly in that procedure. As you know, Fr. Flynn is a retired priest and the archdiocese is not involved in any way in his current difficulties."

Malachy noted that O'Grady skipped over the part about Flynn abusing Pace.

"Treated fairly doesn't sound very promising."

"I'm not going to discuss any priest's assignment with you, period. I know what you've been hired to do. As I said, Bari will be treated fairly."

"Which wasteland are you going to bury him in? Fairly, of course."

"Malachy, is there something else on your mind?" O'Grady asked, as he turned his head to look for his associate's return.

"Yes. There's a shitstorm headed your way because of Flynn. There isn't much time to do the right thing and avoid the worst of the storm."

"Malachy, your language always was colorful and never subtle. There are many complex issues, many competing interests, and no simple decisions. I know you always liked life to be binary—black or white, yes or no, win or lose. I imagine you found jury trials very satisfying—limited in time and with an explicit outcome. The life of the Church is not like that and cannot be like that. Every major decision has profound ramifications with incredibly tangled secondary and tertiary effects that last for decades."

"You stayed too long in Rome," Malachy said.

"Perhaps," O'Grady said. "And perhaps you've spent too much time in the old neighborhood, hanging on to the old ways."

"Could be," Malachy said. "But it suits me. I suppose Rome suits you."

"I'm glad to be back in Chicago," O'Grady said. "It's home, after all."

"Well, back here at home some decisions are simple," Malachy said. "For example, instead of moving child predators from parish to parish, call the cops. That way you prevent this from happening."

Malachy slapped down one of the photos of Flynn in a sexual pose with Pace. O'Grady glanced down at the picture but did not pick it up. He looked up at Malachy.

"That was very dramatic. One of the tactics left over from your former career, I suppose. No one wants anything like that to ever happen to a child, but those unfortunate occurrences do not change how decisions must be made for the Church. Please put the picture away."

Malachy made no move to pick up the picture and asked, "That photo is of Flynn abusing Pace. That means nothing to you?"

"You are making a surprising number of assumptions for somebody trained in the law. What you say is a fact could have any number of explanations. You're not a disinterested party. Put that away or our conversation is over."

Malachy picked up the photo and put it in his pocket.

"It's Flynn, and his stiff prick is all too real," Malachy said. "There is still time for you to do the right thing. If you don't take any action, the shitstorm is going to be intense."

"And of course 'the right thing' includes restoring your client to his former position, which undoubtedly earns you additional money," O'Grady said. "Are you even allowed to have clients as a disbarred lawyer?"

Malachy gave O'Grady a smile to acknowledge the threat and said, "I'm a consultant now, and my client is the committee. We consultants believe in win-win. A shitstorm means somebody loses."

O'Grady looked at his watch and said, "We're approaching the ten-minute mark."

Malachy stood up and started to say good-bye when he remembered something his father told him. He stood quietly staring at the wall, trying to recall the full context.

"Good-bye, Malachy."

Malachy looked back at O'Grady and said, "The old neighborhood must have some hold on you. You never sold your parents' place."

Malachy focused on O'Grady's reaction.

"No, I never did. As you know, my aunt lived there for years after my father died. I believe she even occasionally met friends for lunch at the Shamrock."

"She did," Malachy said. "She liked the fact we have cloth napkins. Actually, bigger and better than those." Malachy pointed to the napkins on the table.

Malachy calculated his tone and words carefully and said, "It's been empty for a while, hasn't it? The house, that is. Expecting the neighborhood to make a comeback?"

"Not really, just never got around to renting it."

"Well, I'm getting tired of apartment life," Malachy said. "If you want sell, give me a call. I'd be interested."

"Of course, Malachy. I'll do that."

Malachy looked at his watch and said, "How about it? Right on time. Good-bye, Augustine."

"Good-bye, Malachy."

Malachy left the restaurant and called the Count. "Mr. William Sutton? I have a job for you, but not much time for planning, unfortunately."

"That bank? You're joking?"

"Not a bank, thank God. Meet me at the Shamrock and I'll explain. My talk with the cardinal was very revealing."

"Does Mr. O'Grady have a job?" Malachy asked his father. *"He's always home."*

"No real job. He takes a stab at something every once in a while. The bottle is his real job, and he's good at it."

"But Mrs. O'Grady doesn't work. Where do they get their money?"

"He had a big job with the city—one with lots of opportunity," Malachy's father said, making a gesture with his hand extended, palm up. "Most guys like that piss it away, especially the drinkers. Not our neighbor, he's the opposite—a skinflint. So I guess you can say his living is in safekeeping in the basement. It doesn't earn him any interest, but there's no paper trail either."

Malachy never thought any more about the answer until the conversation with O'Grady about the old ways. Malachy's father liked colorful language and puns too. Malachy realized his father meant there was an actual safe in the basement where the cash was kept. Malachy doubted there was any cash in the safe now, but when O'Grady talked about renting the house his body language said he was holding a losing hand. Malachy intended to find out why.

†

Malachy and the Count sat at the table in the Shamrock's storeroom. Malachy explained his guess about the O'Grady basement.

"A safe in a basement? Where? How old?"

"A few blocks from here," Malachy said. "The safe would be well over fifty years old."

The Count smiled and said, "Piece of cake. I suppose you do remember what I used to do for a living. I maybe a little out of practice, but it won't take long to open it."

"Will you have to drill?"

"If I can get to the lock, the only equipment needed I can carry in my pocket."

"When we played hide and seek, there was one closet door in the basement that was always locked. The safe is probably in there."

"We will be in and out in less than an hour," the Count said. "What do you think is in there?"

"Not sure, but I know it's not holy cards or his baptismal certificate."

"What about the neighbors? Or a security company? Can't we spend a day doing research?"

"The cardinal is a very organized, tightly scheduled executive. We're clear for today. But, I make him very nervous. I don't want to wake up tomorrow to find out there was an early morning clerical visitor to the house. We need to go in today or tonight."

"Take a guess—which doors are the most secure?" the Count asked.

"The back and side. After all, he is a prince of the Church. Doesn't royalty always go in through the front door?"

"Not this titled person at all times," the Count said. "But today, yes. Let's go!"

"Now?" Malachy asked

"In about thirty minutes," the Count said. "I have what I need in my pocket, but I need to change the sign on the van and prepare a disguise. It is a daylight job after all."

"Change the sign to what?"

"My function for this operation."

"Safecracker?"

"No," the Count said. "AAA Locksmith—24 Hour Emergency Service. It's one of the standard signs I keep in the van. And you should take the time to make yourself look a little less like Malachy Madden."

"Who should I look like?" Malachy asked.

"A trainee locksmith who is on his cell phone dealing with a problem. Ransack the Shamrock lost and found, you'll find something you can use."

"I forgot we have a lost and found. Eduardo makes sure I have all my stuff. Bridget has probably moved it more than once."

"Lots to choose from I'm sure," the Count said. "Most of your customers are drinking and that means they are leaving all kinds of things behind. Ask Eduardo, he'll know where it is. But you'll still have to deal with Bridget. It will be locked and you obviously don't have a key. And your locksmith is busy. The van is in the alley. See you in thirty minutes."

"Thirty minutes it is," Malachy said. "That will give me time to set up my coffee with Valquist tomorrow. Damn, I forgot to tell O'Grady he belonged in the cell next to Flynn."

"Not too late," the Count said. "You can leave him a note in the safe."

Malachy watched the Count approach the O'Grady front door. He examined the old frame house with its wide front porch, impressive front door with one panel of leaded glass, and the standard two-window second floor, all topped by a small dormer. As a young boy, he played all over the house as his mother and Mrs. O'Grady visited in the kitchen.

"There is a standard, simple security system," the Count said in a low voice. "I will need to be out here in plain view for about three minutes."

Malachy adjusted the volume on his cell phone and responded, "Nobody is paying any attention to you. Hell, I don't even know who you are. I had no idea what a change a full beard makes—and of course the skullcap does wonders."

"And you look like a deranged movie star that escaped from rehab," the Count said.

Malachy looked at himself in the rearview mirror. The sunglasses were a sleek wraparound style, and the dirty, red cap was a size too large.

"I'm in," the Count said. "Headed for the basement."

Malachy watched for any signs of interest in the O'Grady house. Pedestrian traffic was light and nobody was paying any attention to the house or the van.

"I see why he put the safe in the basement," the Count said. "It's large and heavy. The combination lock is standard. No more than twenty minutes to manipulate it. No talk while I'm working unless we have visitors."

"Understood."

Malachy kept busy methodically scanning the neighbors' houses, the sidewalk, and the street, looking for anything out of the ordinary. He checked his watch for the time when he thought five minutes was up. Six minutes had passed.

"Open."

"Amazing!" Malachy said in admiration.

"Not really," the Count said. "The last user only gave the dial a half twist when he closed it—for someone of my skill it makes for almost no challenge to come up with the last number in the combination."

"What did you find?"

"Sealed manila envelopes—a stack of them."

"Anything else?"

"That's it."

"Okay," Malachy said. "Take the envelopes, leave the picture, close up, and let's get out of here."

"Last chance to change your mind," the Count said. "Are you sure you want to leave that picture?"

"Absolutely positive," Malachy said, a little too loudly while looking at the church a block away.

It was the parish church and one of the few Jesuit ones in the archdiocese. The Jesuit motto was inscribed in the ceiling over the altar. And in the grade school in Malachy's time the nuns required the motto to be at the top of all homework and on every test. Malachy figured he had seen it thousands of times and O'Grady many thousands more since he had gone on to a Jesuit prep school.

"One more thing," Malachy said. "Do you have a marker pen with you?"

"Of course."

"Print AMDG in big caps across the back of the picture, but invert the G."

The Count took the envelopes and placed them in his bag. He carefully printed the letters diagonally across the back of the picture and placed the picture in the center of the safe, facing the front. He closed the safe door, twirled the dial seven times, checked his clipboard, and left the dial on the same number where he found it. He removed the ring he placed around the dial to aid his calculations.

The Count checked his clipboard and began to go through all the steps in reverse that he performed to gain entry to the safe. The Count was inside the front door when he heard Malachy's voice.

"Female mail carrier on the sidewalk," Malachy said. "Looks headed your way."

The Count quickly stepped back out.

"I'll wait until she can't see the house."

"Understood."

Malachy watched her until she entered the large apartment building on the corner.

"She'll be in the apartments for a while. Let's get out of here."

"Leaving now," the Count said, placing the clipboard in his bag and opening the front door.

"Damn…a female neighbor just came out of her house and is looking at you," Malachy said. "She's headed your way."

"No problem," the Count said. "She'll leave believing all Jewish locksmiths are sexy and charming."

"Amazing," Malachy said again.

"Yes, in all modesty I truly am when it comes to women," the Count said.

Malachy drove at exactly the speed limit following the Count's directions to one of his warehouses. Once in the warehouse, Malachy exited the van and an employee climbed into the driver's seat. Malachy headed to the warehouse office. The Count gave instructions to the new driver in Polish and then joined Malachy in the office.

"I didn't know the cardinal had a connection to the Jesuits," the Count said.

Malachy explained about the parish and the church. The Count didn't respond.

"Go ahead and say it," Malachy said.

"I don't need to."

"Yes," Malachy said. "It's personal now."

"I think it is for Kevin, too," the Count said. "For some reason I don't understand."

"Me either," Malachy said. "You know, O'Grady despises the old neighborhood and the neighborhood code. The neighborhood had more than its fair share of true bad guys—rogue cops, armed robbers, and worse. And yet of all the hundreds of guys that we both knew growing up, O'Grady is the only one who would knowingly send a Flynn to a new assignment where he could prey on children. And he thinks his shit doesn't stink."

"Just make sure rubbing his nose in it doesn't jeopardize our mission."

"Understood," Malachy said. "Let's find out what we have. Pick one of the envelopes and open it."

The Count carefully examined one of the envelopes to make sure it was not rigged in any way. He took out a small penknife and sliced it open and pulled out the contents.

"It's some kind of report," the Count said.

"About what?"

"I have no idea. All the pages are in Latin."

"No doubt they'll all turn out to be for the Greater Glory of God," Malachy said.

CHAPTER XXV

In his office-booth in the Shamrock, Malachy finished his special lunch of corned beef slathered with a horseradish-mustard mix on rye toast. He stared at his yellow legal pad that contained two numbered items—(1) Latin reports and (2) Coffee with Joe Valquist @ 3:00.

He was meeting with the Count after lunch to discuss the contents of the reports. The Count put himself in charge of getting the reports translated without putting the translators on notice of what they were about. The contents of the report would dictate their use and that decision in turn would influence the strategy with Valquist.

Malachy wanted to sip a Jameson while he finished his coffee but restrained himself. He ripped off the page and balled it up and was ready to make the long toss to the wastebasket when Red approached the booth. Malachy noted that Red while still slender had gained a few pounds and his haunted, sallow look was gone.

"Malachy, can I talk to you about something?"

"Sure, Red. Join me in the booth. Do you want a soft drink or something?"

"No, thanks. I want to talk to about Kevin."

"Okay, what about him?"

"He has a lot of rules, a whole lot of rules about the apartment. And I think he's mad at me."

"Why?" Malachy asked.

Red looked down and said quietly, "He found some pot."

"What did he do?" Malachy asked.

"He went through everything in the apartment, everything. I told him there wasn't any more, but he just kept looking."

"And?"

"When he was done, he told me the rule for the apartment was no pot, no drugs of any kind, and no alcohol unless he was present. Then he flushed all the pot down the toilet. He didn't yell or even raise his voice, but he was very serious."

"That's Kevin," Malachy said. "A rule is a rule, no exceptions."

"I don't think it's fair," Red said.

"Life is not fair," Malachy said, pointing to the picture of JFK behind the bar. "We have it on presidential authority. But anyway, why don't you think it's fair?"

"Because you guys drink, and I heard Kevin did drugs, lots of them, when he was younger."

"Both are true," Malachy said. "My dad convinced Kevin to stay off drugs when he lived with us. The house rule was the same except for the alcohol. We were older than you, just out of the Marines."

"How long did he live with you?" Red asked.

"About three years."

"Did you ever do drugs?" Red asked.

"No, not really. I smoked a few joints in high school, but my dad convinced me early on the Irish have all they can handle with alcohol."

"I'm not Irish," Red said.

Malachy gave him a bemused look and said, "Well, like it or not, you've been adopted, so you are now. My best advice is to get used it. And Red, Kevin is not mad at you. He's just serious about rules. He believes rules make outcomes more predictable."

"He's a little scary when he's so serious. Do you have as many rules?"

"Not sure, but I do know this—I have a lot more exceptions. Kevin doesn't believe in exceptions."

"I think it would be easier to live with you," Red said.

"Careful what you wish for Red. Not to change the subject, but I'm changing the subject, I hear from the grapevine you have a talent for Italian cooking."

"Did Kevin tell you that?"

"He did, and Antonella told him. Is there any truth to the allegation?"

"I don't know," Red said.

"Well, let's find out. I'm getting tired of our lunch menu. Do you think you could handle the lunch traffic in the kitchen if we added some Italian dishes to the menu?"

"I guess so."

"I'll take that as a yes." Malachy looked around the Shamrock for Bridget and spotted her coming out of the back room.

"Say, Bridget, join us for a minute!" Malachy shouted.

"Now, what in the name of God do you want?" Bridget shouted back as she came over to the booth.

"I want to add some Italian items to the lunch menu as an experiment, and I want to put Red in charge of selecting the menu and doing the cooking. What do you think?"

"Who's the manager of this joint?"

"You are, that's why I'm talking to you about it," Malachy said cheerfully. "It's my rule—always consult with the manager."

"Mother of God, a miracle!" Bridget exclaimed. "Red, you're the witness. He's actually talking to me about a change at the Shamrock before it's imposed. Will wonders never cease?"

"What about the idea?" Malachy asked.

"I'm objective," Bridget said. "Just because it comes from you doesn't mean it won't work. Red, do you want to try this?"

"Yes, I do."

"Okay, then we'll try it," Bridget said. "We'll make the change at the regular kitchen meeting. Don't say anything until then."

"Got it," Red said.

"Me, too," Malachy said.

"Who are you kidding?" Bridget asked. "The meeting is in the morning when you're still asleep. Tell the truth, did you even know we have a meeting?"

"Of course," Malachy said. "I dream about it all the time."

When Red and Bridget left, Malachy reminded himself to figure out who was doing the talking about Kevin and end it. He thought back to Kevin's "homecoming" and the meeting with his father in his basement workshop where all serious talks between them took place.

"I hear my friend Kevin is really messed up," Malachy said. "I want to go find him and bring him home. Can he stay with us for a while?"

"Yes, of course. Where is he?"

"On the streets in New York," Malachy said. "He's in really bad shape. I'm worried that drug shit is going to kill him."

"You'll need help. I'll go with you. We'll drive out there and get him. We'll have better control in our own car. He'll probably need to stay in the VA hospital for a while. I'll make a few calls and get that set up. Malachy, you understand Kevin will fight you. Talk won't work."

"He coming home with us one way or another," Malachy said. "After all we've been through together, I'm not leaving him to die on the streets in New York."

"How much information do we have? Do we have any idea where he is? There are a lot of streets in New York."

"He's been arrested a few times. One of our buddies saw him when he was in the system. He moves around in Manhattan, that's about all I know."

"We're going to need some help. I'll get that set up, too. When do you want to leave?"

"Tomorrow."

The Manhattan police detective came into the interview room and introduced himself with his last name.

"Gallagher. People call me Gally."

Malachy and his dad introduced themselves.

"Lots of Ms," Gally said. "Easy to remember. Can I ask you guys something? Who are you related to? First, the brass calls me in and tells me to make sure I give all the help you need. He makes it very clear the normal rules don't apply. 'Find the guy they're after and do it fast. If you need help, say so.' Then I get a call from a big cheese in the union. 'Make sure you help these fellas from Chicago. I've made a personal commitment.' So, what's the deal?"

"That's my fault, Gally," Martin said. "I called in a few favors. I guess I did too good of a job. I hope you take it as a compliment and not pressure because I asked for the best. We didn't want somebody who would just go through the motions."

"Duly noted," Gally said. "A couple more questions. Who is the guy we're after? And what is his connection to the two of you?"

"I'll answer those," Malachy said. "Kevin and I are Vietnam vets. Marines. The drug shit started there, especially after he was wounded. I tried to convince him to come to Chicago when we got out, but he ended up here."

"Does he have family here?"

"No," Malachy said. "Actually, no family anywhere. He was an orphan."

"Final question," Gally said. "What's the program when we find him?"

"Put him in our car and take him home to Chicago," Martin said. "After a detox stay in the VA hospital, he can live with us if he wants to."

"And what if he doesn't want to go to Chicago?"

Malachy stated to answer the question, but Martin put his hand on his arm and interrupted. "Gally, sometimes all the rules can't be followed. When we find Kevin, he is coming home with us. We don't expect anybody else to operate outside the rules."

Gally looked at Martin and then Malachy and said, "I've already found him. Let's go and get him. It's way past time he headed home."

Malachy and Martin pulled up behind Gally's unmarked car in a No Parking zone about 100 yards from a small bridge in Central Park. They exited the car, and Gally waved them over to where he was standing.

"He's up there with three or four others," Gally said. "Careful where you step as we get close. There's garbage everywhere, and nobody cares about sanitation."

The three men approached the small group under the bridge. They were huddled around a small warming fire. One of the men looked up and said, "Leave us the fuck alone. We're not bothering anybody."

"Hey, Kevin, it's Malachy."

"Malachy? Malachy, what are you doing here?"

"Came to see you," Malachy said, trying not to show the shock he experienced at Kevin's haggard, gaunt, and near-deranged appearance. "There's somebody I want you to meet."

"Meet? Who?"

"My dad."

Kevin staggered up and brushed off his clothes. He came over to Malachy and hugged him.

"Man, it's good to see you," Kevin said, slurring his words. "How the fuck did you find me? Which one's your dad?"

"This is my dad," Malachy said, pointing to Martin.

Martin held out his hand and said, "Kevin, it's an honor to meet you."

"Mine, mine," Kevin responded in a soft mutter, reaching out his hand to shake Martin's.

Martin firmly took Kevin's hand and pulled him hard toward himself. Kevin stumbled into Martin who quickly released the hand and grabbed Kevin in a bear hug. Martin fell backward to the ground with Kevin on top of him.

"Cuff him, cuff him," Martin shouted to the startled Gally and Malachy.

Gally pulled out the cuffs and grabbed one of Kevin's arms. Kevin started to struggle, but Martin held him tight and Kevin couldn't get any leverage. Gally forced on the cuffs.

"Malachy!" Kevin yelled. "This is not your dad! What's happening?"

Martin and Gally picked Kevin up from the ground. Kevin tried to run, but Martin knocked him down, pulled a bungee cord from his jacket, and tossed it to Gally.

"Wrap it tightly around his ankles while I hold him."

Gally secured Kevin's ankles. Martin and Gally stood Kevin up, grabbed him under the armpits, and started to drag him toward the car.

"Malachy, Malachy, what's going on?" Kevin shouted.

"Kevin, it's time to leave the battlefield," Malachy answered. "Time to come home."

At the car, Gally and Martin put Kevin in the backseat and locked the doors.

Gally turned to Martin and asked, "Why didn't you warn me?"

"It wasn't a plan, it was an opportunity. I realized it was better if the two of us handled Kevin, if you know what I mean."

"Yeah," Gally said. "I understand. Kevin's a real mess. I hope it works out for him."

"Me, too," Martin said.

"What happens now?" Gally asked.

"We drive straight through to Chicago."

"It can get wild when they're coming off drugs," Gally said.

"We've got some water laced with sedatives. If we get lucky, he sleeps for most of the trip."

"Let me know how it all works out, will you?"

"Will do. And Gally, if ever need anything in Chicago, you know who to call."

Malachy skimmed through translations of the Latin reports.

"It's not Catullus," the Count said. "Though there are some gold nuggets in there, but they are surrounded by bureaucratic obfuscation."

"How did you get the translations done?" Malachy asked

"I copied the reports, cut them up, and sent unconnected pieces to Poland by email to get translated. Then I reassembled them. A lot gets lost that way, but it is possible to get the gist of the reports. Essentially, they are the notes of meetings with parents regarding accusations of sexual abuse. We are missing a code key so it is not possible to know the names of the parents or the priest who was accused. But it's clear that the parents are warned off taking any action by intimidation and threat."

"By O'Grady?"

"No, his deputies."

"Not the smoking gun I hoped for," Malachy said. "But still a weapon."

"What kind?" The Count asked.

"Cage rattler. Very effective at long ranges if properly targeted."

"And what's the target?"

"Rome," Malachy said.

"What do you propose?" the Count asked.

"Do as the Romans do."

"Could you be a little more specific," the Count said.

"Okay. Act like a devious Curia bureaucrat trying to bring down an adversary—have the chancery office officially fax the original reports to the Papal Nuncio in Washington, D.C."

"And what does the cover sheet say?" the Count asked.

"How about, 'I am losing my grip and your confidence in me is misplaced, Yours in Christ, Cardinal Augustine O'Grady.'"

The Count smiled and said, "Will you settle for, 'Highly Confidential, No Copies'?"

"If you insist," Malachy said. "Let's divide the task. I'll get the fax number, you send the fax."

"Not exactly an even division," the Count responded.

"Life is not fair," Malachy responded. "But you already knew that. How do you propose to get access to a chancery office phone?"

The Count checked his watch and said, "I need to do my research. The simplest solution is to connect a laptop to one of their numbers. That way I can have everything loaded up and ready to go. I prefer to go in during regular business hours if possible, probably as a repairman. Second best is to be part of the cleaning crew. I'll call you in the morning when I have it worked out."

"Not too early," Malachy said.

"Not too early," the Count repeated. "Just fairly early."

Joe Valquist looked around the coffee shop and then focused on the elaborate Italian espresso machine and the extensive menu on three panels high up on the wall.

"What kind of coffee do you serve in the Shamrock?" Joe Valquist asked Malachy.

"The kind that does not require learning a new language to order it," Malachy said. "But I'll confess a secret. There's a French press in the kitchen and mine is made with that and a special coffee. So if you come in and I'm not there, just tell them you want a Malachy coffee."

"That sounds like code for coffee laced with something," Joe said.

"It's a bar so if you want that just tell them what to put in it—no code necessary."

"I'll remember that. How was the meeting with the cardinal?"

"Well, he didn't offer me coffee or any other beverage. He gave me exactly ten minutes of his time, but I did learn a few things. He was aware Flynn had an abuse problem and transferred him to new parishes anyway."

"He told you that?"

"Not directly, but he told me all the same. Remember, we go way back. He's not a good bluffer. It is clear he is going into the bunker and attempt to ride out the storm."

"The way the Church is run he might get away with it," Joe said. "It makes me sick to think about it."

"Not going to happen," Malachy said.

"Why?"

"He has an implacable enemy."

"Who?"

"Me."

"What are you going to do?" Joe asked

"Make sure he loses his job," Malachy said. "And you can help."

"Me? How? I don't have any influence."

"The meeting of the parents," Malachy said.

"I don't understand. I thought that was what we are going to talk about—if you should attend."

"I am not going to be there, but I want those parents to tell their stories in graphic detail—the abuse and their interactions with the Church officials."

"To who?"

"Richard Riordan."

"The PI attorney? Has he agreed to take the case? Everybody in Chicago knows his name."

"No, he's not going to take the case. Actually, I haven't talked to him about the meeting yet. But he owes me a favor."

"Now I really don't understand," Joe said. "What's the purpose of the meeting?"

"In addition to being an extremely wealthy PI attorney who scares the bejesus out of insurance companies and other wealthy defendants, he is the most prominent Catholic layman in Chicago. He's connected to every major Catholic institution and charity in the area. He is on so many boards he has a special assistant just to keep track of the agendas. And his Catholic connections are national and even international. Get the picture?"

"Yeah," Joe said. "I get the picture. He is part of the problem. He's never going to sue the Church so what's the point of the meeting?"

"To piss him off," Malachy said. "To piss him off royally. And then get out of the way and see what happens."

"You actually think a guy like that gives a damn about these parents? These people are mostly blue collar. They are not powerful, not connected, and certainly not rich."

"You just described Riordan's father. He got screwed by a powerful, politically connected construction company when he got injured on the job. Riordan never forgot it. The happiest day of his life was when he nailed that same construction company, and the punitive damages were not covered by insurance."

"These parents have been through the ringer," Joe said. "I don't want to be part of arranging anything that makes them suffer more. What they don't need is one more powerful person who makes them feel they are just pawns in some game."

"Let's get something straight," Malachy said, the anger rising in his voice. "This is not a game. The only way the right thing is going to be done for those parents and their children is for O'Grady to be forced out as the head of the diocese. You believe he belongs in a jail cell. That's not going to happen. But if he is forced out—and have no doubt about it, if he goes, he will be kicked upstairs, not downstairs—then good things can happen. You know what my job is, and I intend to do it with or without your help. The meeting will help the parents and the kids. Are you in or out?"

Joe looked away and was silent. Malachy took a drink of his coffee and waited.

"Okay," Joe said after a minute. "I'll trust you on this. I'll do my best to get as many parents as possible to come to the meeting. Where and when?"

"Where is easy. One of their homes. When? As soon as possible. Work it out with the parents."

"Are you certain Riordan will show up?" Joe asked

"Absolutely certain," Malachy answered.

"How can you be so sure? You're committing the man, and you don't even know his schedule."

"He'll change his schedule," Malachy said. "I changed mine when he needed me."

CHAPTER XXVI

It was years ago when he was still a practicing lawyer, Kevin was his top investigator, and Maria was alive.

"Malachy, wake up!" Maria said, shoving him. "There's somebody named Riches calling collect on the phone. Should I accept the charges? Wake up, damn it!"

It was a Sunday morning. Malachy struggled to force himself awake. He looked at the clock—6:15.

"Who? What?" Malachy asked.

Maria repeated what she said and added, "The operator wants a decision."

"Riches" was the neighborhood nickname for Richard Riordan.

"Accept the charges," Malachy said, walking around the bed and taking the phone from Maria. "Richard, what's the matter?"

"Oh, thank God, you took the call. I'm in big trouble. I need your help."

"Of course," Malachy said. "What's the problem?"

"Can Maria hear me? I want to keep this between us."

"No, she can't," Malachy said, picking up the phone and moving toward the window. "What's going on?"

"I'm in a motel on Cicero Avenue. She stripped me, took everything—a black hooker. All my clothes, wallet, money, my wedding ring, everything. You've got to help me! I can't call the cops. If Monica finds out, I'm dead. I've got to get my stuff back! Especially, the wallet and the wedding ring. Oh God, you've got to help me."

"Richard, I'm going to help you. Where are you?"

Richard gave the address of a motel one mile north of Midway Airport and the room number.

"I'll be there in an hour." Malachy said. "Now listen carefully to me. Barricade yourself in the room as best you can and figure out what you can use as a weapon. There's always the possibility her pimp will figure out you're a potential gold mine and return. Do you understand?"

"Oh God, I never thought of that. I can't leave. She took my clothes."

"I don't want you to leave," Malachy said. "Just do what I told you. I'll see you in an hour. Okay?"

"Okay, but hurry for God's sake!"

"There won't be any traffic. I'll be there in an hour or less. Everything is going to work out. Hang up now and barricade yourself in."

Malachy returned the phone to the bedside table and headed toward the bathroom.

"Malachy, what's going on?" Maria asked, following him into the bathroom. "You can't go anywhere now. We're due in Church at nine for my parents' anniversary mass—you promised."

"A friend is in trouble. I've got to go help him. It can't wait—it's an emergency. I doubt if I will be back in time for the mass. I'll try and make the party later. Just explain I had a client with an emergency. Your mom and dad will understand."

Maria gave him one of her dark Sicilian stares that always meant big trouble.

"Malachy, my parents wanted the whole family there and you promised. And it is not a client. It's one of your neighborhood friends. You're choosing one of your drunk friends who did God knows what over your family."

"Maria, you know I'd never do that. My family is fine and is not in trouble. My friend since we were in kindergarten together is not fine and is in big trouble, and I'm going to help him. If you want to help out, please pack some of my old clothes and underwear in a bag and make some coffee while I get dressed. If not, I will see you later as soon as I can. I'm sorry, but that's the way it is going to be."

Malachy stomped out of the bathroom. Maria said something in Italian and went to Malachy's closet. Malachy knew she would not talk to him or kiss him good-bye, but she would pack the clothes and make the coffee. He reminded himself to put some toiletries in the bag and to grab a couple of cans of Coke from the refrigerator. Hard to recover from a hangover without being able to brush your teeth.

When Malachy came out of the bathroom, a small duffel bag was on the bed. He put in his spare Dopp kit and listened for Maria. She was in the kitchen. He picked up the phone and called Kevin. He kept his voice low so Maria couldn't hear him. "Kevin, this is Malachy. Sorry, if you have company staying over, but I need your help. Can I pick you up in fifteen minutes? We're headed to a dive motel on South Cicero to rescue a friend. We might need some equipment."

"I'll be waiting outside," Kevin said.

Malachy drove to Kevin's with one hand on the wheel, alternately drinking coffee and taking bites of the peanut-butter-covered toast Maria had prepared for him. She did talk to him, but only to deliver a warning—he'd better make the party and be showered and properly dressed. Kevin was waiting on the corner with an oversized sports bag.

"Sorry to ruin your Sunday plans, Kevin. There's coffee in the thermos. Use the top as a cup. And have some toast. Did you have company?"

"Yes, I did. I explained it was a work emergency. She was a little suspicious when I told her I needed a few minutes of privacy to pack the bag. But she was satisfied when I told her we'd go out to dinner tonight. What's the situation?"

Malachy explained the telephone call and his instructions to Richard.

"Surprising they left him with access to a phone," Kevin said.

"Agreed. And 'they' is the operative word. This is more than some hooker stealing a wallet. When we get there, I'll go up to the room, and you check out the motel. Richard will be expecting me to be alone. He didn't even want Maria to know what happened. He'll feel a little less embarrassed if he meets you after he's had a chance to clean up a little and put some clothes on."

"Let's hope there's time for that," Kevin said. "I'll hang back, but I'm going up to the room with you. You can't be sure he will be alone."

"Okay."

At the motel, Malachy drove the length of the parking lot while Kevin examined the parked cars.

"Nothing unusual," Kevin said. "Let's park across the street. We don't want to get blocked in."

Malachy parked and they exited the car. They walked rapidly toward the two-story motel with Kevin carrying the sports bag and Malachy the duffel. Malachy took the concrete steps up to the second floor two at a time. Kevin followed about ten yards behind him. Malachy found Richard's room and knocked on the door.

"Riches, it's M2. What's the score?"

Malachy knew if there was trouble behind the door his answer would not be their boyhood rejoinder.

"We need more," Richard said loudly through the door. "Thank God you're here."

Malachy could hear furniture being pulled away from the door, and then the door opened.

"Jesus," Malachy said. "I hope you feel better than you look." He reminded Malachy of the street bums that used to populate West Madison Avenue—matted hair, unshaven blotted face, and puffy, red bloodshot eyes.

Richard, holding a towel around his waist, stepped back from the door and said, "I've been throwing up all morning, and I feel like total shit. Did you bring some clothes?"

"Yes, they're in the duffel along with some other stuff. Take a few minutes to get yourself straight in the bathroom. Kevin, my investigator, is with me. We go way back and you don't need to worry about him. When you're ready we need to ask a few questions. Richard, don't leave anything out—no matter how embarrassing. We don't have a lot of time to get your stuff back."

Richard started to protest but stopped in mid-sentence and said, "M2, I'm just so grateful you came. You're calling the shots—we'll do it whatever way you want. Give me ten minutes in the bathroom."

"No problem. And Richard slowly drink at least one of the Cokes while you're getting ready. It'll help—I know from experience."

Malachy waited for Richard to go into the bathroom and then signaled to Kevin to join him in the room.

"He'll be out in ten minutes. You check out the motel. Take something with you just in case. I'll wait here."

Kevin nodded in agreement; reached in the bag; pulled out two weighted, thick baton-like devices; and handed one to Malachy. Kevin placed his up the left sleeve of his jersey. He tested to make sure he could easily extract it. Kevin took out two-way radios, and they clipped them to their belts.

"Codes?" Kevin asked.

"Blue for the cops, red for the hooker's associates, and green for rescue."

"Back in ten minutes," Kevin said, going out the door.

Malachy positioned himself at the front door where he could see any car entering the parking lot. As the ten-minute mark approached, Kevin emerged from the stairwell and gave a thumbs-up signal. Malachy and Kevin entered the room and secured the door. Richard came out of the bathroom, his hair still wet from the shower. Malachy introduced Kevin.

"What do you want to know?" Richard asked.

"How and where did you meet her?" Malachy asked.

"Monica was out of town. I was partying on a boat in Belmont Harbor. Somebody suggested we head to Rush Street in a cab. I was totally smashed by the time we left the last bar and was ready to take a cab home. I was handing out tips like there was no tomorrow. The last place was a fancy one and the head doorman asked if I wanted my cab stocked. I told him yes and gave him some hundreds."

"So, it was just supposed to be a blow job on the way home?" Malachy asked.

"Yeah, in my head I thought we would drive around someplace quiet and dark for a while, and then I'd change cabs. As drunk as I was, I didn't want anybody to know who I was or where or I lived. It was definitely a sex cab. The windows were tinted, and the driver couldn't see into the backseat.

"So how did you end up here?"

Richard looked away for a few seconds and then looked at Malachy.

"I was so drunk things didn't quite work right. She was kind of nice about it really. She said she could fix it and give me some special job but we needed a bed—it wouldn't cost that much more and it'd be worth it.

She was very persuasive in every way. She told me I needed to relax. She had some pot, and we shared some. We ended up here."

"I have a question," Kevin said. "Do you remember if she asked your name and where you were from?"

"Actually, she did," Richard answered in surprise. "I lied and gave her a fake name and told her I was from Springfield. Here for a convention."

"Before or after the pot?" Kevin asked.

"Before."

"Did she check in at the motel office or did you go directly to the room?" Kevin asked.

"It's all kind of fuzzy, but I think we just came up to the room."

Kevin looked at Malachy and said, "It's just a guess, but the odds are she's still on the premises in another room. And her associates will be coming over to extract more cash. The motel may even be home. There are a couple of rooms around the corner that look a little different."

"How do we find the right room?" Malachy asked.

"The office is empty," Kevin said. "Let's start there."

"Agreed," Malachy said. "Richard, what does she look like?"

"It was dark everywhere including this room," Richard said. "All I remember is she's small and slender, a cute face with lots of hair and makeup."

"Do you remember what she was wearing?" Kevin asked.

"Not really. Some kind of gaudy dress, I think. And she wore some kind of fancy thing around her neck."

"Good enough," Malachy said. "Richard, I'm going to walk you over to the car while Kevin checks out the office. You wait in the car with the doors locked and the engine running. If the cops show up, you drive off and go home. No matter what, don't open the doors to anybody but Kevin or myself. Understood?"

"Malachy, I can't just drive away and leave the two of you here—that's not right. I'll just have to take the consequences."

"Look, Richard, I don't need any noble intentions fucking things up," Malachy said.

"Nothing is going to happen to Kevin or me from the cops. If I have to, I'll call in some favors. I came down here to get you out of trouble and *that's what's going to happen. Like you said, I'm calling the shots. Now let's head to the car."*

"Okay," Richard said, almost in a whisper.

At the car, Malachy put the duffel in the trunk and turned to Richard and said, "We have our game plan, no last minute changes. I don't want to have to factor you into our response if we get company."

Malachy hurried across the street and met Kevin emerging from the motel office.

"Last room at the end around the corner is my first candidate. I have jimmies in the bag."

They moved quickly to the front door of the room. Kevin tried the passkey, but the door was secured from the inside. Malachy took the heel of his baton device and began banging loudly on the door.

"Police, open this goddamn door now!" Malachy shouted. "Police! Open it now, goddamn it!"

Malachy and Kevin both banged on the door with increasing force. A half-dressed man came around the corner.

"Police business," Malachy said to the man. "Go back in your room and shut the door."

The man disappeared back around the corner. Malachy and Kevin resumed banging on the door. They heard a muffled voice from behind the door.

"You've got the wrong room! I'm all alone. You've got the wrong room!"

"Open this goddamn door right now or we will break it down," Malachy shouted. "And then we will come in there and break your fucking head open! Open it now!"

"Okay, Okay, I'm opening it."

Malachy and Kevin flattened themselves against the wall on either side of the door. The door opened a few inches constrained by two chains. Kevin hunched down in a crouch holding the heavy sports bag with two hands and placing it on the cement walk. Malachy stepped out, turned around, and gave the door a mule kick and quickly moved back to the wall. From his couched position, Kevin swung the sports bag in an arc hitting the door with the force of a battering ram.

The door flew open as shrieking sounds filled the air. Kevin threw the bag into the room and then dived into the room and rolled. Malachy counted to three and then charged through the door. Kevin was straddling a figure on the bed. Malachy quickly checked the closet and the bathroom for an accomplice. There was no one. Malachy closed and bolted the door and then flicked on the overhead light.

On a large clothes-caddy in the corner of the room, an elaborate wig and a woman's dress and undergarments were carefully laid out along with some items Malachy didn't recognize. There was a large makeup bag on the floor next to the chair.

"Oh, Jesus," Malachy said.

"Don't hit me in the face, not in the face!"

"Relax," Malachy said. "We're not going to hit or hurt you. Just cooperate so my partner can cuff you."

"Roll over," Kevin commanded.

"I get paid for that, honey."

"Not this morning," Kevin said, quickly pulling his captive's arms together and cuffing the wrists.

"You are slender," Malachy said, looking at the short, lean black figure dressed in some kind of tight, woman's exercise outfit and a black skullcap.

"Why, thank you. I work hard on my figure. But you didn't have to break down my door to pay me a compliment."

Malachy marveled at the voice. It was throaty and sexy and certainly sounded like a woman's.

"What's your name? Malachy asked. "And I mean your street name, not your real name."

"My name is Lucy like in I Love Lucy."

"Your way too young to have watched that on TV," Malachy said.

"Reruns, honey, reruns. I watch a lot of daytime TV."

"Well, Lucy, just think of me as an emotional Cuban like Ricky. When I get upset I do crazy shit, and, guess what, I'm upset."

"What's the matter, Ricky, honey?"

"You stripped my friend and took everything he had. Where is it?"

"Ricky, honey, I don't know what you're talking about. I'm just trying to make a living. You can see, there's nobody here."

Malachy walked over and picked up the wig and put it on the bed. He rummaged through the sports bag and took out a large wire cutter.

"Ricky! Honey, what are you doing? That's my big hair. I need that for my work."

Malachy did his best to adopt a Cuban accent and said, "Lucy, you're lying to me and that upsets me. If it happens just one more time, I'm going to cut this wig up and flush it down the toilet."

"Oh, sweet Jesus, don't do that—it cost a fortune!"

"Lucy, listen up! We don't want this episode to end with Ricky cutting up everything you own and putting you out on Cicero looking like that. You can keep the money, I need everything else, everything. Where is it?"

"I can keep the money?"

"Yes, all the money," Malachy said in his own voice. "Showtime is over. Where is it?"

"The clothes are in a garment bag in the closet. His wallet and other stuff are in the fake bottom of the makeup bag. There's a hidden zipper in the ruffle on the side."

"Thanks, Lucy."

Malachy retrieved the garment bag and opened the bottom of the makeup bag and dumped the contents on the bed. It was all there—wedding ring, full money clip, and wallet. Malachy checked the wallet for the driver's license and credit cards. Everything was intact.

Malachy took the money from the clip, held it up, and asked, "Now Lucy, what's the scam? And remember lies make me act crazy."

Lucy leaned back on the bed, gave Malachy a flirtatious smile, and said, "I use my hands while I talk."

"Okay," Malachy said, nodding to Kevin who released the cuffs. "Now start talking."

Lucy rubbed her wrists and said, "The john is supposed to be from out of town. I leave him naked and cuffed to the bed. The Big Man comes over with a Polaroid camera and takes some pictures. Then he blackmails him with the pictures to buy shit with his credit cards or cash a check. If he cooperates, he gives him back his stuff, but not the pictures. He makes a big show of writing down his address and threatens to mail the pictures home if he calls the cops. He leaves him enough money to take a cab back to the hotel. No one has ever called the cops."

"Hard bluff to call," Malachy said.

"Hard is right, honey. There they are naked and scared to death with the Big Man taking pictures, but I'm so good they still get hard when I get it in my mouth."

"Talent wins out," Malachy said. "What went wrong this time?"

"I kind of liked the john. We did some pot together. I was flying when we got here. I went to the wrong room. The working room doesn't have a phone and the cuffs and sex toys are there. In a way, I don't think I wanted to do that to him. He treated me nice. But in the end I got scared and took his stuff."

"When does the Big Man usually show up?"

"After nine, most of the time. He always calls before he leaves to drive here so that the girl is ready to play her part."

"I'd like to wait and pay my respects, but I'm late for church," Malachy said. "How bad does he beat you when things go wrong?"

"He likes to kick," Lucy said. "He'll hurt me if he figures out I used the wrong room. He was counting on this score. He told me to keep working until I found one."

"Time for you to find a new job, Lucy. This scam is going to be shut down anyway. Now, you have a little bankroll to get started."

"A new job? There's no way. You can't get away from the Big Man. He owns this motel and is into all kinds of shit."

"Time to move on, Lucy. The Big Man is headed for the slammer. It may take a little time, but that's where he's going."

"Man, you're crazy. This is no TV show—the Big Man will end up killing somebody."

"Lucy, it's your choice. You can give the Big Man the money and take the beating, or a guy in your business who owes me a favor will take you in. He's on the South Side. He protects and takes care of his talent. He's a businessman who caters to special tastes. Like every good businessman, he likes repeat customers. There's none of this kind of bullshit."

"For real?"

"For real," Malachy said.

"Ricky, you're some strange kind of cop."

"Your choice, Lucy."

"Okay, call him! Oh, sweet Jesus, I can't believe I'm doing this. What am I going to do? All my things are in this room. I can't just walk out and leave everything here."

Malachy walked around the room and looked in the closet. He gestured to two portable closets.

"Filled with your clothes?"

"Yes, honey, filled to the top. And I have to take that makeup table—that's special."

"All the contents of the closets and the table," Malachy said. "Everything else stays."

"Well, Ricky, honey, there are some personal items, of course."

"Of course, Lucy. Every woman needs her things.

Lucy, do any of the cars in the lot belong to the Big Man?"

"Yeah, that big old Cadillac. He uses it as a limo sometimes."

"Okay, we'll use that," Malachy said. "Kevin, any car keys in the office?"

"No, but I can start it."

"Good, park right outside the door and leave it running. And tell our friend, we have his stuff. He can turn off the engine. We'll be leaving in thirty minutes."

"Thirty minutes? Oh sweet Jesus, I need time to get ready!"

"Pick out an outfit and start to get ready," Malachy said. "Everything else is going into the Caddy."

Kevin left with the sports bag to deliver the message and get the Cadillac.

"Ricky, honey, what if the Big Man spots me driving his Cadillac?"

"Kevin will be driving," Malachy said. "He'll make sure you get to your new home safely. Now you get ready while we pack. We're leaving on time."

"The car is packed, Lucy, time to go!" Malachy shouted.

Lucy emerged from the bathroom, dressed to the nines.

"Looking good, Lucy, looking very good!"

Lucy looked around the room and said, "I hope I got everything. I know I can't come back."

"Treat yourself to something new if you forgot anything," Malachy said.

The phone rang. Lucy looked at it as it rang and said quietly, "The Big Man."

Malachy went over, picked up the phone, and answered in a loud voice:

"Chicago Office of Tourism, complaint bureau, may I help you?"

Malachy heard a curse at the other end of the line before it went dead.

"Sweet Jesus, Ricky, honey, you're a strange one."

"Lucy, you're not the first good-looking woman to tell me that."

Malachy drove about ten blocks with Richard, pulled into a McDonald's, and pointed to a phone booth.

"I need to make a few private calls. How about you get us some coffee and something to eat to go? I need about fifteen minutes."

"Sure," Richard said.

Malachy called his client on the South Side and explained the situation.

"The Big Man can't be that big because I've never heard of him," the client said. "You're doing me the favor if he-she's that good. She'll be well taken care of. And yes, we test all the talent. Kevin can leave the Cadillac. I'll get rid of it. One of my men will drive him home."

On the way home Malachy made small talk with Richard about mutual friends from the old neighborhood. He didn't want to embarrass him by talking about the incident or Lucy. Richard did his part, asking about Maria and the girls and Maria's parents. Malachy explained he was headed to the anniversary party. Just before he dropped Richard off, he knew he had to warn him.

"Richard, Lucy is going to be checked out by her new employer. Things sound like they were very confused last night. I wouldn't have relations with Monica until you hear from me that everything is okay. I'm sure it is, but why risk it?"

"I understand, M2. I really appreciate everything you've done. God only knows what would have happened to me if you hadn't shown up."

Malachy got to the anniversary party on time, showered and dressed appropriately. Maria warmed up to him a little, but was very reserved when they got home. Malachy decided not to press the issue.

Early Monday afternoon, Maria called him.

"Malachy, I'm not that mad at you. You didn't need to spend all that money, but the flowers are beautiful and I love the necklace and pendant. The diamond looks so real. But, are you sure you want to spend that much on the show tickets and that fancy restaurant? You really don't have to do that for my parents. I haven't called them yet. Everything is okay, really."

"My guess is the diamond is real, Maria."

"Real? What do you mean you guess?"

"It's not from me. What did the card say?"

"'Sorry to have disrupted your Sunday.' There's no signature and no return address."

"It's from my friend—his way of saying thank you," Malachy said. "Knowing him the diamond is real for sure."

"Oh my God! The diamond is so big. What did you have to do for him? Kill somebody?"

"Not yet," Malachy said. "Anyway, I'm glad you're not mad anymore."

Maria laughed and said, "Not mad! You have my permission to rescue him anytime he's in trouble."

Later that afternoon, Malachy called a friend, an assistant state's attorney, who owed him a big favor. He described the scam, the role of the Big Man, the function of the motel, the stocked cabs.

"Can you provide a victim or a witness?" the friend asked.

"Not possible because of the way I developed the information. But it should be easy to set up a sting or at the very least raid the motel as a whorehouse. It'll make for great headlines, and there is an election coming up. And if the Big Man is paying protection, your boss gets a twofer."

"What's your interest in this? And please don't tell me you're being civic-minded."

"It's a union thing," Malachy said.

His friend emitted a loud, exaggerated, "Huh?"

"It's hard enough to get conventions to choose Chicago because they have to pay union scale to do anything. If word gets out that an attendee might end up naked and cuffed to a bed while a pimp takes pictures of a hooker chewing on his cock, it might negatively influence some votes on the site selection committees.

"Okay, okay, Malachy, I get it. I'll take care of it."

"Good," Malachy said. "Somebody has to and, given the circumstances, better you than me."

CHAPTER XXVII

Malachy muted the TV and answered his cell phone.

"Are you awake?" the Count asked.

"Define your terms," Malachy countered.

"Able to intelligently discuss the plan for the chancery fax and propose solutions for any flaws. You're a consultant now, remember?"

"I do remember and am fully capable of meeting the terms of your definition of wakefulness. Proceed."

"I'm going in as a telephone-line repairman to fix static on one of the lines. My laptop is loaded and ready to go with the Latin reports and an official-looking cover sheet. The number you gave me is programmed. The whole operation will take no more than fifteen minutes. I'm in the van outside the chancery offices. Any flaws?"

"No."

"Are you horizontal or vertical?" the Count asked.

"Relative to what?"

"Your bed."

"My direction relative to my work surface is the same as yours," Malachy said, adjusting the pillows behind his head.

"If you don't hear from me in twenty minutes, come to my rescue," the Count said.

"Absolutely," Malachy said. "Only give your name, rank, and serial number no matter how much they stretch you on the rack."

Malachy got fresh coffee and returned to bed, set his alarm for eighteen minutes later, and resumed channel surfing. He was fully engaged in his TV hobby of watching interviews of political figures with the sound muted, scoring the number of lies told by body language, when the alarm went off. He looked at his cell phone, expecting it to ring. Nothing happened. At the twenty-five minute mark, he got up from the bed and started to pace. The cell phone rang ten minutes later.

"What happened?" Malachy asked.

"A very attractive women, an administrative assistant of sorts. She was having phone problems at home and wanted my expert opinion. So of course I listened. It is a very complicated problem. By the way, the operation went flawlessly. Fax sent and received—no problems."

"Good," Malachy said. "How far did you go?"

"I assume you're asking about the attractive woman and not the fax."

"Correct."

"I told her to call me on my cell, which of course is untraceable, if the solution I proposed did not work and I would fix the problem as a favor, no charge."

"I understand," Malachy said. "Clearly, on the right side of the line between operational necessity and impermissible fraternization."

"Absolutely," the Count said. "One is not allowed to fudge these matters just because the subject is attractive and in desperate need of a long, cool drink of water in a desert of celibacy. See you at the joint chiefs meeting."

In the Shamrock's storeroom, Malachy looked at Kevin and the Count and said, "So far, so good. To sum up, Flynn is out of commission at least for the near term and likely for years to come. We have collected enough information and evidence to prove that Bari did not abuse Pace.

"We have at a minimum caused a little confusion between O'Grady and Rome and perhaps sowed some serious doubts as to O'Grady's competence and control. And, finally, the pressure on O'Grady will increase a lot once Richard Riordan meets with the parents of some of the victims."

"Are you sure Riordan won't just listen and end up doing nothing?" the Count asked.

"Not in his nature," Malachy answered. "He'll take some kind of action. How strong and how direct are the only questions. But no matter what, there will be increased pressure on O'Grady. Knowing Richard, I'm betting on big time, public pressure, locally and nationally. Enough to get more attention from Rome."

"What next?" Kevin asked.

"Well, I have a major proposal to put up for discussion," Malachy said.

"Ready," the Count said.

"All ears," Kevin said.

"We let the pot boil for a couple of weeks without interference."

"Nothing?" the Count asked.

"No action at all?" Kevin asked.

"That's my proposal," Malachy said.

"And when did this brainstorm come to you?" the Count asked.

"Are you feeling all right?" Kevin asked.

"I'm feeling fine," Malachy answered. "I was watching the cooking channel this morning and the chef made the point that sometimes the best results come from taking no action—no stirring, no probing, no checking."

"Are you just out of ideas?" the Count asked suspiciously.

"I'm just doing what the two of you have urged on me many times in the past," Malachy said.

"Okay, I'll bite," Kevin said. "What's that?"

"To be disciplined."

"All right," the Count said. "What do you really have in mind?"

Malachy smiled and said, "I'm serious about letting things boil for a couple of weeks. But I must admit I've a few ideas about how to flambé the final presentation."

"Thank God," the Count said. "You had me worried that some strange malady was afflicting you. And for sure I wasn't concerned about an outbreak of discipline."

"We will never accomplish our mission as long as O'Grady remains the cardinal archbishop of Chicago. So here's my idea for getting Rome to act."

Malachy described his plan in detail for ten minutes without interruption. Both the Count and Kevin smiled when Malachy finished.

"You are asking a lot of our nameless, faceless employer," the Count said.

"A whole lot," Kevin said.

"True," Malachy said. "But he hasn't balked yet. And after all, he's got two weeks to plan."

"He'll need it," Kevin said. "All of it."

"I propose I make the call," Malachy said.

"Agreed," Kevin and the Count said in unison.

Malachy took out the special cell phone and pressed the preprogrammed number. He listened while the call was forwarded numerous times. Finally, it was answered and Malachy gave the code, explained that it was a major request and would take time to describe, and clicked off.

A few minutes later the cell phone rang.

"Malachy, what do you need?"

Malachy launched into a detailed description of his plan.

"Some questions, Malachy," the employer said. "Is this business or personal and why?"

"Mostly business," Malachy answered. "O'Grady must be removed for Bari to be restored to full powers at the Shrine. And that decision will come from Rome. We need to get Rome's attention."

"What's the situation with Bari's accuser?"

"We have the conclusive evidence to prove to him that it was Flynn and not Bari who abused him," Malachy said. "We are going allow the current storm over Flynn to increase in intensity for a couple of weeks before choosing a method to persuade Pace to recant."

"What did you mean by 'mostly business'?"

"The specific number I requested has a 'pissed off' factor in it that is personal. No doubt, the business purpose could be accomplished with less."

There was a few seconds of silence, and then the voice said, "Malachy, we'll count it as an extra bonus. We need to fix a date now and it can't change, even if the cardinal is not in residence. You can choose."

"Seventeen days from today," Malachy said without hesitation.

"Good luck," the voice said.

Malachy looked at the Count and Kevin and said, "Now that we are on leave for a couple of weeks, I propose we get off to a good start with an excellent Italian meal—including a modest amount of good wine and other spirits."

"Taylor Street?" the Count asked.

"Shamrock—Red is doing a great job with his new assignment," Malachy said.

Malachy turned to Kevin and said, "Of course, the Count and I would completely understand if the start of the two weeks of R & R requires you to immediately join Antonella. After all, you are no longer on active assignment."

Kevin gave Malachy a big grin and said, "I'll be breaking bread with the two of you. We are declaring a unilateral cease-fire, but battle could break out at any time. I need to stay focused."

"Such iron discipline," Malachy said. "Remarkable. I shall have to seriously consider the merits of it. Is it difficult to develop?"

"Decide there are no exceptions. It keeps things simple—that way the rules are the rules."

"But," Malachy said, "isn't an exception really just a new rule?"

"No," Kevin said. "An exception is a breaking of the rule, no matter the circumstances. Breaking the rule for Antonella leads to breaking the rule for her sister."

"Antonella has a sister?" the Count asked, hopefully.

"No, sorry, it was a figure of speech," Kevin said. "Anyway, Malachy why are there so many exceptions?"

"One of my rules is to not let imponderables interfere with a good meal—let's eat!"

Bridget entered the back room, looked at the empty wine bottles, and said, "Before you start into the sambuca, there is someone at the bar asking for you, Malachy. He looks official. What do you want me to tell him?"

"How official?" Malachy asked.

"I didn't do a strip search," Bridget said. "But if he sat down with some of the cops who eat here, he'd fit right in."

Malachy turned to the Count and asked, "How long have I been on vacation?"

"Exactly eighty-three minutes," the Count answered, checking his watch.

"There are lots of ways of measuring," Bridget said, gesturing to the empty bottles. "But none of them get me an answer."

"I'm reluctant to return to work," Malachy said.

"Lack of experience, no doubt," Bridget said. "What's the answer?"

"Tell the gentleman I will join him shortly at the bar. And have Eduardo bring us the aforementioned digestive aid and some of the special coffee."

"Right," Bridget said. "That will sharpen your wits."

"Exactly."

"Good afternoon and welcome to the Shamrock," Malachy said, extending his hand.

The man shook Malachy's hand and said, "Thank you for interrupting your busy schedule to see me. My name is Daniel Breen. I was hoping to have a few confidential words with you regarding your current activities."

"You look familiar," Malachy said, looking the man up and down. "North Side or South Side Breens? On the Force?"

The man smiled and said, "South Side and a retired detective, now doing a few special private projects. Kind of like you, if my research is correct."

"Well, you have the advantage on me. I didn't know you were dropping by today so I couldn't do any research. May I ask who is funding your research?"

"And my request for confidential words?" Breen asked, looking around the bar.

"Of course," Malachy said. "Please join me in my office. It's the last booth up there. I sit on the side that surveys the barroom—that way I can spot any errant researchers on a bender. We do serve the university community here, you know."

"I did know that," Breen said. "Your office, it is."

"I'll join you in a minute. Just tell Eduardo what you like to drink. I need to tell my colleagues in the other room to carry on without me."

"Please extend my apologies to Kevin and the Count for the interruption," Breen said. "I tried to wait until your meal was finished."

"More research," Malachy said. "You've been busy."

"Very busy."

Malachy settled himself in the office-booth across from Breen.

"Cardinal O'Grady," Breen said.

"What about him?" Malachy asked.

"That's who is funding my research."

"I hope you got paid up front," Malachy said. "He's from a long line of tightwads and late payers."

Breen laughed and said, "I knew I was going to enjoy this assignment."

"And what is the assignment?"

"To convince you to return certain documents to the cardinal, to give your word that no copies were made, and to cease your campaign against him."

Malachy raised his right arm and said, "I swear to God I'm not the one who took his *Playboy* collection. More like an inside job, I'd say."

"The documents are in Latin and were taken from a private safe belonging to the cardinal that's only a stone's throw from the Shamrock."

"You're wrong."

"About what?"

"The distance to the O'Grady residence. Many a summer night I threw stones from here and never hit the damn house once. And I've got a good arm. Never knew they had a safe, though. I guess if I were a cardinal I'd keep the *Playboy*s locked up too. Can't blame him. Wouldn't want to cause any scandal if you know what I mean."

"My research did not reveal any *Playboy*s. But I do have some witnesses that report a locksmith van was parked outside the O'Grady residence; that the driver resembled one Malachy Madden, a well-known figure in the neighborhood; and that the locksmith who came out of the O'Grady residence was a shorter, older man about the height of your colleague, the retired thief and safecracker known as the Count."

"Damn!" Malachy exclaimed. "Just my luck."

"That there were witnesses?" Breen asked.

"No, the damage to the Shamrock's reputation. Because of some look-a-like, everyone in the neighborhood will be thinking I'm working a part-time job. It will start rumors the Shamrock is failing, and that's never good for business."

"The way I hear it you subsidize the Shamrock," Breen said.

"You have been busy spending the cardinal's money," Malachy said.

"Just doing my job. So here's the proposal—you give back the original documents, give your word there are no copies, cease your campaign, and in return the cardinal does not report the break-in to the police."

"That's very upsetting," Malachy said.

"The proposal?"

"No, the news that the O'Grady house was burglarized. The neighborhood is changing and not always for the better. I won't break your confidence, but if you do go to the police I would like to post a reward for information leading to the arrest and conviction of those responsible."

"Is that your answer?"

"No," Malachy said. "This is my answer. Please tell the cardinal that if he has lost something, it is my strong recommendation that he pray to St. Anthony for its return. I've found it very effective, and I'm sure a cardinal's requests are considered a priority."

Breen laughed and said, "Well, I guess I have my answer. Thanks for your time and hospitality. I do have one favor to ask."

"Ask away!"

"I would like to meet Kevin. In my research I read the citations for the medals he won. It would be an honor to shake his hand."

"Follow me," Malachy said, getting up from the booth. "You ought to shake the Count's hand, too. No public medals but if every fighter had killed as many German officers per year of age as he did, the war would have ended years earlier."

"I didn't know that," Breen said.

"Some facts are very difficult to uncover even with diligent research," Malachy said.

Malachy entered the back room with Breen following behind him.

"This is Daniel Breen, a South Side Breen, a retired detective from the Force, and a most resourceful researcher. Not known yet if he is named after the famous Irish freedom fighter."

"It is an honor to meet you both," Breen said, shaking hands with Kevin and then the Count. "Malachy is fortunate to have such valorous colleagues. And yes, I am named after that Dan Breen. My father was an intense admirer."

"And my father greatly admired Michael Collins," Malachy said.

"A great man who made a disastrous mistake in London by agreeing to a treaty that fell way too short of a republic," Breen said

"Collins was a great man and a pragmatist," Malachy quickly responded. "The essence of the treaty was the power it ceded to the Free State. With that power, all would have been different if Collins had lived. The disastrous mistake was made by all those who chose civil war rather than to accept the vote of the people."

"There was not an all-Ireland vote and therefore it wasn't valid," Breen said.

"North Side, South Side, pro-treaty, anti-treaty—seems like the basis for an interesting afternoon," Malachy said. "Will you join us for some sambuca and coffee?"

"I don't want to interfere with what I assume is a celebratory lunch. Is it someone's birthday?"

"No, and you actually knew that, given the thorough research job you did on all of us," Malachy said. "We are celebrating the start of a two-week vacation."

"It's a bad habit of mine," Breen said with a big smile. "I'm always checking to see if my research is correct. Two weeks off. Well at least I have that to tell my employer along with the bad news that Malachy's declined his invitation.... Sorry, didn't mean to talk shop."

"Not a problem," Malachy said. "May I share our conversation with my colleagues?"

"Of course," Breen said. "But later, please. Now is just social. Sambuca and coffee and good conversation seems just the ticket to ease into late afternoon."

After an hour, Breen said his good-byes. After he left the Shamrock, Malachy briefed Kevin and the Count on the conversation.

"He's damn good," the Count said. "I'm glad it's late in the game and we're ahead. Nevertheless, I think we should check him out."

"Agreed," Malachy said. "Are you volunteering?"

"Yes!"

"That was enthusiastic," Malachy said.

"I like the man," the Count said. "But it will be fun to see if I can catch him coming out of a house he shouldn't have been in. He reminds me of you, so the odds are good I'll have the opportunity."

"Since I'm relaxed from my vacation, I'll take that as a compliment."

"What are the chances that the cardinal will go to the cops?" Kevin asked.

"Not likely at all," Malachy answered. "With the cops, it ends up public. And then you generate a lot of interest and questions, like what was in the safe and why."

They agreed Malachy and Kevin would return to their normal routines at the Shamrock, and the Count would vet Breen.

†

Three days later, Malachy was working in his office-booth on Shamrock business when Richard Riordan called.

"Malachy, what is it you want me to do at this meeting?"

"Just listen."

"And then what?"

"And then I hope you will do whatever you think is right, including nothing, if you think that is the right response."

"No one is expecting me to take their case or anything like that?" Richard asked.

"Absolutely not."

"Okay, I got it. I'll talk to you after the meeting."

"Not necessary," Malachy said. "I just appreciate your responding and changing your schedule."

The next morning Malachy was still in bed when Riordan called his cell phone. It was the second call of the morning about the meeting with the parents. Valquist woke him with a very disturbing report that Malachy responded to with a loud, angry curse.

"Malachy, this is Richard. I need to tell you, the pain and anguish in that room was excruciating. It was harrowing. And, there is something I need to know. I have just one question for you. I hope you understand why I need to ask it."

"Richard, we go way back. Ask your question."

"Everybody in the neighborhood knows that you and Augie never got along. Some of the armchair shrinks figured it was because all the mothers fawned on the smart, charming, and handsome priest-, bishop-, and cardinal-to-be—especially your mom. Is this a jealousy-based vendetta for you?"

"Richard, it's personal now, but it is not a vendetta. Everything you heard in that room wouldn't have happened if O'Grady had just called the cops instead of transferring Flynn from parish to parish. Those transfers were not just bureaucratic fuckups. They were deliberate maneuvers at damage control by O'Grady."

"How do you know that?" Richard asked.

"You know the way I work. I can't tell you how I know. But I can tell you it is a fact. Think about it. You know Augie well. Doesn't that fact fit the pattern?"

"Yes, Richard said. "Sadly, yes it does."

"Richard, there is something else you need to know about last night. One of the kids attempted suicide. The doctors think he's going to make it. According to Valquist the boy blamed himself for the abuse."

"Oh my God! There was one mother who was really worried about her son. Do you know what the boy's name is? How it happened? What hospital he's in?"

"I don't have any of the details. I'll have Valquist call you with what he knows."

"This has got to stop!" Richard almost yelled.

Malachy deliberately kept emotion from his voice and said, "Yes, Richard, it must stop. The question is, who has the clout to help make that happen?"

CHAPTER XXVIII

Malachy sat in his office-booth at the Shamrock drinking coffee and reading all of the articles Sheila culled for him from the local, national, and international press and selected websites. It was the fourteenth day of "vacation," and the pressure on O'Grady was mounting daily from all sides. Big Catholic donors across the nation had formed a committee led by Richard Riordan to restrict giving to only those institutions that had adopted formal plans to deal with allegations of sexual abuse of children and had met strict criteria concerning its prevention.

A movement by ordinary, faithful parishioners to get actively involved in the financial and personnel decisions of their parishes and to demand information and accountability had spread like a prairie wildfire despite specific orders from O'Grady that such groups could not meet on church property. Many pastors simply ignored the directive from the archdiocese. O'Grady was met with protestors at some of his public appearances including celebrating Mass at Holy Name Cathedral.

Sheila found a website that was devoted to reports and gossip about the bureaucratic and institutional side of the Church. There were all kinds of postings about the pressure the Vatican and specific Curia departments were under because of O'Grady. No one in the Vatican wanted to appear to be succumbing to public pressure by recommending O'Grady's removal to the pope, but O'Grady's support from his fellow cardinals and bishops was declining daily as every new allegation was headlined in the press.

Malachy knew his best weapon in this fight was O'Grady himself. He could count on O'Grady being supercilious, authoritarian, bureaucratic, and obsessed with his prerogatives as a cardinal. The bunker mentality would rule the day.

Malachy's cell phone rang, showing Joe Valquist's number. Malachy answered and Valquist said, "I have an invitation from a lawyer to come to a meeting tomorrow with Pace and his lawyer to review some evidence concerning Pace's abuse. Are you behind this?"

"Can't say that I am," Malachy said, carefully parsing his words. "Who's the lawyer?"

"Victor Naples," Valquist said.

"I know him well. He has a good reputation. My recommendation is that you go to the meeting."

"But this isn't your meeting?"

"No, I won't be there. But if Naples had invited me I would go."

"Okay, Malachy, I get it. I've trusted you this far. I'll go."

"Let me know what happens," Malachy said, trying to sound sincere.

†

"Sorry for the cramped quarters," Victor Naples said with a sweeping gesture toward the overcrowded conference room. "I have a two-lawyer practice, and we chose to spend our rent budget on ample offices. But the speakerphone, the AV equipment, and computer are state of the art. The computer will be operated from a remote location."

"Let's review the rules of engagement, so to speak," Naples continued. "I represent a certain client who has evidence relevant to the abuse of Mr. Pace. This is not evidence that can be used in court. My client wants you to see this evidence so that your lawsuit against the archdiocese is properly targeted. To be specific, my client asserts this compelling evidence reveals one Fr. Reginald Flynn to be the priest who abused Mr. Pace, not Fr. John Bari. I do not know what this evidence is and have no control over it. And once the presentation starts, I will be leaving the room.

"My client insists on anonymity, but will be on the speakerphone to direct the presentation of the evidence and to answer any questions you have. You will *not* be given a copy of the evidence. My client is certain that ample additional evidence exists to prove Fr. Flynn and the archdiocese are liable for your client's abuse and that this evidence can be gathered with the normal civil procedures available to litigants."

Naples paused and looked at Anthony Pace, flanked by his attorney on one side and Joe Valquist on the other.

"Are you ready to proceed?"

"Yes," Pace's attorney said. "We're ready."

Naples turned off the mute button on the speakerphone and said, "We are ready to proceed."

Malachy's disguised voice came over the speakerphone.

"What you are about to see and hear is very graphic and disturbing. Anthony, I am sorry that this is necessary because it will be painful and distressing. But it will be even more so if you go through the whole litigation process and do not prevail against the archdiocese because you name the wrong priest as the perpetrator, even if it is an error made in good faith."

"We are certain we have the right priest," Pace's lawyer said firmly.

Pace turned to Valquist with his hands shaking and said, "You've been a good friend through all of this, but I don't know if I can stand this."

Valquist put his hand on Pace's arm and said, "The voice is right Anthony. You don't want to go through it all again only to lose. At least hear the beginning."

"Okay," Pace said just loud enough for Malachy to hear. Malachy didn't hesitate.

"Fr. Flynn did everything he could to convince you than he was Fr. Bari while he was abusing you. Why? He was obsessed with Fr. Bari, going all the way back to Fr. Bari's time in the seminary. Sexually obsessed and jealous. That obsession led him to target you. And to make sure that any repercussions would harm Fr. Bari. The first picture you will see is yourself and next to it is a picture of Fr. Bari, just a couple of years older than you are in the photograph. Please note the remarkable similarity."

The two pictures flashed up on the AV screen in the semi-darkened room.

Pace's lawyer said, "That's meaningless. Lots of people look like other people."

Malachy ignored the comment and continued.

"The voice you are about to hear is Fr. Flynn explaining why he targeted you."

> I don't remember where I first saw his picture but it shocked me—the kid was a clone of Bari. I saw the picture and in that instant the urge overwhelmed me. I found out all about the family's circumstances—his father's death, his mother's devotional practices, as much as I could about the entire family. I was helping out with confession at the parish during that time. It was easy to make sure I was the priest who heard his confession.

Pace raised his voice and said, "My mother's ridiculous mini-shrines in our house were well known in the parish."

Malachy decided he'd better make sure Pace stayed engaged. "Part of the evidence is your mother's testimony in her own voice. Please be patient and let me proceed."

"My mother?" Pace asked in a subdued tone once again.

Malachy ignored this and continued, "The next part is Flynn explaining how he impersonated Bari."

> I knew that Bari was really popular with all the children. He has this Italian accent. I was always good at mimicking and imitating. It was easy to sound like Bari. I knew I had to be careful and never let the kid see me. It's easy to get kids to do what you want—to follow orders when they are confused and scared because you're an authority. And guess what? Many of them are also excited—aroused—and curious about what's happening, but they always pretend they don't want to be doing it.

"As we all know, the abuse started in the church's basement bathroom," Malachy said. "There is no dispute about that. Anthony, what you don't know is that your mother followed you to that bathroom one day…"

"What the hell are you talking about?" Pace shouted at the speakerphone.

"Your mother followed you to the basement bathroom and actually saw the priest who abused you emerge from the bathroom," Malachy said. "Here are her words."

> He had been acting so strangely. Quiet and secretive. Sometimes I heard him crying. At first, I thought it was about his father's accident. But sometimes he disobeyed me about coming right home after school. So that day, I decided to follow him after school. He never saw me.
>
> I followed him to the church and down into the bathroom. He closed the door. I hid myself so that he wouldn't see me when he came out. Then a priest knocked on the door, and the door opened and he went inside. I listened at the door. I could tell they were doing disgusting things. I ran back to my hiding place, crying. First, the priest came out and then Anthony. I stayed in my hiding place, crying and praying.

"Goddamn her, she knew!" Pace screamed at the speakerphone.

"Yes, Anthony she knew, and she also knew it wasn't Bari. Just listen. The male voice you hear is that of the questioner."

> Q: What was the name of the priest you saw come out of the bathroom?
>
> I don't know. I didn't recognize him. He was not a Pius XII priest. I don't think I ever saw him before.
>
> Q: You are absolutely sure the priest was not Fr. Bari?
>
> Yes, I'm sure. That priest wasn't tall. Fr. Bari is very tall. And Fr. Bari is very Italian looking. This priest looked sort of Irish.

Malachy quickly continued, "After some more questions and answers, your mother reiterates the priest was not Bari, but sounded like him. Here she is."

That's very strange. He sounded like Fr. Bari. It wasn't Fr. Bari, but he sounded just like him.

"Oh my God," Pace said. "My own mother didn't help me."

"No she didn't," Malachy said. "And one reason was her pastor swore her to secrecy on pain of excommunication. She never told you or anybody else until this tape was made."

"How did you get that tape?" Pace's lawyer shouted. "I demand you answer that question!"

"I can't tell you that," Malachy said. "Please let me proceed. Brace yourself. The next picture you are going to see is one of the actual abuse taking place."

The picture of an erect Flynn with a naked Pace flashed up on the screen.

"And where did you get that?" Pace's attorney asked, his tone still insistent.

"I can't tell you that either," Malachy said.

"I demand that you give us copies of all this evidence," Pace's attorney said loudly.

"Not going to happen," Malachy said. "Please let me proceed. As you can see from the picture the adult's face is blocked, but his naked body is all too visible. The adult in the picture is Flynn. Note the body type. The next picture is of Bari naked. As you can see, Bari is long and very lean. Flynn is shorter, heavier, and thicker."

The screen went blank.

"Please wait a moment," Malachy said. "And then I will resume."

Everybody waited in silence in the darkened room with the only noise being the computer. Malachy's disguised voice came back on the speakerphone.

"The copy of the evidence loaded into the computer has been permanently deleted," Malachy said. "Now I will answer any questions you have."

"All of this could be contrived," Pace's attorney said. "A big con job to set us off on a wild-goose chase. Everything we saw and heard could be rigged. We need to be able to examine the evidence and to know how it was developed."

"Actually, you don't," Malachy said. "There is only one standard for this evidence."

"What the hell do you mean?" the attorney asked angrily.

"Anthony knows who abused him," Malachy said gently. "It happened too many times, in too many ways, and for too long a time, not to know at some level if the abuser was a tall, almost skinny man or a shorter, almost fat man."

There was silence in the darkened conference room again. Pace started to respond but faltered. He began to breathe loudly and rapidly and tried again to talk but kept stammering.

"It's not fair…not fair," Pace repeated over and over, sobbing.

"This conference call is over," Pace's lawyer said, reaching for the phone.

"No, wait," Pace said. "The voice on the phone is right. I do know. It wasn't Fr. Bari. I can remember one time the man was forcing me to…I can't talk about it…but the blindfold slipped. The light in the bathroom was off, but I could see a little. He lifted up his shirt to wash himself off. It's true…he wasn't tall, and he had a gut. It couldn't have been Fr. Bari. It had to be somebody else."

"I am going to get off the phone now," Malachy said. "Remember, there are two people responsible for the criminal abuse you suffered —Fr. Flynn and Cardinal O'Grady."

Malachy turned to the close-by Count and said, "Naples certainly didn't splurge on the guest office, but like he said all the equipment is state of the art. Do we have it on tape?"

"Yes. Are you concerned Pace will recant?"

"Not really. I'm more concerned about the attorney. The tape is insurance he does the right thing."

"What next?" the Count asked.

"Next you tell me the good news that the cardinal is in residence tomorrow night," Malachy said.

"That is the official schedule according to my new friend in the chancery office."

"I wish I could watch," Malachy said.

"I'd have a stopwatch in hand," the Count said. " Our employer runs remarkably efficient operations."

"Are the pennants ready?" Malachy asked.

"They are. I'm dropping them off tonight at the warehouse in Berwyn as instructed."

"No chance of being traced?" Malachy asked.

"No chance," the Count said. "I printed them myself on my own equipment. And the equipment has already been recycled, so to speak. The blowback from this is going to be fierce. We all have to anticipate search warrants."

"Agreed," Malachy said. "I know you're ready. I assume you will be going through the Shamrock, my place, and Kevin's place tomorrow, clipboard in hand."

"Of course. And starting early with you. What's on your schedule for tonight?"

"An early dinner on Taylor Street with Sheila. I'm paying my debt for all the research."

"Also an early night?"

"Perhaps," Malachy said, smiling.

"When the time comes to make that decision, remember I won't be late tomorrow morning."

"I'll factor that in," Malachy said. "Giving it the proper weight in my complicated, mathematically based decision model."

"Of course you will," the Count said without a hint of sarcasm. "After my inspection, how do you plan to spend the day?"

"Making Bridget happy. I'm going to do Shamrock work all day and into the night and then head home."

"Don't answer any telephone calls in the early A.M.," the Count said. "We don't want any record that anything is out of the ordinary."

"I will be just like everybody else who turns on the TV as they start their morning routine. Final item. What about Breen? Do we have to worry about him?"

"No, and that's fortunate because he's so good."

"Why? And how so?" Malachy asked.

"Because he is in Florida visiting family. I know that for certain because I drove him to the airport and watched him get on the plane."

"What happened?"

"I was following him. When he headed to the third Catholic church, I was going to call you to see if there was some Irish devotional practice I didn't know about. He came out of the last church and walked right up to my car. We ended up having coffee and talking shop. He was just having fun with me by going to the churches. He picked me up as a tail almost immediately. He told me he was going to Florida for a week. He wanted me to know so I wouldn't waste my time—a professional courtesy was the way he put it. I offered to drive him and he accepted."

"Did he say anything about O'Grady?"

"No, and I didn't ask. It seemed impolite."

"So, we may still need to worry about him when he returns," Malachy said.

"Indeed. The cardinal doesn't strike me as a turn-the-other-cheek type."

"He's not," Malachy said, remembering a long-ago incident. "See you in the morning."

Malachy visited his father in his basement workroom.

"I'm going to beat the shit out of Augie," Malachy told his father.

"No doubt he deserves it, but why?"

"Tommy may not graduate from the Academy because of him."

"What happened?"

"He snitched on Tommy. He told their history teacher that Tommy cheated on the final exam and that's why he passed. Now there is some kind of a meeting with a dean and the teacher. Tommy is so nervous about it he's throwing up. He's afraid to tell his mom—she's been so excited about his graduating."

"I know," Malachy's father said. "Tommy's academic career has been a real roller coaster ride. She was telling your mom just yesterday how she had prayed and prayed he'd make it, and she was so grateful her prayers were answered. What's the deal on the cheating?"

"He had a copy of the test. He didn't steal it or anything—he got it from the teacher's daughter. She has a big crush on him. He didn't even

ask for it. She just showed up with it. He used it to study so of course he got a good grade."

"How did Augie find out?" Malachy father asked.

"Tommy opened his big mouth. I told him to shut up about it and not tell anybody, but Tommy can't keep anything a secret."

"How do you know it was Augie who told the teacher?"

"Because when Tommy was teasing him he made some crack about how at least he was going to graduate."

"I see," Malachy's dad said. "Is there bad blood between the two of them?"

"Yeah, Augie started it. He said something about Tommy's dad being in jail. And so Tommy has been riding him about going to the seminary —jokes about not bending over in the shower and stuff like that."

"I get the picture. When is this meeting supposed to take place?"

"Tomorrow at ten."

"You came down here for a reason, didn't you?" Malachy's dad asked.

"Yes."

"Okay, Malachy. I think that family has suffered enough heartbreak. What do you think?"

"I think so too."

"Go and get Tommy and bring him here. And Malachy if you see Augie on the way, be friendly."

"Got it," Malachy said. "Thanks, Dad."

"Well, Malachy, Jesuits can be tough customers. This is going to take a little planning."

"Tommy is going be so relieved."

Malachy's dad looked at Tommy and said, "Malachy tells me you have a problem keeping a secret."

Tommy stared at the floor for a few seconds and then looked up.

"I do and it got me in big trouble," Tommy said.

"Well, let's see if we can't get you out of that trouble, Tommy. But, if I'm going to help, I need to know you've learned the lesson and our meeting here is going to stay between the three of us. And, you are never, ever going to talk about that test again."

"Oh God, Mr. Madden, I swear! I'll never talk about it. Never!"

"Okay, Tommy, I'm going to the meeting tomorrow for you. I'll stop by the apartment later and explain things to your mother. But I need your solemn promise, and Malachy's, that neither of you will touch that holier-than-thou shithead Augustine O'Grady."

Both boys laughed and then promised. "And lay off the teasing," Malachy's dad said.

"Mr. Madden, we were expecting Tommy and his mother," the dean said

Martin Madden looked at the tall dean with his craggy face, untrimmed eyebrows, and long arms and thought he'd be able to bring order to the hallways with just a stare. Malachy's dad nodded at the other man present and said, "I know, Fr. Beale, but I'm here as a friend of the family. Please call me Martin. As you know Tommy's father can't be here so I came."

"Yes, we are aware of that," Fr. Beale said. "But I'm afraid we can't discuss this confidential situation except with a member of the family."

"I totally understand," Martin said. "Perhaps this will help."

Madden handed over a signed power of attorney authorizing him to represent Tommy and his mother. He then turned to the other man, extended his hand, and said, "Martin Madden, good to meet you."

The man briefly shook the proffered hand and tersely said, "Mr. Schwartz, history teacher."

"So what appears to be the problem?" Martin asked.

"We are investigating a serious allegation that Tommy cheated on his final history exam," Fr. Beale said. "Tommy's score on the final exam was far higher than any other test score he previously earned in history or any other exam, for that matter. And Mr. Schwartz has received a credible report that somehow Tommy got the exam in advance. And that is why we need to be able to talk with Tommy directly about the exam and his preparation for it."

"Unfortunately, that won't be possible," Martin said. "The lad is very sick. Frankly, I believe that this situation has contributed to the illness. You see the father is away because of a horrible miscarriage of justice that has caused tremendous suffering for the family, especially Tommy's mother. Mrs. Regan was counting on Tommy's graduation as a ray of hope in the darkness."

"That's too bad," Mr. Schwartz said. "But if Tommy cheated then he flunks the exam and that means he flunks the course and that means he doesn't graduate."

Martin stopped smiling and looked first at Fr. Beale and then Mr. Schwartz and said, "'If' is a very big, two-letter word. If another miscarriage of justice is about to be visited upon that suffering family because of a feud between two teenagers, then I will do whatever it takes to make certain that doesn't happen."

"What do you mean feud?" Fr. Beale asked.

"I mean that Augustine O'Grady, your informant, has a feud going with Tommy Regan and that feud led him to inform Mr. Schwartz of nothing more than neighborhood hearsay."

"My informant will remain anonymous, but it wasn't hearsay," Mr. Schwartz said. "He quoted Tommy himself as saying he got a copy of the exam. That's why we need to question him directly."

"You have no idea of the devastating impact this is having on the family. As I said, Tommy is too sick to be here. Here is his doctor's report indicating he needs complete bed rest and is not to be put under any stress."

Martin handed the report to Fr. Beale.

"May I ask a question of Mr. Schwartz?"

"Of course," Fr. Beale said.

"How is it possible that a copy of the exam could be available to any unauthorized person? Surely you keep it secure."

"I do and I don't know how Tommy obtained a copy. Perhaps he broke into my office or my study at home."

"I see," Martin said. "And of course the fact that a break-in was the crime that his father was falsely accused of has no influence on your surmise."

Mr. Schwartz started to respond, but Martin cut him off.

"Fr. Beale, I make my living as a union organizer. As you can imagine, I get involved in a lot of intense confrontations. Many times after it is all over, the business owners tell me they were totally surprised at two things—first, the high price they had to pay in terms of time, legal fees, employee ill will, and bad customer PR. And second, the tactics I used to prevail.

"I tell them they turned a blind eye to the basic situation—the law and the facts were on my side, and all they had was the power to be arbitrary. And they tell me they were still surprised how far I took things both in court and on the streets. I tell them I have an Irish thing about arbitrary power, but I've actually calmed down a bit—I no longer blow things up.

"In the current situation, we have only one fact—Tommy passed the exam and is entitled to graduate based on the Academy's requirements for graduation. Everything else is speculation and hypothesis..."

"That is exactly why we need to question Tommy," Mr. Schwartz said.

Martin turned and gave Schwartz a hard stare and said, "And you can do exactly that when his doctor says he is well enough to undergo the ordeal..."

"I don't believe he is even sick," Mr. Schwartz said.

Martin turned back to Fr. Beale and said, "I will restrain myself because I'm here to solve a problem, not cause one. I think we all do better if we stick to facts and not conjecture. But just for the record, any man who calls me a liar better have a good dentist."

"I understand everything you have told us Mr. Madden," Fr. Beale said. "And let me assure you that our decision will not be an arbitrary exercise of power. I think it best to bring this meeting to a close. Thank you for your participation. I will call when we have made a decision."

The next day Martin received a call from Fr. Beale's secretary.

"Fr. Beale wanted me to tell you that Tommy Regan will be allowed to graduate, and he hopes that Tommy will be well enough to participate in the ceremony."

Malachy and his parents were guests of Tommy and his mother. At the reception following the graduation ceremony, Fr. Beale approached the group.

"Tommy, I see you have made a full recovery," Fr. Beale said.

"I have, Father. I was lucky."

"Very lucky indeed," Fr. Beale said, looking at Martin. "Lucky to have such committed family friends."

The group talked amiably for a few minutes, and then other families and their graduates joined in. Fr. Beale and Martin ended up talking to each other away from the main group.

"My wife is big on the Christian Brothers," Martin said. "It's kind of *a family tradition. But I have to tell you my money is on the Jesuits—I like your keen sense of justice."*

"If you are referring to the situation with Tommy, the decision was determined by prudence, not justice," Fr. Beale responded. "Administrators must be most concerned with making prudential decisions."

"And how is Mr. Schwartz doing? I haven't seen him today."

"Unfortunately, he is feeling very aggrieved," Fr. Beale said. "It seems he just discovered yesterday that his youngest daughter is sweet on Tommy."

"That's an interesting development," Martin said.

"Yes, it is," Fr. Beale said. "But somehow, Martin, I think you knew that fact."

"Having seen Mrs. Regan's glowing face today, do you regret your decision?" Martin asked.

"No I don't, but I do worry that Tommy will take the wrong lesson away from the matter," Fr. Beale said.

"I see," Martin said. "Well, there's the one I'd be concerned about," Martin said, gesturing toward Augie O'Grady who was across the room. "He knows the Regan family situation well, and he knew how much Tommy's graduation meant to his mother. It takes a stone-cold heart to be the informer that kills that dream."

"Yes, it is a bad combination."

"Combination?"

"A hard heart and cleverness," Fr. Beale said. "If Augustine knew that Tommy got a copy of the exam, he also knew that it came from Mr. Schwartz's daughter. He withheld that information so there would be no extenuating circumstances that would lessen Tommy's punishment."

"Well his little scheme got thwarted," Martin said. "Thanks to prudential Jesuit decision-making."

"With an assist from a fierce Irish union organizer with access to a cooperative union doctor," Fr. Beale said, smiling at Martin.

CHAPTER XXIX

At 3:45 a.m. an officer-down call came over the police radio with an address near the projects a mile southwest of the cardinal's mansion. At the same time all the electricity in the mansion went off, the telephone trunk line was cut, and the cell tower that served the area malfunctioned. At 3:48, all the streetlights near the mansion went out. At 3:50 two convoys of three large garbage trucks converged on the mansion. The headlights were turned off as each truck approached. A large watering truck rigged with a pressure pump and hose joined the six trucks. As soon as the convoys reached the mansion, large construction trucks maneuvered to block the streets with access to the cardinal's residence.

The lead garbage truck crashed through the gate that blocked the driveway, pulled forward ten yards, and stopped. The watering truck pulled around the garbage truck and positioned itself a few feet from the mansion's large brick portico. The lead garbage truck pulled forward and stopped. Two men emerged from the truck's cab dressed in modified hazmat jumpsuits and masks. One man gave a hand signal, and the truck dumped out large cement blocks and long poles on the ground.

The two men quickly pulled the blocks into a circle, attached pennants to the poles, and secured the poles in holes cut in the center of the thick blocks. One of the men gave a hand signal and the first truck pulled away, and the next truck took its place. It positioned itself to dump its full capacity of stinking garbage in the circle made by the cement blocks, unloaded, and pulled away. The men repeated the procedure with the other trucks making sure that the growing pile of garbage was evenly distributed around and within the circle with the help of two more men, dressed the same way, using large shovels and rakes.

As each truck finished dumping, it was steered off the driveway and onto the grounds. The driver and helper then exited the truck, slashed its tires, put their outerwear and masks in a burn bag, stowed the bag in the trunk of a waiting car, and climbed into the car. As soon as the waiting car had four passengers, it drove away and was replaced by another car. Fifteen minutes into the operation a barefoot man dressed in slacks and a T-shirt with a flashlight in hand appeared at the mansion's door yelling, "Stop! Stop! What are you doing? Stop!" Immediately he was hit with a powerful jet of water and retreated inside and closed the door.

A few minutes later, two more half-dressed men with flashlights appeared at the side of the mansion, and they were doused with water and went back inside. The last truck dumped its load, and the water truck sprayed the large mound of garbage and took its place with the other trucks. The two men from the water truck entered a waiting car, and it sped away. The trucks and the men were on the mansion property for less than thirty minutes. No one called 911 until someone from the mansion stopped a passing car and was driven to an area with cellphone service.

There was no interference in the operation except for two late-night revelers from the bars on North Avenue who stumbled onto the operation and tried to take some pictures with their cell phones. Two uniformed police officers quickly appeared by their side, placed them under arrest, cuffed them together, confiscated the phones, and ordered them to sit on the sidewalk, facing away from the trucks and cars. The two officers left in the last car.

†

Malachy checked his alarm clock—6:52 A.M. He got up, used the bathroom, brushed his teeth, returned to bed, poured a cup of coffee from his thermos, and settled in for a long session of channel surfing. He was hoping for at least some national cable coverage of the incident at the cardinal's residence and for lead coverage in the local news channels. The first station was already a minute into the coverage when he turned the TV on with the remote.

"…We cannot show you a close-up of the pennants because of the nature of the images on them. They are very explicit depictions of young boys being sexually abused by a male adult. The boy's faces are obscured, but the male adult is the same person on all the pennants. The images appear to be photographs that were transferred onto the pennants…"

Malachy clicked to another local station. It was showing a helicopter shot of a truck and the garbage.

"…The last garbage truck is being towed away. It takes a massive tow truck to move one of those, and we were told there was a major delay in removing them because the tires on all the trucks were slashed and had to be replaced. The plan is now to remove the garbage. As far as we know the garbage is ordinary refuse, but tests are going to be conducted before the start of the removal process to ensure that there is nothing toxic or dangerous to the workers involved. No group has claimed responsibility for the attack, and the archdiocese has yet to issue a statement. A big crowd has gathered to watch the cleanup despite the smell of the garbage."

Malachy moved to a national cable network.

"…Cardinal O'Grady has been under increasing pressure from a widening sexual abuse scandal. Many Catholics, and even some priests and pastors, in the Chicago Archdiocese are in open rebellion and defying his authority. While there are no official figures, it is an open secret that Sunday donations have fallen throughout the archdiocese. And there is a nationwide movement led by prominent wealthy Catholic donors to deny financial support to any institution that does not adhere to the standards…"

Malachy tuned his bedside radio to a twenty-four-hour news station and adjusted the volume. He continued to scan to the local TV stations and listen to the radio. He calculated that if there was no news from the police of an arrest by 8 A.M. all of his employer's men were safely hundreds of miles away. The eight o'clock news cycle contained nothing new. Malachy put the TV on mute and turned off the radio. He checked his cell phone. Joe Valquist had called at 6:30. He decided it was late enough to call him back.

"Malachy, have you seen the news? Somebody attacked the cardinal's residence with garbage—a lot of it!"

"Yeah, I heard it on the radio a few minutes ago when I woke up. Somebody must have been really pissed off. From what I heard, there were a lot of trucks involved—that couldn't have been easy to arrange."

"And so far nobody has claimed responsibility," Valquist said. "I'm a little worried that the authorities will think Fight Abuse had something to do with it."

"Why? You guys are always very careful to keep your demonstrations law abiding. Have you ever been arrested for trespassing?"

"Never! We always wanted out protests to be completely within the law."

"So, you have nothing to worry about," Malachy said.

"Malachy, I need to ask you something. Did you arrange it? You told me you were O'Grady's enemy."

"Did I? Well, he is certainly no friend. To answer your question, I was home in bed asleep when the dirty deed was done. But I have to tell you the cardinal deserved it. His failure to protect those children stinks to high heaven. And I guess somebody else thinks so too."

"You had nothing to do with it?"

"Nothing," Malachy said with as much sincerity as he could muster.

"I was going to call you anyway this morning," Valquist said.

"Why?"

"To tell you that you were right about Richard Riordan. He is holding a press conference tomorrow to announce a major class-action lawsuit against the archdiocese and the cardinal. He got very involved with the family of the boy who attempted suicide. The more involved he got, the angrier he got. Maybe he had something to do with the garbage."

"Absolutely not," Malachy said. "It's not his style. He makes it happen in the courtroom and without any of the bullshit stunts that those with less talent have to use to win their cases. Not that it will come to trial."

"What do you mean?"

"With Richard on the case, there are only two alternatives for the archdiocese—settlement or bankruptcy."

"O'Grady will never settle," Valquist said.

"It won't be his decision," Malachy said.

"I don't understand. Whose decision will it be?"

"His successor's. Rome expects its cardinal archbishops to keep a tidy house. And O'Grady's mess keeps getting bigger and bigger."

"The sooner the better," Valquist said.

Malachy remembered something his dad had taught him about poker—the amateur has a tendency to relent just before his opponents are busted out of the game, the professional never lets up.

"Well, Joe, maybe you can help speed things up a little. Large, loud protests whenever the cardinal appears in any public venue will send the message to Rome that O'Grady can never clean up his own mess."

"Fight Abuse can arrange that."

"The bigger and the louder the better," Malachy said. "Rome has a hearing problem."

CHAPTER XXX

Malachy was listening to Richard Riordan's press conference in the Shamrock's back room when Bridget entered and said loudly, "Two of Chicago's finest are here to see you. Plain clothes. What do you want me to tell them?"

"Tell them I'm innocent."

"Okay, but are you sure you want me to lie to them."

"Have you watched any of this Bridget? Richard is doing an outstanding job."

"And to think the two of you were in the same classroom together all those years. What happened? Were you asleep the whole time?"

"My skill set is just different than Richard's."

"No shit, Sherlock. Should I tell that to the two detectives who are patiently waiting to see you?"

"No, I'll tell them myself," Malachy said, slowly getting up from the table. "Here, take my Jameson and save it, and have Eduardo bring some extra strong coffee to my booth."

"For sure," Bridget said. "We wouldn't want the detectives to get the wrong idea that you drink in the afternoon."

"It's early evening," Malachy said.

"Right," Bridget said. "Somewhere."

Malachy looked at the two detectives across from him in the booth. They both were young and looked alike—broad faces, high cheekbones, and large foreheads topped with light-colored hair. He glanced at the cards they gave him—he didn't recognize the names and knew he couldn't pronounce them. He marked the cards with an A and a B and put them in his shirt pocket.

"We understand you know some of the old-timers on the force," Detective A said.

"I do," Malachy said. "And even a few young-timers. But, I don't think we have ever met before."

"We haven't," Detective A said decisively.

"I have a question before you start with yours," Malachy said.

"Sure, ask away," Detective B said.

"Are you two related?"

Detective A smiled and said, "We get that question a lot. Not that we know of—but our families go back to a small town in Poland that was always being overrun by armies on their way to somewhere else. So you never know."

"I know what you mean—coastal towns on islands have the same problem. Anyway, how can I help you?"

"We are investigating the incident at the cardinal's residence," Detective A said.

Malachy sipped his coffee and didn't say anything.

"The cardinal told us you had a confrontation with him in the Pump Room and made some threats."

Malachy continued to sip his coffee silently.

"You aren't saying much," Detective B said.

"I'm happy to cooperate and don't want to waste your time," Malachy said pleasantly. "But you haven't asked me a question yet."

"What kind of threats did you make?" Detective A asked.

"I prefer the term 'warning,'" Malachy said. "I told him that a shitstorm was headed his way because of Flynn, and he didn't have much time to do the right thing. It turns out I was right."

"Why did you confront the cardinal?"

"Neighborhood protocol."

"What does that mean?" Detective B asked.

"That means the cardinal and I were raised in a neighborhood with certain unwritten rules. One of those rules requires a warning to a neighbor when big trouble is headed his or her way. It's a neighborhood cohesion thing."

"What was the right thing for the cardinal to do?" Detective A asked.

"In general, to acknowledge it was wrong to move Flynn from parish to parish because he was a known sexual predator and to take the necessary actions to deal with the consequences of Flynn's abuse. In particular, to take the procedural steps to restore Fr. Bari to his role at the Shrine because Flynn, not Fr. Bari, abused Pace."

"This big trouble—the shitstorm—were you going to cause it if the cardinal didn't heed your warning?" Detective A asked.

"No," Malachy said. "It was more in the vein of a weather forecast. The meteorologist doesn't cause the storm. He just sees the conditions developing that lead to it."

"Do you have it in for the cardinal? A vendetta?"

Malachy looked at Detective B and answered, "We haven't seen eye-to-eye on much for many years, if ever. But, we haven't had much to do with each other ever since he left the neighborhood, either. So, no, I wouldn't call it a vendetta."

"Did you show the cardinal a picture during your confrontation?" Detective A asked.

"I did."

Detective A waited for Malachy to tell more about the picture. Malachy slowly sipped his coffee and remained silent. Detective B broke the silence with a low-key request.

"Tell us about that picture."

"Sure," Malachy said. "It was actually two pictures—a before and an after. A picture of Pace before he was abused by Fr. Flynn and one from his press conference announcing his lawsuit. I got them out of the newspaper. I told the cardinal the difference between the two pictures was the result of transferring sexual predators from parish to parish instead of calling the police."

"During your confrontation with the cardinal, did you show him an explicit picture of a child in the act of being abused by a naked, aroused adult male?" Detective A asked in a less-friendly voice.

"No."

"You never showed the cardinal a picture similar to the ones on the circle of pennants that were stuck in the garbage outside his residence?"

"No."

"The cardinal claims you showed him only one picture—and it was like the ones on the pennants," Detective B said.

Malachy remained silent, sipping his coffee.

"Are you telling us the cardinal is deliberately lying—in effect, setting you up?" Detective A asked, trying to keep the skepticism from his tone.

Malachy reached into his wallet and took out the two pictures, unfolded them, and placed them on the table facing the detectives.

"That's what I showed the cardinal. I'm not a detective but from what I've read about the clerical sexual-abuse scandal, I'd rather believe an Irish saloonkeeper than a cardinal when it involves the abuse of children. When it comes to drinking habits, I'd go with the cardinal."

Detective B gave a slight smile in response to Malachy's answer. The detectives continued to question Malachy for another thirty minutes. Toward the end of the time, Detective A thanked Malachy for his cooperation and asked one last question.

"You've been around the block in all kinds of investigations. Do you think we will find whoever trashed the cardinal's property?"

Malachy drained his coffee cup, looked directly at each detective in turn for a few seconds, and then answered the question.

"No, I don't. Of course, I only know what I read in the papers and no doubt you have already developed many sources of reliable information. But the papers say the two policemen that arrested those two barflies have never been found, that the phone service in the residence and in the area was cut off, and that even cell phone service was somehow unavailable. That suggests to me that the operation was professionally planned and executed and not just some stunt a pissed-off amateur pulled off."

"We're professionals, too," Detective A said.

"Yes, you are," Malachy said emphatically. "But every investigation needs a point of leverage. The cardinal pointed you in my direction. Unfortunately for you his motive is tainted. No leverage here."

"Let's see what happens," Detective B said.

"For sure," Malachy said. "There is one other thing I would like noted for the record."

"What's that?"

"I couldn't have been involved—I don't have a license to drive a truck."

"We'll be sure to include that in our report," Detective A said.

Malachy moved from the booth where he was interviewed to his office-booth, reviewing in his mind the answers he gave to note any mistakes that could cause trouble. Bridget came over with his drink in her hand.

"How did it go?" Bridget asked, as she put the drink down in front of Malachy. "Did you convince them that you're innocent?"

"No, but it went okay."

"Good," Bridget said. "I'd be worried about public safety if you were able to persuade them you're innocent. What happens now?"

"They'll be back, maybe with a search warrant or a grand jury summons or both. The cardinal convinced them I'm involved in the attack on his residence. They don't have much else to go on so they'll keep drilling that dry hole, hoping for a lucky break."

"When will it be over?" Bridget asked.

"In a few months, after the cardinal has moved on and there are other, bigger fish to fry."

"Move on? Where is he going?"

"My bet is on Rome."

"You've been around the Shamrock a lot lately. Is this a trend?"

"Actually, I'm thinking about going on a real vacation."

"Good. Stay out of my way until you do. I finally have the place running right and don't need you screwing it up. And keep me posted on how things are going. I hate when you expect me to provide an alibi for you without any notice. Got it?"

"Understood." Malachy looked down at the drink and asked, "Could you add a little freshener? Like you said, somewhere it is evening."

Malachy was in the back room watching the coverage of Richard's news conference. Eduardo came to the doorway and announced, "A man wants to see you."

"Who?"

"Mr. Matt Morse."

"Bring him back here, Eduardo. And find out what he wants to drink. Where's Bridget?"

"In the kitchen," Eduardo answered.

"Good. Don't tell her the man's name, okay?"

"Okay, but if she asks, I tell her."

"If you have to, Eduardo. I just don't want her to go on strike. It just makes your job harder."

"Why strike, Mr. Malachy?"

"Protest against the FBI, Eduardo."

"Sí, now I remember. They don't do their job and the president gets shot. And other bad things happen. The big boss, he wears women's clothes."

"So some say. Please put up the private sign after you get Mr. Morse. And bring me some coffee."

"Okay, Mr. Malachy. I take the Jameson?"

"No."

"What are you watching, Malachy?"

"The news coverage on my friend's press conference. He is suing the archdiocese big time."

"Let me guess, he's from the neighborhood, too," Matt said.

"Good guess. We all grew up within a block of each other. Funny, how things turn out."

"Not funny for the cardinal. He can't catch a break. He's like Linus—wherever he goes, the black cloud is overhead."

"When Richard is after you the storm just keeps intensifying. He has a small army of wicked-smart young associates. Most of the time, they are handling lots of cases, but now all that firepower is trained on the cardinal and the archdiocese. And he is just getting warmed up."

"Kind of makes you feel for the cardinal," Matt said.

Malachy held back his "not really."

"Speaking of firepower, Matt, is this visit social?"

"No. We are trying to find Dino."

"Why? Is he lost?"

"No. He has disappeared. We can't locate him anywhere. Do you know where he is?"

"No."

"Have you heard from him?"

"No."

"When was the last time you talked to him?"

"Not sure," Malachy said. "But I know it's been a while. I could check the phone records, but so could you."

"The last time you talked with him—what was it about?"

"Don't remember that well. But I'm sure it concerned my work with the committee and Fr. Bari. Can I ask a question?"

"Sure."

"When you say 'disappeared'—what are we talking about? The man is totally connected to Chicago, personal and business."

"Off the record, I mean he's gone—lock, stock, and barrel. The wife with him, we assume. And not a word to his young and very classy girlfriend. His wardrobe, his extensive art collection, his antique rugs—everything valuable that he owns. One day he is here doing his normal thing, the next day he and everything he owns has disappeared."

"What about the rest of the family?" Malachy asked.

"Still off the record, the kids got a phone call. Everything is fine, but he and Mrs. will be out of touch for a while. Not to worry."

"Jesus Christ," Malachy said. "I finally get a well-paid consultant job, and the fucking paymaster runs off."

"You think you've got problems—downtown is ballistic."

"Obviously you didn't have him under surveillance. But still to disappear with everything he owns on short notice takes a lot of help. There has to be some trace of the move—a mover, a truck driver, a transportation record, something."

"Nothing," Matt said. "Absolutely nothing. I've never seen anything like it."

Can I ask one more question?"

"You can ask."

"Why do you want to find him?"

"Can't say, even off the record, Malachy. What I need to know is if you know anything about it. Anything? I need help."

"No," Malachy said. "I don't know a thing about it. But I do know where you should look for him."

"Where?"

"Stake out Savile Row—he is bound to show up there sometime."

"I don't think I'll pass that suggestion on," Matt said.

"Okay, but I know I'm right."

"Malachy, there is going to be a grand jury probe on this and other stuff. You are going get subpoenaed."

"Anytime soon?"

"Don't know, why?"

"I'm thinking of going on vacation for a couple of weeks starting next Monday. Tell you what, I'll call you and let you know my itinerary and my attorney's name and phone number. I wouldn't want anybody jumping to the wrong conclusion."

"Where are you going?"

"Some place I can play golf and poker," Malachy said.

"Las Vegas?"

"No, I'm thinking of Ireland."

"Poker?"

"Absolutely. The Celtic Tiger and all that."

"Going by yourself?" Matt asked.

"No, with Kevin. And you have my solemn word that if either of us sees Dino while we're there, we will call you immediately."

"I'm sure downtown will find that very reassuring," Matt said.

"Like I told you, Matt, I like to cooperate when I can."

"I think a more accurate phrasing would be 'when I choose to.'"

"Matt, you look tired so I'm not going to argue a semantic point with you. Would you like something stronger than coffee? It's the end of a long week. A White Sox game is going to start in a few minutes. And Red, the new kid in the kitchen, prepared a special of sausage and peppers. Will you join me?"

Matt looked at his watch and then around the empty room.

"What about customers? Won't some of them want to watch the game?"

"If you join me, the private sign stays up. We'll let Bridget handle any customer complaints."

Matt laughed and said, "Accepted."

"Canadian Club with lots of ice?"

"How did you remember that?" Matt asked

"For some reason, it is easy for me to remember what somebody drinks."

"What's difficult to remember?"

Malachy smiled at Matt and said, "Whatever I choose."

CHAPTER XXXI

Malachy walked through the Shamrock front door wondering what kind of reception he would get after two weeks away. Bridget spotted him and gave an ear-splitting whistle and yelled, "His Lordship has returned. Once again our prayers were for naught."

"It's good to be home," Malachy said, walking over to his office-booth. "Could I get some coffee and something to eat?"

Bridget opened the kitchen door, shouted out the order, and joined him in the booth.

"How did things go while I was on vacation?"

"Great," Bridget said.

"No problems?"

"No Shamrock operational problems," Bridget answered. "And business was decent to good the whole time. I think the word got out you were gone. But you have a backlog in terms of your other business. What the hell did you do? Lose your cell phone."

"I kept it off except to listen to messages and check in with the girls and grandkids. I wanted a real vacation."

"Why? It's not like you were working too hard before you left."

"I needed to think about a few things."

"Well, call Victor Naples. There are now at least two grand juries that would like to hear from you. And Dan Breen wants to see you ASAP."

"I'll call them both right after I eat. Really, no problems?"

"Really. Nothing serious. One small incident involving Red."

"How small?"

"You be the judge. Red stayed with me during the vacation. Somehow he met a guy who's at least ten years older, and the guy started putting on a full-court press. I told him to get lost, but he kept hanging around the Shamrock. So one afternoon when there were only a few regulars around, I took the baseball bat and went over to his table and smashed his drink. Never saw him after that."

"Very small," Malachy said.

"I kept these for you," Bridget said, handing over a stack of newspapers. "Did it play big in Ireland?"

"It did. Very big. They have the same problem over there."

Malachy looked at the headlines: "Cardinal Out" and "Cardinal Resigns." He was up-to-date on every detail of the story. He even knew O'Grady's successor from the website that covered Church politics. O'Grady was scheduled to take up his new job as head of a Pontifical Commission on Canon Law within a week.

"Thanks, Bridget, good reading for lunch."

Malachy made his first call. The phone was answered with "this is Victor Naples."

"Hey Vic, its Malachy."

"You're a popular guy, Malachy. There are now two grand juries desiring your presence."

"I'm ready to appear whenever they want."

"I assume you'll be taking the Fifth, and we'll be using that drawer full of motions."

"No," Malachy said. "I've changed my mind. I will be answering all their questions as best I can. Make sure they know that."

"I don't understand that decision," Naples said. "At least hold out for qualified immunity."

"Change in strategy, Vic. The quickest way to drain the energy out of the inquiry is to confront all their questions head on. Of course, I don't know much, so I'm not going to be of much help."

"You know they're going to look for inconsistencies, Malachy."

"They are not going to find any, Vic, because there aren't any."

"Okay, Malachy, I get it. I'm not going to waste my breath. Just for the record, I'm opposed to your testifying without immunity."

"The record is duly noted," Malachy said. "But I still want you available outside the jury room, just in case there's a curveball I didn't anticipate."

"I'll be there," Naples said. "I'll call you back with the schedule."

"Try and make the appearances in the afternoon, will you?"

"Sure thing, Malachy. It does help to be fully awake when testifying under oath."

Malachy made his second call. The phone was answered with "Dan Breen speaking."

"Hello, Dan. It's Malachy. I understand you want to see me on an urgent basis."

"I do. I know the first day back from a vacation is always hectic, but could I come by this afternoon? Say about 3:00?"

"That works well, Dan. I'm headed up to see my girls and the grandkids at 5:30. Of course, if you're stopping by to tell me you've turned pro-treaty…"

"Not on your life," Dan said. "It's business about my employer."

"Does he need help packing?"

"Not exactly," Dan answered. "See you at three."

Malachy was concerned about the meeting with Dan. It was a wild card that hadn't been covered in the sessions in Ireland. Three days of intense reviewing made sure of time lines and who participated in which activities. Everything was planned, including who remembered what. Dino's disappearance made things much easier. He could carry a lot of freight and wouldn't be available to complain about the load.

Malachy decided as much as he liked Dan and trusted him, it would be necessary to make sure he wasn't wired and that there could be no way the conversation could be picked up.

The Count wasn't home from Poland yet, so no help there. Malachy thought about how to make it not demeaning and decided on an equal opportunity sweat. The sauna would be empty in mid-afternoon. Eduardo could drive them, and Kevin could make sure there wasn't any company. No call, no company. And there is no way anybody could anticipate the location of the health club inside a motel in Skokie.

Dan Breen strode over to Malachy's office-booth with his arm and hand extended, ready to shake. "Welcome home, Malachy," Dan said. "How was Ireland?"

Malachy stood and shook Breen's hand and responded, "Hey, Dan, good to see you. Ireland was brilliant—one good thing after another—music, strong drink, great golf, overserved opposing poker players, even a little sunshine now and again. One small problem I'm hoping you can help me remedy this afternoon."

"What's that?" Dan asked. "Glad to help if I can."

"Stale Jameson trapped inside. Need a little sweat to get my system right. I thought we might discuss business at the same time."

Dan gave a wry, calm smile and asked, "Wet or dry heat?"

"Dry."

"Count me in. Where?"

"A little place I know farther north. Eduardo will drive us."

Dan smiled again and said, "I'm guessing things are getting a little hot outside the sauna, too."

"Good guess."

Malachy turned up the heat in the sauna and joined Dan on the upper bench. Nobody followed them to the motel, and Dan shed his clothing in the too-small locker room and put them in their shared locker without hesitation. And he let Malachy get the towels.

"So, what's happening with Cardinal Augustine O'Grady?"

"He's getting paranoid about you, and I caused it," Dan said.

"Tell me more."

"He thinks you want to put him in jail."

"I didn't know the Vatican still operated jails," Malachy said.

"American jail, like Flynn," Dan said.

"How did he get that idea?"

"Well, it started because of the attack on his residence. He is convinced that you're behind it, and he wanted me to prove it. His theory was you recruited a bunch of thugs from the old neighborhood who owed you favors. The path to your front door would be 'brightly lit' in his phrase. When I told him he was wrong, at first he couldn't quite get his mind around it."

"How wrong?"

"When I finished my investigation, I reported to him that it was a highly professional operation, flawless in its planning and execution. And it took a lot of resources—money and men. At least twenty men, all highly trained. And there is no trace of them, nothing. And I stressed to him how important that was."

"The dog that didn't bark."

"Yes," Dan said. "It takes a lot of money to bring twenty men into Chicago from somewhere, execute a complicated plan with lots of variables, and then remove the men without leaving behind a shred of evidence. A lot of money, but other resources, too."

"Like what?" Malachy asked.

"Deep local knowledge. You can't just go out and rent six garbage trucks filled to the top."

"Don't know that for sure because I've never tried, but I do see your point," Malachy said. "Did the cardinal eventually see it your way?"

"Too well," Dan said. "My mistake was in telling him about Flynn."

"What about Flynn?"

"As part of my investigation, I poked around a little in Wisconsin. There are a lot of retired Chicago cops up there, and it was easy to get connected to local law enforcement. I heard the wild tales Flynn was telling about how you kidnapped him and set him up. Did you know he's going to plead?"

"Really. No, I only know what I read in the papers and that's always a day late."

"He is. But the curious thing is his lawyer had a hell of time working it out. Flynn absolutely refused to plead to the local burglary or break-in charges or any of the federal charges that resulted from the search of his place. In his words, 'I will only plead to something I did.' So they've worked out a deal with the Feds based on sexual abuse and crossing state lines. Flynn provided all the information. All the other charges are going to be dropped."

"Does the deal involve Pace?"

"No."

"So what's O'Grady's concern?"

"I told him I believed the basics about Flynn's wild tales about you," Dan said. "Everything in the church break-in was just too pat. He was soaked in Scotch the night he was arrested. The clincher was Flynn isn't known as a heavy drinker at all. At most, he has a couple of beers."

"The cardinal's paranoid about someone changing his drink?"

Dan laughed and said, "No, he thinks that somehow you have access to some secret organization with lots of resources, and that he's next on your list to try to put in jail."

"The Freemasons have been very helpful," Malachy said.

Dan smiled and said, "I told him I didn't think you were trying to put him in jail, but I would find out for sure. That's why I'm here."

"Amazing, isn't it?"

"What is?" Dan asked.

"The man lived in the old neighborhood his whole life until he left for the seminary, and he never did learn the rules. I suppose he just doesn't get unwritten rules."

"How would you formulate the rule that covers this situation?"

"Fair is fair. And more is unfair."

"Could you be a little more explicit?" Dan asked.

"Flynn is in jail and can no longer abuse children, and O'Grady is on his way to Rome and can no longer facilitate abuse and has no real power to prevent Bari from resuming his role at the Shrine. A fair result I'd say."

"So I can tell the cardinal that you have no plans to try and put him in jail," Dan said.

Malachy looked at Dan and said, "It's all over on my part. No further plans."

"Would it be possible to return the originals of the reports in Latin?" Dan asked. "The cardinal is particularly worried about them."

"Would that help you?"

"Yes," Dan said.

"Okay, then they will be returned to you. Let's consider them an honorary membership certificate in the old neighborhood."

"Accepted with thanks," Dan said. "And I do understand the membership rules. But I'm not changing my opinion about the treaty."

Malachy laughed and said, "Me either. By the way, how much time will Flynn get?"

"No more than ten to fifteen years. If he makes it that far."

"To the sentencing?"

"No, to the end of his term. He won't be doing white-collar time. Child abusers have no protectors on the inside. Too many victims. But you know that from when you were still practicing."

Malachy locked eyes with Dan and said, "Yes, I know that. Too bad Flynn put himself in that situation. Did the cops in Wisconsin tell you about the bicycles?"

"Nobody mentioned any bikes."

"They were in Flynn's storage shed. Children's bikes, wrapped in plastic, all bright and shiny. In all sizes, some even had training wheels."

"I hope the bastard rots in jail," Dan said.

†

"How's your morning going?" Kevin asked as Malachy entered the Shamrock.

"Two problems—my internal clock has not yet adjusted so I woke up way too early. And I'm having trouble adjusting to the pace of life here versus the remote west of Ireland."

Kevin gave Malachy a knowing looking and asked, "What happened?"

"I'm having a quiet cup coffee in that fancy coffee shop down by the university, thinking things over in preparation for our meeting when suddenly this impatient blowhard starts shouting at the kid behind the counter. She didn't make his drink fast enough. He was in a hurry and 'doesn't have time for goddamn incompetence.'"

"Who was the barista?" Kevin asked.

"That very slender, shy Asian girl who looks like she's a walking violation of the child labor laws. I ignored it as long as I could but the guy wouldn't shut up. He is yelling and pointing and eventually she bursts into tears."

"What did you do?"

"I got up and left."

"And?" Kevin asked.

"And positioned myself outside in front of the door. So Mr. Impatience finished his rant and attempted to push open the door in a hurry. The problem was my foot was stuck in front of the door, and the door he is expecting to swing open stayed shut. He smacked into the door, spilling the hot coffee drink with three names all over himself.

"Now he was really going berserk. I kept my foot in the door and won't let him through. He tried to force his way, but I never budged. He was screaming curses at top volume, but I pretended not to hear him and put my hand up to my ear. I think that put him over the top. He backed up and hurled himself at the door. Of course, I pulled it open and stepped out of the way."

"Very polite," Kevin said.

"I thought so. The guy stumbled as he came through the doorway and fell face first onto the sidewalk. So I went back inside and held the doors shut. Now he was practically foaming at the mouth."

"How long did the dance last?" Kevin asked.

"Until the cops came. Mr. Impatience still hadn't calmed down. He didn't seem to understand that it's a bad idea to yell and curse at cops. They arrested him."

"Do we know the cops?" Kevin asked.

"Turns out they eat lunch at the Shamrock sometimes. Told me they like the change in the menu with the new Italian specialties."

Kevin looked serious and said, "I'd like a detailed description of Mr. Impatience. Some guys are slow learners."

Malachy gave a detailed description.

"Did you see Matt Morse?" Kevin asked

Malachy looked around and answered, "No, where?"

"In a car parked down the block. He called on the bar phone and asked if you would meet him in his car as soon as you showed up. I told him your morning schedule was not predictable. He said he'd wait."

"Interesting and strange."

"What are you going to do?"

"Meet him in his car. The Count will be here in a few minutes. Explain the situation. Tell him to call me on my cell if Matt has any company nearby."

Malachy approached the car with coffees in hand. Matt reached over and pushed the door open. Malachy handed him a coffee and climbed in.

"Bridget won't actually attack you know. She only goes on strike."

Matt gave a smile and said, "This visit is off the record. Personal matter I was hoping you could help with."

"I'll try. What's the situation?"

"My son-in-law Jerry was arrested last night. My daughter Mary is really upset. She's very worried about his job. The firm he works for is small and kind of straitlaced. An investment firm with very-high-end clients."

"For what and where?"

"Drunk and disorderly and destruction of public property. In Wisconsin, a small town near Lake Geneva. An outing with some of his old college buddies that got out of hand."

"Not too serious."

"There's more. He was booked under the name of one of his friends. Somehow, they switched wallets. You know the deal—it seemed a good idea at the time as a way of protecting Jerry's job. Routine minor offenses so nobody was paying that much attention. And I guess they look a lot alike."

"That's more serious."

"I know. And if I get involved, it could blow up and makes things much worse for everybody, including me."

"Where are Mary and her husband now?"

"At home, fretting and waiting for my call."

"Matt, you need to stop your involvement right now. My suggestion is to have my former partner Victor Naples handle the situation. And, I have a special investigator in mind that has good contacts in Wisconsin. We need to know a lot more about how they deal with things up there."

"Who?"

Malachy looked at Matt and said, "You're not involved. Your only job is to call Mary and get her and her husband to go directly to Victor Naples's office. Immediately and without talking to any other family or friends. Make sure they understand—not to anybody else, no matter what the relationship. You make that call, and I'll step outside and call Vic and set things up. And tell them to bring their checkbook. It's a normal attorney–client relationship between Jerry and Naples."

"Understood."

Malachy called Vic and explained the whole situation, including wanting to use Dan Breen as his investigator. He got back in the car as Matt was finishing up his call.

"They are on their way," Matt said.

"Good. Vic is expecting them."

"What does he think?"

"Vic is always cautious. So he thinks we don't know enough yet to talk about outcomes. The trick is to make it go away without perpetuating a fraud on the court and without putting your son-in-law's job at risk."

"What do you think?"

Malachy smiled at Matt and said, "I think you made the right decision."

"I really appreciate it, Malachy. And I know you have a lot of other things on your mind. I hear you are going to testify fully. No Fifth."

"That's right."

"They're really going to come after you about Dino," Matt said.

"I already told you where to look for him."

Matt gave a half-hearted laugh and responded, "Malachy, they see you as the key link to Dino. You're all they have. And they intend to turn you inside out to find him. All the investigation has yielded is some uncorroborated information about Dino's connection to a shadowy Italian-Mexican who has gambling interests all over the Caribbean and Europe including Internet sites. They say the guy is some kind of math whiz and supposedly has really big-time money. The rumor is he used to operate out of Chicago. But none of the organized crime units have anything on him. I'm not sure he even exists."

Malachy looked at Matt for thirty seconds without saying anything. Matt looked very uncomfortable.

"Matt, I didn't like last night's decision."

"What decision?"

"Taking out the middle reliever when he was in his groove. What do you think?"

"Malachy, what the hell are you talking about?"

"I am changing the subject to the White Sox because I don't want you to tell me anything as some kind of payback. You asked me for help because a family member is in trouble. There is no quid pro quo. Might I ask for a favor in the future? Sure, but absolutely nothing that compromises you."

Malachy stopped and let his last words sink in while he took several sips of his coffee. Then he continued, "When the situation in Wisconsin is resolved successfully and the Dino investigation has lost its steam, come on up to the Shamrock. We'll have a few drinks and watch the White Sox together. Until then, and it might be a while, I don't want to hear from you or see you. Unless you're on official business and then I expect you to do your job."

"Thanks, Malachy."

"See you then, Matt."

Malachy convened the joint chiefs meeting in the Shamrock's storeroom.

"Matt was definitely by himself," the Count said.

Malachy explained Matt's family problem to Kevin and the Count and what he said about their anonymous employer. The Count told about the successful return of the Latin reports to Dan Breen.

"Are we going to be involved in the Wisconsin thing?" Kevin asked.

"Just if it's the only way to get it resolved," Malachy said.

"Do you have any guess about what happened to Dino?" the Count asked.

"I do. Our employer was informed about Dino's tax scheme at the Shrine. Maybe Dino went to him for help. Or maybe our employer found out on his own. In either case, he sent his small army led by Captain Laconic to pick him up."

"If our employer is involved, the Feds will never find him," the Count said. "Whatever condition he is in."

"Agreed," Malachy said.

"What's your read on the new archbishop?" the Count asked. "Do we have a chance?"

"So far, so good," Malachy said. "He handled the negotiations with Richard personally and settled quickly. He sold the mansion to fund some of the settlement without looking back. Fr. Paul has nothing but good things to say about his actions so far—and he's not easy to impress. The Italian community is pushing hard. We have a chance."

"What time is Bari meeting with the archbishop?" Kevin asked.

Malachy looked at his watch and said, "Right about now. But Bari wants to thank us in person, yea or nay. He's arranged a special lunch for us on at the Firenze on Taylor Street. He said it's a celebration either way because for sure he will be able to act as a fully functioning priest again even if the assignment is not the Shrine."

"I'm sure he will be an outstanding priest," the Count said. "But, somehow I think I will be a more enthusiastic lunch companion if it is a yea."

They spent the rest of the meeting calculating the expenses for the Shrine project. Even without the bonus, the $2,000 a day consulting fee covered all the expenses and left a profit.

Eduardo drove Malachy and Kevin down to the Firenze. They sat in the back together so they could talk more easily.

Kevin looked around the back of Malachy's Merc and ran his hand over the seat and said, "This is an improvement. You didn't tell me that the Count was going to have work done on the inside too."

"The Count didn't tell me either."

"I'm looking forward to the meal at the Firenze no matter what the outcome with the new archbishop. And I know Taylor Street restaurants are your favorites."

"The last remnant of the old Italian neighborhood. Let's hope the bonus works out so the Count will really enjoy what promises to be an outstanding meal."

"No matter what happens with the bonus, it's a good result. I'm glad your plan worked," Kevin said.

"Antonella is a bonus in her own right," Malachy said.

Kevin smiled and said, "That's not what I meant."

Kevin looked out the window and was silent for a few minutes. He turned back to Malachy and spoke quietly.

"If Flynn wasn't stopped by jail, I'd have stopped him."

Malachy noted the "I" and didn't respond right away, remembering something his father had told him.

"You know, Kevin, during that time you stayed with us, I once asked my dad what the two of you talked about so intensely when I would find you alone with him. He told me, 'That's confidential, Malachy, and only for Kevin to tell if he wants.' And then he added, 'But I will tell you this from personal experience, orphans are too often preyed on by the too many viscous bastards with power over them.'"

Kevin turned his head again and looked out the window. After a few more minutes of silence, he turned back.

"Your father was an orphan, too," Kevin said. "He knew what it was like. I swore an oath to myself that when I was older I would never let it happen to another kid if I could stop it. Like I said, I'm glad your plans worked—let's just leave it there and enjoy our lunch."

Malachy tried to think of something to say and settled for "okay."

†

"Malachy, how are you?" Stacy asked. "Your last visit was too-long ago. But today, I get to see everybody—what a treat."

Stacy gave hugs and kisses on the cheeks.

"Bene, bene," Malachy said. "And you look wonderful. Is the Count already here?"

"Of course. I never remember a time when you arrived before him unless you elbowed him out of the way as you came thru the door. He's in the private dining room talking with Fr. Bari. Father asked me what the infamous trio liked to eat and drink, so prepare yourself for all your favorites. Right this way."

Stacy led the way to the private dining room. Malachy wondered if Bari's body language would tell the tale. It did.

"Malachy and Kevin welcome," Bari said, getting up from the table with energy, grasping Malachy's hand and then Kevin's. "Kevin, how good to finally meet you. Antonella has told me all about you. She says you really like Italian food. I know Malachy does. And Leon just told me only Polish cuisine tops it, so I'm hoping everybody will enjoy the luncheon I took the liberty of ordering, with Stacy's help of course."

"I'm guessing we have something to celebrate," Malachy said.

"We do, we certainly do! I'm reinstated at the Shrine!"

"Outstanding," Malachy said.

"Congratulations," Kevin said sincerely, shaking Bari's hand again.

The Count bounded up from the table, clapped Bari on the back, and said, "I take back what I was saying about my instinctive anticlericalism. I must commend the archbishop for his wisdom."

"I thank you all," a beaming Bari said. "I know your efforts made the difference. And I know I wasn't the easiest to work with. I truly appreciate all that you did."

Malachy wondered what the appreciation would turn into if Bari knew all they did. He decided to change the subject.

"I'm thirsty," Malachy said, looking around for the drinks.

"Here is Stacy now," Bari said.

Stacy rolled in a drink cart and on it was a bottle of Jameson and a bottle of Polish vodka with labels Malachy had never seen before. "I'm told you can't buy these in the States. I had some priest friends send them over. I hope I didn't violate any laws."

"Absolution is hereby given," the Count said, picking up the vodka bottle and admiring the label.

Everybody laughed, and Stacy poured the drinks. They sat down at the round table that was set with Deruta plates and extra-large cloth napkins. Stacy had gone all out. When Stacy left, Malachy asked Bari how the meeting went.

"He is a remarkable man and bishop," Bari said. "He was genuinely concerned about my ordeal and how it affected me. At the end of the meeting we prayed together and he gave me his blessing. My emotions were over the top and I wept. I couldn't believe it was all over. In some ways, I still can't. It has been an unbelievable week."

Malachy could tell by Bari's body language there was more to tell but he had no idea what.

"Yesterday I received a call from a lawyer with one of the big Loop firms," Bari said. "I couldn't believe my ears. It's all very complicated but somebody has given me a lot of property. It's all located right in this area—by the Shrine, up and down Taylor Street and by the university."

"Good thing," the Count said. "This is going to be a very expensive lunch."

"Well deserved," Kevin said.

"Any strings attached?" Malachy asked.

"It's very interesting. The anonymous donor requested, but did not require, I use the income from the properties to help those in need of drug rehabilitation. There is going to be some kind of foundation that I control. It's a wonderful opportunity. The legal aspects are truly mind-boggling and I don't understand them at all. But evidently there will be a large amount of income."

"A great opportunity," Malachy said. "And you're just the right man to make sure the money actually does some good."

They were an hour into the lunch and only finished with the second round of appetizers when Bari asked, "Do you always eat and drink at this pace?"

"I always claimed Malachy was the slowest moving Marine in the history of the Corps," Kevin answered. "But when it comes to meals, he sits alone in the *Guinness Book of Records*. I have actually found myself hungry at the end of one our meals because it lasted so long."

"Time is a complex phenomenon," Malachy said. "It moves at different speeds depending upon the activity. For example, it slows down markedly if you climb on an Exercycle, but speeds up when you are enjoying a good meal. So on that basis, I think I've spent too little time at table."

"I think I have my answer," Bari said to general laughter.

Stacy entered the dining room and said, "Sorry to interrupt, but a strong, silent type asked me to give you this note, Malachy."

She handed Malachy a small, sealed envelope. He opened it and read its one line: "I have a cell phone for you."

"Alas, time just slowed down. A piece of business I must attend to. Please excuse me for a few minutes."

Malachy followed Stacy to the maître d' station. There was nobody there.

"He was here just a moment ago," Stacy said. "Wait, here's a package with your name on it."

"Thank you, Stacy," Malachy said, picking up the small box. "I think I'll take the opportunity to get a little fresh air."

Malachy went outside and into the parking lot, waved to the attendant, and walked to the back of the lot to a secluded spot behind the building. He opened the box, took out the phone, and pressed the number three as a small card instructed.

"Hello, Malachy. Congratulations on a job well done."

"Thank you."

"Please excuse the interruption. I want to settle the matter of the bonus. Have you made your choice?"

"Good news travels fast. I'll take the cash."

"I understand your preference for the certainty of cash versus the difficulty to assess odds of reinstatement."

"That was not a factor in my decision," Malachy said.

"No desire to return to the law?"

"Not exactly," Malachy said. "I don't qualify for the reinstatement program. The kid I was defending was innocent, and I promised his mother I'd get him off. Bribing Monihan, who I knew for a fact was totally corrupt, was the only way to get it done. So, same circumstances in the future, same decision."

There was a soft chuckle in Malachy's ear.

"I admire those who can be objective especially about themselves. Do you want actual cash?"

"No," Malachy said. "I prefer a check from the committee."

"I understand. It will be delivered to you at the Shamrock this evening by special messenger."

"Captain Laconic?"

There was another chuckle and the voice said, "No, but I do like the name. It will be delivered by the new chairman of the committee as one of his last duties."

"I hope he doesn't mind the storeroom."

"He is not as fastidious as Dino. The storeroom will suit him fine."

"Dino is a popular fellow at the moment," Malachy said. "It seems like those who want to find him have no idea where to look."

"So I understand. What have you told them?"

Malachy couldn't resist and said, "I told them where to find him."

A cold, hard voice commanded, "Tell me exactly what you said and to whom."

"I told my friend Matt Morse to stake out Savile Row because Dino would show up there eventually. I don't think he was keen on passing on the suggestion."

"Do all the Irish make jokes about serious business matters?"

"Not all, but many do about everything—but especially the serious stuff. There was a famous writer who wrote a comic masterpiece satirizing the saints and the Church and then dedicated it to his guardian angel, assuring him he was only kidding and warning the guardian angel to make sure there was no mistake when he came home."

"Difficult to enforce a penalty if the warning is ignored," the voice said.

"Yes, indeed," Malachy said. "You know I didn't have much in common with Dino but I liked the man. I'm hoping he is not helping Jimmy Hoffa hold up a goalpost somewhere."

"When did you learn about his tax activities involving the Shrine?"

Malachy decided a simple factual answer was in order.

"Many weeks ago. I can get the specific date if it is important."

"It's not important. You never told me."

"Following instructions," Malachy said. "To quote, 'anything else you find out about Fr. Bari which is not relevant to proving his innocence, keep it to yourself.' And I did."

A neutral voice told Malachy, "Fair enough. Is there anything now you want to tell me about your assignment?"

"No."

"Is there any reason for concern about the grand jury investigations?"

"No," Malachy said firmly. "Dino was driving the bus. I was just a passenger who happened to get picked up along the way."

"So your concern for Dino does not extend as far as the grand jury?"

"No, it doesn't," Malachy said, laughing. "I hope that won't ruin my relationship with him."

"No, it won't. No harm, no foul, no penalty."

"Speaking of penalties, Fr. Bari told us about the property donation," Malachy said.

"That matter does not concern you, Malachy. I think our business is concluded. Again, congratulations on a job well done. Please destroy the phone."

"Thank you, I will destroy the phone. What if there is a future development you should know about?"

"Then somebody will bring you a new phone. Good luck."

Based on the conversation, Malachy guessed Dino bought his way out of his problem and was now in a reverse witness-protection program. Probably in a few years, Dino's kids and grandkids would be on vacation somewhere and Dino and his wife would suddenly appear out of nowhere. Knowing his employer's attention to detail, it wouldn't be in London.

Malachy entered the dining room with a big smile.

"Nothing to put a damper on our celebration, I hope?" the Count asked.

"No," Malachy answered. "Routine call to arrange a business meeting tonight at the Shamrock. A client wants to pay off an outstanding receivable. So it's good news."

Stacy and two waiters entered the dining room with covered plates and a new bottle of wine. Another hour went by quickly and they had just finished up the last of the entrées when Stacy came into the room with a large box.

"Kevin, a very attractive woman in an Alfa sports car sent this box in for you with a message—she is ready when you are."

Kevin flushed a little and took the box.

"Ambiguous," the Count said.

"Open it," Malachy said.

"Antonella has always loved dramatic, extravagant gestures," Fr. Bari said, looking at Kevin sympathetically. "I'm afraid this is my fault. I told her about the lunch."

"What fault?" the Count said.
"Open it," Malachy said again.
"Any message back?" Stacy asked.
Kevin looked totally bewildered.
"Please ask Antonella to join us for dessert," Fr. Bari said to Stacy.
"Will do."

Stacy returned laughing.
"Are you sure she's your sister, Father? I quote, 'What I want for dessert is not on the menu. I will sit in the sunshine, have an espresso, and wait patiently.'"
"Yes, Stacy, that's Antonella, my sister," Bari said. "Kevin, perhaps you can persuade her?"
"Or vice versa," the Count said with energy.
Kevin suddenly took charge of the situation. He quickly opened the box; took out an elaborate, feathered pirate's hat; and put it on his head.
"Time and tide wait for no man," the Count said.
"Very dashing," Malachy said.
Kevin turned and said, "Tell Bridget, will you? And look after Red."
"All the arrangements have been made," Malachy said.
Kevin shook hands with the Count and then turned to Fr. Bari.
"Thank you for this excellent lunch. I'm glad that everything turned out so well. Please excuse my early leaving, but Antonella has been very patient with my work schedule and I think I should join her now. I hope to see you soon."
"Well, actually you will. Antonella has invited me up to her place for Sunday supper."
"Good," Kevin said. "See you on Sunday."
Kevin shook Malachy's hand, adjusted the hat to a rakish angle, and strode out of the dining room to an enthusiastic "Bravo! Bravo!" from Stacy.
After forty-five minutes of dessert, espresso, and sambuca, the Count took his leave, mellow and full of praise for Bari and the archbishop. Now that they were alone, Malachy hoped Bari would not ask too many questions.
"The archbishop is even more pastoral than I explained earlier," Fr.

Bari said. "At the end of our meeting, he handed me a manila envelope full of very embarrassing pictures from long ago and simply said, 'These were mailed to the chancery office with your return address. I don't know by whom or whose property they are. I am giving them to you. I've no interest in them. They're not pictures of the priest I see before me now.'"

Bari paused and looked at Malachy and asked, "Do you know anything about them?"

Malachy carefully parsed his answer, hoping that Bari's infallible lie detector was a little off-kilter because of his modest intake of food and wine.

"Well, we know that Flynn had it in for you. He had the opportunity and the malign motive to take the pictures, keep them all these years, and then send them to the chancery office. So my guess is he's the one who did it."

"I still don't understand why he hated me so deeply," Bari said.

"Original sin?" Malachy suggested, hoping to change the subject.

Bari did not even smile and responded, "It distresses me. I worry that I did something, or failed to do something, that spurred him on."

"Men like Flynn count on good people like you having just that reaction. I don't know whether he's morally responsible for his actions or not, but I do know this—jail is the right place for him. The harm he can do there is limited."

"Malachy, I also worry about you. I was called before the grand jury and testified truthfully. I'm concerned that my testimony will cause you legal problems. Many of their questions concerned you and Dino. The only questions I did not answer were about that young man you caught breaking into the rectory. On my attorney's advice, I claimed a priest–penitent relationship and refused to give any information about him other than that you apprehended him."

Malachy knew that the Feds might well ask Bari about their conversation in the future so he was careful in his answer.

"If I ever did know his name, I certainly can't recall it now. That was a very confusing and dangerous situation, and my only concern was your safety. That's why I called Dino to take you somewhere secure. He never did tell me where they took you."

"I don't know either," Bari said.

"As to the grand jury, there is no need for concern. I will answer all their questions. But the person who can give them the information they want is Dino, and, from what I read, he can't be found."

"I hope he's all right."

"Me, too. I was hoping to get some fashion tips from him. But the Count tells me, as do my daughters, that ironing my clothes is the right place to start. What do you think?"

Bari looked at Malachy for a few seconds and then said, "I think you don't want to talk about these matters anymore."

"This is a celebration."

"Yes, it is. I just hope that resolving my situation did not harm you or anyone else on any level."

Malachy brushed aside the wisecracks that came to him and responded truthfully, "I wish I had your strength of faith."

"Malachy, I pray every day that your faith and trust in God will be strengthened."

Malachy felt like he could almost reach out and touch the faith emanating from Fr. John Bari. It reminded him of his mother. He also remembered how strongly his father lived within him.

"Good, I need those prayers."

Malachy's Gloriam

ABOUT THE AUTHOR

"C.M. Martello" was born into a family of Irish-German heritage whose Chicago history on both sides goes back more than one hundred years. He was educated in Catholic schools and then went on to a career in finance and advertising. The author chose the pen name Martello as a tribute to his favorite author, James Joyce. Martello Tower in Dublin is the setting for the opening of *Ulysses* and the site of the Joyce museum. The author was inspired to begin writing after a visit to the tower. *Malachy's Gloriam* is his first published novel.

Made in the USA
Middletown, DE
06 December 2023